Surveyor
Book I of the *Corps of Discovery* Series

Surveyor

James S. Peet

Geo-Mar Publishing
2017

First Printing: 2017

Geo-Mar Publshing
718 Griffin Ave. #295
Enumclaw WA 98022

ISBN: 978-0-9996093-0-9

Cover art by Patrick Turner

To buy this (and future book by James S. Peet) in e-book format, please go to **www.jamespeet.com**.

For my family.

CONTENTS

Prologue	1
EARTH	5
Chapter 1	7
Chapter 2	11
HAYEK	27
Chapter 3	29
Chapter 4	55
Chapter 5	61
Chapter 6	75
A NEW LIFE	81
Chapter 7	83
Chapter 8	103
Chapter 9	115
Chapter 10	135
Chapter 11	143
Chapter 12	161
Chapter 13	171
Chapter 14	185
Chapter 15	197
ZION	207
Chapter 16	209
Chapter 17	221
Chapter 18	227
Chapter 19	237
Chapter 20	253
Chapter 21	261
PLANET 42	271
Chapter 22	273
Chapter 23	279
Chapter 24	289
Chapter 25	297
Chapter 26	303
Chapter 27	315
Chapter 28	325
Chapter 29	333

ACKNOWLEDGEMENTS

Special thanks to all that made this novel possible: Shannon Page, my editor; Mark Teppo, publisher at Resurrection House, who was willing to sit down over beers, wine, and whiskey to give valuable insight; Evelyn Nicholas, owner of *A Good Book and Cafe* bookstore in Sumner, WA, who also gave valuable insight over fires, beers, wine, and whiskey; Pat Turner, the cover artist (who kept the planet in the sky for me, despite his objections); The Beta Readers who provided excellent feedback to make this novel better than what it started out as - Becky Rush-Peet, Domingo Chang, Dave Jeschke, Emily Arfin, Trisha Battistin-Clark, Chris Mauthe, David Morris, Clairese Jorgensen, and Mike Hadley, and last, but definitely not least; my daughter Katie Peet who did the concept art that the cover art is based on.

PROLOGUE

Tim Bowman didn't intend to open a portal to a parallel Earth, it just happened.

The half-Irish, half-Japanese Buckaroo Banzai wannabe was actually working on an attempt at a matter transporter. As a kid, he had watched all the *Star Trek* television shows and decided that he should be able to figure out some way to make the show's transporter a reality. Several decades later, with a PhD in physics in hand, here he was in a small metal shed on his ranchette just outside the small town of Selah, Washington, finessing his latest attempt. His buddy, Dave Jaskey, was sitting on a swivel chair watching him. Dave, dressed for the cowboy action shoot the two were planning on attending shortly, was holding onto a lever-action rifle he had brought with him to show Tim. It sat, forgotten, in his lap as he watched Tim begin the start-up process for his machine. Where Dave was sitting he could see the imposing profile of Mt. Rainier, Washington's largest mountain, through a window at the far end of the shed.

The machine was a simple-looking affair, consisting of two metal-framed gateways separated by about fifteen feet, and a control panel fed by a standard electric cord from an outlet on the shed's wall. The control panel was linked to both gates. According to Tim, once it was activated, one should be able to walk through the opening of one gate and appear from the other. Naturally, Dave was skeptical.

A sacrificial chicken was in a cage next to the first gate. The plan was to push the chicken through the gate and have it emerge from the other. Tim had considered using a goat but figured his wife would be more upset to find one of her milk goats missing than a chicken that had stopped laying eggs. Besides, he figured, it's a chicken. If it died, it wouldn't be missed.

Tim finished fiddling with the control panel, and then said to Dave, "Well, here goes nothing." He flipped a switch and a humming sound emanated from the two gates. Dave's eyebrows raised in surprise.

"Well, at least something's working," he said.

Tim left the control panel and practically ran to where the chicken sat. Opening the cage, he pulled the squawking bird out. Still standing to the side of the gate, where he could keep an eye on the other gate, he reached around and threw the chicken through. It disappeared from sight. He stepped back for a better look at the exit gate, frowning.

"Where's the damned chicken?" he asked.

Dave shrugged. "Beats me."

Tim hurried to the opening of the second gate and looked through it. All he saw was the shed's floor and space between the two gates. His frown deepened, creating deep furrows on his forehead. He ran back to the first gate, and this time actually looked through the opening.

"What the hell?" he muttered.

Dave got up from his perch and walked over to stand by Tim.

"What the hell is right," he said.

The two men saw the chicken, but instead of standing on the floor of the shed, either outside the second gate or between the two, it stood on the ground of a high desert, just like the land surrounding Tim's ranchette. Off in the distance, they could see a mountain that looked just like Mt. Rainier. But they couldn't see any signs of civilization, just an untouched natural environment. Dave did a double take, looking at the mountain through the gate and then at the mountain through the window.

Tim was just about to reach down and grab it when the bird squawked and tried to run away. Its little bird brain had recognized danger, but too late. A tawny bundle of fur leaped in; the two men stood in shock as a large cat with two long fangs bit down on the bird, ending its squawking with a flurry of flying feathers.

Both men stepped back, shocked. Dave grabbed a cartridge from the leather pistol belt around his waist and loaded it into the rifle. He brought it up and aimed it at the lion. The motion caught the attention of the large beast. It turned to face them, dead bird dangling from its mouth between the two scimitar-like fangs. It lay its ears back and crouched as if to attack.

At that point, Dave had had enough and shot the animal between the eyes. It dropped like a stone, still clutching the dead chicken between its jaws.

"What the hell is it?" Tim asked.

"From the looks of it, a freakin' saber-tooth tiger," Dave said, working the lever on the rifle to eject the spent casing, and loading another cartridge from his belt.

Tim stepped back toward the gate, and then, gingerly, poked his head through it. He looked around for a minute, then pulled his head back and turned to Dave.

"You look and tell me what you see, so I don't think I'm crazy."

Dave did. When he looked back at Tim, his eyes were wide, the whites showing vividly around the blue irises.

"A herd of woolly mammoths? Did you just invent a time machine, or what?"

The two men dragged the dead saber-toothed tiger through the gate and into the shed, dead chicken in mouth and all.

"I don't think so," Tim said. "You're the astrologist, can't you figure it out this evening?"

"Astronomer," Dave absently replied. It was a standing joke between them.

"I'm not sure I want to try taking any pictures at night from there," Dave said, nudging the dead lion with his cowboy boot. "Not if there's more like this. Why don't you shut this thing down until we figure out what we're doing?"

"Probably a good idea," Tim said. Giving the lion a wide berth, he went over to the control panel and turned off the machine.

"So, we've got a couple of options here," Dave said, contemplating the dead lion. "Either you developed a time machine and found a way to the past, or you've opened up a portal to an alternate universe, giving us access to another Earth where the megafauna still roam."

EARTH

Chapter 1

"I'm not going."

"What do you mean you're not going?" Bill asked, stunned.

Jessica crossed her arms across her chest. "Exactly what I said. I'm not going."

"But, but, we've planned on this for years."

"No, Bill, *you've* planned on this for years. I didn't. *I* planned on marrying you and staying on Earth while you got a nice job. I *never* agreed to going to another planet. And I'm certainly not up for being the wife of somebody whose idea of fun is gallivanting around wild planets while I sit at home and worry."

Bill couldn't believe what he was hearing. For years he had busted his butt to get into the Corps of Discovery, and he had assumed that his fiance, Jessica, was on board with that. After all, it was pretty much all he had talked about since they met freshman year.

Struggling to understand, he asked, "So, what do you want me to do now?"

Uncrossing her arms, she came up to Bill and wrapped her arms around his neck. "Simple. Take that job offer from the National Geospatial Intelligence Agency. Once you start, we can finally get married."

Reaching up, Bill removed her arms from around his neck and shook his head.

"Sorry, I can't do that," he said, shaking his head. "I only applied for that job as a fall-back in case I didn't make the cut. You're asking me to give up what I've worked for most of my life. I just can't."

"Yes, you can," she said. She crossed her arms again. "Look. Either it's me or the Corps. Your call."

Bill looked at her blue eyes, framed by an almond-shaped face and blond hair tied up in a pony-tail, and shook his head. She meant it: she was actually giving him an ultimate.

Had she changed so much since they fell in love? Or had he ever really known her?

With a sinking feeling in his gut, he said, "That's not much of a choice. Either way, I lose."

"What do you mean you lose? What am I? Some sort of consolation prize if you didn't get your precious Corps?"

Bill leaned forward, gave Jessica a quick kiss on the lips, and said, "I love you, but I'm not willing to stay here and kill my dreams."

With that, he turned and walked out through the open door of her dorm room.

Behind him, he heard her yell, "You bastard!"

He turned around just in time to get hit in the cheek with a small, sharp object.

Bill put his hand up to his face as he looked down. On the floor, he saw the small engagement ring he had given her on Christmas Eve. He scooped it up and put it in his pocket.

Well, I guess that's that, he thought, looking at the closed door.

His cheek stung. When he withdrew his hand, there was a small bit of blood on his fingertips. He wiped the blood on his jeans leg and continued down the hall.

Yeah, this is gonna be fun explaining to "the Colonel."

Supper that evening was "interesting." Along with having to explain to his father (whom Bill thought of as "The Colonel"— always in quotes because that's how it was in his Air Force family) why Jessica didn't join them for his celebratory graduation supper, he also informed his father that he wouldn't be staying on Earth for another day. His father wasn't too thrilled about his only child leaving Earth to put his life on the line just for adventure, which he said was nothing more than somebody else in danger in a faraway land. Supper was a tense affair but fortunately didn't devolve into an argument, as all too many of them had while Bill was growing up. It didn't help that Bill was still in a state of shock from Jessica's behavior, and, in his mind, betrayal.

As the two exited the restaurant on Lake Union, "The Colonel" walked Bill to his old, rusting pickup truck. Bill held out his hand to shake with his father, but "The Colonel" unexpectedly grabbed him in a bear hug. "Be careful out there," he said in a husky voice, then stepped back and added, "Make me proud."

Bill was shaken by the emotion coming from his father. It wasn't just unexpected, it was unheard of. "The Colonel" hadn't even cried at his wife's funeral. Then again, six-year-old Billy was crying hard enough he didn't notice if anyone else was.

"I'll try," he stammered.

"The Colonel" strode toward his rental car on the other side of the parking lot, never turning around for a last look. That was his way. That was how he always left Bill: no backward looks, no regrets, just a forward determination, like a cat.

Bill wrestled his keys from his pocket and opened the Toyota's door, listening to it squeal the entire time. As he backed up out of his parking space, he saw his father in the rear-view mirror getting into his car. Bill had no idea how long it would be before he next saw him.

Chapter 2

Despite the early hour, the road leading up to the Transfer Station was mobbed, and the massive parking lots were filled, mostly with buses. Signs directed emigrants and travelers to different lots, and those lots fed into different parts of the Parallel, Inc. Transfer Station, a large building looking more like a fruit packing station (which it was in a previous life) than the portal to a parallel universe. A number of protesters lined the road leading up to the building but stopped short at the guarded entrance to the lot. Most held signs saying "No Exploitation," "Stop the Infestation," "Gaia First," or similar themes. They were obviously people who had no desire for humans to expand to the new worlds that Parallel, Inc. was opening for settlement and resource exploitation. Passing through the throng of chanting protesters, Bill drove up to the gate separating the Transfer Station from the surrounding land.

At the gate, Bill gave the armed guard his destination and was required to show his driver's license. Another guard waved a wand over, around, and under his truck and eventually gave the first guard an "all clear" signal. *That must be one of bomb detection wands I've heard about*, he thought.

The guard passed him through the gate and Bill spotted the sign for the Corps of Discovery lot. It had the stylized image of Lewis and Clark that was on the envelope Bill had shown "the Colonel" last night, one man pointing outward, the other standing slightly in front of him, holding onto a musket. The sign pointed toward a part of the building separate from the main immigration area. He pulled into a parking space in front of the building, hopped out of the truck, and walked over to the lone door. Over it was a smaller Corps of Discovery sign.

Despite the early hour, the temperature was already rising, and the parking lot still retained heat from the prior day, so it was with some relief that Bill entered the building and discovered it was air-conditioned.

The room was about the size of a small classroom, with a row of computers on one side, each separated by a divider with a chair in front of them; on the other side of the room was a counter with a computer monitor.

An older woman sat behind the counter. A hideous scar ran down the left side of her face from the edge of her eye to her jawline, partially covered by long, silver-streaked black hair, and she was missing her left arm from just above the elbow. Bill was surprised to see her reading an actual newspaper, the type derived from trees, wood pulp, and a printing press. She was dressed in the brown, utilitarian Corps of Discovery field uniform, and was wearing a headset with a boom mike. Above her right pocket were three ribbons, the type the US military used to substitute for medals when worn on undress uniforms. She looked up as Bill entered, then rose and said "Howdy. How can I help you?" as she put the paper down.

"I'm here for basic orientation," Bill said, handing over the letter he had shown his father, "the Colonel", the night before. It stated that Bill had been accepted as a Probationary Explorer in the Corps of Discovery, with a primary designation as a survey specialist.

The woman scanned it and set it down on the counter, then spoke softly into the mike while she looked at the monitor. Bill looked more closely at the ribbons on her chest. He could have sworn one was for the Purple Heart—the purple middle surrounded by two thin white stripes on either side was the same he had seen on his father's uniform. The other ribbons were unfamiliar. One was green in the center with two large blue stripes on either side with what looked like a footprint in the center the other was simply sky blue and had a number of metal pieces on it. They looked like little pine cones.

"Great. Gotcha right here. William J. Clark. We weren't expecting you until next week." The last sentence was more like a question than a statement.

"Yeah, well, things changed, so I decided to come early."

"Not a problem. Did you get the informational packet?"

"Uh, no. What informational packet?"

"It's one we send out to every Probie before they report. Provides basic info about the Corps and Hayek. Well, never mind, you'll figure it out when you get there. Now, if you don't mind, I'll need to do a quick DNA check to verify your identity."

Despite having gone through a rather extensive physical before being accepted, Bill was still surprised. "Uh, sure. May I ask why?"

"You'd be amazed how many people try to sneak into Hayek." She pulled a sterile swab from a container under the counter. "Lots of people want to move there without paying, so they try to steal a Probie's identity. Others want to gain access to the gate so they can destroy it."

Bill nodded, thinking about the protesters he had just passed.

Leaning in, she said, "Open wide." As Bill did so, she none too gently swabbed the inside of his cheek, then placed the swab in a machine under the counter and watched it until it beeped. She then nodded.

"Good to go! Welcome to the Corps. I'm Janice. Janice Goodland," she said, holding out her hand to Bill.

Bill shook it. "Thanks, Janice. What's a Probie?"

"A probationary member of the Corps. Much easier to just say 'Probie'." Janice smiled. Her face lit up, showing what a beautiful woman she was, despite the obvious damage to her person.

"You get a lot of people stealing identities?"

"Enough that we have to be on our toes." This caused Bill's eyebrows to rise in surprise.

"What do I do now?" he asked.

"First step is in-processing. You get to fill out a few pieces of paperwork. After that, we'll get your gear and move you over. Once over, that's it, the point of no return. If you bail, you pay. Once you're on the other side you'll be assigned a place. Orientation for the new probationary class is in four days, so you'll have plenty time to learn about your new home. Meantime, let's get you started." Janice reached under the counter and pulled out a micro-USB flash drive, which she handed to Bill. She pointed to one of the computers against the opposite wall and said, "Have a seat at computer number one and wake it up. I'll make sure it's set for your biometrics. Insert your flash drive before signing anything, and follow the instructions."

Bill sat down and tapped on the keyboard. Once it was running, he inserted the flash drive into the USB port just below the monitor screen. The first instructions came up, directing him to place his thumb on the scanner built into the side of the screen. A greenish light seeped out from around his thumb as it was scanned. A second later, the screen displayed "Confirmed, William J. Clark. Click 'Next' to proceed."

Bill touched the 'Next" button on the screen and a short document appeared, stating that Bill declared himself a responsible adult, accepting all liberties and responsibilities that one got as such. Bill was surprised it used the word 'responsible' rather than the usual 'legal' he saw on most documents. At the end of the form was a signature block, with a computer-generated 'Use the touchscreen to sign your name' box next to it. He touched the signature block, then signed his name on the screen using his index finger. He was also directed to swipe his thumb over the scanner, signifying that he did, indeed, electronically sign the documents.

He repeated the process for the remaining documents. Next was a contract stipulating that he was accepting employment with the Corps of Discovery as a survey specialist, with additional duties as co-pilot and navigator. The contract specified that if he made it through the one-year probation period or died on duty during that time, he would not have to reimburse the Corps of Discovery for his immigration costs (Bill noted that if he died while off duty, part of his insurance would go to paying the rather hefty immigration fee.) While it turned out to be one of the lengthiest documents he would sign, it was only a couple of pages long.

Other forms included an insurance form (with the payout in gold), a basic will (he left all his worldly possessions, including the gold insurance claim to his father, since Jessica was no longer a part of his life), a copy of his health records, emergency contact information, and a couple of human resource-type forms.

He was stumped when he began filling out the payroll form. Not having a bank in Hayek yet, he didn't know where to deposit his salary. He didn't think Wells Fargo would have a branch there. He was about to ask Janice about this when a sidebar popped up on the document saying "No Bank Account on Hayek? Touch Here." Bill did so and was directed to the website of the Parallel Credit Union, a member-supported credit union for the employees of Parallel, Inc. and all its subsidiaries.

Bill knew from his research that Parallel, Inc. was the parent firm for several subsidiaries, such as Interworld Transfers, Resource Management Group, and the Corps of Discovery, but it was still surprising to know that he'd be working for a private enterprise in what would normally be a government-supported role on Earth.

Bill navigated his way to the "New Member" page. He completed the online form but was stumped about his addresses. Again, a sidebar popped up "No mailing address on file? Touch Here."

He did so and saw "If you do not have a permanent address, we can use your work address. Do you want to do that?" Bill touched the 'Yes' button. After he did, he was back at the form, which now had his address listed as the Corps of Discovery headquarters on Sacajawea Base, near Milton, the capital of Hayek.

When he touched the email address block "If you do not have a permanent email address on Hayek, we can use your work address. Do you want to do that?" appeared. Again, Bill touched the 'Yes' button and was returned to the form. He saw that his new address was bill.clark@cod.svc He wondered what 'svc' was, but decided to ask Janice once he was finished.

After entering in all the data, including a password, he was asked if everything was correct. He looked it over, saw everything appeared right, then touched the 'Save' button.

He then saw a statement form showing a zero balance in his account. He wondered why he wasn't given a choice of checking or savings, but, again, figured he would ask Janice.

The screen then showed "If you are satisfied with your banking arrangement, touch 'Yes' to return to the documents. If not, touch 'No' to edit." Bill touched 'Yes' and was returned to the payroll form, where he saw that his new banking information had been automatically entered.

One form Bill didn't miss signing was the income tax form. There wasn't an income tax on Hayek, so there was no need for that type of form. Of course, he expected he would still have to pay his federal income tax, at least until such time as he revoked his US citizenship for a Hayek one.

Once Bill was finished signing and thumb scanning every form, the computer showed "Congratulations! You are now a Probationary Explorer in the Corps of Discovery. Please click 'Here' to save a copy of your signed forms on the external storage device you inserted in Drive F. You may pick up your identification card at the front desk. The Explorer at the desk will give you instructions on its uses."

Bill touched the 'Here' button and, after seeing that all the documents were saved, extracted the flash drive.

He got up, put the drive in his pocket, walked over and let Janice know he was finished. She reached under the counter and brought up a card, handing it to him. It looked like a combination of a driver's license and credit card. On the front was a headshot of him, along with his full name and a security chip. The Corps of Discovery emblem constituted the background. A magnetic stripe and a barcode were on the otherwise blank back.

"This isn't just your Corps identification card, it's also your medical card and your debit card for your bank. So, any time you change any info, you'll need to get it updated, usually at HQ. The chip contains data on your date of birth, blood type, religion, medical allergies, et cetera."

He asked Janice about the lack of choice between checking and savings.

"Oh, we just have bank accounts—they aren't broken down further. Nobody uses checks anyhow, only cash or electronic transfers. Some people tried to get credit cards working, but most merchants wouldn't use them, so you probably won't ever see one. By the way, unless you've got a special reason to hold onto it, you'll want to get rid of whatever US currency you have—it's worthless on Hayek."

"Good point. Not that I have much, but where can I do that?"

"There's a currency exchange inside before you cross over," Janice said, nodding at the door leading into the rest of the huge building.

Just then, the front door opened and another young man entered. Both Bill and Janice turned to face the newcomer. In contrast to Bill's average height and looks, he was short and lean, with sharply defined features and bright blue eyes.

"Is this where I check in for the Corps of Discovery?" he asked in a surprisingly deep voice with a strong Southern accent.

"Sure is," Janice replied. "Give me a minute and I'll be right with you." Turning back to Bill she asked, "Do you have any personal effects you're taking over?"

"Yeah. My pickup is parked outside with all my stuff in it."

"In that case, grab one of the carts out front and bring it all in here. Unless somebody else is taking your truck, you'll want to sell it. If you want us to sell it, then bring the keys in here after you've emptied it. You do have the title with you, don't you?"

"Oh yeah," Bill replied.

"Great. Well, off you go, then. I'll pull up a power of attorney for you to fill out when you get back."

Janice turned back to the new guy. As Bill was walking away he heard Janice ask, "Okay, then. What's your name?"

The newcomer answered, "Matt Green," in his deep Southern drawl.

Stepping outside, Bill grabbed the four-wheeled garden cart next to the door. The day had warmed considerably since he had been inside. Even with the cart sitting in the shade, heat transferred from the cart's handle to his hand. Unlike western Washington, which seemed to have a perpetual cloud cover, eastern Washington didn't seem to suffer from a lack of sunshine. The hot sun began beating down on Bill's head as he crossed the lot, pulling the cart behind him. By the time he arrived at the truck he could feel sweat breaking out on his forehead and armpits.

After unloading his truck and stacking everything in the cart, Bill was starting to wilt, and sweat stains were becoming visible on his shirt. He couldn't wait to get back into the air-conditioned building.

As he headed back, he heard something hard land near him. Turning to the sound, he saw a rock skitter across the macadam. Several of the protesters near the gate were reaching down to pick things up from the ground. He picked up his pace, keeping an eye on the small crowd. A few more rocks fell near him; the protesters yelled obscenities. One young woman in a flowing dress and her hair in dreadlocks yelled "Killer of planets!"

Back at the building Bill had to hold the door open with one hand while pushing the cart in with the other. As the door closed he could feel the air conditioning hit and begin cooling him and drying his sweat.

"Rowdy crowd out there," he said to Janice.

"Luckily, they're not on Hayek," she said, sliding a document over the counter. "Here you go."

Bill parked the cart beside him while he looked over the power of attorney. Seeing that everything seemed legitimate, he signed the document.

"Well, I guess that's pretty much it," he said. "Where to now?"

Janice pointed to the second door in the room. "Just go through there and follow the signs for the Corps of Discovery. We've got our own gate. A little small, but it's all ours." She smiled. "Don't forget to stop at the currency exchange. You'll want real money on you when you go over. You'll also want to make sure that any electronics you've got with you are accessible. We scan everything for viruses once you pass over. Also, if you've got any firearms, you might want to unload them and keep them packed. I don't recommend wearing them out in public until you've gone through orientation."

"Oh. Okay. What about the cart?"

"Take it with you. It'll be returned once you're finished with it."

Bill grabbed the handle of the cart. "Thanks."

"No problem. Stay safe out there."

As he headed for the door he saw that Matt Green was engrossed in filling out his own forms, not even looking up as Bill passed.

Bill stepped into a cavernous room, deafening with the cacophony created by what seemed like thousands of occupants. There were people of all shapes, sizes, colors, and ages, although there weren't as many older people (as would be expected considering Earth's demographics). Many of them were standing next to carts that were either hand-pulled or pulled by animals. Very few motor vehicles were in sight. It reminded Bill of an old Heinlein novel he read once, about a tunnel in the sky.

He surveyed the scene for a minute, getting his bearings. A bright flashing sign indicated the currency exchange to his right, about fifty feet away. The gate was in the opposite direction, against a far wall. There was nothing flashy or shiny about it, just a simple sign above showing the Corps logo and the words "Corps of Discovery Gate."

Bill pulled his cart to the currency exchange and joined a line of people. The line moved fairly fast as there were several people working behind the desk. In short order, it was Bill's turn.

He approached the desk and saw behind it a sign showing the exchange rates. Gold was selling for 5,000 US dollars an ounce, and the currency fee was two percent. This meant that for 5,100 dollars, one would get an ounce of gold. Bill didn't have to worry about that, as he didn't have all that much money left.

"How may I help you?" asked the young woman, giving him a toothy smile.

"I'm moving to Hayek and I need to get rid of my US currency."

"Very well. Would you like that in gold, silver, certificates, or a direct transfer to a bank?" she asked.

"Uh, what's a certificate?" Bill asked.

"Oh. Well, rather than carry gold or silver everywhere, all banks issue gold and silver certificates. Sort of like US currency, but actually backed up by real gold or silver."

"Gee. I'm not sure. Which do you think would be best? I've already got a credit union account on Hayek. Can I do a combination?"

"Certainly. How much would you like to convert?"

Bill pulled out his wallet and took out his remaining US currency, all one hundred twenty dollars of it. "It's not much, but it's all I've got."

The young woman counted out his currency, then tapped a computer keyboard hidden by the counter. "At today's rate, that would be a little under a fortieth of an ounce of gold or one point two ounces of silver. The only way we could pay you in gold would be a deposit to your account, as that amount is too small to handle physically. We could accommodate most of the silver in coin or certificates if you like, with only a bit as an electronic deposit. The transaction fee would only be point zero two four ounces of silver which we would have to take electronically."

"Okay. Let's do it that way, then," Bill said.

"Great. I'll need to see your bank card".

Bill dug his newly printed card out of his wallet and handed it over. She inserted it into a card reader on the counter and tapped the keyboard again. Then she handed Bill's card back to him, along with three silver coins.

"Here you are. One point one five ounces of silver. The remainder has been deposited in your account. Don't spend it all in one place," she finished with another smile.

Bill fumbled as he attempted to put the coins, his card, and his wallet away. The coins went into a pocket, then the card into the wallet, and the wallet back into its pocket. After completing this masterful act, he looked back at the young woman and said, with his own smile, "Thanks. I'll try not to."

Bill grabbed the cart handle again and begin walking toward the Corps of Discovery gate. The room had gotten even more crowded since he had first entered it. After several minutes of winding himself through groups of people, he finally arrived.

The Corps of Discovery gate had an actual metal fence surrounding it, keeping unwanted people out. A young black man, older than Bill by a couple of years, but still in his twenties, was sitting at a desk behind the fence, reading from an e-book. Like Janice, he was dressed in the Corps of Discovery field uniform, with the same ribbons on his chest. Unlike Janice, he had a pistol strapped to his side. As Bill approached, the young man looked up and put the e-book face down on the desk. "Can I help you?"

Bill nodded. "Sure can. Janice at the Corps office told to me come here to cross over to Hayek."

"Great," he said, standing. "Got your ID? I'll also need to take a DNA sample."

Bill figured he ought to be getting used to the DNA thing by now, considering just how many people obviously wanted to leave Earth. And this was only one of many such buildings scattered across the globe.

The man pulled out a DNA swab from the desk before opening the gate so Bill could enter. A quick swab, a run through the analyzer, and the check was complete.

"Congrats. Looks like you're you," the man said. "Why don't you go stand by the gate over there?" He pointed toward a large metal frame, the size of a single-wide garage door, in front of the gray wall that made up part of the building. On the floor before it were yellow stripes in the middle and red stripes on either side. Arrows on the right side pointed toward the gate and arrows on the left side pointed away from it.

"Go to the right-side lane, just in case anyone's coming over this way. When you get on the other side there'll be somebody there to help you out and get you started. It'll be another ten minutes or so. I heard there's another guy lined up to cross over, too."

Bill walked over to the gate, pulling his laden cart. As he approached it, he heard a clang. Turning around, he saw that the gate was closed and the young man was sitting down at his desk again, reading the e-book. It was then that Bill noticed the man had an artificial leg, as a titanium rod could be seen between the man's shoe and pants cuff.

Sure are a lot of amputees here, he thought.

Bill was full of questions, but it was apparent that the man had no interest in talking. Eventually, Bill pulled his tablet out of his messenger bag to search for the cell phone network, or maybe an open wi-fi. The screen came alive, showing his screensaver of a wooly mammoth on a hill. He touched the settings button. A public wi-fi was available.

Bill checked his old email address one last time, hoping to see if there was one from Jessica. There wasn't. *Well, what the hell did you expect?* he thought. *It's not like you didn't tell her she was wasn't worth it or anything.* There were three emails, though, one from his former college roommate, Joe, one from the university he just graduated from, and one from the Corps of Discovery. He went through them in order.

Joe's email was short, wishing him good luck, and letting Bill know that anytime he wanted to, he was welcome at Joe's place. Bill replied, thanking Joe, and telling him to look him up if he was ever on

Hayek.

The university email was also short, announcing that his diploma would be sent in a couple of months to the forwarding address he had provided and that his official transcripts showing that he had earned his bachelor's degree were now available.

The Corps of Discovery one was a bit longer, and unexpected. It welcomed him to the Corps and advised him of his email address and how to set the password. A link was provided to the server, with a comment that access to the server and email were only available on Hayek, and he should save this email on his hard drive or write down the information. It also gave him a schedule for the first couple of days, beginning in just a few days. *The Corps moves pretty fast*, he thought.

Bill noticed that the first day was for an introduction to the Corps and Basic Militia Training orientation and equipment issue. He wondered just how much equipment would be issued, and what the training would be like.

Just as he was finishing the final email, he heard the man at the desk say, "Hi. How can I help you?"

Bill looked up and saw Matt Green.

"I'm here for the Corps of Discovery," Matt said. It sounded to Bill like, "Ahm he'e fo' tha Coah o' Discuvry".

After the same process Bill had just gone through, Matt joined Bill in line.

Bill held out his hand. "Bill Clark."

Matt grasped Bill's hand in return, a firm, dry hand. "Matt Green."

"I heard. So, what's the Corps got planned for you?" Bill asked.

"Co-pilot. You?"

"Survey Specialist," Bill answered. "Although I've got additional duties as copilot and navigator, apparently."

"That's awesome. Maybe we'll be working together. My additional duties are navigator and exploration surveyor."

"Exploration surveyor?"

"Yeah, you know, the guys on the ground who walk around

exploring. They're the ones who do the actual cataloging of data."

"Wow. How'd you get that?"

"Growing up, I was that one kid who spent more time hunting and fishing than I did in school. When I decided to go to college I studied zoology and did a lot of outdoor stuff. As a matter of fact, I worked as a NOLS instructor for the past three summers."

"NOLS?" Bill asked.

"National Outdoor Leadership School. You know, the guys who lead six-week backcountry adventures. I spent a lot of time outdoors doing basic backpacking and survival stuff."

"Well, I hope that you never need that survival stuff." Just as Bill said that, the young man at the desk stood up and announced, "Gate opening in two minutes. Stand by and be ready to enter it as soon as it's open. It burns up a lot of neutrons, so let's not waste any."

A flashing yellow light above the portal turned on.

Bill put his tablet away and grabbed the handle of his cart. He was feeling extremely nervous now, his heart rate accelerating and his palms and armpits getting clammy with sweat. He hated his reaction, but it was one he'd always had when facing the unknown.

"One minute," the young man said.

Shortly thereafter, a green flashing light above the door lit up, and the yellow light shut down. The blank wall behind the portal disappeared and was replaced with another room, much smaller than the building they were in. Bill and Matt looked at each other and then walked forward.

"Okay, head on through. Stay safe out there," the young man said.

As they were walking through, they passed a small group of tired-looking men and women, all dressed in Corps of Discovery dress uniforms, walking the other way. One was limping, which made Bill think about amputees again. All three had long hair, and two of the men sported beards. All had the same three ribbons that Janice and the man at the gate wore. Each pulled an empty cart behind them.

HAYEK

Chapter 3

The crossover from Earth to Hayek was completely uneventful—just like walking through any other garage-sized door from one room to another.

Once Bill and Matt entered, and as soon as the other Corps members were through, the gate shut down. A blank cinderblock wall now stood where there had been a large room teeming with thousands of people and animals. The sudden quiet was deafening.

"Welcome to Hayek," Bill heard. He turned to see two members of the Corps sitting beside a table. Both had laptop computers in front of them; a small stack of folded papers was between the laptops. One was a blond woman in her late twenties, the other a man in what appeared to be his early thirties. Both were extremely tanned and had short hair. Both wore the sky-blue ribbon, but not the other two ribbons that Bill had seen on all the other Corps members so far. The greeting had come from the woman.

Next to the man was a small booth containing unfamiliar equipment—Bill presumed it was the gate controls, as he hadn't seen anything on Earth that looked like it could control the gate.

"Thanks," Matt said as he advanced to the desk. Bill followed, not uttering a word.

"You must be Matt Green, and you must be Bill Clark," the woman said, looking at each of them.

They nodded.

"Well, now that you're here, let's get you settled in. First off, let's check your ID."

Both men handed over their new identification cards, which the woman inserted into a card reader on the table. "You're you," she said after each card was read. She typed a few keys on the laptop, then handed the cards back.

"Okay. What happens now is we scan all your electronic devices for viruses, and when that's done you head to Sacajawea Base. Place your devices on the table. Don't want any of those nasty Earth viruses on Hayek," she finished with a smile.

The two men did so. For Bill, it wasn't much of a pile, just his tablet, iPod, and phone. Matt's was slightly bigger, including a laptop and digital camera.

The woman pointed to the phones. "If you plan on using those on Hayek, you'll want to get a compatible SIM card. There are a couple of cell phone providers, so you can decide which company to go with once you get through training. You won't be using them until then anyhow. On the other hand, the Corps will issue you a phone, one that's a whole lot better than what you've got, so you might not want to waste your time upgrading yours."

The man at the table scanned each device, and once sure they were all clean, handed them back to their respective owners.

"The skytrain is owned by Parallel, so since you're in the Corps, you won't need to buy any tickets. Just be sure you've got your ID with you when you ride it. Ride the skytrain to the base, check in there, and they'll assign you housing. I know you're probably excited about being on Hayek and checking out the sights, but hold off until tomorrow, or at least until later today. It ain't goin' nowhere." She smiled again.

Picking up one of the folded papers, she handed it to Matt and said, "Seein' how you're both going to the same place, here's a map of Milton. The skytrain you'll want to take is highlighted on the map, as is our location and the base. You'll have to show your ID at the base entrance. They'll tell you where to go. There's also a cart return area, so once you're done with the cart, park it there and somebody will return it to the entry point. Any questions?"

Both men shook their heads, looked at each other, grabbed the handles of their carts, and headed toward the exit.

"Stay safe out there," the young woman said as a farewell.

Just as Bill pushed the door open, he heard the older man say, "Good luck, guys. Stay safe out there."

Everyone keeps saying that, Bill thought. *I wonder if it's a Corps thing or a Hayek thing?*

Bill and Matt stepped out into the sunshine of Hayek. It felt just like the sunshine in Selah, yet also somewhat different. The air was cleaner. It was also hot, just as hot as it had been in Selah. Bill thought, *That makes sense. The only difference between the two planets is that humans never developed here.*

In front of the building they had just exited was the skytrain station. The skytrain was a suspended rail system, consisting of concrete towers spaced every hundred yards with a rail running between them and suspended from them by a metal latticework. The towers were fifty feet tall, and the rail cars ran underneath the latticework. The bottoms of the cars were suspended twenty-five feet above the ground.

The station was very basic, consisting of a covered platform with stairs leading up to it from either end and an elevator in the middle. Bill noticed that there was a single-lane road running alongside the station, with paved macadam paths along both sides. There appeared to be solar panels along the top of the latticework and the station roof.

Bill and Matt walked along the short walkway between the building and the closest path and then over to the station. Bill pushed the elevator call button and asked Matt, who was still holding the map, "Which train do we get on?"

"A Line East, looks like," he said, showing Bill the highlighted map, indicating their station and their final destination. The two locations appeared to be about fifteen miles apart. The skytrain had five different routes, all with either an east-west or a north-south direction. The A-Line was the longest, and the only one stretching up the Naches River Valley. The rest were clustered within the city, and all linked at a central location marked Intercontinental Station. Bill wondered if that was where one could catch trains from Milton to other cities across North America.

They rode the elevator to the platform and waited. It wasn't long before a suspended train silently pulled into the station.

An overhead voice announced, "A Line East now boarding on track E." The train stopped, doors opened, and several people got off. Bill and Matt entered, awkwardly maneuvering their carts. There were seats at the ends, but the center area was clear, with only support poles. Each man grabbed a pole to hang onto.

The doors closed and the train accelerated. Bill looked at a map above the door. There were only two more stops in Milton, then a long stretch until they arrived at the base.

As the train moved the two men stared out the windows, enraptured by the view. It was an amazing sight; their first parallel city. Mt. Rainier jutted into the sky to their west, and they could see the Yakima River to their east. Between the river and the skytrain was the city of Hayek, built on the same site as the little town of Selah on Earth.

The city was laid out in a grid, with a combination of houses and short multi-story buildings, most in the three- to five-story range. Bill could see that of the closer buildings, the bottom floor or two were for business, and from the third floor up they were residential. The architecture reminded him of Vancouver, British Columbia. Lots of glass and porches.

The single-family homes were smaller than what he was used to, hearkening back to pre-automobile North America. He could see porches on the front, with larger backyards than front yards. He didn't see too many automobiles, and the ones he saw most resembled old Willy's Jeeps or little cab-over pickup trucks.

As a geographer, Bill loved looking at backyards. Looking into those in Milton gave him some insight into the type of culture he could expect to encounter. He could tell that many of the residents were attempting to be self-sufficient. The gardens he saw weren't just simple little plots but instead were full-scale urban agriculture, taking up the majority of the backyards. He even saw several large outdoor aquaculture systems—large fish tanks that fed hydroponic plants.

Nowhere did he see telephone poles or power lines. Bill knew the reason for the former from his studies of the planet—everything was either buried fiber optic or cellular. As to the power, he knew that it was a combination of renewables and nuclear, but he didn't know why he couldn't see any transmission lines. He figured that since Hayek used nuclear power, there must be some leading from the power plants to the cities, but none were visible.

The few remaining passengers got off at the last stop in Milton. Nobody got in their car. The doors closed, and the train began its final leg to the base.

Leaving the city was quite sudden. The landscape went from urban to agriculture, with no extended suburbs. Bill could see orchards, vineyards, and some pasture with sheep grazing, but what he found noticeably different from the agriculture he was used to was the lack of cattle. Bill pointed out this to Matt.

"Yeah, well, y'know Hayek limits cattle imports," Matt said.

"Pretty odd for a supposed libertarian society."

"Yep. But then again, it ain't full-on anarchy-type libertarianism. They do have some rules. Guess they're trying not to destroy this planet like people did on Earth."

"I bet you're right. Probably trying to avoid 'the tragedy of the commons' type scenario," Bill said.

"Tragedy of the commons?"

"You know, when everyone has free access to something so they use it as much as they can 'til it's gone. From an old story about cows on the common meadow in a town. Nobody owned it, and everyone wanted to maximize their gain, so they each put so many cows on it that all grass got eaten and the cows starved."

"Gotcha," Matt replied.

They rode in silence after that, watching the landscape pass by. After a while, Matt nudged him and said, "Hey, look at that!"

Bill turned and saw what looked like an oversized drone with four propellers flying parallel to the train and slightly above it. This craft was actually carrying a person inside it. "Wow, an actual flying car!" he exclaimed.

They watched the flying car until it veered off near the final stop.

The fifteen-mile trip from the gate took less than fifteen minutes, even with the stops in Milton.

The doors whooshed open. Bill and Matt stepped out on the platform, carts in tow, and were immediately assaulted by the heat. It must already have been in the low nineties, and it wasn't even noon.

They headed for the elevator's open doors. At ground level, they stepped out and saw a large wooden sign that said: "Welcome to Corps of Discovery Sacajawea Base: New Probationary Members Check in at In-Processing." A map was next to it showed the streets of the base. The streets were named, but the buildings only had numbers. A legend identified each building. The In-Processing building was listed as Number 2; headquarters was listed as Number 1.

Before they could exit the skytrain station, though, they had to present a security guard their ID card before she opened the gate.

Fortunately, the In-Processing building was adjacent to the train station, so there was little opportunity for the two men, or just about any Probie, to get lost.

Bill and Matt made a beeline for the building. A Jeep was parked in front of the building. Bill thought it was a Willy's CJ-3B, the old high-hood Jeep, but he thought, *That can't be. There weren't that many produced on Earth, and most of those are trashed. This thing looks brand spanking new.*

Upon entry, they found, with great relief, that it was air-conditioned. The room was quite large, with a long counter bisecting the front from the back. The counter had signs suspended above it, breaking the alphabet down into eight sections of three letters each. Above all the signs was one stating "Last Name begins with…" Below each sign was a computer monitor and a card reader, identical to the ones they had already been exposed to. Bill headed for the spot under the ABC sign, while Matt headed for the GHI sign spot. Before either man made more than a couple of steps, a young Asian girl with short hair waved them over to the last sign. She was dressed in the Corps field uniform with only the sky-blue ribbon on her chest.

"Just come on over here. Not much of a crowd, so I think I can handle the two of you," she said. "Wait another couple of days, though. This place'll start jumping."

After they arrived at the counter, she put them through the same ID check they'd been through several times already. "Well, it looks like you two are who you claim to be. Welcome to the Corps. I'm Amy Ito."

Bill nodded while Matt said, "Hi."

"Next step is to get you some housing," Amy said. "After that, you're free to do whatever you want. I, personally, suggest reading the Base Information pamphlet that you'll find in your cabin, if you haven't already read the one sent to you in the information packet. That'll bring you up to speed on what's what on base. Lunch in the Probie cafeterias starts at noon, so make your way to one and join the other Probies that came early. Some of the cadre will be there and glad to answer any questions you have."

"Great," Bill said.

"You guys want to room together?" Amy asked.

Matt and Bill looked at each other, shrugged.

"Sure," Bill said.

"Why not?" Matt agreed.

"Great. Let me get you set up."

Amy typed for a minute, then inserted each man's card into the card reader one final time before handing them back.

"Okay. I've got you set up in a nice little four-bedroom cabin on Jaskey Lane. You'll have two other roommates, who are already there, so don't be surprised. You might want to announce yourself when you arrive. Your ID serves as your key, so don't lose it. It'll also grant you access to the safe in your room. You'll want to reset the bio-code once you open it. And if you've got any firearms with you, I'd suggest storing them ASAP."

Amy picked up a map of the base and using a pink highlighter, marked the cabin's location, along with the In-Processing building. She then highlighted the most direct route, which was about a quarter of a mile.

"Just head up Floyd Boulevard until you get to Jaskey Lane, then turn left. The address is 117 Jaskey Lane, on the west side of the street. Any questions?"

Bill asked, "Bio-code?"

Amy said, "Yeah, your fingerprint. Most safes operate on bio-codes, either fingerprints, palm prints, eye scans, or DNA samples. We use fingerprints on base for personal safes."

Matt asked, "Where's the closest cafeteria?"

Amy highlighted it on the map.

"Right here, at the corner of Floyd and Rosen. About two blocks from your cabin."

"Thanks, Amy," Matt said.

"What do we do with the carts once we're done?"

"Bring them back here after lunch. We'll send them back to Earth for the next bunch of Probies."

Turning to Bill, Matt asked, "Well. Shall we?"

Bill responded, "We shall" rather formally, with a quick nod of his head.

The two men grabbed their carts, bade Amy farewell, and headed back out into the hot sunshine of Sacajawea Base.

117 Jaskey Lane looked like a small, two-story board-and-batten cabin from rural Washington. It sat almost on the sidewalk in front of

it, with three broad steps leading up to a small porch. On the porch was a double-wide swing and two Adirondack-style chairs, and a couple of small tables.

Bill took the lead. Dropping the handle of his cart, he walked up the stairs and rang the doorbell. He heard motion inside, and the door was shortly thereafter opened by a black man, obviously in his early twenties, and just as obviously trying to grow a mustache. He was similar in stature to Matt, short and lean.

"Can I help you?" he asked, staring at Bill with gold-flecked hazel eyes.

"Hi. I'm Bill Clark, and this is Matt Green," Bill said, pointing back to Matt, who was standing by the carts on the sidewalk. "We're your new roommates."

"Oh, hey. Great. C'mon in," the young man said, opening the door wider and giving them a welcoming gesture.

"I'm Jordan. Jordan Washington. Our other roomie is in the can, but he should be out soon." Jordan held out his hand to Bill.

Bill took it and gave a brief, firm shake, and was rewarded with the same type in kind.

"Let me get my stuff," Bill said.

Meanwhile, Matt had already figured out that pulling the cart up the stairs was not a happening thing, so he had grabbed a box and was heading up, passing Bill on the way.

"Hi," he said to Jordan, nodding instead of trying to balance a box and try shaking hands.

"Nice to meet you, Matt. Welcome. Just pile your stuff up in the main room and I'll give you guys a tour. We've got two rooms left so you'll have to fight over them."

Bill and Matt quickly emptied their carts, creating a small pile in the main room. Thankfully, the cabin was air-conditioned.

As Matt was bringing in his last box, he heard the sound of a toilet flushing, and then another young man stepped into the main room. This man was also in his early twenties and short, but barely clearing five feet, black-haired, and quite obviously of Asian ancestry.

"Hey Thep, meet Matt and Bill, our new roomies," Jordan said.

"Hi," Thep said, shaking their hands. "Actually, my real name is Thepakorn Daeng, but everyone calls me Thep." Despite speaking in fluent American accented English, it was obvious that it was Thep's second language.

"So, how about the grand tour?" Jordan asked the group.

"Lead on," Matt replied.

Jordan spread his arms and waved around. "This, well, this is the great room, living room, main room, whatever you want to call it." The room Jordan indicated contained a small leather sofa and a couple of leather chairs, a coffee table, and a few end tables with lamps on them. There was nothing else: no television, no stereo, no pictures, just blank walls. The wood floor looked like it had seen some heavy use, but was still in good shape.

"Follow me," Jordan said, and led the men into a kitchen with a small dining nook attached to it. "This is where we fix the occasional meal, and, more importantly, where we store the beer. Most meals are in the cafeteria, so we don't do much cooking here."

Next to the kitchen was a utility room with a washing machine and dryer. "Here's where we try to clean clothes, and our 'guest' bathroom." Bill could see the appliances and suspected that the toilet was hiding behind one of them. He saw a door leading out to the backyard through the room.

Jordan led the three men back to the main room, and then up a flight of stairs. There were three doors at the top landing, one in front of the stairs and one to either side.

"That," Jordan said, pointing to the front door, "is your bathroom," then pointing to the other two doors, "and those are your bedrooms. Thep and I have already claimed the first-floor bedrooms, so these ones are yours."

Matt said, "I've got no preference. You choose."

Bill considered it for a moment. "If you don't mind, I'll take the one on the left." Considering just how hot it got in eastern Washington for the summer, and that they were in the same location here on Hayek, he would rather have a north-facing room in the summer.

After making his decision, Bill opened the door to his room and looked in. It was pretty sparse: a single-bed with only a bare mattress, a small built-in desk, a work chair, a closet, and a small gun safe. He was curious about why they each had a safe and asked Jordan about it.

"From what I understand, everyone's supposed to keep all firearms locked up if they aren't in direct control of them. Since we get issued several rifles, I suspect the Corps don't want us losing them or having them stolen. You can read more about it on the Base Information Pamphlet."

"Oh. Any idea where this pamphlet is?" Bill asked.

"Downstairs. I'll get it for you after you get moved in," Jordan said.

All four men returned to the main floor, where Bill and Matt began the process of moving their belongings to their rooms. It didn't take long.

Bill set most of his stuff on the floor, with the exception of the duffel bag, which he placed on the bed's mattress.

Then he spent a couple of minutes figuring out how to operate the safe. There were instructions on the safe's top. The first step was to insert his ID into a slot just above the door. After he extracted the card, a fingerprint sensor above the door handle would light up where he was to place his thumb and then his index finger. He was advised to do so several times at slightly different angles, then remove his ID card. The safe would then be active and ready to be opened.

Bill was able to open the safe within a couple of minutes. He closed the door and did a dry run to see how fast he could open it again. Within seconds the door was open.

Over at the bed, he pulled clothes and bed linens out of his duffel, eventually exposing his rifles and pistol case.

He pulled the first rifle out, a Ruger Mini-14, checked the

chamber to ensure it was empty, and set it in the gun safe. The second rifle was a rather unique one, a break action single shot carbine manufactured by Thompson Center Arms. It was a Contender carbine, designed to allow the user to switch barrels for a variety of calibers. Bill had two barrels, one in 6.8 SPC, and the other in .22 long rifle.

Bill broke the rifle open and checked the chamber. Seeing it was still empty, he closed the action and set it in the gun safe, then retrieved his final firearm. He opened the case and extracted the pistol, a Glock 19. Holding it in his right hand, with his finger down the side of the trigger guard, he pulled the slide back, checking the chamber to ensure it, too, was still empty, and there was no magazine in the magazine well. Seeing it conformed to all the firearm safety norms he was taught, he released the slide and placed the Glock on the shelf that was inside the safe on top.

He debated putting Jessica's ring in the safe, but decided to keep it with him. *Never know when you'll find a good pawn shop*, he thought

Satisfied, he closed the safe door and heard a click indicating it was locked.

Once they all congregated back in the main room Jordan handed Bill a pamphlet. "You'll want to spend some time on that, but maybe after lunch. Whaddaya guys say? Should we go get our feed on?"

Bill looked at his old-fashioned analog watch and discovered that it was almost noon. "I'm up for it."

"Me, too," replied Matt.

Thep just nodded his head and started for the door.

Bill set the pamphlet down on the coffee table and joined the exodus.

Stepping outside, the group was met by a veritable heat wave.

"Gonna be another scorcher," Jordan said.

"How hot you figure it's going to get?" Matt asked.

"According to the weather report, all the way up to 38."

"Huh?" Matt said. "What's that in English?"

"Oh, a bit over a hundred Fahrenheit, I guess. Nobody here uses the English system, other than gold and silver ounces, which are really Troy ounces, so you better get used to going metric."

"Yeah. Never could figure out why you Americans used that old system, anyhow," piped up Thep. "Even the English and Canadians gave it up a long time ago."

"I guess we're just stubborn," Matt muttered.

"So, how long have you guys been here?" Bill asked Jordan and Thep.

"Well, I got here two days ago, and Thep arrived yesterday," Jordan said.

"Wow. For some reason, I thought you'd been here longer," Bill said.

"Nah, but we've made the most of it," Thep said.

"Ah, here we are—the Culinary Institute of Sacajawea Base," intoned Jordan, as the group arrived at the cafeteria, getting a chuckle from them all.

The cafeteria, in addition to being air conditioned, was large, capable of seating 250 people at a time. Most of the round tables were empty. Bill saw that there was at least one uniformed member of the Corps at each of several tables, surrounded by people who were dressed in civilian clothing. Some of the uniformed members had long hair, though most had short.

As they loaded up their trays, Bill saw that some foods were labeled 'vegan' or 'vegetarian'. He elected to try a vegan lasagna along with a large scooping of cantaloupe for dessert, along with a tomato based drink, much like the V-8 he used to enjoy on Earth.

Once their trays were filled, the four men sat down at a table occupied by two young women in civilian clothes and a tall, young, Polynesian-looking man in a field uniform. Bill noticed that there were no ribbons on the man's uniform.

"Howdy," said the Corps member. "Jordan, Thep," he said with a nod. Turning to Bill and Matt, he added, "I'm Luke. Luke Kanehama." After handshakes and introduction, Luke gestured to the two young ladies. "This tall brunette is Kim Smith, and the shorter gal is Brenda Lightfoot." Kim appeared tall, even sitting, while Brenda appeared like she might be a Native American. Bill thought the table looked like a liberal professor's ideal version of diversity, despite the fact they all probably shared the same ideology and desires.

Once they were seated, Luke asked, "So, I guess you guys are full of questions?"

Matt and Bill nodded.

"Thought so. Most Probies are, so that's why I'm here."

Bill asked, "I couldn't help but notice, the people on Earth who greeted us were amputees. Is that common?"

Luke swallowed a mouthful of food before chuckling and responding.

"No, not really. But, it does happen. And once you lose a limb, you're pretty much toast for field ops. That doesn't stop people from wanting to serve, so the Corps will usually put them in positions that they need filled, but don't need all the body parts."

"How do they usually lose limbs?" Matt asked.

"It depends. For many, it could be an equipment failure, like a plane going down. For others, it might be nature. Like Janice Goodland, who was probably the one who checked you in on Earth. She was attacked by a smilodon on a survey. Damned lucky she only lost an arm and got those scratches. Smilodons usually kill whatever they attack. That woman's one tough cookie. In her case, the smilodon lost," he finished with a tight smile.

"Ouch," muttered Matt.

Bill grimaced, then asked, "I noticed that a lot of Corps members have ribbons on their chests. What do they represent?"

"Hmm. The most common ones are Survey medals, Purple Hearts, and Trekker medals," Luke said. "Survey medals can be for ground or aerial surveys, and they're awarded for completing a survey. Purple Hearts are the 'I forgot to duck' medal. They're similar to the US military Purple Heart, but in this case, it's for any injury sustained in the line of duty while on a survey. See, most of what we do is dangerous. You're out there, mostly all on your own. Even a minor mishap could lead to some serious consequences. So, a horse falling on you and crushing your leg, or a branch coming down on your tent in a storm qualifies you. You don't need to be shot at or in a war, although the militia and the standing army give out the Purple Heart for those reasons."

"Oh, so that would explain why Janice and the other guy at the gate had Purple Hearts," Matt said.

"Yep. If I'm correct, they also had the Trekker medal," Luke replied. "As a matter of fact, I know Goodland does."

"What's that one?" Bill asked.

Luke set his fork down and put his elbows on the table, lacing his fingers in front of him. "It's the one you don't want. Technically, it's called the Survival Journey medal, but we just call it the Trekker medal. It's the one given to anyone who has to trek back to the local base, IP, or civilization after something went terribly wrong. In Goodland's case, her survey flight went down on the east coast here on Hayek about twenty-five years ago. It was just a routine mapping survey. She and the navigator were the only ones to survive the flight, and that's because they bailed out before the plane crashed that they survived. Anyhow, they had to trek halfway across the continent until Goodland got rescued. She lost the arm and the navigator on that trek. Hence, the three different medals."

Matt and Bill raised their eyebrows at this, as did all the Probies around the table, with small mutters of "whoa" and "holy shit" came from those seated at the table.

"There's also medals for saving lives—one just for saving a life, and another for putting your own life at risk to do so. You'll see a lot of those. Of course, there are also some that one can earn in the Militia or the military that Corps members are authorized to wear, including military medals from Earth, if it's a real thing, not just a 'been there, done that'."

Luke took a sip of his coffee and continued. "Typical military medals are campaign medals, and medals for bravery. Anyone involved in a shooting match, and I'm talking real combat, gets the Combat Action Badge. It's similar to the US Army's CAB, but here we don't differentiate between a Combat Infantry Badge and a CAB, everyone gets the same thing. After all, if it's a shooting war, and you get into action, it don't matter if you're infantry or a cook. It's all the same thing."

Luke took another sip of coffee. "Anything else?"

Kim asked, "Why do some Corps members have long hair, but most don't?"

"Ah, great question. Notice my hair is short?" Luke pointed to his head. "You might have noticed that those with the long hair also have a Trekker medal. The Corps requires short hair, but they decided that anyone who can survive a trek could pretty much do what they damn well please when it comes to their hair length. It's actually usually pretty long by the time they show up in civilization, so it's not so much growing their hair as it is just not cutting it. They're also allowed to grow beards, while the rest of us peons can only have a mustache. Of course, you Probies can't have any facial hair, so you'll have to wait a bit if you want a stache"

At this point, Jordan rubbed his small mustache and made a face.

Brenda asked "What about women? They won't require us to cut our hair like the guys, will they?"

Luke shrugged. "Actually, they do. You've seen the women in Corps with the short hair?"

Both women nodded.

"Well, they're the same as you and me, Corps members who haven't had to trek. You have to keep in mind, Hayek has probably one of the most egalitarian cultures out there and the Corps is even more so. Of course, that can sometimes cause angst, especially for those who like to differentiate between genders or races, but it is what it is."

Luke took another sip of coffee, while the others continued to eat.

"So, where are you guys from?" Luke asked Matt and Bill.

"I'm from Memphis," Matt replied.

"Where's that?" Luke asked.

It was at this moment that Bill realized that Luke might not be from their Earth.

"Uh, it's in Tennessee," Matt replied.

"Ah, one of those states around the Appalachians," Luke said.

"Actually, more along the Mississippi River," Matt said.

"That would explain the accent," Luke said, nodding his head in understanding.

Luke then looked at Bill expectantly.

"Oh, I'm a military brat. My dad was in the Air Force, so I've lived all over the place. I've lived in Seattle for the past four years, attending U-Dub."

Matt asked "U-dub?"

"Yeah, the University of Washington, the letters U and W, shortened to U-Dub to describe the school."

"I've seen it a couple of times. Didn't know it was called that," Luke said.

The other four had been quietly eating during this exchange, but then Thep asked, "So, where are you from Luke?"

"I grew up in a small city on the other side of the Cascades, Tahoma. It's pretty much in the same place as Earth's city of Tacoma. Originally, I'm from Earth, but my folks migrated here when I was a toddler, so I'm not too familiar with Earth, other than the occasional notification or recruiting trip."

"What's a notification trip?" asked Kim.

"Next of Kin notification. You know, 'Sorry to inform you Mrs. Smith, but your boy got eaten by a terror bird while on a ground survey' type thing," Luke answered.

"Is that common?" she asked.

"Unfortunately, all too common. We lose several members every survey. Usually to beasties, but sometimes to equipment failure, nasty bugs, or just plain stupid shit. I knew one guy who got killed when a tree branch fell on him. Talk about some bad karma," Luke said with a sad shake of his head.

"You did know about the mortality rate before you signed up, didn't you?" he then asked the group, looking at them intently.

All of them nodded their heads. Brenda said, "Yeah, but you figure it won't happen to you."

"There is that," Luke said.

Matt turned to the others. "So, where's everyone else from?"

Brenda said, "I'm from Colville—it's a small town just north of here on Earth, close to the Canadian border. Unlike dog boy here," she said, pointing at Bill, "I went to Wazzoo. Go Cougs!" she finished with a hoot.

"Wazzoo, what the heck is that? Sounds like a body part you sit on," Matt said, with a slight upward curl of his lips.

"Washington State University. Easier than saying that or WSU," Brenda answered looking slightly miffed.

Matt raised his eyebrows. "That makes sense, but why did you call Bill 'dog boy'?"

"Because I went to U-Dub, home of the Huskies," Bill answered for her.

The others laughed slightly.

Kim spoke up. "I'm from San Antonio, Texas. My dad was also military, but he was stationed in Texas most of the time."

"I thought Texans had the same kind of accent that Matt does. Why do you sound more like Bill?" Luke asked.

"Because my folks weren't from Texas," she said. "My dad was from New York and my mom was from California. I guess I picked up their speech patterns. And I graduated with my master's from UT Austin."

"UT Austin?" Luke asked.

"The University of Texas at Austin. That's the state capital of Texas, and they've got a great geography program, which is what I studied."

"Hey, a fellow geographer," Bill said. "I studied GIS and remote sensing. How 'bout you?"

"Same thing. I guess that makes us geo-nerds," Kim said, visibility brightening up.

"What's GIS?" Matt asked.

"Geographic Information Systems," Kim said. "It's basically computerized mapping, but with the ability to analyze spatial data. You know the map app on your phone to get directions?"

Matt nodded his head.

"That's a simple network analysis, one of the functions of a GIS. There's a whole bunch more but no sense in boring you with this geo-nerd stuff," she finished with a smile.

Matt turned to Thep. "Well, roomie, what about you?"

Thep replied, "I'm from the Chiang Mai. You've probably never heard of it. It's a little place in the northern part of Thailand. In the mountains, so it's not quite the tropical paradise you would think. Also, not enough action for me, and too many rules."

"Sounds like Seattle," Bill said.

"Probably, but without all the people and things to do, unless you like water buffalo, if you know what I mean," Thep said. "Anyhow, I got my degree in tropical botany from Chulalongkorn University in Bangkok."

Jordan volunteered, "I'm from East LA." Everyone turned to look at him. "I decided that it wasn't for me, so I got a scholarship to Stanford, and busted my butt to get into the Corps. Yeah, unlike my friends and family members still there, I ain't dead or in prison."

"Why would they be dead or in prison?" Luke asked, looking perplexed.

"Ah, you know. Gangs and the War on Drugs stuff," Jordan said. "Most of the guys I knew growing up were either using the shit or selling it. And if you're selling it, you're in a gang. And you know how gangs in LA are."

"I've heard of all that, but luckily we don't have it here," Luke said. "No need for a war on drugs or prisons for drug users. Drugs aren't illegal. No need for gangs, either, because our society frowns on that kind of collectivist grouping for violence." Then he grinned. "Except when it's the Militia; I guess we're nothing more than one big collectivist mob for violence."

"So, what did you study?" Matt asked Jordan.

"Biology," Jordan answered proudly. "I figured with all the new worlds being found, there'd be plenty of opportunity for me."

"You ain't kiddin'," Luke said. "Biologists, botanists, and zoologists are top hires. Not just in the Corps, but also for many of those migrating to the newer planets. Of course, so are mining engineers, mechanical engineers, civil engineers, agricultural experts. Well, you get the idea," he finished with a smile.

"In other words, if you've got a useful degree, you're wanted," Brenda said.

"Actually, it's more like a useful education," Luke replied. "Degrees count, but most places care more about practicalities and common sense than they do degrees. As a matter of fact, here on Hayek, we look at the total picture, not just to see if you've got a degree or two. Of course, graduating from Hayek University or the University of Milton, or even Cascadia Tech shows you've got a pretty decent education."

"Wait," Jordan said. "You mean you've got colleges and universities here?"

"Of course. What do you think we are, home-schooled inbreds? Look, we've got close to sixty million people on this planet, and lots of things to do. Of course, we've got colleges and universities. Most focus on practical learning, unlike some of those silly programs I've seen for Earth universities. Didn't you read the pamphlet the Corps sent you?"

Bill shook his head. "Actually, I never got it. I guess it was still in the mail when I reported in."

"Well, you might want to pick one up or do some research. Lots to learn about Hayek."

While Bill knew that a lot of people were migrating off Earth, he'd been unaware that the number of people on Hayek was so large. *I think I better do some research, like ASAP. Damn, I wish I'd gotten that packet.* Bill had planned on doing more research on Hayek and the Corps after graduation and before reporting, but Jessica's behavior left him in a bit of a tailspin and accelerated his move.

"Did you go to one of those schools, Luke?" Kim asked.

"Yep. Cascadia Polytechnical School. I've got a degree in Exploration Science."

"Exploration Science? That's an actual degree?" Jordan asked, sounding surprised.

"Of course it is," Luke answered indignantly. "You only studied biology at Stanford. At Cascadia Tech I studied zoology, botany, physical geography, geology, remote sensing, GIS, resource identification, and aviation science. I also had to study some civil engineering, metallurgy, and field repair. As a matter of fact, with more Hayekers graduating with an Exploration Science degree, the Corps is starting to phase out recruitment from Earth. I'm betting in five years no Earther will be able to get admitted to the Corps."

"Wow. Guess we got in under the wire" Matt said.

The others nodded.

"Then again, if the Gaia Firsters get their way, there won't be a Corps of Discovery," Luke said.

"Gaia Firsters?" Matt asked.

"Yeah. I guess on Earth you'd call them Earth Firsters. They put the natural planet above the needs and wants of humans. They're always interfering with gate operations to stop exploration and settlement."

Bill hadn't heard about this, though he remembered the protesters at the gate. He asked Luke to expand on it.

Luke told them about a group of people who called themselves "The Gaia Liberation Front;" their slogan was "Gaia First." They had been responsible for a number of attacks on the company, the Corps, and several gates on Earth. "Fortunately, since Parallel controls the gates, not too many of those whack jobs made it to Hayek to cause any problems. I'd hate to see what they would do if they got over here."

"How come we've never heard about any of this before?" Kim asked.

"Beats me. It's always big news here whenever a gate gets attacked or an Explorer gets killed. We've even had the Militia called up a couple of times."

The group continued with their lunch, probing Luke about the Corps and Hayek. They also wanted to know what the rules were about leaving base.

"Other than when you've got to be somewhere, you're free to go anywhere you want. I'd just suggest holding off a couple of days until you've learned enough to survive out there unless you've got a guide. Hayek's a lot different than Earth. Safer, but also easier to get into trouble if you don't know what you're doing. Tell you what, though. If you guys like, I'll take you into Milton tomorrow. But you've got to promise you'll listen to me and do what I say."

"I'm game," Bill said. The others agreed.

They decided they would meet for breakfast, then explore Hayek as a group.

"Make sure you've got enough in your accounts for any goodies you may want," Luke cautioned. "I don't want to start you off in debt to somebody."

"Where can we check our bank accounts?" Bill asked.

"The base has secure wi-fi all over the place. Just check online. The password is in your cabin," Luke answered.

"I'll show you where it is," Thep said to Bill and Matt.

After lunch, the group split up, with the four men of 117 Jaskey Lane heading back to their cabin. Bill put his card in the lock's card slot to see if it would work. It did, and the four went inside.

Thep pointed to a piece of paper tacked to the wall near the front door. "Here's the wi-fi and password info. They apparently don't change it too often."

Bill picked up the Base Information pamphlet and sat down in one of the chairs so he could read up on his new home.

On the inside cover of the pamphlet was a map of the base. It looked rather large, extending from the outskirts of Milton on the east to the crest of the Cascade Mountains on the west, and from the Yakima River Canyon to the north to a ridgeline several miles south of the Yakima River. It still caused a bit of a disconnect for Bill, seeing names he was used to mixed in with names of towns and cities that weren't on Earth. He knew that the volcano he knew as Mt. Rainier had once been called Tahoma, but seeing it on the map as such was disconcerting, to say the least. He wondered why some names remained the same, while others were replaced or gone.

The first page was a welcome letter from the Commandant of the Corps of Discovery. The usual fluff, as far as Bill was concerned.

The next page showed a more detailed map of the main base area within the Naches River Valley. Bill saw that about a mile south of the valley was the airfield, Bowman Field, and to its west were firing ranges. Bowman Field, named after the inventor of the gate and the founder of Hayek, was rather large, with two parallel runways and a third that transected it.

Bill learned that the base was named after Sacajawea, a Lehmi Shoshone woman who helped the United States Corps of Discovery in 1804, led by William Clark and Meriwether Lewis. The purpose of that Corps was to explore North America for the US government. Bill chuckled upon reading this, thinking, *Well, here's another William Clark in another Corps of Discovery.*

Pages showed the contact information for the many facilities and the heads of each department, including an emergency number for medical or life-threatening emergencies, along with the hours for each facility.

After reading the pamphlet, Bill set it back down on the coffee table and went to his room to retrieve his tablet. Back in the main room, he saw Matt reading the pamphlet. Thep and Jordan had decided to flop down on the sofa and were engrossed in their tablets.

"Hey, guys. Anyone interested in seeing the museum?" Bill

asked.

"I'm up for it," Matt said.

"Naw, I saw it yesterday morning," Jordan replied.

"I'll join you," said Thep.

"All right then," Bill said. "Let's go."

"Have fun, guys," Jordan said as the three men headed out into the summer heat of Hayek.

A short walk later, they arrived at the museum. It was larger than Bill had expected. He was used to military museums on military bases, which were typically only a couple of rooms in a regular-sized building. This museum was the size of a small gymnasium, and two stories tall.

As they entered, they breathed a sigh of relief when hit with the cool air inside.

The first thing they saw was a lifelike representation of a man on a horse, a lever-action rifle held in one hand, the reins in the other. He was wearing a brown felt fedora, a work shirt, blue jeans, boots, and had a revolver in a holster strapped around his waist. The horse wore a Western saddle with saddle bags behind and on the horn. Bill realized that the statue was the man responsible for discovering the gate, and Parallel, Incorporated's founder, Timothy Bowman, Ph.D. The statue represented him on his first journey onto Hayek, when he and several others made a trip to the Blue Mountains, in the area Bill knew as Baker City, Oregon, to gather the gold necessary to finance the start of the process of opening up Hayek and other parallel planets for exploration and settlement.

As the men walked around the first floor of the museum, they saw many large photographs of that first journey, including landscapes that were vaguely familiar, unshaped by the hands of man, and plenty of megafauna, including mastodons, giant beavers, a smilodon, North American lions, a cave bear, a pack of dire wolves, and herds of elk unlike anything seen on Earth in over a hundred years.

A display of David Jaskey was in one corner of the first floor. It was because of him the first expedition went in armed sufficiently to protect themselves against carnivores who had no fear of humans. Most of the first party had either 45-70 lever-action rifles, the same one carried by Dr. Bowman in the statue, or civilian versions of the M-14 military rifle, the M1-A. The M1-A fired a 7.62 mm bullet, which was considered suitable for any animal up to 1,000 pounds and was the same caliber issued by the Corps to its survey members today. The display had photographs of him prior to crossing over, and on Hayek. He was a nondescript man in his mid-fifties, with a balding pate, graying hair, and a bit of a pot belly. A brief description of his life and the impact he had on that first expedition was attached to a large sign on the wall.

A Grumman Goose twin-engine seaplane rested in the center of the first floor, looking ready to take off at a moment's notice. Bill knew, from his readings about Hayek, that this was the plane that had taken the second expedition to California's gold country.

As the men toured the museum, they saw stuffed animals from various parallel Earths, including some that looked like small dinosaurs. There were plenty of megafauna, along with normal-sized animals (at least, normal-sized to Bill and the others). Pictures of past Corps members in various stages of exploration or training abounded, as did displays of the various pieces of equipment used.

There was a special section on the second floor dedicated to trekkers. A pink marble wall listed the names of all trekkers, with a star next to those killed in the line of duty. The wall had almost five hundred names, of which more than half had stars. It was a sobering display.

It also showed the tools trekkers used, and those developed along the way. There were obsidian knives, fish hooks made from bone, nets and snares made from rawhide or wood fibers, and a complete outboard rigger canoe. The display reminded Bill of some of the Hawai'ian and Native American museums he had been to, where the natives made everything from natural things, such as plants, rocks, and animals. He hoped he'd never be put in that position.

The final display was one honoring those who had died in the line of duty. It was a long, white marble wall with the names carved into it. Each name was painted gold, so the name stood out in bright, bold color. If the trekker display was sobering, this one was doubly so. Almost two thousand names were listed, including those from the trekker wall. While the number seemed large, one had to take into account that it was over a forty-year period, reaching back to the gate's discovery, through the beginning of the mass exploration and migration period twenty years ago, to the present.

By the time the men finished at the museum, it was supper time, so they headed for the cafeteria. Along the way, they saw many new people hauling carts onto the base. It was actually becoming somewhat busy on base with all the new arrivals.

"Looks like it's starting to get busy," Matt said on seeing the increased activity. "I wonder how many crossed over after us."

Chapter 4

When they arrived at the cafeteria, they were surprised at how crowded it was. While the lunchtime crowd had been pretty sparse, now at least half the large room was occupied. A lot of people were talking, that, with the sound of cutlery on dinnerware, created quite a din.

Thep pointed across the room. "There's Jordan. Let's get some food and join him."

Bill saw Jordan half out of his seat, waving to them. He was with three different women than the ones they ate lunch with. Bill waved back and joined the line to get his food.

When Bill got to the table with a bowl of venison stew and a couple of biscuits, Thep and Matt were already seated, wolfing down their meals.

"So, whaddya think of the museum?" Jordan asked.

"Sobering," Bill said. "Makes you realize just how dangerous the job is."

"It is that."

Jordan introduced the men to the women. Two were from New Hampshire but had actually met at the Massachusetts Institute of Technology, and the third, Nicole Andrews, was from Christchurch, New Zealand. The two Americans still exhibited their winter paleness, but Andrews' face and arms showed a tan, due to her hemisphere of the planet just finishing up their summer and fall.

Bill mentioned that he had always wanted to visit New Zealand, but it looked like it wouldn't be happening anytime soon.

"That's too bad," Nicole said in her Kiwi twang. "But, then again, where we're going will probably be a thousand times better. So, which of you boys is a pilot?"

Matt raised his hand and said, "Well, actually, I'm listed as a co-pilot. Does that count?"

"Me, too," said Bill.

Nicole laughed. "Me, three. That's why I was asking, to see if I'd be working with any of you."

The eight sat, ate, and chatted for almost an hour, then decided to hit one of the bars on base for a beer or two.

It was obvious that Matt and Nicole were hitting it off. Bill suspected that if they spent much time together, Matt might do the same thing his college roommate Joe did—disappear as a roommate. Watching the two of them caused Bill to experience a flashback; he and Jessica sitting on the quad at UW, with the cherry blossoms in full bloom, along with the smell of her, something that Bill always found attractive. It was so real it caused him to experience a sudden physical feeling of loss and aching. He almost gasped out loud but didn't. Luckily, nobody noticed.

Did I do the right thing? he wondered. *Either way, it's done, and I can't go back. Not unless I can come up with a hundred grand to pay back the gate fee.*

The bar they decided on was a small, relatively quiet establishment. A sign above the door declared it the Cave Bear Cave, with a painting of a cave bear emerging from a cave beneath the name. The air temperature was cooling down, so the group decided to take a table in the outdoor beer garden. Light music was playing over a speaker system strung on poles around the garden, and the volume was quite tolerable. Bill hated going to places where the music was loud enough to burst eardrums. He didn't go to dance clubs or to very many live concerts.

An older woman came over and asked what they'd like to drink.

As none of the group had ever had a drink on Hayek, they didn't know what to ask for, so Thep asked for a beer menu. The woman laughed pleasantly and pointed to a chalkboard hung by the door. "There's the beer menu. Take a minute and look at it, and I'll be back to take your order.

She was back in less than two minutes. "Well, what'll you have?"

The group had decided on a pitcher each of the pale ale and a brown ale.

"Great. I'll be right back with them."

As she left, one of the girls from New Hampshire, Eileen Finerty, exclaimed, "Wow. She never even asked for my ID. That's a first."

Jordan explained to her that there was no drinking age on Hayek, hence no need to check IDs.

Eileen thought about it for a couple of seconds. "I knew that. I guess it never really sank in until now."

The waitress returned with the two pitchers and eight pint glasses. "Enjoy. I'll keep a tab going for you until you're ready to pay."

As none of them were required to be anywhere the next morning, other than the proposed trip with Luke to Milton after breakfast, the group stayed out quite late and consumed much beer.

Matt picked up the tab, saying he had sufficient funds to cover it, but that he expected payback in the near future. Then he and Nicole disappeared into the night while the three remaining roommates made their way back to their cabin.

Bill was still too wound up from the day's activities, so he decided to grab his tablet and do some reading to wind down. He automatically connected to the Wi-Fi and checked his email first. Nada. Pretty much as he expected. When you don't really know anyone on a planet, it's pretty futile expecting they would email you.

He decided to do a little more research on his new home, particularly since Luke had left him feeling quite ignorant. *How the hell was I supposed to know Hayek had universities?* he thought. *It's not like there's actually much about Hayek's demographics and culture covered on Earth.* Most of what Bill saw on the news on Earth related more to wars, crime, and celebrities rather than news of other planets.

He found a website that described the geography of Hayek, showing the major and minor settlements and the transport systems between them.

It turned out that the west coast was the most heavily settled, with some settlements on the east coast, and in what he knew on Earth as Europe, South Africa, Australia, and New Zealand. It looked like most of the population was settling in the more temperate climates.

What he knew as North America was called Ti'icham. South America, he saw, was called Suyu. The entire Eurasian continent was simply called Eurasia, rather than being broken down between Europe and Asia. Africa was still called Africa. Antarctica was still Antarctica, but Australia was Nura. Bill was again puzzled by the fact that some names remained the same while others were different, particularly since he couldn't identify where the different names came from.

He noticed that places with native names remained the same, but those with European names were changed, other than places in Europe. He recalled that Mt. Rainier was called Mt. Tahoma here, and that Luke came from Tahoma, where the city of Tacoma existed on Earth.

The continents were broken down into cantons, based mainly on climate and bioregions, rather than some esoteric line drawn on a map. Cascadia, to his west, extended along the Pacific Ocean encompassing that part of Ti'icham that consisted of a marine west coast climate. On Earth, that would have been from Northern California to Alaska. Bill was currently in Yakama Canton, what was known on Earth as the Columbia Basin Plateau, a dry plateau in the rain shadow of the Cascades.

He still wasn't sure about the whole concept of cantons but figured he would learn more about it later, as it was becoming quite late and he was now feeling the effects of the excitement of the change, the long day, and (perhaps) the beer.

The door opened and in stepped Matt, looking quite happy, and slightly inebriated.

"Yo, dog," he greeted Bill.

"Hey. How'd it go?"

"Totally awesome. She digs me," Matt said.

"So, when's the wedding?" Bill asked.

"Not soon enough," said Matt. "Hell, I'd marry her today if she would agree." All the alcohol Matt had consumed had made his Memphis drawl even more pronounced.

Bill chuckled at that. "Fell a bit hard, did we?"

"We most certainly did," Matt agreed, heading up to his room.

Bill followed, putting his tablet to sleep and making his way upstairs.

After brushing his teeth and using the toilet, Bill crawled into bed for his first night's sleep on Hayek, and within seconds was sound asleep. The adventure had begun.

Chapter 5

Bill awoke early the next morning, as was his habit. Unlike the day before, though, he had managed to sleep past 5 a.m. Quietly, he went downstairs, found a coffee maker and coffee, and started a pot brewing.

While he was in the kitchen waiting for the coffee to finish, he heard a noise. Looking out, he saw Jordan exiting his room. To put it mildly, Jordan looked like something the cat dragged in. His eyes were bloodshot and his hair was matted.

Jordan entered the kitchen. "Coffee?" he croaked.

"Almost done," Bill said. He looked in a couple of cupboards until he found some mugs and pulled two down.

When it looked like there was enough coffee in the pot, Bill pulled it off the burner and filled Jordan's cup and then his own, then replaced the pot under the filter.

"So, when are we meeting with Luke?" Bill asked.

Jordan grunted while taking a sip of coffee. "Don't ask me anything in the morning. My brain doesn't function until the second cup." He abruptly turned away, walked back into the main room, and plopped down in one of the chairs.

Bill thought that was a bit rude, but made his way to the sofa facing Jordan anyway.

After the first cup Jordan started perking up. He still didn't speak but went back for a second cup. Upon his return to the main room, he managed to utter a few words.

"Sorry, dude. My brain truly does not function in the morning without coffee. What did you say?"

"I asked when we were going to meet Luke."

"Not sure. Gimme a couple minutes and I'll check my messages. I'm sure he sent us a time and place."

Eventually, Thep and Matt joined them. Both men made a beeline for the coffee, returning to the main room with cups in hand.

"Okay. I'm almost human. Lemme check my email," Jordan announced, setting down his cup on one of the end tables, then going to his room for his tablet. "We'll join Luke for breakfast at the dining hall, then head out at 9:00," he said, after reading his messages. "He says dress cool, 'cause it'll be hot as hell."

After finishing a second cup of coffee, Bill went to take a shower.

He wasn't surprised to discover that the showerhead was a low-flow type, with a button that would allow him to turn the water off at the head temporarily, rather than with the handle. The purpose was to allow the user to get wet, turn the water off and lather up, then turn the water back on and rinse off. Since Bill had been doing that for years, it was natural to him.

While he was showering, he saw a squeegee hanging on a hook on the wall under the showerhead. He knew immediately what that was for. "The Colonel" had instilled in him the need to squeegee shower walls to minimize mold growth.

After his shower, he was glad to see the mirror above the sink hadn't fogged up too badly. *It's probably because of the dry climate here*, he thought.

He took a battered mug and shaving brush out of his toiletries kit. The mug had old, used soap chips that Bill used instead of shaving cream or shaving soap, *why spend the money when old, used soap chips worked just as well and didn't cost any extra?* He shaved quickly, then put his supplies in the medicine cabinet, making sure they were all on the same shelf, leaving room for Matt's toiletries.

He dressed in shorts and a short-sleeve shirt, displaying the pale complexion of a western Washington dweller—the aqua tan, as they called it. He knew a guy from Sitka, Alaska, who referred to it as the Beluga tan.

He grabbed his tablet on his way downstairs, then opened his new email account and saw the same message that Jordan had read aloud to them.

While he waited for the others, he decided to do some more research on Hayek, this time looking at educational systems. He was surprised to find out that not only were there universities, colleges, and trade schools scattered about, but there didn't seem to be any public schools. It appeared that all education on Hayek was private. He even found several online venues for learning, all the way from elementary grade level up to post-secondary. Looking more closely at Milton, he saw numerous schools, most of which seemed to specialize in specific programs, and most offering tailored education.

Wow, he thought. *That must be great. What I would've given to go to something like that, rather than taking all those b.s. classes in high school and college.*

It was then he realized just how bad the monopolized educational system he grew up in was. Here he was, on a planet that valued competition and free market systems, extending that to their educational system, and he could see just how much variety there was. He wondered, though, how good it was. He made a note to ask Luke when they met.

Jordan was, again, the first to join Bill, followed shortly by Matt, and finally, Thep. The four left the cabin and made their way to the cafeteria.

When they arrived, they found Luke already seated, eating a meal while chatting with the two women from lunch the day before, plus Nicole. Bill wondered if Matt had had a hand in that, and asked him.

"I might've said something to her," he admitted, smiling and waving at Nicole when he saw that she had seen him.

After grabbing trays of food, the four men joined Luke and the three women. Matt made sure he sat next to Nicole.

"You guys ready to explore?" Luke asked.

"Damn skippy," Matt said. The rest just nodded, most with mouthfuls of food.

"Great. As soon as we're done, we'll head out. Now, the first thing to understand is that the culture here is a lot different than what you're used to. Don't be surprised to see things here that you wouldn't see on Earth. The most shocking thing to most Earthers is the fact that most Hayekers are armed."

That raised some eyebrows, particularly among the women.

"Why is that?" Nicole asked.

"Well, a couple of reasons. First, since there's little law enforcement like you're used to on Earth, people are used to protecting themselves. That means that people also help protect each other. Also, since we've still got a healthy predator population that hasn't learned to fear man, people need to protect themselves from nature. It's also part of our culture. While we may not use pistols all that much, all of us practice monthly with our rifles or peeders for the Militia."

"What's a peeder?"

"A Personal Defense Weapon or PDW, but we just call it a peeder. It's what's issued to Militia members who aren't basic infantry, like doctors, nurses, truck drivers, you name it. There's also a version we carry when exploring. Some of you'll be getting one, along with your rifle, when you start Militia training tomorrow," Luke said.

"Is that where we have the mandatory meeting regarding living on Hayek?" Thep asked.

"Yep. You'll get a little taste of it today, but tomorrow the real understanding begins. Remember, when we go out, be nice. As Heinlein said, 'An armed society is a polite society.'"

After the meal, Luke led the group outside. As they walked to the skytrain station, they chattered like a bunch of excited children on a school outing. In a way, they were.

The morning was still cool, but it was apparent to Bill that it was going to be another hot one. He was glad he was wearing shorts but was slightly embarrassed by his Seattle tan, or lack thereof. Most of the others in the group had a start on a tan, except for Jordan and Thep, who had natural tans due to their heritage.

The wait for the skytrain wasn't long. When it arrived, the train disgorged a motley collection of cart-hauling men and women, most of whom were in their late teens to early twenties, all of them looking slightly confused. Bill guessed correctly that they were fellow Probies just arriving.

Luke shouted to the new Probies, "In-Processing is just next door. Show your ID card to the security guard at the gate, go through the gate, and turn left."

The small group of explorers entered the skytrain, and soon were traveling along the same route Bill and Matt had taken the day before. Two stops later, they got off at the City Center station.

Luke spread his arms out, and said, "Welcome to Milton!"

Turning back to the group, he added "Now, before we go wandering, here's another tip: pay attention to signs as you enter stores to see what type of payment they accept. Some only take gold or silver, some'll take electronic transfers, and some are willing to take bank certificates."

"What's a bank certificate?" Jordan asked.

"Well, it's sort of like the money you're used to—it's a paper certificate that's backed up by gold. Here, let me show you." Luke pulled a wallet from his back pocket. Opening it, he extracted a single colorful piece of paper and passed it around.

It was similar to the Canadian currency Bill had used on his occasional trips to Vancouver, British Columbia. It was colored with a transparent streak bisecting it, with a watermark visible. In big letters were the words *1/20 Gold Ounce* and *Backed by the Parallel Credit Union*. There were images of the Corps of Discovery symbol on one side and a herd of mastodons on the other.

"Much easier than carrying gold or silver, and a bit more

private than using your card," Luke said as Bill was inspecting the certificate.

After they had all looked at it, Luke put it away in his wallet.

"So, remember, check for signs about payments, don't gawk, don't steal anything, and be polite. You're not only new to Hayek, but you're also representing the Corps of Discovery, so act like it." Luke smiled.

Bill was able to see more of the city center, now that they were stopped for more than a minute. It was actually a square, much like one would find in most small towns scattered across the American South. A large park-like setting, several acres in size, was surrounded by streets laid out in a grid pattern. Those streets adjacent to the park had the tallest buildings Bill had seen on Hayek so far, some as much as five stories, but most around three or four. Most of the buildings appeared to be a mix of retail on the bottom floor, with residences above.

On the street were a number of vehicles, but only a couple of different types, including a couple of the aircars he and Matt had seen the day before. Bill saw a couple of new-looking Jeeps like the one he saw on base and a number of small cab-over pickup trucks that had a bikini top over the bed. One of the pickup trucks that passed the group had several passengers sitting on benches which ran along the sides inside the truck bed.

Thep said, "Hey, just like a baht bus."

"What's a baht bus?" Jordan asked.

Thep pointed to the truck. "A pickup truck that's been converted to carry passengers. They usually run along a fixed route, but deviate a bit to help the passengers. We call them baht buses because it used to only cost a baht to ride them. A baht's the currency of Thailand," he finished, shrugging.

"We call it a Kenji," Luke said. "They're made by Kenji trucks over in Tahoma. Other than taxis and the skytrain, they're our main source of mass transit. You'll find them all over Hayek. On Earth, you call them jitneys."

"Hey Luke," Bill asked, "what's with all the old Jeeps I see running around?"

Luke laughed. "Old? Most of those Jeeps are pretty new. They're also made in Tahoma. As a matter of fact, I worked on the Willy's assembly plant for a couple of summers, and part-time when I went to school."

"You've got a Willy's Jeep plant here?" Bill asked.

"Yeah. Funny story about that. One of the founders was a real Willy's Jeep fan, so when they got enough gold to open Parallel, he went over to Asia and bought an entire Jeep assembly plant and brought it here and named the company Willy's, keeping with the tradition.

"Probably the biggest difference between the new Willy's and the old one is some of the modifications. As you can see, most have roll bars, but what you probably don't see is that they're diesel, not gas. They've also got air conditioning, heating, radios, and adjustable front seats. Other than that, though, they're pretty much stock. The Corps uses a lot of them for overland surveys."

"It sounds like Tahoma's got a lot of manufacturing," Thep commented.

"One of the biggest manufacturing cities on Hayek," Luke said. "It's because Tahoma has great access to the oceans, but is still protected from most bad weather. Other cities are springing up around Hayek, mostly around resource-rich areas, but most people prefer to live in the temperate zones."

"Enough chit-chat. Let me show you Milton," Luke said and took off down the street.

The streets were macadam, with macadam sidewalks between the street and the buildings, but there were also broad areas between the sidewalks and the streets that were vegetated. The plants looked natural to the area, not the unnatural transplants Bill was used to seeing. Looking around, he saw no Scotch broom visible—the yellow flowering plant was an invasive mainstay of Washington State, growing on every highway median and shoulder, it seemed. Most of the trees were an oak variety that Bill had seen before, but wasn't sure of the exact type. He saw the same type trees in the town square, but, there they were much larger and obviously much older.

As they walked along they saw numerous small cafes, with tables on patios that extended out into the sidewalk. They passed a small grocery store, one that reminded Bill of pictures he had seen of early 20th century America—with large bins of fruit and vegetables on display outside. A small Asian woman came out of the store carrying groceries in two canvas bags, with a couple of paper bags sticking out of one of them. Apparently, plastic bags weren't in much use on Hayek.

Luke turned back to the group. "If you see anything you want to explore more of, just go on in, but let me know you're bailing. We'll meet for lunch over there, at the Hungry Mastodon." He pointed to a restaurant at the end of the block.

One of the stores that caught Bill's attention was Milton Alcohol, Tobacco, and Firearms. A sign in the window advertised that they bought gold, silver, and jewelry. He nudged Matt and asked, "Want to check it out?" The irony of the name was not lost on either of them.

Matt turned to Nicole and asked if she'd be interested; she agreed. "Mind you, I'm not quite the gun nut that most Yanks seem to be, but I do enjoy shooting, so this should be quite fun."

Bill told Luke what they were doing, and after a warning from Luke not to break anything, the three peeled off from the group and entered the store.

Bill was used to gun stores in Washington, where handguns were kept in glass cases on display, and rifles were hung on walls behind the glass cases. Usually, there would be shelves and displays scattered about the store holding ammunition, holsters, targets, and other shooting paraphernalia. The first thing Bill saw when they entered was a stack of boxes labeled "Dynamite." He also saw cases of "Plastique Explosive – C5 Composition" and "Plastique Explosives – Semtex." Rifles were on the walls, but so were what appeared to be machine guns and rocket-propelled grenades.

The only things that seemed remotely similar to what Bill was used to were the handguns and the shooting paraphernalia. He even saw a mortar on display, with a crate of mortar rounds next to it, both with price tags on them. Not used to the currency, he wasn't quite sure how much it converted to in dollars, but he thought that a half ounce of gold was pretty inexpensive for a small artillery piece.

On display cases sat bottles of spirits, along with boxes and humidors of cigars. Bill even spied some cartons of Marlboro cigarettes.

"Howdy," said an older gentleman sitting on a stool behind one of the cases.

"Hi," Bill replied. Nicole answered with a, "G'day" and Matt just nodded.

"Can I help you with anything?" the man asked.

"Not yet," Bill said. "We're new here and this is our first time in a gun store, so we're just checking things out. This is amazing!"

"I hear that from a lot of noobs from Earth," the man said with a chuckle. "Well, if there's anything you'd like to look at or check out, let me know."

"Thanks."

The three then took their time walking around the store, looking at the various implements of destruction, with occasional exclamations of "Wow! Look at this" and "Whoa. This is awesome."

Eventually, Bill approached the store owner and asked what it would take to buy one of the weapons if he could afford it.

"Give me the money and I'll give you the gun," the man replied.

"That's it? No paperwork or background checks?" Bill asked, surprised. "Even for the explosives?"

"What for? This ain't Earth, it's Hayek. You decide to use a gun wrong, you'll pay for it. Ain't nobody's business what you want to buy or own, just as long as you don't steal it or use force to get it."

"I know where I'm coming after I get my first paycheck," Matt said.

"Me, too," Bill said.

"Well, I don't think I'll be joining you blokes," Nicole said. "Since the Corps is giving me guns, I don't think I need to spend my own money on one."

"Ooh, smart, good-looking, and fiscally responsible," Bill said. "Don't let her get away," he told Matt.

"Not if I can help it," Matt replied, grinning at Nicole who smiled back at him.

Bill turned back to the owner and asked if he'd be willing to buy a piece of jewelry.

"Sure. Watcha got?" the old man asked.

Bill dug into his pocket and retrieved the diamond ring that Jessica had thrown at him just a couple of days ago. Setting it down on the glass cabinet, he said, "This. I don't have a need for it anymore."

The man looked at him sympathetically. "Turned you down?"

"Not really. She gave me a choice, her or the Corps."

"Tough choice," the man said, picking up the ring and looking more closely at it. "Sure you want to sell? If you like, you could put it on consignment. That way you'll get more for it."

Bill thought about it briefly. "How long do you think it'll take to sell?"

"Nice ring like this, not too expensive but still nice. Shouldn't be too long."

"Okay. Let's do it, then."

Bill provided the owner with his name and contact information and signed a brief contract giving the man permission to sell his property in lieu of a small commission. He also gave the man his email address so he could be notified when the ring sold.

The three thanked the store owner, then left the shop, stepping out into the growing heat of the day.

For the next two hours, the trio explored downtown Milton, being sure not to try to purchase or break anything. It was obvious that Matt and Nicole were interested in Bill's story, but he wasn't up for talking about it and made that pretty clear.

They noticed that most people in Milton seemed to dress rather casually, to the point where Matt mentioned that he hadn't seen a tie or suit since he arrived. It appeared that comfort overruled outdated fashions. They noticed plenty of women wearing light dresses, and both men and women wore shorts and short-sleeved shirts, with a few men wearing utility kilts. Bill was used to seeing utility kilts in Seattle, but it was apparent that it was something novel for Matt. The first time he saw a man wearing one, his jaw practically dropped.

Stores were pretty similar to what they were used to on Earth, only smaller. There were several grocery stores, but they reminded Bill of the small corner stores he saw in Earth cities. There were also none of the chain stores they were used to seeing, not even a Starbucks, which, for Bill, was a shocker. In Seattle, he'd see a Starbucks on just about every corner. Most of the coffee shops just had "coffee" listed, along with some teas and other beverages. While he saw signs for lattes, mochas, cappuccinos, espressos, and the like, none of the stores announced the brands of coffee they sold.

Curious, Bill asked one of the staff members of a coffee shop about the apparent lack of choices.

The employee shrugged and told Bill that there weren't all that many coffee plantations on Hayek yet, most being in the Hawai'ian Islands.

Matt treated Nicole and Bill to a coffee, telling them not to worry about paying him back.

"I've got a pretty large chunk of money that I don't plan on holding onto, so we might as well enjoy it," he explained. Bill thought there was more to the story, but decided to wait until he knew Matt better before asking.

The trio sat at a covered table on a sidewalk part of the café, enjoying watching the people pass by. It was pretty easy to tell the locals compared to those that who were new to Hayek.

Bill overheard a couple next to him talking about the large number of newcomers.

"Looks like a fresh group of eff oh geez. The Corps must be starting a new class."

"Yeah. Look at all them fresh faces. Wonder how many of them will be able to adapt to Hayek?"

Bill was intrigued by the phrase, so he did something he rarely did, turned and asked the locals what it meant.

"Ah, it's a term we use for noobs," replied the man, a tanned old-timer. "It means 'Fresh Outa the Gate'. It's a take-off on FOB and FOP from Earth, you know, Fresh Off the Boat and Fresh Off the Plane."

That caused the trio to raise their eyebrows in mild surprise. It isn't often that you're not only told that you're new to a place, but that you're so new that you're clueless. But, considering that it was true, none of them took offense.

"I guess that makes us FOGs," Nicole said, smiling at the couple.

"Don't take no offense at it, sweetie," the older woman replied. "We were all FOGs one day, except those born here, and most of them ain't as old as you noobs the Corps brought in."

Perplexed, Nicole asked her, "How did you know we're with the Corps?"

"Hell, that's easy, honey. Just look at you. Early twenties, in good health, and not out scrambling for a job the minute you crossed over. If you weren't Corps, you wouldn't be sitting here sipping on joe and asking me questions. You'd be waiting on me or at some other job this time of the day." The woman chuckled.

"Fair enough," Nicole responded, with a nod and a smile.

Looking around, Bill noticed that the woman's description fit most of the people wandering around the square. Not only were they pretty much uniformly the same age, but they were walking around in small groups, gawking like country bumpkins fresh to the big city.

"So, where are you kids from?" the woman asked.

"Now, honey, you know that's not a polite question," the man said to her.

"You hush. These kids are here because they want to serve in the Corps. They ain't running from something."

Turning back to the trio, the woman awaited their response.

"I'm from New Zealand," Nicole told them.

"Memphis," Matt said.

"Pretty much all over," said Bill.

"Sounds like me," the man said. "My dad worked for the embassy and dragged me all over Earth. How about you?"

"Air Force," Bill said. He usually didn't go into discussing his upbringing, as he had discovered years ago that most people either didn't care, didn't believe, or tried to one-up him. It was better to keep it simple. It was hard explaining how he had moved every year or two, with the longest time in one place being his four years in Seattle while attending the University of Washington.

The old man nodded in understanding.

The woman told them that she was originally from Tallahassee, Florida, but had moved to Portland, Oregon in her youth, then migrated to Hayek when they opened the gate to immigration twenty years ago. "Met this old coot way back in the beginning," she said, indicating the old man.

"Best thing ever happened to her," the old man said dryly. He immediately yelped, as he received a sharp kick to his shins under the table.

"What do you do now, if you don't mind my asking?" Nicole asked, grinning.

"We're pretty much retired," the woman said. "We opened one of the first bars in Milton, and then got several others opened in the other cities, so now we're just kickin' back and enjoying life."

Matt, looking at his watch, realized that it was close to the time they were to meet Luke and the rest of the group and told Nicole and Bill.

Bill drained the last of his coffee while Matt reached into his pocket and pulled out several pieces of silver. He dropped them on the table, causing them to clink together.

They waved to the older couple as they exited the café.

The older man said, "Stay safe out there."

"Nice-lookin' bunch of kids," the old woman said.

"Yep. Sure are. Hope they make it," Bill heard the old man say as the trio walked away.

Chapter 6

The three arrived at the agreed-upon meeting spot, finding only Luke.

"So, what do you think of Milton so far?" he asked.

"Pretty amazing," Matt said.

"It is that," agreed Luke. "A bit more civilized than the other cities, but only a bit."

"How did it become so, well, civilized, in such a short time? I mean, it's a city carved out of the wilderness," Nicole said.

"The first thing you've gotta remember is that it's actually closer to forty years old than twenty," Luke said. "The founders laid it out and brought in people to build it before they even told the world about the gate. Sorta like a private club. Actually, a bunch of the cities are older than twenty years, but it's been mainly since the gate opened that they've grown."

As Luke was talking, the rest of the group showed up. "You'll find things on Hayek aren't really as they're represented on Earth," Luke told them all. "I guess you could say that it's a lot of disinformation. Of course, it doesn't hurt that the news on Earth isn't really news, so much as sensationalism. If it was, people on Earth would know more about us."

Luke looked at the gathered group. "I don't know about you, but I'm hungry." He turned and strode through the open door of the Hungry Mastodon.

The rest followed him. As Bill entered, following a hand-holding Matt and Nicole, he heard Luke telling the hostess their party size, requesting someplace cool.

The interior of the restaurant consisted of darkened wood, booths and tables scattered throughout, with an outdoor dining area visible through glass doors at the rear. Walls held a combination of color and black-and-white photographs of the local fauna. There was even a poster inviting "Like-minded Libertarians" to migrate to Hayek. The poster showed a picture of a man riding a horse, holding a rifle, looking at a herd of Mastodons in the background.

Once the group was settled around a large table near the rear of the restaurant, Bill looked at the menu and realized that, like the base cafeteria, the food was heavy on the veggies and light on the meat. But the meat was unlike any he had seen before. Mastodon, mammoth, elk, bison, and even giant sloth were listed, all part of grander meals.

Luke ordered a stir-fry consisting of a mixture of vegetables and giant sloth ("my favorite" he whispered to the group). Bill decided to try the mastodon pot pie. While the bison stew was tempting, he figured he'd expand his horizons. Plus, he loved pot pie and hadn't had a decent one for years.

Bill ordered an iced tea. Matt ordered a sweet ice tea. Having lived a bit in the South while growing up, Bill suspected that the tea would give Matt a sugar high for the rest of the afternoon.

The talk around the table soon turned to the similarities and differences between Milton and a comparable city on Earth. The biggest differences all noted were the lack of chain stores, the lack of vehicular traffic, and the lack of pollution.

"Why is everything so clean here?" Eileen asked.

"What do you mean?" Luke asked, clearly puzzled.

"I mean, there's no litter in the streets, the sidewalks are clean, and I haven't seen a bum anywhere asking for money"

Luke laughed softly. "That's probably because we care for where we live. Remember, there's nobody here to pick up after you, so we sort of 'encourage' people to take responsibility for their actions. As to bums, that's an easy one. You want a job? There's plenty of work for you. Don't wanna work? Don't expect anyone to support you. Pretty much everyone on Hayek works. Hell, we've got more jobs than people. Also, it's in our ethos to keep things clean. Seriously, who wants to live in a pigsty?"

"But, doesn't that fly in the face of the 'Tragedy of the Commons' scenario?" Eileen pressed. "I mean, isn't everyone out for themselves, and to hell with everyone else?"

"Well, that's a yes-and-no answer. Are we all out for ourselves? Of course we are. Everyone is, even those helping others. It makes them feel good to do so. As to the tragedy of the commons issue, that doesn't really apply because just about everything is privately owned."

"What about the roads?" Brenda asked

"Privately owned or community property," Luke said. "For example, this downtown area, all the roads belong to those owning businesses and living here. They meet annually to discuss what work to do and how to pay for it. You'll find most communities are the same way, pretty much like homeowner associations in the US. Out in the country, it's usually landowners building them, which is why what you'll mostly see are dirt or gravel roads. On base, well that's company property, so they build and maintain whatever types of roads they need."

The waitress returned with their orders and the table fell silent. Bill was amazed at the pot-pie—the meat tasted like nothing he'd ever eaten before. A bit chewier than beef, but not as tough as some bison he'd had, with a slightly different flavor.

After, lunch, Luke asked if they wanted to continue to explore or return to base. Half the group wanted to return, and the other half wanted to explore, so Luke agreed to stay with the explorers. Bill figured he'd have more time to explore later on and elected to return to base with Jordan and Thep. Matt told them he'd join them later, as he wanted to spend more time with Nicole.

Getting on the skytrain, Bill saw more Probies towing carts on their way to Sacajawea Base. Continuing his newfound extroversion, he struck up a conversation with a small group of them, telling them about his experiences on Hayek to date. Occasionally, Thep or Jordan would jump in with a comment or clarification, or to expand on something Bill had mentioned.

When they arrived at the base's station, Bill guided the new arrivals to In-Processing then he, Thep, and Jordan headed toward their cabin.

Once there, Bill checked his email, hoping that information on the following week's training would be there. It was. He, along with all the other recent migrants, was to report to the main auditorium at 0800 hours the following Monday for basic Corps of Discovery orientation, followed by basic Militia orientation and Militia equipment issue. Bill was assigned to Training Platoon 3 of Training Company A. The email also gave a link to the schedule for Basic Militia Training, known as BMT. Bill wondered if there was an advanced Militia training regimen.

Bill followed the link and saw that training lasted eight weeks. The first focused on basic matters, such as understanding the military rank structure, field hygiene, and establishing fighting positions. Two weeks were for basic firearms training, a week for field medicine, a week for weapons and equipment familiarization, a week for close-quarter combat, a week on insurgency tactics, and a final week of field maneuvers.

Bill looked up from his reading. The others were also engrossed in their tablets.

"Training ought to prove interesting," he said.

The others nodded. Jordan said, "You ain't kidding. I never figured I'd be in the military when I signed up for this gig. I mean, I know we're all supposed to be in a militia, but I never figured it meant this much training."

"I reckon they're pretty serious about having a strong militia," Matt said. "Think about it, everyone who migrates to Hayek goes through this. I don't know about you guys, but if I was a leader of a country thinking of invading Hayek, I'd think again. It'd be suicidal."

For the next week, Bill spent time exploring Sacajawea Base, Milton, and the surrounding areas. He also managed to get in some fly fishing on the nearby Naches River.

On the morning that he tried to find out where to get a fishing license, Luke told him not to worry about it. "Don't need one here," the Explorer said. Bill assumed he was referring to the waters on base and left it at that.

His friendship with his roommates grew, and he was surprised at how little friction existed between the four. Bill was used to at least one overbearing sonuvabitch trying to rule the roost, but that wasn't the case here. He even got to enjoy mornings with Jordan, usually telling him something, and then an hour later, asking the Californian about what he had told him. Jordan would usually wind up giving him a blank stare, not even recalling the conversation.

On Sunday morning he got an email from the gun store owner, telling him his ring had sold. That gave Bill a little more breathing room financially. That evening he treated his roommates, and the female companions who had joined them at the Cave Bear Cave, to a couple of rounds of drinks.

Thinking about Jessica's "contribution" to the event left Bill feeling more than a bit melancholy, so he left the gathering early. Walking back to the Jaskey Lane house by himself in the gathering dark, he wondered if he'd made the right choice.

He still wasn't certain when he went to bed, and that uncertainty kept him up long after the others had returned and the house was reverberating from the sound of their combined snoring.

A NEW LIFE

Chapter 7

Bill was awake by six o'clock the following morning, feeling nervous all over again. He always felt this way just before something major. It was the same feeling he had before he broke the news to "the Colonel" and before crossing the gate to Hayek.

He hopped out of bed and went straight to the bathroom, finding the door closed. He knocked, and Matt called out, "Occupied!"

"I figured that out myself, Sherlock," Bill said. "How long until you're done?"

"I'll be out in a minute."

Bill stood by, hoping his bladder wouldn't explode.

After what seemed like an eternity, but was probably less than a minute, Matt stepped out of the bathroom. "All yours." Bill made a dash for the toilet, not even bothering to close the door.

Thus relieved, Bill made his way downstairs and joined the others in coffee consumption.

After taking his first sip, and feeling the warmth of the beverage and the jolt of the caffeine start to kick in, Bill asked the others, "You ready?"

"Ready as I'll ever be," Matt said.

Jordan, perhaps due to his Southern California upbringing, with all the movie industry there, looked up at Bill from his tablet and replied in his best John Wayne accent, "I was born ready." Everyone chuckled.

"Right. Well, we'll see about that," said Thep, rolling his eyes.

When they arrived at the cafeteria a half hour later, they found it almost half full. It looked like many of the new arrivals had the same idea: be sure to eat before orientation. None of them knew what to expect from this point on. Bill suspected that Militia training would be similar to the stories he had heard of boot camp, with instructors yelling, tearing up made beds, and generally making life hell for the recruits. He wasn't looking forward to it.

After a quick meal, and not seeing Luke or any of the women from the day before, the four made their way to the auditorium, managing to secure seats near the front. Again, Bill was a bit worried, thinking that their location would make them a prime target for the dreaded drill instructors.

On the stage stood a lone microphone stand in the center, with a large projection screen suspended from the ceiling behind it.

The four chatted while awaiting the start of the orientation. As they did, the auditorium continued to fill up, until almost every seat was filled just before eight o'clock.

Nicole appeared at the end of the aisle, and that's when Bill noticed that Matt had saved a seat for her. She scooted past Bill, Thep, Jordan, on her way to her seat. Bill couldn't hear what Nicole and Matt said, but it was obvious they were glad to see each other.

Finally, a lean man with a shaggy head of red hair, obviously middle-aged, and dressed in the Corps field uniform, took the stage.

He stood there, unmoving behind the microphone, until the chatter settled, and eventually ended. All eyes were upon him.

"Welcome." His voice boomed throughout the auditorium. "My name is Jack Lewis and I'm the Commandant of the Corps of Discovery."

A murmur went through the crowd.

"First off, I'd like to officially welcome you to the Corps of Discovery," he continued. "You've just entered what will probably be the most exciting phase of your life. But, before you can begin your duties as Explorers, you have to first begin your duties to Hayek, the most important being the protection of our freedom. This means that for the next eight weeks you'll go through Basic Militia Training. If you don't finish it, we send you back to Earth or give you a second chance. If you still don't finish it, you definitely get sent back to Earth."

Lewis looked around the auditorium at the sea of attentive faces.

"Now, for those of you who grew up hearing about boot camp and other horror stories of military indoctrination, I think you'll be surprised by BMT. Our goal on Hayek isn't to transform you into unthinking, order-following killers; our goal is to provide you with the basic training necessary to help keep Hayek free. In other words, to fight against any aggressor. So, one of the first things you'll be learning about during your orientation is Hayek's constitution, and exactly why every responsible adult is required to be a member of the militia."

For the next several minutes Lewis spoke about the Corps of Discovery and the duties each person was expected to perform. He also gave them some further information about what it was like to live on Hayek. Bill's big take on that part was "with great freedom comes great responsibility."

The Corps orientation was brief, certainly not as long as Bill expected, and soon Lewis was bringing their attention back to BMT.

"Now, I know you'd probably love to hear me ramble on for hours," Lewis said with a smile, "but I do believe there are others more qualified to educate you than me."

He motioned to the side of the stage furthest from Bill, where a lean black woman with short-cropped hair and wearing what appeared to be a uniform was climbing the steps onto the stage. Her outfit consisted of an open-necked long-sleeved khaki shirt, with the sleeves rolled up above the elbows, khaki pants with cargo pockets on the leg, and brown leather boots. There were some ribbons above her left chest pocket that Bill couldn't quite make out, along with what he presumed were rank insignia on her collars tips, and a badge on both her sleeves just beneath the shoulder. She also had a small carbine hanging across her back by a shoulder strap that went over her right shoulder. Bill wondered if that was one of the PDWs he had heard about.

"This is Captain Rowe," Lewis said. "She's a member of Hayek's Defense Force, and her job here is to educate you on our constitution, our defense force, and just about anything else you can think of that relates to the Militia." Turning to Rowe he said, "Captain Rowe," indicating that she should take his place at the microphone.

Rowe approached Lewis, shook hands with him, and approached the microphone. Assuming the military position of "at ease," her hands clasped behind the small of her back and her feet set apart to shoulders' width, she began speaking to the assembled crowd.

"Good morning ladies and gentlemen. As Commandant Lewis stated, I'm Captain Mykhala Rowe, a regular officer in the Hayek Defense Force. I, along with my training staff, who are also regular members of the HDF, will be providing you with the necessary skills to serve in Hayek's militia in the event we're ever invaded or anybody tries to take over our planet. Part of that training includes a basic understanding of our military structure and an in-depth look at Hayek's constitution, both of which I'll be covering this morning. We'll be covering the material this morning in fifty-minutes blocks with ten-minute breaks, so if you need to use the toilet, I'd ask that you please hold off until the break.

"Now, for those of you who think that an invasion by outsiders is out of the realm of possibility, let me disabuse you of that notion right here and now. We've already had two Earth governments try to take over the gate and our way of life—we didn't let them do it then, and we sure won't let them do it in the future." This was a surprise to Bill, as he had never heard anything about an invasion of Hayek by any Earth armed forces. Then again, considering the reliability of the news in the United States.

"We've also had to call out the Militia on the Gaia Liberation Front once when they tried to seize a gate. And trust me, they are not nice people."

Rowe reached into a pants pocket and pulled out a remote controller, then activated a projector suspended from the ceiling. The screen behind her lit up with the logo: a stylized porcupine with the words "Hayek Defense Force" above it and "Don't Tread On Me" underneath.

"For those of you from the US, you'll probably recognize our logo from the Libertarian Party. That's because our founders were libertarians, and felt that the best form of government was the one that governed least. As such, our government serves two basic purposes – to protect your individual rights and to protect the public good."

It seemed that Rowe looked into the eyes of every person in the auditorium as she spoke.

"The HDF is charged with protecting the first purpose. Toward that end, we maintain a small, professional defense force designed to act independently as well as in conjunction with the Militia. We also have a reserve force, separate from the Militia, which can be called up in time of invasion or to assist with disasters. Our constitution makes it very clear that the HDF is for defensive purposes only, just like the Swiss on Earth.

"Of course, it helps that Hayek is pretty much united and that those who don't want to be here can leave anytime they like," she said with a smile. "So, let's look at the structure of the HDF and the Militia."

Rowe clicked the remote again and a slide comparing the two organizations was displayed.

"As you can see, the HDF comes under the organization of the federal government, while the Militia is under the organization of the individual cantons. This means, for you, that the governor of Yakama Canton will be the one to determine if you need to be called up. This only happens, by the way, in the event of an invasion."

For the next forty-five minutes, Rowe described the Hayek Defense Force, focusing mainly on how the rank structure was designed, the table of organization, and what type of units existed. Bill was glad to hear that the rank structure was similar to that of the US Army, which made sense considering that most of the founders and initial settlers were former Americans. While the HDF had the typical combat branches of infantry, cavalry, artillery, and aviation, he was somewhat surprised to learn that there were no armor branches. Rowe never explained why, so Bill figured it was something he would have to research himself. The non-combat branches included engineers, intelligence, medical, logistics, and finance. Interestingly enough, there was no judicial branch.

The Militia structure was somewhat similar in structure to the HDF but without many of the non-combat support roles. Most of the Militia were considered either light infantry or cavalry, with some specialized units consisting of artillery and aviation. The HDF handled medical, logistics, and engineering.

Rowe pointed out that everyone, even conscientious objectors, was required to be in the Militia, but nobody who was opposed to killing for any reason was required to go through firearms training or were even issued a firearm. Mostly these were people in the medical field, so it was probably best for all that they focused on saving lives as opposed to taking them. Bill wondered if the Corps had any conscientious objectors.

After fifty minutes, Rowe announced that everyone could take a ten-minute break. Apparently, a lot of people had had coffee with their breakfast, because there was a large movement to the restrooms.

After the break, Rowe discussed Hayek's constitution.

"For those of you with a good knowledge of history, you'll see that Hayek's constitution was based upon the Swiss and American models—creating a republic form of government. We are most definitely *not* a democracy! Hayek is a federation of individual cantons. As I mentioned earlier, its purpose is to protect our rights and to protect the public good."

Rowe started another slide show. The first slide was one showing three branches of government. "The federal government consists of the executive, legislative, and judicial branches. The legislature is both elected and appointed. The governor of each canton appoints one representative, with the rest elected by voting citizens. The elected representatives are based on population and serve in the Elected Legislature, while the appointed representatives serve in the

Appointed Legislature. The elected legislators serve for a term of three years and are limited to two terms in office, and the appointed legislators serve for six years and are limited to one term. An elected legislator can be appointed, but an appointed legislator can never run for an elected legislative position.

"Our legislature operates quite similarly to the US Congress, with bills being introduced and voted on by the elected legislators, with the appointed legislators only passing or denying the bills. All bills must pass with a supermajority of a two-thirds vote, and any bill related to the budget must pass by a supermajority of three-fourths in both legislatures."

She clicked on the remote and another slide appeared. "As you can see, a 'voting citizen' is one who has served at least two years in a capacity in which he or she risked their life, or potentially risked their life, for the greater good of us all. This currently includes members of the HDF, peace officers, and, believe it or not, Corps of Discovery Explorers. This means that in two years you'll be eligible to vote," she said up with a dazzling smile.

"There are a couple of exceptions, mostly involving HDF reservists and volunteer firefighters. For them, ten years of service will grant them the privilege to vote. One major exception is that any resident involved in defending Hayek from invasion is automatically granted the right to vote. Let me be clear about this. Voting is not a right on Hayek, it's a privilege that one earns!"

Bill learned that only voting citizens are allowed to hold office, including the judicial branch.

"The executive branch is run by the president, who is not only the head of the government but also the head of state, much like the US president. The president also serves a three-year term and is elected by the legislature, much like the parliamentary method. Like the legislature, the president is limited to two terms.

"Our judicial branch is actually pretty small and appointed by the executive branch during his or her term. The goal on Hayek is to limit the influence of any of the branches and to prevent long-timer's disease from setting in" Rowe explained. "Actually, with very few laws, there isn't much to quibble about, other than to ensure that the rights of citizens aren't trampled."

Rowe went on to explain the basic rights that all citizens of Hayek had, including the right to self-ownership, self-defense, privacy, and private property ownership. Bill noticed that there were no special provisions for free speech, religion, and other things he was used to hearing from the US Constitution. Rowe went on to explain that the right of self-ownership basically included those aspects that other constitutions had to define. As the right of self-ownership meant that one had complete control over their body, one could do whatever they wanted as long as it did not interfere with another's rights. Most of what Bill heard sounded very similar to that of the US Constitution, but it was obvious Hayek's constitution was far more protective of the individual.

Now Rowe got quite animated. "Probably the most important part of our constitution is the non-aggression principle that applies to government. As all of you have heard, Hayek is militarily limited to self-defense in the event of an invasion. That's because the non-aggression principle limits Hayek's governments to only responding with the force necessary to stop the unlawful force. This means, if we're invaded, we kick the bastards off our planet, but we don't go into their planet with a follow-up attack. This ain't Earth with all its petty governments, including the US, attacking everyone willy-nilly. If we're attacked, we defend ourselves. If we're not attacked, so what? There's nothing to fight about."

Rowe looked down at her watch, and announced, "Okay, looks like it's time for another break, so be back in ten minutes." Again, there was a dash for the restrooms, with Bill joining in this time. Two hours of sitting and listening had caused his butt to go numb. Several people headed outside, presumably for a cigarette. That was one thing Bill was glad he never picked up. Then again, when he was old enough to buy cigarettes, he was living in a state that basically prohibited cigarette smoking, but allowed people to buy and smoke marijuana. Quite confusing.

After the break, Rowe announced that everyone would be assigned to a training platoon. As everyone was in a four-person living unit, that group would comprise a sub-squad, also known as a fire team, and that two fire teams would constitute a squad. Three squads made up the training platoon.

"Each of you was sent an email last night listing your training platoon and company," Rowe said. "What I'd like you to do now is head outside to the front of the auditorium. Your training platoon sergeant will be holding up a sign with your unit designation. Introduce yourself to him or her, then line up behind them. Once we're organized by platoons, we'll start issuing equipment."

Nobody moved. Rowe softly said, "That meant now, folks." At that, people started moving.

Once outside, the four roommates made their way over to a burly Asian HDF soldier holding the sign for their platoon. Bill saw that he was a sergeant from the three stripes visible on his collar tabs. Like Captain Rowe, the sergeant was wearing cargo pants and a long-sleeved shirt with the sleeves rolled up over his elbows. Bill could see what looked like a nasty scar on his left forearm. As they approached, the sergeant said, "Fall in behind me if you're Company A, Third Platoon."

They did. The sergeant repeated his litany several more times until there were twenty-four Probies lined up behind them, most chatting amongst themselves. It was a mixed gender group, with a few more men than women.

After a few more minutes, nobody else was standing between the auditorium doors and the platoons, other than Captain Rowe and Commander Lewis. The two shook hands, then Lewis walked away while Rowe faced the large crowd.

In a voice that was surprisingly loud and carried well, Rowe yelled out, "Platoon leaders. Take charge of your platoons."

The platoon leaders saluted her, holding their salutes until she returned them. Then Bill's platoon leader turned to his charges and announced, "Good morning Probies. I'm Sergeant Renard, and I'll be your platoon leader for the next eight weeks."

Renard pulled a tablet from a cargo pocket of his pants, tapped it, and looked up at the attentive faces. "Call out when you hear your name. If you don't hear it, let me know, 'cause you're probably in the wrong place." He began calling off names until everyone had been accounted for.

"Great. Looks like we've got everyone. Okay, first thing we're gonna do is get through logistics and get your uniforms and most of your equipment. After you get all your uniform items, I'll want you to change, have lunch, then meet me back at the Logistics Center at one o'clock. Any questions?" He looked around at the men and women surrounding him. Nobody asked him anything. Bill wondered if they were either unsure what to ask or what to expect, or too afraid to look stupid by asking a question worthy of getting their head ripped off, despite being told BMT wasn't like military induction.

"Well, let's go, then," Renard said, turning and walking down the street. Bill saw that the other platoons were doing the same. *Great,* he thought. *We'll all be trying to get the same thing at the same time. Like this won't take forever.*

Equipment issue didn't take too long, however. Everyone was given a duffel bag. When it was Bill's turn, he wasn't surprised by all the equipment he was issued, having grown up in a military family.

In just a few minutes Bill received just about everything he needed. He was issued five pairs of used uniforms (at least, he hoped they had been used before because they were certainly stained). His equipment consisted of a pistol belt and ammo pouches, a poncho, an entrenching tool (which was nothing more than a small folding shovel), a helmet, backpack, canteens, and other militaria. Basically, all the equipment one needed for war. The only things missing were boots and a rifle. Bill asked about those and was told they'd be issued later.

The clerk said, "You'll get to keep everything except the uniforms. Those get turned in at the end of training and you'll be issued two sets to keep. Okay, head outside and wait for the rest."

Bill grabbed the duffel and slung its strap over his shoulder. He was surprised at the weight and felt somewhat awkward walking out of the building, apologizing to the fellow Probies he accidentally bumped into with it.

His roommates were waiting outside, in the shade of a large tree. The four sat there for about thirty minutes, when the last two Probies in their platoon finally came, trailed by Sergeant Renard.

Renard told them they would now be fitted for boots, but before that, they would assemble their equipment on their bodies. "After getting your boots, take your gear home, get in uniform, and break for lunch."

Renard had all the Probies extract their pistol belts, suspenders, butt packs, rifle ammo pouches, and canteens with cups and covers, and showed them how to assemble them into what was called the load-bearing equipment, or LBE. The platoon promptly assembled their LBEs, and soon everyone was wearing one. It took a few minutes but wasn't too difficult. The setup was similar to the US military's, which Bill was familiar with, thanks to "the Colonel."

Renard then led them into another room on the other side of the building. Pads were on the floor in front of the manned counter, with small dumbbells on either side of the pads.

Renard said to the first person in line, "Drop your gear, go stand on that pad, grab the two dumbbells, and hold them until told to put them down." As she did, Bill could see a glow emitting from where her feet were.

A clerk behind the counter looked at the computer screen in front of him. He briefly disappeared into the back room and returned with a pair of brown leather boots.

"Try these on." He indicated a bench on the wall adjacent to the door. "They're gonna feel a little wide, but that's okay. They're designed so your feet can spread while carrying forty pounds of equipment."

The Probie headed to the bench. Renard said, "Okay. Spread out. One on a pad, and line up behind them."

When it was Bill's turn, he held onto the two dumbbells and felt a warm glow on his feet. He thought it resembled a scanner and mentioned that to the civilian.

"Exactly what it is," the chubby, gray-haired woman said. "You can put the dumbbells down now," she said, walking back to the shelves. She was shortly back, handed Bill a pair of boots, and instructed him to try them on.

Once everyone had been issued boots, Renard repeated the instructions to take their equipment home, change into a uniform, and then go have lunch. "Your uniform of the day consists of boots, pants, underwear, belt, shirt, boonie cap, and LBE. We'll meet back here at one o'clock."

"Welcome back, boys. Ready for some real fun now?" Renard asked the roommates as they arrived after lunch.

"I was born ready," Jordan said, again using his best John Wayne accent. The others groaned; Matt asking if this was going to be a common saying from Jordan from now on.

"I reckon so," replied Jordan, sticking his thumbs in his belt.

"What's next on the agenda?" Bill asked Renard.

"Weapons issue. As soon as everyone's here, or it's thirteen hundred, we'll head in."

Precisely at one o'clock, Renard faced the group and said, "Okay. Looks like everyone's here, so first, we'll draw your weapons, and then we'll head over to the training building where we'll be spending the rest of today and the next several weeks."

Bill was issued two firearms, a rifle and short sub-machine gun-looking weapon that was identical to what Captain Rowe had been carrying. When he asked the lady behind the counter about it, he was told it was a Personal Defense Weapon, or PDW, colloquially called a "peeder." Each weapon came with a sling and seven magazines.

After signing for the two weapons, he took them, in their cases, outside where he was told to wait for the rest of the platoon.

As he was waiting, Bill asked Renard if this was a permanent duty or something the professionals took turns at.

"Naw, it's a two-year stint. I'll spend another year training new migrants, and when that's up, it's either to my old unit or a new posting."

Bill wondered how often Renard trained a new platoon and was surprised to hear he went through six training cycles a year. Renard went on to explain that he sometimes he would split a training cycle so he could get time off.

"Do many fail?" Bill asked.

"Not often. Most people who migrate to Hayek want to be here, so we do what we can to make sure they make it. Heck, even the Corps occasionally has a Probie or two who can't quite make it the first time, but we usually get them through with remedial training."

As they were talking, they were joined by more Probies laden with cased firearms, all interested in hearing what Renard had to say about the Militia and his role in the HDF.

One of them, less diplomatic than the others, asked Renard about the scar on his arm.

"Oh, that thing. Got it in the action in Iran during the war."

Bill thought about that for a second. It didn't seem to jive with all that he had learned about Hayek. Particularly since the Iran War was one initiated by Iran's attempt to destroy the US and Europe with high-altitude nuclear attacks. The attacks were designed to create electromagnetic pulses that would destroy the electrical infrastructure and all electronics on the two continents, but fortunately for Americans, Canadians, and Europeans, the detonations were more fizzles than explosions. That didn't stop the US and the Europeans from responding with their own conventional attacks. Thus, the War on Terror continued more than thirty years after it started with the collapse of the Twin Towers in New York City.

"Wait a minute," Bill said. "How is that possible if the HDF isn't allowed to fight off Hayek?"

"Excellent question," Renard said with a smile. "That's because I was on leave from the HDF to fight in a merc battalion."

"Merc battalion?" one of the other Probies asked.

"Mercenary battalion. A private military force that fights for those who pay them. We just happened to fight for the French under their Foreign Legion banner during the Iran War. The HDF usually wants us career types to get some combat experience, so we take leave and go fight on Earth occasionally."

Bill and the others had never heard about any merc battalions, but that wasn't surprising. Only embedded journalists were allowed to go with the troops, and only with specific units.

Bill asked Renard if volunteering for a mercenary unit violated Hayek's non-aggression principle.

"Not really. It would if we were the ones who initiated the aggression, but since Iran started the war, those who were attacked were allowed to respond with a like force. Hell, the Allies could've nuked Iran and it would've been acceptable, but they didn't want to turn all that oil into radioactive sludge, hence the conventional war."

Soon, all the Probies were outside, and Renard led them to a training building to learn more about their weapons. The afternoon was spent in weapons familiarization and firearms safety. Bill noticed that not everyone had been issued a PDW and, at the end of the day, asked Renard about it.

"Well, if you've got a skill that could possibly be something used in a headquarters or support role, they issue you a PDW. What's your specialty in the Corps?"

"Aerial survey specialist," Bill replied.

"So, you might be working in a Military Intelligence role. It makes sense for you to have a PDW."

"But why issue me a rifle?"

"Everyone gets a rifle. Don't matter who you are or what you do, everyone needs to be familiar with them," Renard said.

Bill was fascinated by the PDW. Of course, Bill was fascinated by just about any firearm, so it wasn't too difficult for him to be interested in the afternoon's lecture.

The PDW was the HDF's response to a personal weapon that was better than a pistol, but lighter than a rifle. Usually issued to noncombatants, it was carried on a sling over the shoulder or back. It had a short barrel, barely a foot long with a composite foregrip, a sliding stock, and a magazine well in the grip. The magazine held 20 rounds. The sights were iron, more circular than the traditional post and blade that Bill was used to. There was also a picatinny rail on the top, a means of attaching a rifle scope or aiming device. The design made for a compact weapon with few protrusions.

Bill learned that the PDW had only a safety function and a three-shot burst function. There was no single shot or fully automatic function as he expected.

Renard explained this, telling the platoon that experience showed that a single shot was usually ineffective (but not always) and that people tended to burn through a full magazine on full auto with a single burst. As the idea was to stop the enemy, the PDW-3 was designed to function with only a three-shot burst, which most people could control.

"Recoil's pretty negligible, so basically anyone, no matter how small, can handle it."

The sights, Bill learned, were designed as "ghost ring" sights, a design suitable for rapid target acquisition, not for distance shooting.

"The purpose of the sights is to get on target and get rounds downrange as fast as possible. They don't take a lot of getting used to, and besides, we're not talking long distance. Most shots with a peeder are expected to be within 100 meters. My experience has been that most shots are less than fifty meters."

An afternoon spent learning about the PDW-3, tearing it apart and reassembling it, gave the platoon a solid foundation in the fundamentals of its operation.

That evening, the four roommates went out after supper. Once again, their destination was the Cave Bear Cave. They were joined by Nicole and her roommate, Bridgette. Again, they elected to sit in the outdoor beer garden, where they were waited on by the same waitress as before.

The talk soon turned to the first day of BMT. All agreed that it was far different than what they had expected, with no screaming, yelling, or general abuse thrown their way. They speculated as to whether this would change as the training progressed.

"I hope not," said Bridgette. "I'm all for learning, but I don't see the need for stressing people out."

A debate then developed between the men and the women as to the need for stress in military training. As with most debates like this, nobody changed their view on the matter.

Deciding that one more beer wouldn't hurt them, the group proceeded to have a second, but it was agreed that there'd be no more. Nobody wanted to be even slightly hungover when dealing with firearms.

Discussions ranged from the politics of Earth to the types of music each enjoyed. Bill was into the classics, like One Republic, Imagine Dragons, and Jack Johnson, while Kim was into real classical music, and Thep was into techno-pop. Jordan, surprising everyone, was a country music type. "Yep," he declared, "I like both types, country AND western." Matt enjoyed similar music to Bill, but went a step further, enjoying classic rock from the 70s and 80s, with a bent toward folk rock.

Matt spied a guitar in the corner of the beer garden, went and picked it up, and plucked a few strings. He adjusted a couple of tuning pegs, played a quick warm-up, and then walked back to the table.

Sitting down, he faced Nicole and began playing John Denver's *Follow Me*.

Damn, thought Bill. *He's already proposing*. It must have looked like that to the rest of the group, too.

"Hey, why don't you get down on your knee and propose

properly?" Jordan joked.

Matt stopped playing in mid-strum, looked at Jordan, and said with a smile, "I will, just not right yet. Gotta have the right ambiance."

That caused Nicole to blush a bright red. "Well, I'm sure we'll see the right 'ambiance' one of these days," she stated with a demure smile.

Bill had heard of people falling in love at first sight, but he had never seen it before now. That wasn't the case with him and Jessica, at least on her part. *I swear, if he asked her to marry him right now I'm betting she'd say yes.*

After that song, Bill played several more, mostly older tunes from John Denver, Jim Croce, and Gordon Lightfoot. Despite his accent, he had quite a good singing voice, clear and able to carry a tune.

Soon it was time to head back to their cabins, so the group settled with the waitress. Bill was glad to have enough money to afford a couple of beers, and even paid for Bridgette's.

Bill headed back to his cabin with Jordan and Thep while Matt walked Nicole and Bridgette back to theirs.

The day's heat was dissipating quite nicely, so it was a pleasant walk back, though it was even nicer to step into the air-conditioned comfort. Each grabbed their devices and gathered in the living room to surf the net.

As promised, the email from Renard was waiting, instructing the Probies what uniform to wear. Bill noticed that it was more detailed than just a simple uniform, which consisted of pants, long-sleeved shirt, and the boonie cap: rather, they were required to wear more of their issued equipment: their PDW, as well as their LBE. They were also supposed to report with their PDW with the issued magazines. Renard wanted the platoon assembled outside the training building by eight o'clock, ready to go.

The three roommates were still in the living room when Matt got home, but not for long. Six o'clock comes pretty early, especially if you're straight out of your senior year of college, where most don't crawl out of bed until after ten.

For the rest of the week, the Probies were taught how to construct fighting positions (or "foxholes" as most of them had learned in their youth), hasty and deliberate ambushes, basic squad maneuvers, and basic field hygiene. Shaving in the field was interesting, especially since water was rationed, and seldom heated. Bill was glad, for once, that he didn't have much facial hair.

The second week kicked off the part of training that Bill enjoyed: firearms.

For the first week of firearms training, the Probies learned the basics of shooting—how to load and fire their weapons (and keep them safe), how to sight in and get on target, and how to shoot from various positions. The most difficult for Bill, and many others, was the standing position. It was a bit easier with the lighter PDW, and fortunately, the targets were closer, too.

Bill managed to qualify as an expert with both weapons, and was happy to see that Matt did, too. Bill became particularly fond of the PDW. With its three-shot burst and minimal recoil, he found it easy to consistently stay on target. Of course, the combined weight of gun and ammunition were far less than that of the R-1; the lesser weight was one of the many things about it that Bill found pleasurable.

The second week was spent shooting at targets at various ranges while moving. It wasn't really maneuvering so much as walk, target pops up, shoot it type thing. It reminded Bill more of a video game than anything else. It was designed to get the platoon used to making a decision while moving, not to just expect all contact to be from a fighting position.

The third week was the most exciting. Using some of the maneuvering techniques they learned the first week, the platoon was broken down into fire teams of four, then squads of twelve. First in fire team formation, then in squad formation, and with a lot of coaching by Renard, the platoon worked its way through a live fire exercise with pop-up targets. "Remember, no shooting on the other side of your team or squad. Face outward and only, I repeat, ONLY shoot in the direction you're facing. This ain't a real war, so no need for anyone to die by friendly fire."

Bill was disappointed when firearms training ended, and found field medicine rather boring, having already done a lot of medical training through Boy Scouts.

Weapons familiarization piqued his interest, though. For a week the platoon learned about the various weaponry in the HDF arsenal: explosives, such as hand grenades and directional mines, grenade launchers, anti-tank rockets, machine guns, and even some weaponry of potential enemies (Bill was slightly amused when one of the weapons was US Army standard issue M-4).

The next to last week of training focused on close-quarter combat. This not only included how to fire and maneuver in buildings and urban settings, but also some basic hand-to-hand combat. Bill was pitted against Thep at one point and figured he would have no problem taking the smaller man down. It came as a surprise when he found himself flat on his back on the ground, the breath knocked out of him, and a smiling Thep staring down at him. "You all right, man?"

Weekends for Bill were a combination of fly fishing the nearby Naches River and its tributaries, forays into Milton, and hanging out with his roommates and various female companions at the Cave Bear Cave. The pain over losing Jessica was still fresh and deep enough, that he didn't form any attachments with the various women, but he did enjoy their company.

Finally, training was over, and the platoon joined formation with the other platoons. Each was recognized and given a graduation certificate and an assignment to the local militia. Bill noticed that it was to Sacajawea Base.

That evening Renard treated the platoon to drinks at the Cave Bear Cave, letting them know he'd be proud to have any one of them in his platoon if they ever decided to leave the Corps and join the military. Bill figured he was just saying that because nobody had shot anybody by accident. Nevertheless, Bill enjoyed the drinks while also catching glimpses of Matt and Nicole enjoying drinks and each other's company.

Later that night, while lying in bed, Bill took stock of his situation. While things were certainly different than he'd expected, they were also more exciting, despite the fact that he was doing pretty much mundane things any new recruit in any military on Earth would be doing. He had enjoyed the firearms training and was looking forward to more of it, as it was always something he enjoyed. It was one thing that he and "the Colonel" did together. Thinking about that got Bill wondering how his father was faring—a widower and all alone on Earth, his only son gone off on an adventure on a different planet. It reminded Bill of his grandmother's stories about how it was to have a son go off to war, never knowing if he'd make it home, and watching it all on television. *At least they aren't broadcasting this live,* Bill thought.

Eventually, Bill got to sleep, and his alarm woke him all too early. He still hadn't adjusted to the whole "early to bed, early to rise" thing that the Corps seemed to revel in (at least, from his perspective as a Probie going through basic militia training).

Chapter 8

Finally, after almost nine weeks on Hayek, Bill and his fellow Probies were about to begin their actual training for the jobs they'd been hired for.

On Saturday morning Bill woke early with only a mild hangover, attacked it with a glass of water and a couple of aspirin, started a pot of coffee for the gang, and then checked his email. Sure enough, there was a message from the Director of Training, Corps of Discovery.

Bill was to check in at the auditorium for orientation on Monday at eight o'clock in the morning, followed by equipment draw. He was to report to the Remote Sensing and GIS Department after lunch, to evaluate his knowledge skills and then to train him on the Corps' methods and equipment. Further training would be assigned based on his completion of all necessary development and training.

Bill decided to spend the weekend relaxing and doing some fly fishing on the Yakima River, a river he had yet to try, so he did a quick search to see what kind of guide services existed. Instead, he discovered a business that rented one-person inflatable pontoon boats. He could rent the pontoon, be dropped off on the north side of the Yakima Canyon, then be picked up downriver on the south side of the canyon.

Bill called the company and was pleasantly surprised when somebody answered at the other end, despite the early hour. He was able to reserve a boat for the afternoon. It was already too late for the morning bite, but he should see some action for the evening bite. Bill asked about where he could get a fishing license and was caught off guard when the person on the other end of the line laughed out loud. "You ain't commercial fishing, are you?" Bill replied in the negative and was told that he didn't need no stinkin' license.

After reserving the boat, Bill helped himself to a cup of coffee and then read some news. His first stop was *The Explorer* where he saw an article about the incoming class of Explorers, with all of their names, a headshot, and a brief biography about each person. Bill's was a condensed version of the bio he filled out when he applied to the Corps.

Coffee finished, Bill went back upstairs, showered, dressed, and headed out for breakfast. The others were still sleeping. *Probably trying to sleep off hangovers, considering how much they drank last night,* he thought. *Then again, that was one helluva party.*

The cafeteria was a lonely affair, with very few Probies in attendance, none of whom he recognized. He got in the very short food line behind a young woman, almost as tall as he, with short red hair. She was wearing shorts and a tank top, so even though she was facing away from him, Bill could see she was tanned. *Huh, I thought redheads only burned.* As she reached for a bowl of fruit, Bill could see her facial profile. Her nose was slightly upturned and there was a smattering of freckles along the bridge. All in all, from what Bill could see, it was a rather pleasant-looking face, and not one he recognized from dining in the cafeteria for the past nine weeks.

Once his plate was full, biscuits and gravy with a helping of fresh fruit, he sought out a table alone. As he was passing the table where the redhead was seated, he changed his mind. "Mind if I join you?"

"Sure," she said, looking up.

Bill sat down and introduced himself, holding his hand out to her.

Taking it, she said with a smile, "Meri Lewis." Bill noticed that she had perfect white teeth when she smiled and that they stood in stark contrast to her tan and her bright blue eyes. He remembered reading somewhere that only one percent of the human population had that combination of hair and eye color, and he was fascinated by it.

Bill thought for a second, then laughed a short laugh. "Now that's too funny. Lewis and Clark in the Corps of Discovery."

"I was just thinking that," she replied, still smiling. "I guess this is the future adventures of Lewis and Clark."

"Not to sound presumptuous, but I don't recall seeing you around before," Bill said, taking a bite of biscuit and gravy.

"That's because I haven't been around. I just got in yesterday."

Bill raised an eyebrow at that. "Didn't you go through BMT?"

"Oh, yeah. I did that years ago," she replied.

It then dawned on Bill that Meri was another Hayeker. "Ah, I got it. You're local."

"Yep. Born and raised. You?"

Bill told her briefly about his upbringing and education.

"That must be difficult, moving all the time," she said. "I've only lived on base. I didn't even go away for uni, just took the skytrain to Hayek U."

"It's not too difficult, especially when it's all you've known. I always thought it strange that people didn't move every year or two. So, what did you study?"

"Ah, the norm for Explorers," Meri said. "Exploration Science, with a minor in frontier economics."

"I've heard of Exploration Science, but what's frontier economics?"

"Oh, just the usual stuff—economics as it applies to the frontier environment. You know, what types of industries are best to bring in, where to locate communities to optimize resources, et cetera."

"Sounds almost like economic geography."

"There's certainly a lot of that included," Meri replied with a smile. Bill noticed that when she smiled her entire face seemed to light up.

They talked about geography, economics, and exploration until they had both emptied their plates. Bill even got them both second cups of coffee so they could continue the conversation.

Eventually, the two realized that they were the only ones left in the cafeteria, and decided they should beat a retreat.

"Say, I'm going to be gone the rest of the day, but could I meet you for supper tonight?" Bill asked Meri as he held open the cafeteria door as they stepped out.

"I'd like that. What are you doing that you won't be here today?"

"Fly fishing on the Yakima."

"I love fly fishing!" Meri exclaimed. "I hope you don't think I'm being forward, but would you mind some company?"

Bill couldn't believe his good fortune. And here he was thinking about how lucky Matt had been to find Nicole. *Hah!* he thought, *how about them apples?* Any thought of Jessica was now an ephemeral one, quickly being replaced by this new and exciting woman.

"Mind? Nope, I don't mind at all. I'd love it. Problem is, though, I only reserved a single-seat pontoon boat."

"Who did you rent with? They might be happy to trade up to a drift boat."

Bill told her the company's name, and Meri told him to call them back and see about upgrading. "Since I invited myself, I'm in for half the cost."

Bill called, and sure enough, the company was happy to upgrade.

"Great. It's settled. I'll get my gear and meet you at the station. What time?" she asked.

"The reservation's for two, and I was planning on doing lunch in Milton. How about eleven?"

"That works. I'll see you then." She gave Bill a smile, turned, and walked off. Bill just watched her walk, and was pleasantly surprised when she turned around, smiled at him again, and then resumed walking.

Back at the cabin, Bill gathered his fishing equipment: fly rod, net, waders, wading boots, fishing vest with flies and nippers, and his ventilated hat. The fly rod was a four-piece St. Croix 5 weight he had bought in his junior year of college and had only used a couple of times around Seattle. It was a great, fast action rod, but really only good for smaller fish—definitely not a salmon rig. The rest of the gear was new, recently acquired and used only a couple of times on the Naches and a couple of its tributaries, all on base. Everything went into a small duffel bag that he could easily carry slung over his shoulder.

Despite the time spent gathering his equipment, Bill realized he still had another hour until he would meet Meri. He couldn't believe how antsy he felt. *Damn, is this how Matt feels all the time?* he thought.

He headed downstairs to bide his time on the internet. He was surprised to see Jordan in the living room, slumped in one of the chairs and nursing a fresh cup of coffee.

"Hey, look who's risen from the dead," he joked.

"Yeah, dead. That's me. Wish I really was, the way I'm feeling," Jordan mumbled.

"Water and aspirin, buddy, water and aspirin," Bill said, dropping the duffel on the floor.

"Ow, do you have to be throwin' that stuff around?" Jordan complained, wincing.

"I'll try to be more quiet," Bill said, plopping himself down in the other chair and activating his tablet.

Gradually, the other roommates materialized, each getting a cup of coffee and looking like something the cat dragged in.

Finally, it was time. "See you guys later," Bill said. "Don't wait supper on me." He received grunts in return.

Bill arrived at the skytrain station shortly before eleven and was surprised to see Meri already waiting for him. Along with a duffel, she had her militia rifle slung over her shoulder. Feeling a bit chagrined, he asked her about the rifle.

"You never know when you'll need it. Seein' how the Yakima Canyon isn't developed, anything might pop up. You have to remember, animals on Hayek aren't particularly afraid of humans yet, so to them we're just another meal. And there's always the Gaia Firsters we've gotta watch out for."

Bill hadn't even considered that and admitted as much to Meri. "Should I go back and get mine?" he asked.

"Naw. One should be enough," she said. "After all, we'll mainly be in a boat near civilization. Not likely we'll get attacked by anything on the water."

The two entered the station and chatted amiably while awaiting a train. Soon, one showed up, with only a few people getting off, most in Corps uniforms, but with some children sprinkled among them. Bill was used to this: most of the children were dependents of Explorers and other employees of the Corps.

Meri and Bill entered a train car and were soon on their way.

Lunch was at a small cafe in Milton near the skytrain station. The ambiance wasn't great, but it also wasn't a cafeteria on base. The two enjoyed each other's company and compared fishing techniques. Bill pumped Meri for information on salmon fishing on Hayek and wasn't surprised when she pulled out her tablet and showed him a picture of a Chinook she had caught earlier in the spring.

"It topped out at over 30 kilos," she said. Bill was impressed. Compared to the largest one he had ever caught, a 35-pounder (or about 16 kilos in Hayek's terms), it was huge.

After lunch, they caught the skytrain again. They transferred trains once and were soon at the last station at the mouth of the Yakima Canyon. Exiting the station they spied the boat rental shop across the street. *That's convenient,* Bill thought.

Inside the shop, they found a small retail area with an assortment of fishing and hunting paraphernalia lining the walls and on racks between the entrance and a counter near the rear of the store. A young woman set a tablet down on the counter and said, "Hi. How can I help you?"

"We reserved a drift boat for two o'clock," Meri answered.

"Right. Well, let's get you guys set up so you can get on the river."

Meri worked through most of the transaction while Bill stood, watched, and learned. While it wasn't his first financial transaction on Hayek, he still felt a bit intimidated while striving to learn the social mores of his new home.

The clerk told them about a restaurant adjacent to the boat rental shop that would be glad to cook their catch. "They've got the most amazing way of cooking trout with a hazelnut crust. On top of that, all the veggies they serve come straight from their own farm."

Soon, the two were riding in the back of a Kenji along a narrow gravel road through the Yakima Canyon, following the river upstream. Bill had been surprised to hear that the boats were kept upriver during the day, taken up early in the morning, before sunrise, and rented out on a first-come, first-served basis. He was further surprised to find out that some boats were still available. When he asked why, he was told that most people were switching from trout fishing to salmon as the salmon season was beginning in earnest on the rivers of Cascadia, with some being reported in the Nch'i-Wana, which Bill knew as the Columbia River. He would have loved to go salmon fishing, but with only a weekend off, he didn't have time to get to one of the coastal rivers, particularly the northern ones where the salmon runs were in full swing. He figured he would enjoy fly fishing for trout with reduced crowds, especially with his newest companion.

Once the Kenji arrived at the boat launch, the driver got out to help Meri and Bill load and launch the drift boat.

"Okay. You got your PFDs in the bottom here. There's four, so that should be more than enough. You can see both oars. Just lock 'em in the oarlocks before heading out. Don't want 'em falling out, 'cause that would kinda suck. Here's a map of the river," he said, handing over a plastic-encased topographic map to Bill, "and remember, the limit is two keepers each. Leave something for the rest of us." He smiled, "You two ever use one of these?"

"Oh, yeah. Lots of times," Meri replied.

"Great. See you downriver at the end of the day then." With that, the young man hopped back in the Kenji, started it up, did a three-point turn in the boat ramp area, and headed back down the gravel road, through the canyon.

Bill and Meri loaded their gear into the boat, donned their wading gear, and then pushed it out into the river, each jumping in as their section of the boat began floating.

Soon they were drifting down the river, making short casts from seated positions in the boat. Occasionally they would pull the boat to shore, anchor it, get out and fly fish while wading.

It seemed the trout were in a frantic feeding frenzy, as both had continuous strikes. While drifting and wading, the two kept up a continuous chatter. Bill learned that, like him, Meri was an only child, and that her mother had passed away when she was young. He was a little disconcerted to learn that her father was also the Commandant of the entire Corps of Discovery.

Bill told Meri about his aborted engagement, and how he had chosen the Corps over his fiance.

"It still hurts, but I guess I'm in recovery mode now."

Meri sympathized with him and commented on how it was a tough choice for the two of them, each making a decision that was counter to what the other wanted out of life.

Approaching dusk, the two wound up at the landing behind the boat rental shop. Both had elected to keep one of the numerous fish they caught, deciding that hazelnut-crusted trout with fresh vegetables would make for a great evening meal. Packing their waders, boots, and other gear into their duffels, and hoisting their catch by the stringers, they checked in with the shop, letting the woman behind the counter know that the boat had, indeed, been returned and not sunk to the depths of the Yakima River. Then, carrying their packed duffels and strung fish, headed off to the restaurant.

Upon entering the restaurant, they were greeted by a middle-aged woman with streaks of gray running through her otherwise jet-black hair. "Welcome. Looks like you've brought your own entrée. Here, let me take them and get them to the chef. Grab a seat on the porch," she indicated the back of the restaurant with a flick of her head, "and I'll be right back."

Bill and Meri stepped out onto a porch overlooking the Yakima River. As the sun was behind the Cascades, they knew they wouldn't be pan-fried like the trout, nor would they be blinded by the setting sun. They'd been fried enough already in the late summer sun on the Yakima.

The porch had a number of tables, of which a few were occupied by couples and small families. Meri chose a table against the railing. Meri draped her rifle over the back of her chair, using the rifle sling to support it. The hostess returned carrying two glasses of water and a pair of menus tucked under an arm.

"You'll find all the variations for your catch here. We don't mind mixing and matching, so just pick out how you want your trout done, and what you want with it. Drinks are listed at the front, with desserts in the back. I'll be back to take your order."

Bill and Meri looked through the menu, both deciding on the hazelnut-encrusted trout with asparagus and roasted baby red potatoes. Bill looked at the wine list but figured that since he knew nothing about wine, he shouldn't bother with it. Meri, on the other hand, had apparently grown up in a wine-drinking family and recommended they split a bottle of a red blend from a vineyard just downriver on the Nch'i-Wana from where the Yakima River flowed into it.

The waitress returned and Meri gave her the wine and dinner order. She told the couple that the hazelnuts were from a family member's orchard in south-central Cascadia. When the waitress left, Bill, who knew where Cascadia was, wasn't quite sure of the exact location and asked Meri.

"It's the long valley south of Nch'i-Wana, extending from the river to the mountains, and between the Cascades and the coastal range. You probably think of it as Oregon."

"Oh, yeah. We call it the Willamette Valley."

"So do we," Meri said.

Soon the waitress was back with the wine. She poured Meri's glass first, then Bill's, and told them it'd only be ten or fifteen minutes until their meals were ready.

They sipped wine and talked while watching the undersides of the clouds change hue as the sun sank lower below the mountains.

After the first glass was almost gone, the waitress arrived with their dinners.

The food looked and smelled delicious, and within seconds the two were attacking their meals with gusto. Bill still couldn't get over the difference between meals on Hayek and meals from Earth. On Earth, food looked good but tasted bland. Here, food not only looked good but was vibrant with flavor. He suspected it was because almost everything was locally produced, and not grown for shipping and looks.

Food devoured, and with a half glass each of wine left over, the two relaxed while the waitress removed their empty plates.

"Dessert?" she asked.

Meri raised an eyebrow at Bill. "Sure," he said, knowing well that while he was full, there was always room for dessert.

Meri ordered a crème brûlée while Bill chose a dessert called Death by Chocolate: a brownie covered with chocolate ice cream smothered with melted chocolate.

The two continued chatting while drinking their wine, then eating their dessert. Soon, the plates and glasses were empty.

"Well, I guess we better pay and get going," Meri finally said. The sky was dark and filled with the early evening stars.

Bill motioned the waitress over and claimed the check. "Hey, you got us the boat. It's the least I can do."

With the account settled, the two grabbed their duffels, Meri her rifle, and they headed out to the train station.

All too soon they arrived back at base, despite it being almost ten o'clock in the evening. By far, this was the best day Bill had had in a long time. He didn't want it to end but recognized it had to.

Exiting the station, duffel slung over his shoulder, Bill asked Meri if he could meet up with her for breakfast.

"Unfortunately, I'm meeting my dad for brunch, and then we're spending the day together. How about Monday, though? We could meet up before the orientation."

Bill couldn't quite hide his disappointment, which drew a slight smile from Meri.

"Sure, that'll work. Say about seven at the cafeteria?" Bill said.

"It's a date."

Giving him a quick peck on the cheek, she turned and walked away. He didn't remember the walk back to his cabin, but soon he was on the porch fumbling for his card to unlock the door.

Chapter 9

Monday couldn't come quick enough for Bill, and by 6:45 he was already waiting for Meri outside the cafeteria. Any memory of Jessica was not only fading fast but was being obliterated by the red-headed beauty that had entered Bill's life. Even though it was early in the morning, it was quite warm, being the third week of August and still the height of summer. Bill figured it probably wouldn't start to cool off until mid-September. He couldn't wait for the cooler weather, but he had finally started acclimating to the climate. Luckily, he had finally built up a base tan strong enough to wear shorts and short-sleeved shirts all day, which was how he was currently dressed. He had also gotten smart and had bought a small case to carry his tablet in. The case had a shoulder strap and was currently hanging off his right shoulder.

Bill spotted Meri from several blocks away. She had a nice walk, he observed. Like him, she was dressed in shorts and a short-sleeved shirt. Instead of wearing sneakers, as he was, she was wearing ankle-high hiking boots.

Finally, she was before him. "Hi. I'm famished. How about you?" she said, immediately heading toward the entrance. She was inside before Bill could get the door for her.

They got their food, took a table, and began eating, chatting between bites. Just as Bill took a bite of food he heard a voice over his shoulder. "Got room for two more?"

Bill looked up and indicated that Matt and Nicole should join them. The two sat down and Matt extended his hand toward Meri.

"Hi. I'm Matt, Bill's roommate. This is Nicole."

Meri and Nicole shook hands and exchanged greetings.

"So, this is what you were up to Saturday?" Matt asked Bill. "I thought you had gone fishing."

"We did," Meri said. "I heard you were a bit 'under the weather' that day," she finished with a hint of a smile on her lips.

Nicole nudged Matt in the ribs with her elbow. "Oooh, she got you on that one, sport."

The talk after that was light, especially since they had to finish and be at the auditorium soon. Neither Thep nor Jordan joined them, and Bill didn't even notice.

Shortly before eight o'clock the foursome entered the auditorium and took seats near the front. The room filled up fast. Precisely at eight o'clock, Commandant Lewis stepped out onto the stage and walked to the center of it. His hair wasn't quite as shaggy as the first time Bill saw him at the initial orientation. It only took a couple of seconds before the room was quiet.

"Good morning," Lewis said. "Today begins the fun. Not that I'm sure you didn't have fun with BMT," he added with a chuckle. The audience also chuckled, but moans could also be heard. "But this'll be a lot more fun, mainly because it's the reason you're here.

"So, today's going to be a bit like the first day of BMT training, in that you'll get a little more orientation and then equipment issue. After today, you'll look like Explorers, but don't think you are. That only happens when you finally go through the gate onto a planet that the Corp will be actively exploring.

"All of you have had sufficient training and education in the position you were recruited for. But, we do things a bit different here. So, after equipment issue, you'll report to your assigned sections and undergo a more thorough evaluation. Consider this diagnostic in nature. There's no right, wrong, or perfect scores. Our goal is to determine how much you really know about the jobs we've brought you in for. After we determine the extent of your knowledge, we'll fine-tune it and bring it up to our standards. Depending on your specialty, that could be anywhere from a day to several weeks or even a couple of months. Mostly, that's up to you, but we want you up to speed as soon as possible."

"Equipment issue and haircuts will be done alphabetically," he continued. "Once you're dismissed from here, you'll report to an Explorer outside who will be standing with a sign with letters on it. You go to the Explorer who's holding the sign with the first letter of your last name.

"As I told you eight weeks ago, you're entering what will probably be the most exciting stage of your life. It'll also probably be the most dangerous. Toward that end, and because we'll be investing a lot of time and money in you, we want you to succeed. To do that, you have to try. No half-assed attempts, so try to do things right the first time.

"Once you've gotten your hair cut and been issued your gear, you'll be told how to assemble it and what all you need to have with you at all times. And I mean, at all times!" he emphasized. "You'll be given a master list of gear that you should always have with you, and occasionally you'll be required to have something in addition to what you'll normally carry. If you're caught without what's required, your pay will be docked. We take having the right equipment seriously in the Corps.

"The whole kit and kaboodle will belong to you. That means if you lose anything, you'll have to replace it because you can't operate fully without all the stuff you're required to have. Is that understood?" he asked the crowd, looking around.

Satisfied that just about everyone nodded their agreement, he continued, "Once you've been instructed on the wearing of the uniform and equipment, you head back to your quarters, change into a uniform, and don the appropriate equipment. You can then go to lunch. You'll get an email shortly telling you exactly what equipment you'll need and where to report to after lunch.

"Any questions?" Lewis asked. There were none.

Lewis pulled out a remote control and turned the projector on. The image of the Corps of Discovery came alive on the screen behind him.

"First, a little history," he said. "About forty years ago, Timothy Bowman, who had a PhD in physics, discovered the process that allowed him to open portals to parallel worlds." An image of Bowman appeared on the screen.

"Knowing a bit about history, particularly what happened when Europeans invaded the Americas during the Age of Exploration, which led to the death of millions through the introduction of diseases, he decided to keep his discovery a secret until he could ensure that no mass extinction or dying off would take place. To that end, he founded the Corps of Discovery. Our primary objective is to survey new parallel planets to ensure that no other humans or hominids exist there before opening them to settlement. That is our number one priority!" Lewis emphasized. "Anything beyond that is just pure gravy.

"The Corps currently consists of four branches; Aviation, Ground, Logistics, and Training." The screen changed to show the four branches listed. "As you've probably guessed based on your acceptance letters, most of you will initially be in either Aviation or Ground. Logistics and Training are pretty much reserved to those who have been there and done that."

The screen changed to show four aircraft, which Bill identified as a high-altitude survey plane, a twin-engine seaplane, and two twin-engine cargo planes. "Aviation is not only responsible for our initial surveys, but it also works closely with Logistics to keep Ground supplied. We operate four main aircraft." Lewis clicked the remote. An enlarged image of the survey plane appeared. It had long narrow wings and a Plexiglas bubble on the top of the fuselage.

"This is the S1, 'S' standing for 'Survey'. We call it the Monarch. It's designed to travel around the world non-stop and can support a crew of four for three weeks. It manages this by using a hybrid system of biofuel and solar energy. Note the long wings—that allows for greater altitude possibilities while also housing the solar panels. The Plexiglas bubble is for taking sun and star shootings for navigation. You'll also notice that it has four engines. Two of those are electric and tied into the solar panels, and two are regular aviation gas."

An interior image of the S1 appeared on the screen. "Here you can see the working arrangement—pilots up front, aerial survey specialists behind them. The specialists operate a variety of remote sensing platforms to identify possible sites of human or hominid settlement. No other surveys take place until the initial surveys using one of these fine crafts are complete and no sign of human or hominid habitation is identified.

"We're quite proud of the S1, as it's a homegrown aircraft, designed for our special needs and built exclusively on Hayek," Lewis said with a smile. "As a matter of fact, all craft we use in the Corps are made on Hayek. We do this so we aren't reliant on Earth or other planets to fulfill our needs."

The image changed again, this time showing a seaplane.

"This is a Bombardier CL-415. Originally made in Canada on Earth for fighting wildfires, we obtained the license and manufacture our own version here. We use this craft mainly for logistics purposes and in low-level maritime and terrestrial aerial surveys and mapping. We've specially modified them to extend their range to 3,000 nautical miles. That may sound like a lot, but considering how big the planet is, it really isn't."

The third craft to appear was the twin-engine cargo plane. "Considering where we operate, we selected the C-123, also known as the Provider, as our main initial ground support craft. Now, if you thought the 415 was old, this puppy's got it beat. While the design might be over a half-century old, it's still a great plane, hence our reason for choosing it. Like the others, we build the Provider here. We use the Provider to get supplies close to the Ground teams, hence the term 'initial ground support.' It's a multi-step process. Logistics identifies where to develop airfields, Aviation flies in and parachutes the crew in that'll build the field, and then the necessary construction equipment is brought in using a low-altitude parachute extraction system." Lewis used his laser pointer to show an image of a Provider using the method, barely a couple of meters above the ground, with a parachute pulling what looked like a bulldozer out of the back of the plane. "After everything's on the ground, Logistics builds the airfield.

"Then, Aviation brings in more fuel and supplies, and then the final craft, the deHavilland Caribou, or DHC-4 is brought in." An image of the twin-engine cargo craft appeared on the screen. Much like the venerable Provider, the Caribou sported high wings and a tail end that slanted up toward a high tail to allow for the rear-opening cargo door.

The image changed to show the Caribou and Provider side by side. The Provider was the much larger of the two.

"The Caribou, much like the CL-415, provides low-level aerial surveys and close logistics support for Ground teams. As you can see, it's a bit smaller than its bigger brother, which means it carries less than the Provider and has a much shorter range than either the Provider or the CL-415. Its one major advantage is that it can operate from much shorter fields. Both it and the Provider have short take-off and landing capabilities, but the Caribou's is shorter, therefore better for our operations.

"We use the three types of cargo craft because each serves a different purpose. Some teams are better served from waterborne operations, while others require support further inland. Each plane has its own operational demands, so we use the craft to their best capabilities.

"For those of you wondering why we use the older planes, rather than newer ones like the Osprey, the answer is because we can control the manufacturing here on Hayek, and the newer birds require a lot more infrastructure to build and maintain than the older birds. If we don't have control over all aspects of a craft, and it takes a lot to maintain, we don't use it.

"Each and every one of you will ride in some of these four planes several times during your career, so be sure to familiarize yourself with them and their crews. After all, they'll be the ones bringing you your food and toilet paper when you're way the hell and gone," he said with a smile. The last statement elicited light laughter.

"Ground survey is where most of you will wind up," Lewis continued, as the image on the screen changed from the airplanes to a group of photos showing Explorers walking, riding horses, or riding in Jeeps. All the Explorers shown were holding rifles.

"This is where most of the excitement, and danger, exists. Although, you'll find that danger is pretty much in every aspect of our job. The role of Ground is to get feet on the ground, look around, and see what exists. Initial ground surveys are by foot and horseback. Only if no humans or hominids are identified do we bring in the Jeeps for more detailed surveys. If we do find humans or hominids, we pull back and halt all exploration of the planet, and then quarantine the planet to settlement.

"If you don't already know how to saddle, care for, and ride a horse, this'll be quite the learning experience for you. It's also the most physically demanding branch, so don't think it's a walk in the park—it's not."

The screen changed again, this time showing a collage of stacked pallets, shelves of equipment, a bulldozer on an improvised airfield, and a small cargo ship. "Next to Ground, Logistics is the largest branch. It provides all the logistical support to the other branches. Basically, without logistics, you die.

"Logistics works closely with Aviation to supply Ground, and it has its own navy—small cargo vessels that transport people and equipment between the continents. Along with those duties, they're also responsible for developing airfields, marine ports, and depots for fuel, parts, food, and medical services.

"You'll notice that medical services isn't its own branch; rather, it's a part of Logistics. You'll be happy to know that we've got a top-notch bunch of medical care providers, more and more of whom are graduating from our own schools. I think you'll appreciate having physicians who are more used to the types of medical issues you'll face than somebody trained in clinics where all sorts of specialized medical equipment are available 24/7."

The image on the screen changed again, this time showing a series of photos of people in classrooms.

"Training is the final, and smallest branch. It's where you begin, and where you might wind up if you live and gain the experience necessary to pass on to others. Here is where you'll get updated on our methods and equipment. It's also the branch responsible for teaching you how to survive on your own if you need to. Toward that end, each one of you will be run through our survival school before going on your first mission. All of your trainers have survived on their own, stranded on an unsurveyed planet, some for several months. Listen to them. They know what they're talking about.

"Now, about the rank structure. We're somewhat of a paramilitary organization that way. As you already know, I'm the Corps Commandant, responsible for the entire Corps of Discovery. Under me is the Assistant Corps Commandant, Lisa Ragnar." Lewis gestured to a woman who had just walked on stage. She was a trim forty-something-year-old, dressed in the Corps uniform. She waved casually to the assembled audience.

A table of organization appeared on the screen and Lewis walked briefly through it, announcing the names of each Branch Commander and Branch Executive Commander.

"Each survey crew will be assigned a leader, but other than that, there are no ranks except Explorers or Probationary Explorers.

"Okay, that pretty much sums up your orientation. Head out and get outfitted," he commanded.

This time all the Probies got up and made an orderly exit without needing a second warning.

Bill split from Meri, Matt, and Nicole, but not before making arrangements with them to meet for lunch, and made his way to the

Explorer holding the sign with the letters "A-D". He was happy to see it was Luke Kanehama. He hadn't seen the Explorer since the first week of his arrival on Hayek. The two shook hands and Bill asked where he had been.

Luke told him he had been on a ground survey and was back for two weeks' leave before heading out again. Bill was impressed. Luke looked a bit thinner and darker. *Must be all that time spent outdoors,* he thought.

Luke asked Bill to hold the sign so he could take roll, then pulled a tablet from his pants cargo pocket. Bill could see a list of names on the screen.

As each Probie arrived, Luke asked them their name and checked them off.

Soon there were several Probies surrounding Luke, and nobody else was exiting the auditorium.

Luke put his tablet away. "I guess that's all. Let's head out and get your stuff first, and then you can get your haircuts." With that, he took the sign back from Bill and began walking. The small gaggle of Probies around him followed.

Other groups were doing the same thing, all heading toward the logistics center, the same building where they drew their Militia equipment.

This time the groups separated by matching the door numbers with the last-name letters. Bill's group wound up at Door Number 1.

"Okay. Go in, get your stuff, then come out," Luke said. "Once everyone's out, we'll go sit in the shade and I'll show you how to arrange it. Be sure to read the list of required equipment before you start getting kitted out."

As Bill approached the counter, the Explorer behind it, a grizzled old fellow with a gray beard, said, "Last name first, first name last."

"Clark, William" Bill responded. The man turned and limped into the bowels of the building. He soon returned with a cardboard box which he set on the table. Without a word, he turned and walked back between the shelves. After two more trips into the building, he said, "Let's unpack this stuff, go through it, and make sure you've got everything."

The first thing he pulled out was a tablet, similar to the one Luke used. Small, but rugged looking. The man turned it on.

Handing it over to Bill he instructed him to enter his information to activate the software. Bill entered his name at the prompt, then his Corps of Discovery identification number, which he had memorized. Once the information was complete, a message popped up on the screen. Bill saw it was from the Logistics Center, so he opened it: a list of equipment.

"Great. Looks like it's working," the old Explorer said. Let's go through the list and ensure you've got everything."

The two did, and rather rapidly. Bill was surprised at the amount of equipment he was being issued. Not only did he get uniforms and boots, but also flight suits, Nomex gloves, a survival vest, a backpack, a scoped bolt-action rifle with three twenty-round magazines and a five-round magazine, another PDW (*why do I need two of these?* he thought) with three-twenty round magazines, a hammock with rain fly, web belt with suspenders, a butt pack, a hatchet, knife, and the list went on. As each item was checked off, he put it in a large brown duffel bag, much like his Militia duffel, only a different color. The rifle and PDW were left in their cases. A brimmed hat, with a stiff crown that was vented, went on his head. It reminded Bill of the old Tilly hat his dad had worn for decades.

The final item he was issued was a phone with a SIM card. "You know how to set one of these up?" the old Explorer asked. Bill nodded and replied, "Yep."

After everything was packed, the old Explorer instructed Bill to sign a digital document signifying he had received everything. "That's it. You own it now, so if you lose anything, you'll have to pay to replace it." Looking past Bill, he hollered, "Next!"

Bill placed his new tablet into his tablet case, which was still slung over his shoulder. Then, with some effort, he hoisted his duffel onto his back, placing his arms through the bag's shoulder straps, picked up a firearm case in each hand, and headed out the door. Luckily, one of the Probies waiting for her turn to draw equipment held it open for him, because it would have been awkward to do so otherwise.

Outside, Luke directed him to a large oak tree a short distance away. "Wait over there. It'll be a while, but you can start by looking at the list of equipment you need to have with you at all times. If you want, you can start assembling it. I'll be along shortly to help out if you've got any questions."

Bill walked over to the tree and set his weapon cases down, then shucked off his duffel. Pulling his new tablet out, he studied it. It was lighter than his personal tablet but appeared more rugged. The screen was about twenty centimeters, about the same size as his eight-inch tablet. It also had the words "Waterproof to 10m" on the back. Considering the lifestyle he expected to experience with it, he wasn't surprised that it was designed to be so rugged.

He activated it, found the email application, and opened it. There were two new emails, one from the Logistics Center and one from Operations. Bill opened the one from the Logistics Center first and saw it was the receipt for his equipment draw. The email from Operations provided a list of all the equipment Bill was expected to have on him at all times in his Primary Survival Kit. It was rather extensive and made perfect sense for somebody who might have to be on their own for an extended period. The list also provided graphic instructions on the best way to assemble the equipment for wearing. The web belt was designed to carry a canteen, a hatchet, survival knife, survival pouch, and a magazine pouch that carried three twenty-round magazines for the bolt-action rifle. Lightweight suspenders were to be used with the belt. Just like his Militia equipment, Bill noticed the canteen came with a cup, but it also came with a cup lid and a small stove, all of which nestled in the canteen cover.

The hammock and rain fly went into the backpack, along with a mess kit that fit into a small wood-burning stove, a reloading kit with ammunition components, collapsible water bottles, a small hygiene kit, a first aid kit, and his modular sleeping system. The instructions called for clothing to be packed, but Bill decided to wait until he got home before sorting that out.

The hygiene kit consisted of a small, quick-drying absorbing towel, a small soap carrier, dental floss and a toothbrush, and a small showerhead that fit on the bottles. It was similar to the Simple Shower™ he carried as a Boy Scout at Philmont Scout Ranch, but slightly smaller and without the air tube.

The modular sleeping system was made up of several layers of sleeping bags, each providing a different level of comfort, from the silk liner that served as a lightweight summer bag, to the heavier bag that was designed to keep him warm at minus 18 degrees Celsius. It also had a radiant barrier that was designed to work with his hammock. Even though it consisted of several bags, the entire kit weighed less than a kilo.

Strapped to the outside of the pack was to be a small ax, an entrenching tool, almost identical to the one issued by the Militia, and a bush knife that looked more like a small Japanese samurai sword.

Equipment he was required to carry in his pockets included his tablet, a pocket knife, spork, fire starter, basic sewing kit, small toothbrush, dental floss, compass, bandana, and several means for killing small animals. Fishing line and hooks he already knew about, along with snares, but he had also been issued a bowstring along with several break-away arrowheads and fletches to make a bow and arrow set. He suspected that the rubber tubing was designed to be used to turn a forked stick into a slingshot.

In the survival vest pouches, there was more built-in redundancy, with more survival equipment, including another knife, more instruments of death (as he termed the equipment necessary for killing game), and a couple of 1-liter collapsible bottles. *They must really love knives here*, he thought: he had been issued four knives, a sword, a hatchet, and an ax. One very interesting item that went into a pocket on his vest was a small waterproof paperback book entitled *CoD*

Survival Guide. Flipping through it briefly, Bill discovered it was a veritable treasure trove of survival tactics.

The final item on his list was a chronograph watch with a nylon web strap. That made sense, considering all his duties were supposedly in the air. Bill was pleased; his watch was not only old, but the crystal was scratched and getting hard to read. He took off his old watch, stashed it in the duffel, then put the chronograph on his left wrist. Checking his tablet for the exact time, he then set the chronograph. The instructions indicated that it was an automatic mechanical watch. This meant it had no battery and never needed winding, but operated off the kinetic energy of his arm and wrist.

One web belt, the butt pack, a canteen setup, the PDW, and a poncho and liner were extra emergency equipment that was attached to the crash couch of whatever aircraft Bill would be flying in.

Bill realized there was redundancy built into the equipment, not only for killing game, but for water, fire, health care, and personal hygiene.

He decided to assemble those items he could easily wear until he went back to his cabin before lunch. He assembled the web belt and suspenders to put his personal equipment on. As the instructions had said that the placing of many items was at the wearer's discretion, he decided to put the knife on his right side and the hatchet on the left. The canteen setup went over his left rear pocket, while the ammunition pouch went on the front, to the right. He was surprised to find out how light the canteen, cup, and stove were, and then he saw they were made from titanium. *They don't spare any expense,* he thought.

The final item, the survival pouch, went on the front, to the left. Snapping the suspenders in place, he felt ready to try the whole thing on. By this time several other Probies had joined him under the tree and were reading their tablets.

Opening his rifle case, Bill extracted two of the three magazines and put them in the magazine pouch on his belt. He looked at the remaining one and wondered why he was given a five-round magazine. Seeing a curled sling in the case, he picked it up and unfurled it. He then pulled the rifle out of the case and, after checking it to ensure it was unloaded, attached the sling to it. While doing so, he noticed that there was space in the bottom of the stock that looked like it was designed to fit the five-round magazine. On a hunch, he picked it up and inserted it into the space. Sure enough, it fit like a glove, clicking into place.

He also noticed that the rifle's forearm had an integrated bipod. While scoped, the rifle also had iron sights, the rear one being a ghost ring type. Looking at the barrel he discovered that his rifle was called an ER-1, and fired a 7.62 mm by 51 mm round, basically NATO ammunition. *Huh. I wonder why they're using NATO ammo here,* he thought. The 7.62 NATO was the standard round for light machine guns and was used in rifles before the lighter 5.56 mm NATO round, fired in guns like the M-16, was adopted.

He inspected the rifle a bit further, removing and replacing the bolt several times just to get the feel of it.

After surveying his new rifle, he placed it back in the case and snapped the latches secure.

Bill stood up, picked up the assembled gear, and put it on. The belt was a bit loose, so he adjusted it, but not so snugly as to not fit over other clothes.

Then he loaded the backpack with all its prescribed equipment. Thinking about his days spent backpacking, he tried to pack it the same way he did then: heavier stuff to the front, lighter stuff further from his back. Even though it would all be going into his duffel bag until after lunch, he wanted to get a head start on getting it ready.

The ax, machete, and shovel were attached to special straps on the pack, making the ensemble complete.

Next came the survival vest. This took the redundant equipment for gathering game, the second survival knife (smaller and lighter, not the heavy-duty version he wore on his belt), and a host of other items, such as first aid, sewing, hygiene, and fire-starting equipment. The two water bottles had clips on them that would allow them to attach to the vest, a web belt, or a pack. They rolled up and went into separate pouches on the vest. The final item was a pocket chainsaw; a tool that looked like a chainsaw chain, but was designed to be held by grommets at each end and worked back and forth like a regular saw.

Looking back at the email from Operations he figured out how to pack his Secondary Survival Kit. Another web belt with a canteen, cup, cover, and stove went into it, along with a survival knife, the poncho and liner, and a lightweight mesh hammock. The final items were the three PDW magazines and ammunition. The PDW stayed in the case. Bill figured that he'd put it in the butt pack when he had to.

Finally, with the exception of the boots and clothing, the backpack and butt pack were packed, and both placed next to the duffel. He decided to place the butt pack and the PDW case in the duffel bag, leaving him with only three things to carry back to the cabin, rather than five. *I guess I'll have to wear the pack and carry the duffel. Damn, that's gonna be a bitch.*

By this time, all the Probies had arrived under the tree. Several were getting organized as Bill had done, while others were still reading.

Luke arrived, looked over the crowd, and said "Your attention please," then waited until everyone was looking at him.

"Everyone take a look at Clark," he said, pointing to Bill. "As you can see, he's got most of his gear together. Notice how his belt is configured. Yours should look the same, or similar."

Luke had him come over and stand in the center of the group. "Clark, you stay here and act like a display model. The rest of you, take a good, hard look at how his gear is arranged and then do the same. We'll work on your packs next.

"After you finish up here, you can swing by the barber and then take off for lunch. After lunch, you'll go directly to training. You should have an email telling you where to go. Be sure you show up in uniform, carrying and wearing all the gear you're required to have, that means survival vest, belt, backpack, and rifle. You don't have to carry it when off duty, but you better have it with you at all times when you're on duty."

Luke indicated to several Probies with two gun cases. "If you've been issued both a rifle and a PDW, along with a backpack and a butt pack, carry only the rifle and the backpack. If you're carrying the PDW and the butt pack, that means things went seriously wrong. They're the backup for the backup for those of you on flight status.

"Any questions?"

Nobody raised a hand.

"Great. Also, when you get into your uniform, the absolute minimum is boots, socks, shorts or pants, shirt, and bush hat. You can wear shorts and long-sleeved shirt, or pants and short-sleeved shirt. It's up to you. The only time we require specific attire is at formal events and ceremonies. Uniforms are required during working hours and when on surveys, but when you're off duty you can wear whatever you want, or don't wear anything. Your call."

After several minutes, Luke told Bill he could leave if all his gear was in order. He told him how to get to the barber along with the advice of doing it sooner, rather than later.

Bill thanked him and decided to follow his advice. Before doing so, he sent an email to Meri with his new tablet, with the simple word "Lunch?"

Picking up his pack, he shrugged it onto his shoulders. The weight wasn't too bad. *Then again, there's no food, water, or clothing in it*, he reminded himself.

He grabbed the rifle case in one hand and the duffel in the other. The duffel weighed more than the pack, so Bill made the decision to switch the two, wearing the duffel on his back and carrying the pack.

The barbershop wasn't far, but a line had already started to form. Bill got in line, setting his case and pack down, but keeping his duffel on. Soon it was his turn, and the barber didn't say anything other than "Sit!" Bill sat. Soon he was the proud owner of a new haircut. It actually wasn't too bad. Not quite a military high and tight, but pretty close.

He noticed that women were allowed to keep their hair nominally longer, but none had any hair that came remotely close to touching their shoulders. Bill wondered what Meri would look like with short hair. *Probably still gorgeous,* he figured.

Upon arriving at the cabin he dumped everything from the duffel onto his bed. The next thing he did was to strip and dress in a uniform: brown shorts with cargo pockets, a short sleeve shirt, brown wool socks, brown leather boots that reached barely above the ankles, and the wide-brimmed hat. Only after putting on the shorts did he notice that the seat was reinforced. *That makes sense,* he thought, *considering how much time we'll probably be spending sitting on the ground or logs.* Now that he had a base tan built up, he was more comfortable wearing short-sleeved attire and less worried about burning. He didn't wear the issued underwear, but he did notice they were more like a fine mesh than the cotton briefs he normally wore.

Reading the instructions again, Bill decided to pack the requisite clothing. This consisted mainly of four complete uniforms, four sets of underwear and socks, a raincoat with a removable liner, fingerless mittens, two pairs of brown long underwear that he saw were made from silk, and a balaclava.

Once he got everything packed and assembled, he reassembled it on his person. First to go on was the vest, followed by the web belt, and finally the backpack. While it didn't quite weigh as much as the backpack he wore at Philmont, Bill was still aware that he didn't have any food or water weighing him down. He decided that it would probably be best to at least have his canteen filled. Slinging his rifle over his shoulder, he went downstairs and filled the canteen at the kitchen sink.

About that time the newly shorn Thep and Jordan arrived, lugging all their gear. Bill noticed that neither had a PDW case with them. *Lucky bastards,* he thought, considering how the additional weight of his crash couch survival equipment had made his trip from the Logistics Building more difficult.

The three exchanged greetings before the new arrivals

disappeared into their respective rooms to get organized.

Bill placed the filled canteen in the canteen cover on his belt, snapping it shut after it was seated.

"I'm heading to the cafeteria," he said loudly. "Anyone want to join me?"

Both men claimed they needed time to get organized, so Bill decided to head out on his own. As he opened the door, he saw Matt walking up the steps. Like Bill, Matt had most of his gear organized and was wearing it, carrying his duffel and rifle case.

"I'm about to grab lunch," Bill told him. "Want me to wait for you?"

"Sure, gimme a minute to drop this stuff off and get into uniform."

Matt headed up the stairs. Bill sat on the front porch steps with his rifle across his legs and watched the parade of laden Probies as they slogged from the Logistics Building to their residences, lugging all their newly issued gear.

Within a couple of minutes, Matt reappeared, wearing his pack, vest, and belt, and carrying his rifle.

"Damned if we don't look like a bunch of Explorers from *Far Afield*," he said, citing a popular movie about a Corps of Discovery team that found space invaders on a parallel planet.

"Yeah, but those actors were better-looking than you," Bill quipped back, standing and retrieving his pack.

The two arrived at the cafeteria and headed in. Neither Meri nor Nicole were inside, so Bill and Matt picked a table and put their packs down on a couple of chairs, claiming the table. Neither felt it was prudent to leave their rifles, so they kept them slung over their shoulders and got in line for food.

Back at the table, they removed the packs from the chairs and noticed that the chairs had a notch on the top of the seat back, which was ideal for placing the slings of their rifles in. They found the rifles rested quite nicely, with the butts just inches off the floor, but the entire thing out of the way of sitting. As they were sitting down they were joined by Meri, who set her pack on the chair next to Bill. Bill was right; even with her hair cut short, she was still beautiful. And somehow, the shorter hair seemed to highlight her blue eyes, making them appear even brighter.

"Let me get some food and I'll be right back," she said.

Nicole, also with much shorter hair, arrived and went to get food as well. Soon all four were sitting, eating, and enjoying each other's company.

"So, who's going where this afternoon?" Meri asked.

"Flight line," Matt drawled. "Get to play with some of them there aerocraft thingees," he added, exaggerating his Southern accent.

"Me, too," Meri said after swallowing a bite of food.

"Training Building for a GIS evaluation," Bill said. "Looks like it'll be a while before I'm on the flight line."

"Aw, that's too bad, Bill. We'll think of you when we're flying up there," Nicole said with a smile.

"Gee, thanks, guys," Bill said, acting forlorn. He was actually looking forward to seeing the GIS systems used by the Corps and getting up to speed on them and the remote sensing systems.

After eating, the group put their trays away, grabbed their packs and rifles, and headed outside. The three waved bye to Bill as they headed off to the airfield. Bill was actually feeling pretty good, knowing that his walk would be a lot shorter than theirs.

Chapter 10

Bill arrived at the Training Building, but having forgotten which room to report, he pulled out his tablet and opened his email. A quick glance informed him that he was to report to Room 204 at 1300 hours. Guessing that 204 would be on the second floor, Bill entered the building, found the stairs, and took them up a flight.

Looking through the door window of 204, he saw a typical computer lab, with rows of machines set up on tables. He opened the door and saw an older man, obviously an Explorer by his attire, sitting at a desk in the front of the room reading on a tablet.

The grizzled veteran looked up and said, "C'mon in if you're here for GIS evaluation. If not, you're in the wrong place."

"Guess I'm in the right place then." Holding out his hand to the man, he introduced himself. The man shook his hand briefly, introducing himself as Jim Merriman, then looked down at his tablet.

"Yep, looks like you're in the right place. Leastways, your name's here. Grab a seat. You're a bit early, but we'll be starting in about fifteen minutes. I'm expecting several more Probies."

Bill chose a seat near the front of the class, next to the window. He wasn't sure if he sometimes suffered from ADD, but it always made him feel better being able to look out and see something natural, rather than just a classroom. He set his pack down beside him, then looked around.

"Uh, Jim," he asked, "any suggestions on where I should put my rifle?"

"Oh, sorry. Yeah, the rifle rack by the front door," Jim pointed toward a long rifle rack that Bill hadn't noticed when he entered. "Each rack has a number that correlates with your computer, so put it in there."

Bill placed his rifle in the rack, then returned to his computer station and sat down.

The classroom soon filled up, and he spotted a few Probies that he had seen around base. As they entered, Merriman told them to put their rifle on the rack and take a seat at the computer that matched the rifle rack's number.

Kim Smith, whom Bill had met at his first meal on Hayek, sat down next to him.

"Hey, fancy meeting you here," she said.

"Yeah, about time we finally got to actually use our skills," he said.

Precisely at one o'clock, Merriman stood up. "All right, let's get started. I'm Jim Merriman, and this is Geographic Information Systems Diagnostic Testing. You'll each be given a series of problems to complete using the GIS that we use in the Corps. If you hit a problem you can't solve, let me know, and then continue on to the next one. The whole purpose of this exercise is to see just what you know and what you'll need to work on to bring you up to speed.

"Considering everyone here has at least a bachelor's degree in GIS or a GIS emphasis in their degree, I doubt that many of you'll need much, if any, remedial training.

"Okay, let's get started."

Bill tapped on the keyboard and the monitor brightened. He saw that he needed to log in. He typed his usual login username and password and was granted access.

The "Start Here" document was in the lower left corner of the screen. Bill opened it and begin reading. It consisted of a series of activities he was to do in order, starting with opening the geographic information system software and importing a data layer. The instructions stated where all the GIS data was stored, so Bill opened the GIS and saw it was the exact same type he had learned at UW. *Thank goodness for small favors,* he thought.

Once the software was running, he added the first data layer, which consisted of a base map of Sacajawea Base. He then added layers showing the buildings, roads, water towers, and airfield. All the data to this point was vector data – simple data consisting of points, lines, and polygons.

His first operation was a simple route analysis between his residence, the training center, the rifle range, and then back to his residence. That took him only a couple of minutes. *Hmm, I wonder if this is their way of saying 'you get to go to the gun range next?'* Bill gave the route a name and saved it.

Several more route analyses were performed, each a little different and bit more detailed. Each analysis was named and saved. Bill tried to name them in the order they took place.

The next analysis was another simple one, creating a circular buffer around Discovery School for one mile (the distance students were expected to walk to school). Again, simple. But the next analysis incorporated routing, in that the buffer could only be applied along the actual route that students could take. Bill noticed that both the Naches and Yakima Rivers were within the original circular buffer. He knew of only one person who could walk on water, so he knew, even before the analysis was complete, that it wouldn't be a circle; rather, it would be a truncated circle with the areas along the opposite sides of rivers from the school being mostly eliminated. Sure enough, only one area across the Naches was actually within the buffer, at a point where a bridge existed.

He was then required to do some bus routing, with only those students living outside the buffer being eligible. He opened the student layer and saw points scattered across the map. He suspected these weren't real students as some were listed as being at the airfield. This required the creation of a new layer by joining the truncated buffer and the student layer and then dissolving all the points within the truncated circle. Once only the points outside the buffer were available, he then performed a least-cost route analysis—one that required the least amount of time and fuel to complete.

The next activity was to measure distances between points, which Bill did with ease. He then was required to do the same, but this time using ground units of measurement taking into account changes in elevation. Again, relatively simple, but more complex than just a straight line.

The first change analysis operation had Bill looking at the changes over time to the base, from its founding and in ten-year increments. He had to show what additions took place. For this, he imported raster data—data in pixelated format and ran the analysis. There were distinct areas of change visible.

The rest of the afternoon went on like this. Bill kept plugging away, analyzing change, identifying man-made structures, developing topographic maps using digital elevation models derived from more raster data. It seemed that Bill was running through every aspect of GIS that he had learned.

Merriman announced, "Okay, guys. Five o'clock; day's over. Shut it down, and I'll see you here tomorrow at eight. And don't forget to take your packs and rifles!"

Bill was surprised when Merriman spoke, as he was deep into his work and hadn't even noticed that four hours had slipped away. He suddenly realized he was thirsty and needed to use the restroom.

Kim spoke what he was thinking. "Wow, where did the time go? I thought we had only been at it for an hour or so."

"Well, you know GIS," Bill said, and then tried to sing the verses from "GIS State of Mind," a parody of the old song "Empire State of Mind".

Kim covered her ears. "Noooooo. That came out of UT-Austin!"

Others in the class joined in briefly for the chorus, and that ended the song.

After shutting down the computers, the Probies filed out of the classroom. Bill made a beeline for the restroom. When he came out, everyone was gone, so he started down the stairs on his own, making his way to the cafeteria. It was then he realized he hadn't even checked his tablet all afternoon, so he pulled it out of cargo pocket.

Sure enough, there was an email from Meri, but not the type Bill wanted to see. She was having supper with her dad again, and couldn't join him, but would meet him in the morning. Feeling dejected, Bill went on to the cafeteria.

The next morning, Bill and his roommates were all on the same playing field, leaving the cabin and having breakfast together. As usual, Nicole joined them, and luckily for Bill, so did Meri. Bill introduced Meri to the Jordan and Thep, both of whom greeted her warmly.

Meri told Bill about her first day as a co-pilot, explaining how they started out doing transition flights with the Caribou.

"It's much more complicated than anything else I've flown so far," she said. "I'm multi-engine rated, but the Caribou is a lot larger than anything I've ever flown before. So far we've done a couple of touch and goes, but most of the time has been spent in the simulator."

"So how long do you think it'll take to get up to speed?" Bill asked her.

"Don't know, but I don't think too long. They want us up to speed on all four aircraft before they move us to our secondary duties training. How about you? How's the GIS stuff so far?"

"It's been pretty much a bunch of stuff I know already. If there isn't much more, I'm sure we'll be through the GIS soon and on to remote sensing. I wonder how long it'll be before they have me learning the aircraft?"

After breakfast, Meri agreed to join the group for supper, telling Bill that she would be eating lunch at the airfield for the foreseeable future.

"It's a mile to the airfield, and it doesn't make sense to spend my entire lunch walking," she explained.

"Yeah, that makes sense," Bill agreed. He wasn't too happy about it but tried not to show his disappointment.

Meri picked up on it anyway. "Hey, there'll be other times."

The group gathered their backpacks and rifles and headed out the door, each going their separate way.

Soon, Bill was entering the Training Building and climbing the stairs to the second floor. Upon entering the room he placed his rifle in the rack and went to the same computer he'd used the day before.

"You're a little early, but you can get started if you want," Merriman told him.

Bill did just that, and was soon importing digital data, mostly in raster format, performing analyses, and creating maps.

Eventually, he was done with all the tasks put to him. He looked up and saw that, unnoticed by him, the class had filled in while he was working. Kim Smith was sitting next to him diligently working away, ignoring him as he had ignored everyone else.

Not sure what to do next, Bill raised his hand. Merriman got up and came over.

"Yeah?" he asked in a quiet voice.

Bill quietly told him he was done with the exercise and asked what he should do next.

"Take a break. We're about to mix things up in the next half-hour, so sit back and read something. Just don't leave."

Bill pulled out his tablet and brought up *The Explorer* to see what new stuff was happening in the world of discovery.

Shortly after Bill began reading, a message came across his computer monitor. It advised all Probies to remain seated after completing the assessment until dismissed.

Bill could tell others were finishing up by the increase in bustling noise and activity in the room.

Precisely at noon, Merriman called out, "Listen up. Most of you have finished your GIS assessments, and they look pretty good. For those that haven't, you'll get to do so tomorrow morning. For those that have, you'll begin working on the remote sensing assessment in the morning. This means we'll be testing to see how well you know the various platforms and how to get the data from image capturing to analysis. After that, you'll be introduced to our equipment and methods.

"We'll be mixing it up in the afternoons, so after lunch report to the rifle range. Make sure you've got all your required equipment, which most especially means your rifle," he said. "You'll report to the range master when you get there. Be prepared to do a bit of shooting. See you tomorrow."

Bill walked out of the class feeling pretty good, knowing that he was the first done, and had apparently passed the initial assessment.

Kim joined him on the walk to the cafeteria. "So, what do you think so far?"

He thought about it for a couple of seconds. "Interesting.. so far. I mean, other than giving us some set tasks, it seems pretty fluid. You?"

"Pretty basic. I mean, most of what we've done so far is standard GIS. Although I gotta admit, I wasn't too keen on that metadata development exercise," she finished with a grin.

"Metadata. Yeah. I hate dealing with it, but I guess it's a necessary evil. Without it, how'll anyone be able to understand what your data's about? Or even in what projection?"

It was quite warm as they walked toward the cafeteria, but his body had already begun adapting to the sunnier, drier climate in the rain-shadow of the Cascade Mountains.

When they arrived, Bill realized that not only would Meri be absent, but Matt and Nicole were also on the airfield. Bill hadn't realized until then how close he and Matt had become—the two were practically inseparable—well, whenever Matt wasn't with Nicole, that is.

Bill's olfactory senses were assaulted with the smell of spicy food as he walked through the door. *Smells like curry today,* he thought.

He spotted Jordan and Thep sitting at a table with Brenda Lightfoot, so he and Kim made their way over to them and dropped off his gear.

"Hey, how goes, so far?" he asked.

Everyone nodded to him, as they all had full mouths. Thep even went so far as to give him a grunt. Bill saw that they were eating the red curry noodle soup that was a specialty of one of the cooks. That got Bill's salivary glands working overtime, so he dumped his backpack and rifle at a spare seat and headed over to the serving line, trailed by Kim.

Soon, Kim and Bill were back at the table digging in. Their soup was spicy enough that it slightly burned Bill's lips and started clearing out his sinuses.

After a bit, conversation resumed. It turned out that while Bill and Kim were playing with computers, Jordan and Thep were identifying various creatures and plants. They were required to analyze them, describe them, and then try to place them in a taxonomy table.

"It's actually quite challenging in some aspects," Thep said between bites. "Not only have I never seen some of these plants, I've never even heard of them."

"Yeah, but at least we're dealing with real plants and animals, not just pictures," Jordan said.

"What are you guys up to?" Brenda asked Kim and Bill.

Kim said, "Mainly running through a bunch of GIS problems. This afternoon we're supposed to report to the rifle range. I guess we'll be breaking in our new rifles." She indicated the rifle slung over the back of her chair.

"We're scheduled for the range tomorrow morning," Thep said. "I guess they don't want us getting bored doing the same thing all day."

Bill looked at his new watch and said to Kim, "Hey, we better get on our way. It'll take at least fifteen minutes to get there." He cleared his tray, put his backpack on, picked up his rifle and slung that over his shoulder, and waited while Kim did the same before heading out.

Saying their farewells, the two headed out the door to the rifle range.

Chapter 11

After a bit over fifteen minutes, Bill and Kim arrived at the rifle range. Along the way they had been joined by a couple of other Probies they recognized from the GIS class.

All of the Probies had been to the rifle range before, during the firearms training portion of the BMT, so they were familiar with the layout. The known distance range was on one side, and the "action" range adjacent to it. The "action" range was where the pop-up targets had been during BMT, and Bill suspected it was also where they would face pop-up targets of potential predator threats that they would face during surveys.

Rather than going directly into the classroom, one of the instructors, an Explorer based on his clothing, waved them over to the shade of some oak trees. The Explorer had longer than regulation hair, a sparse beard, and a trekker medal visible on his chest.

"Gather 'round," he hollered to the group, who made their way to him, grateful to get into the shade. "Set your gear down, crack the bolt on your rifle, set it on your pack, and take a seat."

Bill placed his pack on the ground and unslung his rifle. Working the bolt, he opened it, exposing the chamber. He set his rifle on the pack, ensuring it wasn't pointed at anyone else and had the barrel tilted slightly toward the ground. He noticed that the others did the same. He sat down behind his pack facing the instructor. Closer to the ground, the smell of dried grasses wafted up to him.

"We'll give it a couple more minutes until everyone's here. I don't want to repeat things," the instructor said, pulling a tablet from the ubiquitous cargo pocket of his uniform shorts.

Soon, others arrived, until all the Probies who had been in the GIS class were seated around him.

After taking roll, the instructor introduced himself, along with several other Explorers who had joined the group.

"I'm Doug Gerrup, the lead firearms instructor. Today we're gonna break in your rifles and get you sighted in. Over the next several days we'll be doing some serious firearms training—the kind needed when exploring new planets." Gerrup looked around the seated Probies, making sure they were all paying attention. They were.

"Other than your main duties and survival school, this is the one area you want to be the most proficient possible. Sometimes that proficiency can mean the difference between life and death—literally. Just ask any Trekker. This means coming to the range or hitting the simulator on your time off. If all you do is the basic, it might not be enough.

"Now, how many of you have been issued peeders?" Gerrup asked. Everyone raised their hands.

"Okay, then. We'll work on those after basic and advanced rifle handling. Today is basic rifle handling. You'll become quite familiar with your rifle, sighting it in, and learning how to use it properly. That means prone, kneeling, sitting, and offhand. Now, I know you've done all that in BMT, but you'll find the ER-1 is a little different."

Picking up a Probie's rifle, Gerrup proceeded to go through the differences, pointing to each item with his right hand while holding the rifle with his left. "First, you'll notice, it's a bolt action. Not like the automatic action of your R1 or peeder. Second, it's got an integral bipod in the foregrip. This means you can use the bipod for greater accuracy. Third, it's scoped. This means, once again, more accuracy, and over a further distance. Fourth, it's got a space in the buttstock for a spare five-round magazine, and one for a cleaning kit."

"To insert the magazine, just place it in the magazine well and push up until it clicks. Just like the R1. You all appeared to have figured out how to charge the rifle, but how many of you know how to remove the bolt?" Only a few hands went up. Most of the Probies, especially those not from Hayek or the United States hadn't handled firearms before BMT.

Gerrup showed them how to extract and replace the bolt. "You'll want to do that when bore sighting, a technique we'll show you on the range."

Handing back the rifle to the Probie, Gerrup told the group to gather their gear and head into the classroom next to the rifle range for rifle familiarization.

As Bill entered the classroom, he was glad to feel the cool air hit his skin. Even though he was getting used to the heat, he always enjoyed it when he could get a break from the heat.

This was only Bill's second time in the building. During BMT the Probies had only accessed the classroom once, with most of the time on the actual range. Most of their rifle training was done in the training building in the main part of Sacajawea Base. There were tables set up in rows, with only a single seat behind each table.

Gerrup said, "Pick a table, put your gear under it, your rifle on it, and take a seat."

Bill did so, once again winding up next to Kim.

Once everyone was seated, Gerrup stepped to the front of the class, in front of a table that had two boxes on it. "What's the first rule of firearms safety?"

"Treat every gun as if it's loaded," yelled the Probies.

"What's the second rule?"

"Never point it at anything unless you intend to shoot it," they responded.

"Great. Keeping that in mind, go ahead and extract your bolts."

There was a fair amount of clacking and clicking while the Probies worked on extracting the bolts from the rifles.

"Hold up your bolt when you've got it out," Gerrup told the class.

It only took Bill a couple of seconds to extract his bolt, having done it several times already. Holding it up in his right hand, he waited until Gerrup told them they could put the bolts back into the rifles. That took Bill even less time than removing it had.

"Most of you have trained with iron sights, but shooting with a scope is a whole different animal. In some ways, it's easier. In other ways, it's a bit more complicated.

"The scope you've got is pretty basic, a 1.5 to 5 power by 20 mm objective. The power refers to how much an object is magnified. In this case, it can range from one and a half times up to five times as big as normal. The objective just means how big the front of the scope is. In this case, it's 20 millimeters in diameter. The larger the number, usually, the more light it lets in. That's great for shooting at twilight or long distances, but for the most part, it adds additional bulk and weight you don't need."

An image of the view through a scope appeared on the white-screen behind Gerrup. It was circular with the typical cross-hairs, but it also had dots evenly spaced along the cross-hairs extending from the center outward. There was also a red dot in the center and a small circle around the dot.

"These dots are called mil-dots—that's short for milliradian dot. A milliradian is nothing more than a part of a radian. More specifically, 1/1000ths of a radian. So, what's a radian? Gerrup asked the class.

Next to Bill, Kim Smith raised her hand, tentatively.

"Yes?" Gerrup asked her.

"Isn't it just a measurement for a circle, something involved with pi?"

"Exactly—it's a way to measure a circle. More specifically, there are 6.28 radians in a circle, of which 3.14 is half of. Hence, the pi! So, if there are 6.28 radians in a circle, how many milliradians are there?" he again posed to the class.

Just about every Probie muttered the answer "Six thousand two hundred eighty," or a variation of that.

"Correct again, but just to make life simple, we go with 6,400 milliradians—much easier to remember, just because!" he finished with a smile.

"So, each one of these dots," Gerrup gestured to the image of the scope on the white-screen, "represents one milliradian dot, or mil-dot as we'll call it from now on, from the other mil-dot. That's center of dot to center of dot. Mil-dots are great for measuring distance, which is why we use them. They also allow you to accurately shoot something without having to make adjustments to your scope or guess. There are ten dots up and down and ten dots across. Note that the center dot, very small and light, is not a true mil-dot, but it can still serve as one. This means you've got five mils between the center and the edge of the scope, or ten mils from edge to edge.

"Here's how it works in a nutshell. One mil on your scope is the equivalent to 10 centimeters at 100 meters. So, if you place your scope on a target that's 100 meters away, the distance between two mil-dots will cover 10 centimeters. This works proportionally, so at 200 meters the distance between mil-dots will be 20 centimeters, and at a thousand meters it'll be one meter. Everyone understand this?" he asked, looking around for confirmation.

Bill thought the way Gerrup was explaining it made it very easy to understand. Like the others, he nodded his understanding.

"So, the next thing you need to understand is how to tell how far something is away from you. This is also pretty easy. If you line up a dot at the bottom of the object and get one near the top, and you've got a rough idea on how tall it is, you can do the basic math and come up with the distance. The easiest way to figure this out is to take the size of whatever it is you're looking at, multiply that by a thousand, then divide that by the number of mils covering the target. That'll give you the range."

This time an image of a deer appeared on the screen, behind the scope image, looking as if the scope was centered on the deer's chest.

"Look at the mil-dot near the bottom of the deer, at the feet."

Bill did so, then looked for the mil-dot near the top of the deer, spotting it just above the back. There were three dots from the bottom to the top.

"Now, most deer stand about one meter tall at the shoulder, so how far away do you think this deer is?"

Bill raised his hand.

"Yes?" Gerrup asked.

"It looks like it's about 500 meters out," Bill said.

"Explain how you figured that out." Gerrup folded his arms over his chest.

"Well, if the deer stands one meter at the shoulder, and there are three dots between the top and the bottom, then that means it's being covered by two mils: then one thousand divided by two is 500, so it's around 500 meters away," Bill explained.

Gerrup nodded his head and unfolded his arms. "That's correct, and the exact way to figure this out. Knowing this, of course, means you stand a better chance of actually hitting what you're shooting at, depending on if you know the bullet drop of the round you're using. By the time we're done here, this stuff'll be ingrained in you. You'll also be well versed in the various critters out there, and how tall they are.

"Right now, though, we want to get you sighted in. Our goal is to have you shooting dead-on at 200 meters. This gives a rise of about 5 centimeters at 100 meters and a drop of 5 centimeters at 300 meters. Most kill zones of larger animals, the part where you want to shoot them to kill them quickly, is about 15 to 20 centimeters. That's a little bit smaller than a football, or for those of you from America, a soccer ball. This means you'll be able to rapidly line up and shoot into the kill zone of most animals between 100 and 300 meters without having to do any range calculations.

"So, if everyone's got it, let's head out to the range. The first thing we're gonna do is boresight your rifles and then fine-tune them. You'll get individual instruction on that as we go, so be patient, others need help, too." Gerrup chuckled.

"Leave your pack, but keep your belts on. On your way out the door pick up a pair of earplugs and eye protection." He pointed to earplugs and protective eyewear sitting in the boxes on the table at the front of the room. "Grab a shooting lane when you get out there. Somebody will be by shortly to work with you."

Bill was soon standing behind the red line on the shooting range, waiting to be told the range was hot. He had put on his eye and ear protection as he walked from the classroom to the shooting lanes. At the shooting position was a bench with a table attached to it, creating a platform he could sit and shoot from. He could see targets set at the 30- and 200-meter range.

A voice came over a speaker system, "The line is hot. I say again, the line is hot. Shooters may approach the shooting position at this time and may handle firearms."

Bill approached the bench and placed his rifle on it, facing the muzzle downrange. He then opened the bolt to show anyone walking by that the rifle was unloaded. He sat, and then waited for one of the many instructors to approach him. The wait was almost twenty minutes, while the instructors made their way down the line going from Probie to Probie. Those who were the first to get attention were now shooting. Even with his hearing protection on, Bill could hear the shot. He could also feel the concussive force of those closest to him when they shot.

Eventually, one of the instructors appeared at Bill's side.

"Remove the bolt and let's get you boresighted in," he said to Bill by way of greeting. "You'll want to use your bipod for this."

Bill removed the bolt and placed it on the shooting table. He then extended the short bipod legs, resting them on the table, so the barrel was facing downrange.

"You ever boresight a rifle?" the instructor asked.

Bill nodded.

"Then this should be easy. Just look through the barrel until you've got it lined up with the target at the thirty meter line." Bill did so.

"Now, look up through your scope. Does it line up pretty close to what you're seeing through the barrel?"

Bill could see it was slightly off center, a tad to the left, and told the instructor.

"Great, almost there, then. Put the bolt back in the rifle and I'll want you to fire three rounds." He placed a box of twenty rounds on the shooting bench and said, "Put these in your five-round magazine. We'll use just that for now."

Bill opened the box and extracted one round at a time, feeding them into the magazine, then seating the magazine in the rifle.

"Fire when ready," the instructor said.

Bill looked through the scope, lining the crosshairs up on the center of the target. Taking the safety off, he gently squeezed the trigger until the rifle fired, surprising him when it did, exactly as he'd been taught. That slow steady squeeze, instead of a yank of the trigger, meant that Bill couldn't anticipate when the rifle would fire, so when it did, it came as a bit of a surprise. Slowly, he repeated the process twice more.

The instructor used a pair of binoculars to better see the target and told Bill, "Great grouping. All nearly touching, but about two and a half centimeters left, and two centimeters high. Let's fine-tune this puppy. We're aiming to zero in at 200 meters, and since the point of impact at 200 meters is the same as it is at 30 meters, we're gonna want it to be dead on at 30 meters. So, let's adjust the windage first, then we'll get your elevation fine-tuned."

"Now, at 100 meters, one click equals one-half centimeter. Since we want to sight out to 200 meters, how many clicks equals one centimeter?" he asked Bill.

"Two."

"Exactly, so, since we're actually at 30 meters, which will give us the same point of impact as two hundred meters, which is where we want to hit, how many clicks will you need to move your windage point of impact to be dead on?"

Bill had to think this one through. *Let's see, one centimeter at 100 meters, which means it's about a third of a centimeter at 30 meters, and I'm off by two and a half centimeters, so two point five times point three is.. seven and a half.*

"Seven and a half?" he answered tentatively.

"Yep, but since you can't move a half click, what do you think you should do?"

"Um, set it either seven or eight clicks."

"Yep. I recommend going with seven, and we'll see how it works out at 200 meters, and adjust from there."

He then told Bill how to adjust his scope by removing the bezel covers on the top and right side, and turning the bezels a certain number of clicks. "Each click you'll feel is point 1 milliradians, so you want to move it seven clicks to the right and six clicks down."

As Bill turned the top bezel, he could feel, more than hear, the click as the bezel briefly locked into a slot before moving on to the next. He finished with the windage and then adjusted for the elevation.

"Load up three more rounds and let's see how she shoots," the instructor said.

Bill did so and repeated the fire sequence. This time all three rounds wound up in the center of the target.

"Looking good," the instructor said. "Now, load up three more rounds and take a shot at the 200-meter target. You might want to adjust the scope power for that for optimal sighting," he suggested.

Bill increased the scope's power to the maximum of five, ejected and reloaded the magazine, and inserted it back into the rifle.

"Ready when you are," the instructor said.

This time Bill took a bit more time and care in shooting.

Instead of using binoculars, the instructor set a shooting scope on the bench and looked through it. Bill could see on the side of the scope that the power range was 20 to 60.

"Good shooting. Take a look," the instructor told Bill.

Looking through the scope, Bill could see that all three rounds were in the center circle of the bullseye, all grouping within what looked like two centimeters, and just a hair under the exact center.

"Looks like you're good to go. Go ahead and fire the remainder of the rounds. We'll do more after everyone gets sighted in. Make sure you put your rifle on the bench with the bolt open once you're done shooting."

The instructor moved on to the next Probie in line while Bill fired the remaining two rounds. He reloaded the magazine, this time with five rounds, and commenced firing. He did this until he ran out of ammunition, which wasn't too long, considering he had started with only twenty rounds. Once done, he retracted the bipod legs, cracked open the bolt of his rifle, and set it down on the shooting bench table. Then he decided to stand up and stretch a bit, stepping behind the red safety line.

With nothing better to do, he struck up a conversation with Kim. Bill wasn't surprised to hear that she had grown up with firearms. *Doesn't everyone in Texas have multiple guns?* he thought. She was having as much fun as he was, and was looking for more firearms practice.

"This is a lot more fun than spending all day at a desk," she said.

Soon the sound of shooting faded away until there was only silence from the firing range, along with the heavy scent of burnt cordite. All the Probies stood behind the red line.

A voice announced over the speakers, "The line is now cold. I say again, the line is now cold. Everyone should be standing behind the red safety line at this time with rifles on the benches and bolts open. Do not, I repeat, do not touch a firearm. Instructors, check the range."

Several of the instructors came walking by, making sure everyone complied.

"All Probies report to the classroom for further instruction. Leave your rifles on the bench. I say again, leave your rifles on the bench," announced the speaker.

Once more the Probies filed in. They sat at the same tables they had before, where they'd left their packs.

Gerrup came in just as the last of the Probies were filing in, with a rifle slung over his shoulder. "Now that you're all sighted in, it's time to start the advanced training," he began. "How many of you have ever shot a bolt-action rifle before?" He asked. Bill, Kim, and a few others raised their hands. "Well, whatever you knew about shooting bolt actions, forget it! Today's lesson is on how to reload in the presence of dangerous critters."

Gerrup then unslung the rifle and turned to his left, holding the rifle at the ready. Everyone could easily see the rifle and action. He rapidly cycled the action, making sure there was no cartridge in the chamber or magazine in the magazine well. He then put the rifle up to his shoulder, aiming at the wall. "Let's say you've got to shoot something," he said, squeezing the trigger. Everyone could hear the firing pin 'click' as it slammed forward onto an empty chamber.

"Now, most of you probably do this," he continued, grasping the bolt and working the action, all while keeping the rifle aimed at the wall. Once complete, he lowered the rifle and looked at the classroom full of Probies. "I don't ever wanna see you do that Hollywood bullshit again. You're not snipers in some hero action flick. Here's how you do it from now on."

Raising his rifle again to aim it at the wall, he squeezed the trigger, then dropped the rifle down to the ready position and cycled the bolt. Bill could tell that the bolt cycling was much more forceful than what he was used to.

Once the bolt was cycled, the rifle went back up to the shoulder, Gerrup squeezed the trigger again, shooting the imaginary animal, and repeated the bolt cycling operation, dropping the rifle to the ready position and being forceful with the cycle.

"Anyone know why I do it that way?" he posed to the class.

Silence greeted his question.

"It's real simple. If I keep the rifle up like this," he explained, raising the rifle to his shoulder, "then I lose a lot of visibility. Note how the barrel and scope occupy my field of vision?" He gestured to the objects with his right hand.

"By dropping the rifle, I can see more. Remember, some predators hunt in pairs or packs. If you can't see what's around you, then you can't react. If you can't react, you're dead. It's that simple.

"Now, when I'm charging the rifle, notice how I use a fair amount of force to pull the bolt back. Don't be afraid to do that. The rifle's stronger than you. Just yank that bad boy up and back. You'll see the brass fly. Take a quick glance down at the chamber as you're forcing the bolt forward just to make sure you're loading a cartridge. Remember, close that bolt with authority!

"Let me tell you, the last and loudest sound you'll ever hear if you screw up is this," he said, squeezing the trigger. The 'click' the firing pin made coming down on the empty chamber sent chills running up and down Bill's spine.

"Everyone got that?" Gerrup asked. All nodded, even if he wasn't looking directly at them. "Great. From now on, your charge your rifle like that *every single time*. No exceptions.

"All right. For now, head over to the ammo depot and pick up a can of ammo. I'll want you to fill all your magazines. You're going to be shooting off the entire box today, working on the various shooting positions. By the end of the day, you should be hitting the dead zone at 200 meters.

"If you need to use the restroom or drink some water, do so now. Once you've picked up your ammo, head back to the shooting line and await word from the instructors. Since everyone here's done most of this before it shouldn't be much different, other than the actual rifle handling.

"That's it, take five, then get your ammo and get on the line. I'm gonna show you the safest way to reload when you're in the field."

Bill didn't need to use the restroom. He had partially drained his canteen after shooting, so he took advantage of the break to fill it and take a few more sips of water.

At the depot, they lined up at the Dutch door. As each approached it, they were handed several targets and small metal ammo can containing 220 rounds of ammunition. Having hunted deer and elk, Bill was interested in what size bullets were being issued: 165 grain. *I guess that's just about big enough for anything up to an elk. I wonder how well they work on lions or smilodons?*

Back at his shooting lane, Bill stood behind the red line filling up all four magazines. Then he stood waiting and chatting with Kim until they were told to place targets in the 100, 200, and 300 meter stands. An instructor came by with large staplers and handed them out to several of the Probies, telling them to share. Kim was one that received a stapler, so Bill joined her on the walk down the shooting lane.

Soon all the targets were set in place and the Probies back on the shooting line, ready to "kill" the many pieces of harmless paper.

The rest of the afternoon centered on shooting from prone, kneeling, sitting and standing positions. Most of the standing position shots were offhand. This meant that the shooter just shot the rifle from their shoulder without using any type of support, such as a bipod or shooting stick. As one instructor explained, "You're most likely to be attacked by a big predator when you're walking along, so little chance to get into a more stable position."

The only time the Probies had a chance to use the bipods was in the prone position. Other than that, all shooting was done supporting arms on legs or knees, or not supporting the arms at all. And every time the Probies charged their rifles they did it the way Gerrup had taught them. After the first 100 rounds, it practically became natural, although Bill knew from martial arts training that it would take at least 3,000 actions before it became part of his muscle memory.

Bill's shoulder was starting to hurt at the end of the day, and his sense of smell had been deadened from all the cordite, but he was thoroughly enjoying himself. He was also quite pleased to see how well he was doing. Of course, it didn't hurt that the instructors were spending time with each Probie giving them individual instruction. Bill could see the improvement from his first few shots to the last few, and it was impressive. Even at 200 meters, just about every round was hitting in the kill zone, even standing and shooting offhand.

Finally, the day was winding down, and the Probies were told to gather their gear and replace their empty ammo cans with full ones.

"From now on," Gerrup announced, "you'll carry full magazines. The spare ammo in the can is what you get to shoot each day. You should have 65 rounds of ammo on you at all times.

"All right, see you tomorrow," he said.

As the Probies left the rifle range they intersected the Probies leaving the airfield. The latter were easily identifiable by the fact that they were wearing flight suits instead of the traditional Explorer uniform. Just as Bill was wondering if he'd see Meri, he spotted her in the merging crowd. She was looking his way; he waved and caught her attention.

Bill caught up to Meri, who was waiting for him.

"That doesn't look like any GIS I'm familiar with," she said with a smile, looking at his rifle.

"Yeah, well, if you'd been at lunch you would have found out that they were sending us out to the range in the afternoons. Guess they don't want us getting all cooped up."

"So, you gonna be out here tomorrow?" she asked.

"That's the plan."

"Great. That means we can eat lunch together! The cafe's not the best out here, but it's better than walking a half hour. So, how'd the shooting go?"

"Great. They do a fantastic job getting you familiar with your rifle, and I actually managed to improve my offhand shooting. Tomorrow we begin advanced rifle handling, whatever that is. What'd you do today?"

"More manual and simulator time, mostly on failures, and then a couple of laps around Mt. Tahoma," she said. "You should see the west side—totally green, unlike the dry stuff around here. Quite the contrast."

Bill thought back to his days at UW, which was only nine weeks ago but seemed longer, with a bit of nostalgia. "Yeah, in a way, I miss living on that side. Even on Earth it was always green and didn't scorch your brains. I wonder what it looks like here?"

"We've got a three-day weekend coming up soon. Want to go over and do some salmon fishing?" Meri asked. "Our family's got a fishing cabin right on the Nisqually River with easy access to the Salish Sea and the sockeye are just starting to run."

Bill couldn't believe his luck. Here he was, being asked by a beautiful woman to spend the weekend together, fishing.

He stammered, "Yeah. Sure, that sounds great."

"Great. I'll talk to Dad, then, and see if we can add you to the trip."

"Dad?" Bill asked.

"Yeah, silly. Did you think I'd be spending a weekend alone with a guy I barely know?" She grinned and punched him in the arm.

Bill didn't flinch, but he was certainly impressed with the punch and had a hard time not reaching up to massage his arm.

"I guess you're right," Bill said with chagrin. "Don't know what I was thinking."

"Well, I certainly do," she laughed.

Bill, feeling his face flush, immediately changed the subject. "So what's your training schedule look like with the birds?"

"Well, first we'll finish the transition with the 'bous, then on to the Providers, then the 415s, and finally wrap up with the Monarchs. They expect to spend at least two to four days on each bird, not including book time. Naturally, that's only for a co-pilot rating. We won't really transition to pilot for a year or two."

"Looks like we're both doing book time in the morning and fun stuff in the afternoon," Bill said.

"When we come out to the airfield in the morning I've seen others going to the range, so I guess they're staggering us."

As they approached the living part of the base, Bill asked, "Join me for supper?"

"I thought you'd never ask after I scared you off with my dad."

"Ah, not scared, just cautious. After all, I'm sure he's got a gun or two."

"Ha, more than one or two," Meri interrupted.

"Like I said, not scared, just cautious."

"Whatever you say."

"Anyhow, back to supper," Bill said. "If you don't mind, I want to drop this gear off and take a shower, so meet you in about a half hour?"

Meri agreed, so the two went their separate ways.

At his cabin, Bill put his rifle and ammunition in the gun safe, stripped, showered, and dressed in civvies. His roommates joined him on the way out, and the four of them made it to the cafeteria just before the rush. Bill didn't see Meri sitting inside, so he waited outside in the heat for her, wishing he was inside.

Meri soon arrived, and the two of them joined the other. Nicole had already arrived and was seated next to Matt.

After supper Meri excused herself. "Lots of reading to do if I want to get transitioned."

"Me, too," Matt said.

"Me, three," chimed in Nicole.

As the three co-pilots in training left, Bill, Thep, and Jordan looked at each other with a *what do we do now* look.

"Well, I'm gonna get a beer at the Cave Bear," Jordan said. Bill and Thep thought that was a pretty good idea, so they joined him.

The next day came around early, but Bill was ready. The trio hadn't stayed out late, and nobody got even mildly tipsy, so everyone was feeling pretty good as they made their way to breakfast, where they were joined by Nicole and Meri.

Bill's next several days were spent with mornings in the classroom learning the particulars of the Corps remote sensing platforms and software, including how to troubleshoot some of the problems that might develop with the hardware. Afternoons were spent at the range.

Bill found the former fun, but the latter even more fun. He had always enjoyed shooting, so the afternoons for him were like time spent in a candy store for a kid.

The advanced rifle training was unlike anything Bill had ever experienced. While he had hunted, it had usually been while holding a rifle, ready to shoot at a moment's notice. This training emphasized the fact that if he was out in the boonies for an extended period of time, especially if he were trekking, then he wasn't expected to have a rifle in his hands. Rather, he was trained to go from walking with his rifle in a sling over his shoulder (while wearing his pack and all his other gear) to a shooting position rapidly. This didn't mean the rifle was on his back rather, the sling was one that kept the rifle in front of him, across his middle with the barrel pointed downward and at a slight angle away from him. This method made the rifle easily accessible at all time. It was a matter of grasping the rifle and bringing it on target rapidly. Bill managed to master this in a couple of days, and several more after that he had become competent at shooting at oncoming targets, most of which were large predator cats.

He also got to spend some time with his PDW. Because of his experience with the PDW-3 in BMT, the transition to the PDW issued by the Corps, the PDW-1, went well. But, it took him a while to get used to the fact that the PDW-1 was a semi-automatic instead of a three-shot burst variety. When he asked one of the instructors why it was only a semi-auto, he was told that it was because it was for survival, not killing people. "You want to be able to eat what you shoot," the instructor said, "not blast it full of holes. We're going for a killing shot that saves ammunition, not a 'spray and pray' scenario."

Soon Bill had mastered all the GIS and remote sensing aspects of his job, so he began his flight training. He still had to show up with all his equipment, but he was happy he didn't have to bring his flight survival kit. "We save that for the real surveys," one of his instructors told him. "Besides, every craft here has spare kits on board, just because of the training. Don't make sense to have Probies lugging all their equipment out to the airfield every day."

Chapter 12

At last, it was time for the three-day trip to Cascadia.

The trip over the mountains was via a high-speed magnetic levitation train into the city of Tahoma. Meri explained that most short distance routes were simple maglevs, but the longer ones, particularly cross-continent, were E-tubes: supersonic trains operating in evacuated tubes.

Just like in Milton, Bill didn't see any major highways and asked about that.

"Most people use mass transit, such as the skytrain or jitneys in cities, or the maglevs and E-tubes between larger cities. Most cargo is carried in maglevs or the E-tubes, with smaller trucks used for intra-urban transport. I guess you could say we're not as automobile-centric as Earth. Although, those who live in the country usually have some form of mechanical transport, be it a Willy's, a Kenji, or a flitter." During his time on Hayek Bill had come to learn that the aircar he had seen on his first day was colloquially known as a flitter.

Bill felt a sense of déjà vu as they crossed over Snoqualmie Pass. The last time he had crossed it was in his rusting pickup truck on a six-lane concrete highway. Now he was in a high-speed maglev train, the road beside the track being only gravel for cars winding up and down the pass. Bill was surprised to see a ski resort in the same location as on Earth.

Seeing Mt. Si was also a bit of a shock, in that it looked the same. He had always equated seeing Mt. Si as the gateway to the Cascades, with the bustle of the Puget Sound on one side and the dark green fir forests on the other. This time, though, there was just the forest.

Their trip to Tahoma was quick, taking a little more than a half hour from Milton. Tahoma, like Milton, was mostly modern-looking with low buildings in the core and smaller houses in the surrounding area. Bill could see small ships in the seaport in the protected bay. They were nothing like the huge container ships and large gantry cranes that he was used to seeing in Seattle; instead, the smaller ships had their own onboard cranes for cargo handling.

Grabbing their rifles, salmon rod cases, and duffels, the two headed out of the station to look for the skytrain that would get them closer to the Nisqually. Soon they were heading out of the small industrial city. "Y'know, I figured that with Tahoma being the industrial heart of Hayek, there'd be more pollution," he mentioned to Meri while the train silently glided along the tracks.

"We don't have many rules here, but that's one of the biggies: no polluting the air, ground, or water," she answered.

As they rolled out of town Bill spotted fields of what looked like marijuana. "Is that pot?" he asked.

"Pot? No, it's industrial hemp. Don't you have that on Earth?"

It took a few minutes to explain to her that all marijuana production, possession, and consumption was banned in the US at the federal level, with only a few states actually allowing it, despite the federal laws.

"How weird. Why would they ban it?"

"Good question. Because they can?" Bill asked.

Meri just shook her head over the inaneness of Earth's politics.

In less than fifteen minutes they arrived at a station on the north side of the Nisqually River. As they disembarked Meri told Bill that they'd be on foot for the next mile. They crossed the river over a small bridge, where Bill spotted a small general store. "That's pretty much where everyone around here gets their basics," Meri told him.

The two followed a gravel road until they came to a driveway that led off to the right, toward the river. Over the driveway was an arched sign that simply read "Lewis Landing."

"My grandfather put that up," Meri said as they crossed under it. "Apparently, he was a real Mark Twain fan and sort of pictured this place as one of those places on the Mississippi River he read about."

The house was more a country retreat than a year-round residence. Like the cabins at Sacajawea Base, it was a small two-story board-and-batten building, but it also had solar panels on the roof, a small water tower next to it, and a small shed nearby. Bill could see the river behind it.

Meri stepped onto the porch, set her duffel down, and unlocked the front door using an old-fashioned key. Opening it, she said, "Welcome to Lewis Landing!"

Inside, Meri pointed to a set of stairs to the right of the entrance. "Our rooms are upstairs. Dad's room is over there" she said, pointing to a door opposite the stairs.

The house had a simple great room with a kitchen, a dining bar, and a living room all in one. In the center was a large stone-faced fireplace that Bill recognized as a masonry heater.

Meri placed her rifle in a rifle rack by the front door, so Bill followed suit.

"There are some hooks out back on the porch. Hang your waders there, but keep your boots inside—the mice like to eat them," Meri said as she dug her waders out of her duffel. The two put their waders on the hooks and then Meri showed Bill his room and pointed out the shared bathroom where he could put his toiletries.

After getting settled, in he came downstairs to find Meri grabbing a couple of bottles of beer out of the refrigerator.

"I figured you'd want one after the week you've had," she said. "I know I do, after that forced alcohol abstinence for flight training." Meri opened the two bottles and handed him one.

"Sure. So, when do we go fishing?" Bill asked, accepting the proffered beer.

"After beer and supper. We'll catch the evening bite. Dad said he'd be here around sevenish, so I want to make sure supper's ready when he gets here."

Bill looked at his chronograph; it was just past six thirty. He and Meri had left Sacajawea base at exactly five o'clock when the Corps was dismissed for the long weekend. Despite the fifteen minutes spent walking from the skytrain, and more than 150 miles on three different trains, they had only spent a bit over an hour and a half traveling. *Huh. Had this been Earth, it would have been at least three and a half hours, and that ain't including traffic,* he thought.

As it was late summer, the sun would remain up for more than an hour with an extended twilight—plenty of time to eat and go fishing after.

Meri rummaged around in a small pantry and pulled out pasta and spaghetti sauce, commenting on the lack of food in the cabin due to everyone being in Milton. "We usually do some shopping on the way, but since we're here only a couple of days, it doesn't make too much sense. We'll pick up some veggies at the corner store tomorrow."

Bill offered to help, but Meri told him he'd just be in the way, and to go explore a bit. Taking his beer, Bill unlocked the back door and stepped out on the porch overlooking the river. He decided to wander down, and as he got close he could see schools of sockeye salmon, their distinctive red bodies and green heads visible through the water. He watched them for a while until Meri called.

Making his toward the cabin, he was greeted by Commandant Lewis stepping through it onto the porch.

"Welcome to Lewis Landing," he said, holding out his hand. A beer was in the other.

Bill took the offered hand and shook it. "Thank you, sir. And thanks for having me here."

"My pleasure," Lewis said, releasing Bill's hand. "It's not often Meri invites anyone to the Landing, so it's great to have you here."

Meri announced supper was ready and asked Bill to help her set the table on the porch.

As the trio sat down to eat Lewis peppered Bill with questions on his background, family, education, and thoughts about Hayek and the Corps. Meri quietly ate, watching the interchange between the two men. By the time supper was finished Bill felt as if he'd been waterboarded at Guantanamo. When Lewis stepped out of the room for a moment, Meri told Bill this was her first time bringing any male companion home to meet her dad. "Most were scared off once they found out who my dad was."

When Lewis returned, Meri said, "All right Daddy, you can let up now. I brought Bill here to go fishing, not be interrogated like a criminal." Nodding to Bill, she said, "Grab your gear and let's go catch some salmon."

Bill was relieved to have an excuse to escape the "interview." He and Meri put on their waders, boots, and fishing vests. Rods in hand and rifles slung over shoulders, the two waddled their way down to the river. Meri showed Bill a small path, barely visible, that wound along the bank to a gravel bar, where they emerged from the surrounding forest and were able to safely wade into the river.

"Keep an eye out for bears," she cautioned.

Meri was downriver, so she cast first, and then Bill cast. As his line drifted downriver he took a moment to look around. Nobody else was in sight. For him, this was a first. He couldn't remember a time salmon fishing in Washington when there weren't others scattered along the river, sometimes shoulder to shoulder. *I guess there's really no need for 'combat fishing' around here.*

Soon both had fish on their lines, and the battle was on. For the next hour, they fished, mainly doing catch and release, but keeping a couple.

At one point a grizzly bear came down to the water downstream from them. Meri moved a bit closer to Bill and both kept an eye on the large bear until it eventually caught a fish and moved back into the forest on the opposite side of the river.

Bill remarked to Meri how weird it felt to fish without a fishing license or catch record. She gave him a puzzled look. "Whatever would you need a license for? You're obviously not commercial fishing, and what's a catch record?"

Bill explained what licensing was like on Earth and that a catch record was a sheet that anyone fishing for salmon had to write down information on every salmon they caught and kept, such as date, type of salmon, and river caught on. He then asked her to explain why some people didn't need licenses, but others did.

"Hmm. How familiar are you with the land and sea rights on Hayek?" she asked.

"Uh, not very."

"In that case, let me try to make this real simple. Parallel owns the entire planet. They don't just govern it, they outright own it. Anyone who lives here has agreed to abide by that. It's part of the Responsibility Oath you took. Anyone who lives here either buys land from them, rents land owned by them or by another landowner, and purchases concessions for resource extraction if they want to mine, fish, log, or do any other commercial venture. This includes *all* resources. Parallel doesn't require anyone to have a license to fish for personal consumption or cut down trees to heat their home, but if you want to catch fish or cut timber and sell them, then you're required to purchase a license and abide by the rules that Parallel's Resource Management Division set up. Hunting's a bit different, in that hunting seasons are limited to certain times; unless you're way out in the boonies and need to hunt to survive, then there really is no season.

"Another thing about Parallel is that they don't sell vast tracts of land. The best you can do is maybe 100 hectares for agriculture, such as the farmers in the Palouse," she said, referring to the land in the southwestern part of the Yakama Canton, "and they keep the right of first refusal in the deed. The Founders saw what happened on Earth and didn't want it repeated here.

"I guess you can say it's a bit idealistic, but it's what I've grown up with and it makes more sense than what I've seen or read about Earth."

Bill thought about it and had to agree; it certainly made more sense in some ways, but he wasn't sure about having one company control a whole planet, even if he did work for that company.

As twilight started to become night, they gathered their salmon and headed back to the house. Bill offered to filet them and Meri took him up on it, showing him where the fish cleaning station was. Before cleaning the fish, the two put away their fishing gear. They hung the waders up to dry and put the boots on a special drying rack near the back door.

"How'd it go?" Lewis asked from an easy chair in the great room, setting a tablet down in his lap.

"Lots of action," Meri said, while Bill held up the two salmon to show Lewis.

"Nice. Looks like fresh salmon for breakfast. I bought some eggs, so they should go well together."

While Bill cleaned the fish Meri poured each of them a glass of wine. She set his glass down on the porch table and started sipping from hers while waiting for him. As soon as the fish were clean Meri helped Bill put them in a container to put in the refrigerator, and then the two sat down on the porch to talk, drink wine, and watch the stars come out.

Lewis joined them for a glass of wine and regaled them with tales of his adventures, and more humorously, his misadventures, as a young Explorer. Bill couldn't get the image of a young Explorer Lewis, interrupted while heeding nature's call, running from a pissed off glyptotherium, pants around his ankles, screaming for help. "Bullets just bounced off his armored skin."

The Commandant also talked about the threat posed by groups such as governments on Earth and non-governmental groups, such as the Gaia Liberation Front.

"We've got enough problems with some of our Explorers questioning the need to open new planets without having to deal with the Gaia Firsters," Lewis said. "Last year, alone, we had over a dozen attacks on Earthside gates by these lunatics. Believe it or not, we're actually working with some of Earth's governments to try and put a stop to this."

Bill told them about his experience crossing over, and the protesters outside the gate. He thought about the problems of the Earth Liberation Front on Earth, and how they caused extensive damage to commercial operations throughout North America, and asked Lewis what could be done.

"We're working on a few things," he said. "Most of the problems come from the developed countries on Earth. That helps us, and it also hurts us. Because most of those governments are authoritarian, they've got some pretty good databases on their citizens. Of course, asking any of those governments for help also puts us at a disadvantage, particularly if they're after somebody who came to Hayek or through one of our gates. This is especially true because we don't have any extradition treaties with them, other than for murder."

He took a sip of wine and continued. "Of course, the biggest threat is posed by those governments, who want to control the gates. As you know, we've already had two of them attack us. Luckily, the gates are controlled on Hayek, so those attempts didn't work out too well for them."

Later that evening, as Bill was about to retire, Meri came over to him, wrapped her arms around his neck and said, "This has been a great day. Thanks for putting up with my Dad." She then kissed him, let go, and went to her room, leaving Bill thinking, *Wow! Just, wow!*

The rest of the weekend went far too fast for Bill. Not only did he get a lot of fishing in, but he and Meri became closer, although nothing beyond what propriety would allow, especially since Commandant Lewis always seemed to be around.

I wouldn't exactly say that he's protecting his daughter's virginity, but he's sure acting like he is, Bill thought on his last evening at Lewis Landing.

Lewis left late the following morning, proclaiming, "Others may get three days off, but I never do."

Before he left he pulled Bill aside. "Damned glad you came, son. I haven't seen Meri this happy since her mother died. Try to keep her that way."

"I'll try, sir," Bill replied seriously.

Turning more serious as well, Lewis then told Bill about possible threats to Meri's life from the GLF. "Intel tells me they're planning on taking more action, this time against me and my family. Keep your eyes and ears open, and your powder dry."

Along with the increased affection that Bill experienced for Meri, he also discovered that he enjoyed her father's company. The commandant turned out to have quite a sense of humor and was never at a loss for words. Bill was sad to see the weekend end, but he was also looking forward to getting back to training so he could begin his career.

Chapter 13

On the walk to the station, Bill asked Meri about the GLF threat. She shrugged it off, saying "Dad's always worried about something or other. He wouldn't be Commandant if he wasn't. I wouldn't worry too much about it."

The ride back to Sacajawea Base was just as thrilling for Bill as the ride out. He got to see the land from different angles, so new things came into view. The late afternoon approach to Tahoma really showed the north-south running hills that were drumlins left over from the last ice age, more than 10,000 years ago. While populated with small houses, it had nowhere near the density that Bill was used to.

As the two walked from the skytrain station to a restaurant in Tahoma, before hopping the maglev back to base, Meri held out her hand for Bill, so he took it in his.

"So, are we a couple now?" he asked her, partly in jest, partly serious.

"Well, duh. What do think?" She grinned up at him, then reached over and gave him a quick kiss on the lips—more a buss than a kiss, but enough to thrill him even so.

The restaurant was near the maglev station and had a great view of the bay. The Puyallup River, milky white with glacial flour sediment, flowed into the bay, which was larger than on Earth, and with far fewer, and smaller, cargo vessels. The one dock Bill could see looked like it held a small stack of shipping containers, but none of them were larger than Earth's smallest, the twenty-footers. He pointed that out to Meri, who shrugged and said she didn't know much about cargo shipping but didn't recall seeing any larger containers her whole life.

Supper done, and with the sun set, they made their way across the street to the maglev station.

While they didn't hold hands during the train rides, and there were no more public displays of affection, they did hold hands between stations and from the final station outside the base to Meri's cabin. It turned out she didn't live too far from Bill. Then again, not many Probies lived too far from each other.

When they arrived outside her cabin, she gave Bill another kiss, this one much deeper, which caused his heart rate to increase dramatically, among other reactions.

Laughing, she said, "Whoa, down boy," as she released him. Another quick peck on the lips and she said, "See you at breakfast," then disappeared inside.

Bill walked back to Jaskey Lane practically floating. When he got home, he found his roommates sprawled on the seating.

"Damn, look at you!" Jordan said.

"Yeah, what's with the stupid grin?" Matt asked.

"That must've been one helluva weekend," Thep said.

"Why, yes. Yes, it was," Bill said, and without another word, headed up the stairs to put his stuff away and go to sleep.

Early the next morning Bill checked his email, something he hadn't done for several days. He discovered that he would begin flight training that morning and was to report to the airfield with his primary survival equipment and wearing his Nomex flight suit.

Now it was Bill's turn to spend evenings cracking the books to learn about the different aircraft.

The first morning was spent covering aspects of the Caribou and putting the Probies into simulators and having them do simple actions, such as start up, take off, a short flight, and landing. The harder simulations, such as engine failures or fire, would come later.

After a quick lunch at the airfield cafe with Meri, who was going through firearms training, Bill was back at the airfield, ready to fly.

As he was doing his first pre-flight with the instructor, the smell on the flight line brought back the memory of the first time he had pre-flighted. He was fourteen years old and "the Colonel" was teaching him how to fly in an old, battered single-engine Cessna. "The Colonel" was walking him through the pre-flight, making sure he had the checklist and followed it accurately. "If you don't have the checklist, you might forget something. And if you forget something, you might die. Never pre-flight without a checklist," "the Colonel" admonished.

Four years later Bill had his commercial pilot's license with single-engine, multi-engine, and water certifications, along with his instrument flight rating. These came in handy when he started school in Seattle, as he was able to finagle a part-time flying job with an airline that flew seaplanes out of Lake Union. Even then he'd known the certifications would come in handy for applying to the Corps.

Pre-flight done, the instructor and Bill boarded the Caribou through the lowered ramp in the plane's tail. Walking up through the body, the two set their rifles and packs into storage spaces behind the cockpit. They then entered the cockpit. The instructor took the pilot's seat and gestured Bill into the co-pilot's seat to his right.

The instructor walked them through the start-up checklist, with first the port engine starting and revving with a whine, and then the starboard engine. Bill watched as each engine started, just in case a fire broke out.

After getting clearance to take off, circle, and do a touch and go, the instructor taxied the plane to the end of the runway, ran up the engines, and began the takeoff roll.

"Keep your hands on the yoke and follow my lead," he told Bill.

Bill did as he was told, and as the instructor pulled the yoke back to take off, Bill could feel it move in his hands.

Soon they were circling around the field, and then the instructor lined up the twin-engine plane on the runway and brought it in for a landing, walking Bill through all the steps. Immediately upon landing he upthrottled the plane and told Bill to take it back into the air. Bill did so. It was little more difficult than any other plane he had flown before, mainly because it was also bigger than any of them.

The instructor continued to walk Bill through the flying. They did several more touch and goes before he was satisfied that Bill had the basics well in hand.

At one point the instructor pointed at what appeared to be a small convoy of trucks lined up on the apron. These included fuel and regular cargo trucks. "Looks like a survey's about to get replenished. See them all lined up at the Survey Gate?"

Looking down, Bill could see the trucks and what he assumed was the gate—a simple affair that looked exactly like a giant gate—one big enough to drive a C-123 through.

"Let's wrap this up. Set this bird on the ground, and don't bend anything," he said, sitting back and crossing his arms over his chest, leaving Bill on his own.

Bill managed to get the plane back on the ground without bending anything and taxied it to the parking ramp. It took him a bit, but he finally figured out how to turn the plane around so it was on the apron facing the runway and ready to fly again.

The instructor held out his hand to Bill and said, "Great first flight. Let's complete the post-flight."

Once the post-flight inspection was complete, the instructor told Bill he was done flying for the day, but to check with the head instructor to see what he could do until the end of the workday. He found the head instructor in the simulator room next to the cafe and told him what the flight instructor had said.

"Take some time to read up on flight and cargo characteristics. It'll come in handy for tomorrow's simulations," Bill was told. He dug his flight manual from his pack and sat down on one of the easy chairs scattered around the airfield's waiting room and began to read.

He was deeply engrossed in reading about overcoming engine failure when he heard the bustle of others moving around. Looking at his chronograph, he realized it was quitting time. Soon he was walking down the road toward the main part of the base and meeting up with Meri in front of the shooting range.

On his second day of flight training, things went horribly wrong.

The morning had been spent in classes and flight simulation, so Bill was glad to finally get in the Caribou after lunch.

After take-off, the instructor told Bill to get to altitude and fly toward the Salish Sea. Bill had brought the plane up to the specified altitude and was heading north toward Snoqualmie Pass when, without warning, the airplane jolted. To Bill, it felt like he was a ping-pong ball inside a tin can getting hit by a baseball bat. The yoke was wrenched out of his hands and the plane made a sudden lurch to the left and downward.

Before Bill could ask the instructor what was going on, he was drenched in a warm fluid. Grabbing the yoke wildly with one hand while clearing the fluid out with the other, he turned to the instructor. What he saw froze him in shock. It took several seconds for the shock to wear off and his brain to kick into overdrive. Pulling the yoke back and to the right to try and stabilize the ungainly bird, he keyed his radio.

"Mayday, mayday, mayday. This is Tango Zero Five declaring an in-flight emergency, over."

Ground control came up immediately. "Tango Zero Five, state your emergency, over."

"I think a prop blade just came through the cabin. I've got a runaway engine and the pilot's been decapitated, over," Bill practically yelled into the microphone, over the howl of the wind coming into the cockpit at more than 250 knots per hour.

"Roger Tango Zero Five. Engine out and no pilot. Your status? Over."

"I think I'm okay. Stand by, over."

Bill heard the control tower calling again but he concentrated on flying the plane. Bill killed the power to the port engine, leaving him with only the starboard engine, then wiped his sleeve across his face to remove as much of the pilot's blood as possible.

Looking around, he could see the plane was stabilized in flight, but the controls were mushy. He didn't see any signs of fire. *Thank God for small miracles*, he thought. His heart was beating so hard he thought his chest would explode. The adrenaline dump that the incident has caused left him hyper-aware and he felt everything was moving in slow motion. He could swear he could see the individual propeller blades of the starboard engine as they spun around at thousands of revolutions per minute.

"Tango Zero Five."

"Go ahead Zero Five, over."

"I'm stabilized, running on one engine. I think some hydraulics have been cut. Advise closest field, over."

"Zero Five, can you RTB? Over."

"Ah, roger that... I think. Over"

"Zero Five, you are first in line. Crash trucks standing by, over."

"Roger that. Turning now, over."

Bill gradually turned the plane around in a shallow bank until it was on a heading to Bowman Field.

As the plane lost altitude, Bill could feel the controls getting mushier. He could see the field in the distance.

"Tango Zero Five. Field in sight, over."

"Copy, Zero Five. Field in sight. Tango Zero Six, can you do a fly by on Zero Five? Over"

"Tango Zero Six. Roger. We've got him in sight. Zero Six to Zero Five, you copy? Over."

"Roger, Zero Six."

Several more minutes passed as Bill continued to fly southward, losing altitude. He soon saw another Caribou flying in formation off his port wing.

"Zero Six to Zero Five, over," he heard on the radio.

"Go head Zero Six, over."

"Zero Five, you're missing a blade on the port prop, and there's a gash in the cockpit. Other than that, you look stable from this side, over."

"Copy, Zero Six. What about the rest? Over."

"Stand by, we'll do a fly around, over," the pilot of Tango Zero Six said. She had the calming voice of one who had been there, done that, and it helped Bill calm down a bit.

Another minute passed.

"Zero Six to Zero Five, over."

"Go ahead, over."

"Zero Five, it looks like you've got some hydraulic fluid leaking down the bottom. Other than that, no visible damage, over."

"Copy Zero Six. Hydraulic leak, no other damage," Bill affirmed. He suspected that was what was causing the control problems.

As Bill approached the airfield he deployed his landing gear. All lights indicated they were properly deployed, but he wasn't very trusting of the plane at this point.

"Zero Six, Zero Five, over."

"Go ahead, Five. Over."

"Can you confirm landing gear status? Over."

Several seconds passed before Bill heard, "Zero Five all landing gear deployed and looks locked, over."

"Roger, Six. Thanks."

Bill then addressed the control tower. "Tango Zero Five on final, over."

Bill concentrated on getting the plane on the ground. As he came in on final approach he could see crash trucks scattered on either side of the runway. By now the adrenaline had caused his eyesight to narrow, so the closer he got to touching down, the less peripheral vision he had until he no longer saw the trucks, only the rubber-streaked concrete runway.

The Dehavilland DHC-4 Caribou was designed to stop with two engines by running the props in reverse. Bill knew if he attempted that he would probably roll the bird, so instead, he throttled back the remaining engine and feathered the prop when the plane touched the ground. *Glad I was reading about this shit last night*, he thought as the plane slowed, gently applying the brakes.

Only now did Bill notice how tightly he was gripping the yoke. He attempted to release it, but his hands were frozen. It took several attempts before he could get his blood-covered hands free from the now sticky yoke. By then, the plane had stopped rolling. Bill could hear the sirens as the crash trucks approached.

He shut down the remaining engine, unbuckled from his seat, took one look at the decapitated, blood-soaked body of the instructor, and promptly vomited all over the floor of the cockpit.

Bill was taken to the base hospital for evaluation, both physical and mental. Fortunately, he had suffered no physical injuries, but they decided to keep him overnight, regardless. After showering and being given a mild sedative, a counselor came to his room to help him deal with the post-traumatic stress disorder that was sure to develop.

Later that evening Meri came by. She didn't say much, just hugged Bill and told him how happy she was that he was okay. She stayed by his bed until he finally faded out to sleep.

The next morning, after breakfast in bed, Bill was discharged and told to report to an accident review board at Bowman Field. He was also ordered by the attending physician to check in with the counselor weekly for therapy. "It's a common practice in the Corps," the physician said. "We get a lot of trauma cases and deaths every year. We treat the whole person, not just the physical injuries. So don't miss the appointments."

Bill was given a ride to the airport. As they approached the airfield, he could see a line of Caribous parked on the apron.

"They've all been grounded until they discover what the problem was," the driver said.

Tango Zero Five was at the end of the apron, with a number of mechanics climbing all over it. Bill could clearly see the port engine with its missing propeller blade. The blade was no longer embedded in the cockpit.

Bill was dropped off at the entrance to the ready room and told: "They're waiting for you inside."

Entering the room, he saw several older Explorers sitting at a table in the front. On the opposite side of the table was a lone chair. Upon seeing him, the two men and one woman rose and gestured for him to come in.

The woman walked around the table as Bill approached. "Tango Zero Six," she said, extending her hand.

Bill was swept with emotion. Here was the one person who was there with him in the sky, watching over him as he struggled to fly, and land, the damaged plane. He couldn't answer, as a lump had developed in his throat. He could only shake her hand and nod.

Once they were all seated, the older man, sitting in the middle, said to Bill "That was one hell of a flying job yesterday, son."

By now, Bill's voice had returned. "Thank you, sir."

"As you're probably aware, this is an accident review board. Our job is to find out what happened so we can prevent it from happening again. If we can't prevent it, we want to know how to deal with it. Now, we're not here to place blame on you. You did an exemplary job. What we want to know is exactly what happened. So, can you take it from the top?"

Bill did, beginning with the original pre-flight inspection

through the final moment of landing. The only thing he left out was his final action, which added to the cockpit's slurry mess. Several times he was redirected to immediately before and after the propeller came into the cockpit.

"We know we're pushing you here, son, but we've got to have all the facts."

Finally, after several hours, the grilling was done, and they broke for lunch. Tango Zero Six, whose real name was Janet Babbitt, asked Bill to join her for lunch in the airfield's cafe.

"I can't give you an advance insight, but let's just say that you're not to blame and everyone thinks you did one helluva job," she said, taking a bite of her sandwich.

"Thanks," Bill said. "Also, thanks for being there. If it wasn't for you I'd have probably continued freaking out."

"Naw, you were doing fine," she said with a wave of her hand.

That evening Bill met Meri for supper and then the two of them went for a long walk.

He told her everything he could remember about the incident, including how afraid he was and how he froze up. "If it wasn't for Babbitt calming me down, I don't know if I would have survived."

"Well, you did. As a matter of fact, everyone's talking about how great you handled it. I don't think I could have done as well."

Sleep didn't come easily to Bill that night, and when it did, it didn't last long. He woke up covered in sweat, his heart racing, and wiping his face to clear the instructor's blood off it. Once he realized what he was doing, he stopped trying to clean blood that wasn't there.

He finally managed to sleep but woke up feeling groggy when the alarm went off.

A quick breakfast with Meri, who picked up on his mood and didn't push him, then off to the airfield for more classes.

Caribou flights were still canceled while the technicians went over them, looking to see if the same issue that affected Bill's 'bou was affecting them. The Probies were told it would be another day or two until they got back up into the air, so the afternoon was spent in more class and flight simulator time.

By suppertime, Bill was feeling a bit more human and interacted a bit more with everyone. He didn't talk about the incident, and nobody asked. He was grateful for that.

When Bill reported to the airfield the next morning, he was sent to the same room where the accident review board had met. When he entered the room he saw Janet Babbitt sitting at the table. On the table in front of her was a thick file folder. She gestured for him to close the door and join her.

Once seated, Janet slid the folder over to him and said, "This is in strictest confidentiality. Don't discuss this with anyone, even your girlfriend. The only reason I'm showing it to you is because the review board, and Commandant Lewis, think you deserve to know. Especially after what you've been through."

Bill opened the folder and flipped through it, scanning through the report and photographs. After several minutes, he closed the folder, set it down, and said, "So, it was sabotage?"

Janet nodded. "Yep. Somebody deliberately removed the cotter pins on that prop. When the nuts finally let loose, the bolts sheared, and that's what caused the prop to go flying."

"Who would do something like that?" Bill was shocked.

"We're not certain, but we think the Gaia Liberation Force."

"The Gaia Firsters?"

Janet nodded. "It's possible that they've got a mole on base. That or they snuck in. Either way, it complicates things."

Bill was alarmed. He recalled his conversation with Commandant Lewis on the last day at Lewis Landing, where Lewis warned him of the threat posed by the GLA.

"What do we do, now?"

"Carry on as usual, but just be more vigilant. At least, if you see something, you're armed and can take action."

Bill didn't want to shoot anyone. That was one of the reasons he worked so hard to join the Corps; to avoid getting swept up in the US's ongoing War on Terror and all the killing that came with it.

Janet continued. "We've already changed the training protocols - from now on, all props will be checked during the pre-flight inspections. I know, it's like closing the barn door after the horses got out, but we don't want a repeat of that."

"You okay to go back to flying Caribous?"

Bill nodded. "Yeah, just having nightmares. I think I'll be all right, though."

"Well, let's give it a try. And don't miss those meetings with the therapist. Trust me, it's better to talk to them than to suffer PTSD long term."

After Janet dismissed Bill, he reported to the head flight instructor who assigned him to Tango Zero Six for the remainder of his Caribou training.

The days that followed, like the weeks before, were pretty standard. Simulation and classes in the morning followed by flying in the afternoons. Soon Bill was type rated for the Caribou, then the Provider, then the 415, and finally the Monarch.

While all four planes were twin engines, the Monarch was unlike anything Bill had flown before. Unlike the other three, it was an extremely light bird with a wing surface that was practically designed for a glider. Takeoffs and landings were more like floating than flying. It took a while to get to altitude, but once up, it seemed like it would stay aloft forever with little input by anyone or anything. The entire top, wings, and fuselage, were covered with lightweight solar cells that powered the electric motors when they were at altitude.

Another thing that separated the Monarch from the cargo planes was the inclusion of living quarters. It wasn't much, just a small galley, some hanging lockers, a really small lavatory, and four bunks with curtains across them.

The main cabin also included two workstations and two crash seats for the aerial survey specialists.

Bill thought that flying the 415 and the two cargo planes was relatively straightforward, but then he discovered that they were like driving a bus compared to the Monarch, a more nimble craft.

The thing Bill enjoyed the most was being able to see more of Hayek, albeit from several thousand feet in the air. The juxtaposition of what he saw with what he remembered from Earth still threw him for a loop sometimes. Particularly disconcerting was when the flights took them over Cascadia and around the Salish Sea. There were only a couple of small cities, instead of the sprawling megalopolis that had engulfed the Puget Sound region. There was no Tacoma Narrows Bridge, no floating bridges across what he knew as Lake Washington, no large naval bases or airfields. Mostly what he saw was forest. Lots of forest. Despite the growing population, which was approaching a million in Cascadia alone, it was still mostly untamed. Of course, the lack of a dairy industry also meant that land that was in agriculture on Earth was still unsettled and virgin on Hayek at best, or lightly settled at worst.

As with all good things, flight training came to an end, and Bill was checked off as a co-pilot for all four planes. Of course, his favorite was the Monarch, just because of its lightness, its nimbleness in flight, and the fact that it could climb high enough that he felt he could see halfway across the continent.

When he landed the Monarch on his last flight, his instructor shook his hand and said, "Too bad you didn't try for pilot. You're a natural."

Hearing that made Bill a bit homesick, as it was something his father had always said. He could just hear "the Colonel" as he would say, "Y'know, Bill. You're a natural at this. You oughta try for an Air Force commission." Bill thanked the instructor then thought, *Hell, dad, this is way better than anything the US Air Force could have ever provided,* and the feeling of homesickness disappeared.

Chapter 14

Survival training turned out to be the hardest training yet. Once again, Bill was with his GIS cohort, so he and Kim Smith paired off.

It turned out that Janice Goodland was the lead instructor. She had the Probies pull out the *CoD Survival Guide* they had been issued on the first day of training. After ensuring everybody had one, she told them to put them away in a pants cargo pocket. "You never know when your tablet will die or break."

Sweeping her graying hair out of her eyes, she told the assembled Probies, "It doesn't matter what all you've learned from your other training, this is the only training you'll get that may keep your asses alive.

"Look at me." She gestured to herself with her one remaining hand. "This didn't happen sitting at a desk, in a cockpit, or driving a Willy's. This happened because there are hungry animals out there with no fear of man. Or the more dangerous of the species, woman," she finished with a chuckle. "Our goal is to ensure that this doesn't happen to you. I can't say that you won't be eaten or attacked by some nasty critter, but we hope that we train you sufficiently to prevent this from happening.

"The training you're about to go through will be difficult, but not impossible. As with everything in the Corps, it's designed to ensure you're the best trained possible. We invest a lot of time and money into you, and we want to recoup that investment.

"As with your other training, we'll be doing a combination of classroom and fieldwork. You will note that all of your instructors have the Trekker medal. We've all been there, done that. So don't think you know better than us. Unless you've got a Trekker medal, you don't. Do not forget that!

"Now, you're all properly trained in firearms, so let's get you up to speed on the rest of it."

Goodland outlined the course schedule. The first two weeks were to be spent at Sacajawea Base going over basic survival skills— threat analysis, water and food procurement, shelter building, fire starting, hygiene, and the myriad skills necessary to maintain life without civilization. During this time the Probies would also get training in emergency medicine, hopefully enough to help them live in the event anything bad happened to them. The third week would be spent learning survival skills in an arid environment. The fourth and fifth involved learning how to build boats and survive at sea, and the final week would focus on jungle survival.

Each phase would take place at a different location. It was the first time that he heard that there was more than one Corps of Discovery base. Apparently, there was another in Yakama Canton, small and dedicated to arid lands survival training. Most of the Salish Peninsula, which Bill knew as the Olympic Peninsula, was a training base and nature reserve managed by the Corps. This base served for sea, mountain, and arctic survival training. There was also a training base in the Yucatan Peninsula. Bill was excited to hear about that, as he had never been that far south. With his father in the military, most international travel for dependents was frowned upon due to the threat of kidnapping and terrorism. Of course, on Hayek, it wasn't really international travel, but it would still be quite a journey for Bill.

Goodland led the entire first session, going over the most important things about emergency situations ("Keep your cool") and explaining the rule of threes. "You can survive without air for three minutes. Without shelter for three hours. Without water for three days. Without food for three weeks. Of course, that depends on having all your prior needs met. So, you need to ensure you've got access to all four within those time frames.

"I think we've all got an understanding of the breathing thing. If you're underwater, get above it. If you're at too high an altitude, get down as soon as possible. Believe it or not, some people die of hypoxia—not having enough air at altitude. You'll know when that's happening by your body's reaction." She then went on to explain the symptoms of altitude sickness, such as headaches, blurred vision, vomiting.

"Most of you will probably never be at that altitude, but for those of your running initial aerial surveys, it's always a distinct possibility."

The first morning the Probies spent time learning how to locate water and build shelters from available materials. They were also taught the importance of fire

"One thing we've learned in forty years of exploration is that wild animals hate fire. They instinctively understand how dangerous it is, and will do anything to avoid getting caught in a wildfire. They smell smoke, they run in the opposite direction. For that reason, the one thing you always want to do when setting up camp is to get a fire going as soon as possible."

She then launched into the concept of threat awareness and analysis with respect to survival situations.

"I'm sure most of you were taught to stop, think, stay calm, and wait for help to arrive. Well, that's not what we teach. You do that, you die. It's that simple. We want you thinking, but we also want you moving. And when you're moving, or even staying still, we want you cognizant of the dangers facing you. It's not just animals, although some of them are pretty nasty; it's also the terrain, the environment, and just about everything under the sun, including the sun.

"Our goal is to get you thinking about what's around you at all times. First, let's start with predators because those are usually the scariest, but not the worst threat you'll face."

She showed pictures of the types of animal threats the Probies could be expected to encounter. While the usual suspects were displayed, such as the big cats, bears, and canines, there were also some fine feathered friends included. One such was the terror bird, mostly found in the isthmus area between Ti'ichum and Suyu and throughout most of northern Suyu. Bill still had to translate local geography to the Earth geography he grew up with. *Okay, that's North and South America, so the isthmus must be the Panamanian Isthmus.*

"When you're walking or stopped, always look around near you first, then expand your search outward, looking for movement. And, don't forget to look up. You'd be surprised how many times people are jumped by cats or snakes hanging out in trees."

Other animal threats included alligators, crocodiles, snakes, spiders, and the various sharks of the seas. But, most interesting to Bill was the threat posed by hoofed herbivores.

"Do not get near these if you can avoid them," Janice warned, "other than to kill one for food. While they won't hunt you, they will protect their young, and heaven help you if you're in their way when they decide to stampede. Moose, rhinos, hippos, elk, bison, mammoths, mastodons. They're all dangerous, so don't think they're just dumb grass-eating herd animals. They'll kill you just as dead as a smilodon."

A discussion on water-borne threats, such as viruses, bacteria, parasites, and worms, followed, and then a discussion on the dangers of terrain.

The two main physical geography features Goodland lectured on were cliffs and water. These two killed more people than animals. The Probies were told how to safely ascend and descend cliff faces, and more importantly, how to avoid having to do so. "Avoid the threat," was Goodland's mantra.

Water threats were numerous, having to cross oceans, rivers, lakes, swamps, and frozen bodies of water, including glaciers.

"You won't get field training on glaciers until you get to Salish Base, so I won't tell you much beyond the basics." She also spoke about how to identify avalanche zones, and when conditions were ripe for an avalanche.

The threat analysis class lasted all morning. By lunchtime, Bill was seriously reconsidering his career choice. While he knew, both from his reading up on the Corps before applying, and more recently from his walk through the Corps museum, that life in the Corps could be dangerous, he wasn't quite expecting it to be this dangerous.

That afternoon the class had the students stringing up their hammocks, most for the first time, and building shelters from materials they found in the surrounding forest. Bill came to appreciate the hatchet and ax they were required to carry.

He was also surprised at how the hammock worked. Rather than enter from the side, as with most hammocks, one entered from the bottom in this one. Goodland explained to the class that the design was a refinement of the Hennessy Hammock developed on Earth in the mid-1980s. While the bottom entry at first felt strange, and most thought they would fall through the entry, Bill discovered that once inside, the bottom sealed up quite nicely from his weight pressing on it. The mesh above the sleeping portion protected the user from bugs, and the detachable rain fly protected him (or her) from rain or snow. There was even a lightweight reflective material that served as insulation by fitting into the double bottom on the underside of the hammock. The double bottom also provided an additional barrier to hungry mosquitoes and other bloodsucking insects. As a final thought, there were even four rain collectors that attached to the rain fly. Each collector was designed to work with the issued canteens and collapsible water bottles. In total, the entire system weighed slightly more than a kilogram. There were several different sizes of hammocks. To Bill, that made sense. *No sense having small people carry more than they need.*

The following day was dedicated to finding and treating water, along with field hygiene.

"Trust me," Janice said, "the one thing you'll want to do, other than avoid getting eaten by a nasty critter, is to stay clean." Looking around the assembled Probies, she asked, "Any of you men ever have crotch rot?"

A few tentatively raised their hands. Janice selected one and asked him to tell the class the particulars, including the circumstances.

"Well, I was on an extended backpacking trip and didn't have a chance to shower or wash my clothes. After a few days, it showed up. Definitely not fun," he finished while the class chuckled at his discomfort.

"That's exactly it. Not fun!" Janice exclaimed. "Let me be clear, if you don't take care of yourself, your clothing, and your equipment, bad things can happen. And crotch rot is one of those bad things. There's a reason we include hygiene equipment in your survival gear. You're gonna be traveling for quite some time if you go down in the boonies, and since we're spending so much money on you, we want you back, healthy!"

The Probies were then taught how to use the small showerhead that fit on a bottle. Bill had used one in the Boy Scouts, so he thought he knew the right way. It turned out he was wrong. Goodland showed them a technique that was guaranteed to get them wet with the minimal amount of water. Stripping down unabashedly in front of the group, she grabbed the shower, which was attached to a water-filled canteen. Holding her hand palm up, she grasped the funnel shape of the shower between her thumb and index finger, and then lifted it straight up, inverted. The water flowed down her arm, armpit, side, and leg. She then moved her arm so the other side of her body got wet, telling the class, "If I had two arms, I'd switch the bottle from one hand to the other, which is what you should do." She then circled the bottle around her head, front and back.

"There, completely rinsed," she said as the water finished draining out of the bottle. The Probies could see that there wasn't a dry spot on her. "For basic hygiene, that's all you need. Of course, soap comes in handy, but that requires two or three liters of water."

The Probies were then surprised when they discovered Goodland expected them all to perform the same act. It was obvious that some of the students came from cultures where stripping down in front of others, particularly those of the opposite sex, was either forbidden or not encouraged. Bill was one of those and felt somewhat embarrassed stripping down, but he did so. *If everyone's doing it, then nobody will be looking at anyone* he thought, and then changed his mind as he realized he was admiring the women in the class and noticed that some of them were eying him. He couldn't help notice that pretty much everyone appeared fit, with not so much body fat that you couldn't see the muscle definition. It was also obvious that most of them had "Explorer Tan," with dark faces, necks, arms, and legs, but pale elsewhere. Even the black and Asian Probies had some semblance of the tan.

Soon, all the Probies were soaked, and Goodland had them dry off with the small towels that they had been issued. Once dry, the Probies rapidly dressed.

"You might as well get used to being naked in front of each other," Janice said. "After all, most of you'll be spending a lot of time in close proximity to each other out in the boonies when you're on a mission, and there ain't no shower curtains to hide what you've been blessed with.

"Now, who knows what this is?" she asked the group, holding up a toothbrush.

Everyone chuckled and held up their hands.

"Great. It's also another one of those important things. You forget to brush, you might get cavities. And let me tell you, there ain't nothing worse than an infected tooth when you're thousands of miles from a dentist. Be sure to use it and the dental floss you're issued."

Goodland instructed them on the proper care of feet, toenails, hair, and just about every body part that needed taking care of.

By the time she got done Bill was wondering if he even knew how to properly care for his body, despite having lived with it for twenty-two years.

The training was intense, but by the end of the first week, Bill felt comfortable in his knowledge of basic survival skills, the most important of which was using his brain.

Despite the intensity, Bill was enjoying himself. Days were spent

in training, with evenings spent mainly with Meri. As both had passed
their primary and secondary skills training, they weren't spending time
cracking the books at night. More often than not they would be joined
by Matt and Nicole.

They also attended several of the weekend gatherings hosted by
Goodland, usually at the Cave Bear Cave. It gave the Probies a chance
to talk to her and other Explorers in a more casual environment, a
setting she fostered.

Emergency medicine was an eye-opener for everyone. It wasn't
just a matter of taking two aspirin and slapping a band-aid on. They
learned how to properly clean and dress a wound, how to deal with
problems induced by heat and cold, and how to suture a wound. They
even learned how to amputate and cauterize a wound using a campfire
and a knife. Goodland was emphatic about learning that one. "If I
hadn't known to do that, I'd be dead a long time ago," she told the
crowd.

For the third week of survival training, the class went into the
Channeled Scablands of Yakama. There they were taught how to find
water, protect themselves from the heat, get food, and all the other
survival skills needed to live in a desert. Bill and the others were quite
surprised at just how cold it could get in the desert at night.

The training area was a smaller base than Sacajawea, and the
Probies had to remain there the entire week. This meant they got to use
their equipment, including the hammocks, which served mainly as tents
in the practically treeless environment. It also meant they got to eat
emergency rations, which was definitely not the highlight of the week.

A weekend back at Sacajawea Base, where Bill discovered Meri
had just started survival training, and then he was off to the Salish
Peninsula for two weeks of training. The first week was mainly survival
at sea training, with the second week encompassing mountain and
arctic environments training. Salish Base was the largest base operated
by the Corps of Discovery, covering most of the Salish Peninsula, an
area that encompassed beaches, mountains, alpine glaciers, rivers,
coniferous forest, rainforests, and plains.

Bill thought the sea survival training would be mostly about how to catch fish and eat them raw, but it turned out to be far more. While the Probies did learn how to fish using a plastic circular reel called a Cuban Yo-Yo reel, they also built an outrigger canoe, just like the ancient Polynesians used to, using only an adze and an ax. They learned how to distill sea water with a poncho. They learned about the various sea plants and how to utilize them for food. They were taught, and were forced to memorize, the global wind patterns, particularly the Trades and the Westerlies. They also learned how to prepare meals without the benefit of fire ("you do not want fire on a boat in the middle of the ocean," one instructor explained).

Salish Base was also where they learned the various methods of preserving food for long treks. They learned how to smoke various meats, how to make pemmican, the best ways to dry fruits and berries, and how to turn otherwise inedible foods into edible ones. Bill had heard that Native Americans used to live on the otherwise inedible acorn by leaching them, but he didn't understand what that meant until he was actually required to do so: shelling the acorns and boiling them several times until the water no long turned dark with the tannins. Only then could the acorns be ground into flour for use.

Making clothing out of animal skins was a new one for Bill and many of the Probies. Along with hunting game for several of their meals, they were required to turn the skin of whatever they killed into leather suitable for clothing. This was tied into the food preservation training, in that the fat and meat from the game was used in making the pemmican, while the brains were used in tanning the hides. They also learned how to turn sinew and skin into rawhide for bow strings and other implements that required rope or twine. Of course, they learned how to make rope and twine from plants, too.

It was at Salish Base that the Probies learned how to make useful tools from simple sticks and stones. Naturally, a spear, along with a bow and arrow, were among the first tools they produced. They even got to build their first boat, a simple outrigger dugout canoe.

And for the first time, the Probies got to see some of the

megafauna that Hayek was famous for. They not only saw a small herd of mastodons, but they saw several giant beaver, and one Probie claimed he caught a glimpse of a lion. Of course, nobody believed him.

Having lived in Washington, Bill was aware of the difference between the two sides of the Salish Mountains, with a rainforest on one side and the rain shadow effect on the other, practically creating a desert. Many of the Probies, new to that part of the world, were not only unaware of this geographic phenomenon but were quite shocked when they had to spend part of a week on the beach on the rainforest side. It seemed nobody ever truly dried out.

Another weekend at Sacajawea with Meri, and then off for the final week of survival training in the tropics. The Probies boarded a C-123 Provider for a two-day, very long, very noisy flight to Maya Base deep in the Yucatan Peninsula. They were told it was part of their training, and to learn to get used to riding in the Provider.

While training in the tropical climate of the Yucatan, Bill decided, *Maybe the temps aren't too bad in Yakama.* Along with high temperatures, the Probies had to deal with the high humidity. And bugs. Lots of bugs. Nasty, biting bugs. Lots of nasty, biting, blood-sucking bugs. Of course, the Probies got their revenge by eating several of the bugs as part of their training. *Turnabout's fair play*, Bill thought as he crunched into some grubs cooked on a rock over a fire.

Bill discovered a deep, profound respect for his hammock during tropical survival training. This respect was most especially for the bug netting and the double bottom that prevented some of said nasty, biting, blood-sucking bugs from getting to him while he slept. He was also most grateful to the designers who decided to make the uniforms, and particularly the underwear, lightweight, sturdy, and quick-drying. He also found out just how useful his handheld shower and towel were, as compared to several other male Probies, who failed to use theirs daily. Bill winced just watching them walk during the final days. Bill still didn't feel totally comfortable stripping down in front of women he wasn't about to enjoy the company of in the carnal sense, but he was starting to get used to doing so.

Halfway through that week's training, Bill heard a loud commotion followed by several gunshots. Whipping his rifle up, he pivoted his head around, looking for threats. More shouting, and Bill, along with the other Probies, made their way to the uproar. They found several Probies surrounding what appeared to be a very dead, very large bird. One Probie was practically yelling, "Did you see him attack me? Huh? Did you? Did you? I had to shoot him. The fucker was gonna kill me!"

One of the survival instructors arrived, and told the assembled Probies, "Threat analysis, what should you be doing?" at which point many of the Probies remembered that they weren't in Kansas anymore and resumed their watchful vigilance.

The instructor identified the bird as a terror bird, one of the largest flightless predators of the avian family.

"You got lucky," he told the Probie. "These things'll usually tear you apart before you even see or hear him."

The Probie was still in shock but seemed to appreciate hearing this. The instructor then looked down at the bird and said with a grin, "Guess it'll be fowl for supper."

Bill had thought some of the instructors were joking about terror birds because he had read they ceased to exist over a million years ago. *I guess that's just on our timeline,* he thought. This led to another train of thought: *I wonder what else survived on this timeline?* to *I wonder what's survived on other timelines?* Then the thought of encountering dinosaurs kicked in. *Man, I hope I don't see any of those* as images from *Jurassic Park* passed through his mind.

Finally, survival training was complete and the Probies returned to Sacajawea Base on board the same Provider. The long flight, which only took one day this time with stops for fuel, made it back to base early Tuesday morning. Unfortunately for Bill, Meri was at Salish Base for her third week of survival training.

As they landed at the airfield, they were met by Janice Goodland. As she shook Bill's hand she said with a warm smile, "Glad you made it Bill. I was rooting for you." He didn't know why, but that comment made him feel extremely proud, like a kindergartner being told his being able to write his name legibly was a great accomplishment; but it did, and he felt his chest swell with pride.

"Thanks," was all he could manage to say, before letting her hand go.

"Go join the group over there." Janice pointed to a point where the disembarked Probies had gathered. "I'll be along shortly."

Bill and his fellow survivalists watched as Goodland greeted every disembarking Probie, then joined the group.

"This is great! Nobody died. This bodes well for y'all," she said. "I know you're all tired, but I want you to go back to your cabins, clean your gear, and then yourselves—in that order. Once you've done that you can eat or crap out, but I want you to meet me back at the Survival School for a wrap-up. I'll see you at 1300 hours. Don't be late!"

Chapter 15

Bill was glad to finally be back in the cabin, and after getting all his equipment clean he spent a considerable amount of time in the shower, enjoying the steaming hot water. Unlike the quick showers he had taken during training, which only rinsed him off, he was now able to soap up and rinse off numerous times. He was finally getting most of the grime out from under his fingernails, but it seemed the dirt was well and truly ground into the whorls of his fingers. After some serious scrubbing using a washcloth, he even managed to get those parts clean.

Of course, nothing feels quite as good after a shower as getting rid of a week-plus worth of facial fuzz, so off came the stubble. After rinsing the lather off, he ran his hand across his chin, marveling at the smoothness of it. *Damn, this feels good to be clean. Here's hoping I don't have to go through that again.*

Bill changed into a fresh uniform, leaving off his socks and boots, and took his dirty uniforms and dumped them into the laundry. He had a half hour until they would be ready, so he set alarms on both his phone and on his nightstand clock, crawled onto the bed and was instantly asleep.

A moment later, it seemed, the alarm clock, immediately followed by his phone's alarm, brought him back from the dead. Groggily, he sat up and fumbled for both devices. By this time, he was almost fully awake, well, at least enough to get moving.

Putting his socks and boots on he went downstairs and found his clothes washed. He put them in the dryer and decided he had enough time to hit the cafeteria and get some lunch, along with a healthy dose of coffee. Grabbing his now-clean pack and rifle, he headed out the door, wondering when his roommates would return.

Arriving at the cafeteria, he saw Kim Smith sitting alone at one of the tables.

"Won't Meri get jealous?" she asked with a smile, as he slung his rifle over the chair's notch.

Bill set his pack down on the floor. "Naw, she knows you're not a cradle robber."

"Cradle robber? Why, you diaper-clad youngster..," she sputtered, as Bill laughed and headed for the food line.

Over the past several weeks the two of them had gone through most of the same training, so a friendship had evolved, much like an older sister with a younger brother. They were now comfortable together, except for the stripping in front of each other, which still caused them all a bit of nervousness, with their prudish Earth morals. The native-born Hayekers didn't have those same issues, as Bill learned from Meri when they were talking about survival training one evening. "It's just a body," Meri said when Bill tried to explain his reluctance to undress in front of strangers. Of course, she didn't strip down in front of him, saying, "That's different" when he mentioned it.

Bill returned to the table with his tray. "Wow, real food we didn't have to kill or dig up," he said, setting the tray down at the table and taking a seat. Kim said nothing, as her mouth was full of food.

After they ate, Kim said, "Well, off to see what Goodland's got planned for us this afternoon. Any idea?"

"Haven't a clue. As a matter of fact, I haven't a clue about anything, especially since I haven't even checked my email or the news since before we took off for that tropical hell hole."

Upon being reminded of such things, both Probies pulled their tablets from their cargo pockets. There was nothing from Janice indicating what the afternoon portended.

Bill did have an email from Meri letting him know how her training had gone, and that she was looking forward to seeing him soon, which made him feel good. He sent her a response saying that he was done with survival training and was awaiting word.

The walk to the Survival School was actually quite pleasant, especially after the heat and humidity of the tropics. It was just cool enough to be comfortable, but no need for a jacket. Bill suspected that within a week or two the temperatures would start to dip as November approached, but right now the mid-day sun felt good.

Bill and Kim made their way to Goodland Hall where they joined a growing body of Probies. The classroom they were directed to was set up like one of the many lecture halls Bill had sat in while attending the University of Washington. Seats were arranged in tiers with a space at the bottom for a speaker. That space was occupied by Janice and Commandant Lewis. As they filed in, they were told to fill up the first couple of rows, so they did.

"Good afternoon, ladies and gentlemen," Janice greeted the Probies. "As of today, you have all completed the formal portion of your training. Congratulations." She gave a warm smile. "I'm sure some of you wondered if you would, particularly during the past couple of weeks.

"Commandant Lewis is here to hand you your Explorer Training Graduation Certificates along with your first assignment, so when you hear your name, come on down. After you get your certificate take a seat."

Bill was one of the first to be called, right after Kim Smith. When he got to the front, Lewis extended his hand. "Congratulations Bill," Lewis said as they shook hands. "I always figured you'd make it, even with all you've had to endure. I'm sure Meri would have been happy to be here to see this." He handed Bill a large envelope. "As soon as she's done, I'd like to have the two of you up for supper."

"Thanks, sir. I'd like that." Bill took the envelope.

Back at his seat, Bill sat down and opened the envelope to see what it contained. Next to him, Kim was doing the same.

The first thing he saw was a certificate, much like his university diploma which had only recently arrived on Hayek. It proclaimed to all and sundry that he had passed the Basic Explorer Training and was fully qualified to serve in the capacity of an Explorer in his area of specialty. Both his primary and secondary fields were listed. Bill decided that he'd get the certificate framed and hang it on the wall next to his university diploma. *Damn, I'm getting to be like "the Colonel" with my very own "I Love Me" wall.*

Sliding the certificate back in the envelope he pulled out the next piece of paper, which was his first official assignment as an Explorer. He was to assist in the secondary aerial mapping survey aboard a Bombardier CL-415 crew on Zion, a planet that had already had an initial survey, and was now in the process of the secondary survey prior to opening it for settlement. Crew CL-415-Z21 was currently on Zion and he was to join them on Monday by 0800 hours. *Five whole days off,* Bill thought. He was to bring all his Explorer uniforms and equipment, including the Secondary Survival Kit. Personal items could be left at his residence.

From his training, Bill knew that secondary surveys were more focused on producing accurate maps and doing ground surveys for the purposes of ensuring there were no humans or other hominids, along with identifying flora and fauna, particularly dangerous fauna. Of course, one the best things about secondary surveys was that there was more support in the event something bad happened, such as a plane going down, a ground crew getting injured, or a survey or cargo vessel getting stranded or having mechanical problems. The dangers really weren't any less, but there was definitely more support than one would find on an initial survey.

Bill was pretty excited about this and leaned over and showed Kim his letter. She smiled and showed him hers. Aerial mapping survey aboard a CL-415 on Zion. Crew CL-415-Z21. The same crew! Bill raised his eyebrows, but neither one of them said anything as the ceremony was still in progress.

Soon, all the Probies were seated again, and Commandant Lewis gave a short speech, explaining that they were about to embark on a truly grand adventure, but that danger lurked around every corner, so they should always remember their survival training.

"Since you've been here, all of your communications about training have been via email, so I'm sure some of you are wondering why you got an actual paper letter for your first assignment. Simply put, it's tradition. We found out that when we transitioned from paper to digital decades ago, people would print out their first assignment email and frame it with their diploma. A memento, if you will. So, for this one assignment, we reverted back to printing it on real paper and giving it to you with your certificate. Do with it what you will, but be sure to report to the right location at the right time," he said with a chuckle.

"This wraps up your initial training. More will come later as we get new equipment, software, and skills. As of now, you're no longer in training. You are now Explorers assigned to an exploration, but still on probationary status. Congratulations, and stay safe out there."

Janice Goodland then said, "If you plan on celebrating tonight, all well and good. But don't get carried away. The last thing you want to do if you have to report tomorrow is show up and impress your new co-workers with just how hungover you can get." As an unexpected bonus, Janice announced, "I'll be at the Cave Bear Cave starting at seven. The first round is on me if you want to come by. Maybe I'll even tell a war story or two," she finished with a dry chuckle.

As they stood, Bill said to Kim, "Damn, I hope I'll be able to see Meri before we leave."

"Doesn't she have the weekend off?" Kim asked.

"I think so."

Better send her an email," Kim replied. "Matter of fact, why don't I take a picture of you and we can send that to her? That way she won't forget what you look like."

Once the two were outside, Kim used Bill's tablet to take a picture of him with Mt. Tahoma rising the background. He sent it to Meri, along with the news of his assignment.

Then Kim and Bill decided that getting prepared for their upcoming assignment, despite being five whole days away, took priority over food and grog, so they said their farewells and went to their respective residences.

Back at the cabin on Jaskey Lane, Bill went upstairs and reviewed the list of all required equipment he was to bring with him. He pulled everything out of his pack and then repacked it, making sure that all the requisite equipment was enclosed. He checked all the pouches on his web belt and went through every pocket on his survival vest. He made double sure the *CoD Survival Guide,* now well-thumbed, was in the correct vest pocket. Finally, he went through every pocket of his uniform.

Satisfied that all his primary survival gear was in order, he then pulled out his secondary survival gear and went through the same process. Once he was happy, he set the PDW and his rifle in the gun safe and the two sets of survival equipment on the floor by the door.

What's missing? he thought and then realized that while he had many pictures of Meri on his tablet, he didn't have a physical one. Having one he could pin up to his workstation sounded like a great idea, and this got him looking for a way to print one out. He decided to print one from their long weekend at Lewis Landing, where she was holding up a sockeye salmon and grinning from ear to ear.

Hopping online, Bill discovered that pictures could be printed and laminated at the base exchange, so he headed out. It felt strange not wearing his survival vest and belt and to not have his pack and rifle strapped over his shoulder. He *felt* like an Explorer.

It wasn't Bill's first time to the base exchange, but since he didn't visit too often, it took him a couple of minutes to find the copy center. After tucking the picture into his left pocket, he a decided to explore the base exchange a bit more before supper. He still had several hours to kill before meeting Kim, but not enough time to go back to the cabin, grab his fishing gear, and hit the Naches, despite the fact that the salmon were running.

It was then that he thought of "the Colonel." *Damn, I should've written him a long time ago,* he thought, and looked around the exchange for a flash drive and padded envelopes, finding them in the office supply section. Then he returned to his cabin to type a letter.

It took him quite some time to sum up what all he had been up to since crossing over, and letting his dad know that he was about to go out on his first mission. He made sure to include a return address knowing, though, that letter writing was something "the Colonel" rarely did. Once finished, he saved the letter onto the flash drive and included several pictures, a few of which included Meri. Some of the pictures were taken on the flight line, some in the air, and several were of the flora, fauna, and landscape of Hayek. The picture Kim had taken earlier in the day was included, with the comment "Taken today after graduation."

He made his way to the base's small post office and inquired about mailing the envelope to the United States on Earth.

"Not a problem," he was told by the clerk. "Let's just figure out the postage and get it on the way."

The postage was about ten times what he was used to paying. When Bill remarked on that, he was reminded that the envelope had to go through a gate, and gates cost a lot of money to operate. Bill nodded. *That explains why all Earth made stuff is so expensive.*

By now it was practically supper time. Walking toward the cafeteria he was happy to see other Probies going in the same direction in all their gear, while he was practically naked, wearing only his uniform. It was what separated those in training from those in exploration.

He arrived at the cafeteria in time to catch Kim just entering. "Perfect timing," she said.

"That's me, perfect Bill," he quipped.

They sat together while eating and talked about their upcoming adventure. Both had a basic understanding of what was expected, but neither was totally sure. The anticipation was both exciting and nerve-wracking.

After supper, they swung by the Cave Bear Cave for a quick beer (on Janice's dime) and then parted ways, both wanting to get as much sleep as possible to make up for all the lost sleep of survival training.

Bill received an email the next morning explaining the check-in procedures. He was to be at Bowman Field at least thirty minutes in advance of crossover, which was at 0800 hours, wearing the proper attire and with all the required equipment. Included was the list of equipment he was to bring, most of which had been sitting by his bedroom door since the day before. As his duties involved flying, his duty uniform was a flight suit. This meant including his flight suits in his gear, something he hadn't considered.

Upon crossover, he was to check in at the Field Manager's Office and then report to his assigned crew. His crew, CL-415-Z21 was led by Explorer Mindy Hubert.

The next couple of days were spent relaxing and salmon fishing. Bill also sat down with the counselor and worked out some of the issues still plaguing him from the Caribou incident.

Meri made it back for the weekend, so the two of them spent practically all their time together. They made it a point to enjoy a night out on the town in Milton, where Meri introduced Bill to something other than food and grog—live theater. It was Bill's first time seeing a live performance, and he found it to be quite enjoyable.

Bill spent the afternoon before crossover washing and packing his uniforms into his duffel. As all his gear had been ready since the day of graduation, nothing else needed doing. Matt and Thep were off on survival training, and Jordan was still doing his secondary training, which was, surprisingly enough, as a mechanic. It turned out that Jordan was one of those shade tree mechanics every town seems to sport. He apparently used to make enough money from it that when he went to Stanford he was able to pay his living expenses from his savings and doing mechanical jobs for students and professors on the weekends.

Supper was spent with Meri. The two enjoyed the fine culinary skills of the Sacajawea cooks, before heading to the Cave Bear Cave for a single beer each. Neither wanted to have so much as a hint of a hangover for the upcoming week's adventure.

As Meri headed up her cabin steps after saying goodnight to Bill (in a manner that left him breathless), she turned and said, "Stay safe out there." She then disappeared into the cabin, leaving Bill with a warm feeling.

ZION

Chapter 16

Bill and Kim trudged across the crushed rock airfield. Dressed in their flight suits and light jackets, they practically staggered under the weight of their gear. For the first time since equipment draw, they were lugging their equipment belts, survival vests, backpacks, butt packs, rifles, and PDWs. Both primary and secondary survival kits had to be stashed in the CL-415 before take-off. Despite all the equipment they were encumbered with, their heads were on swivels. Other than Hayek, this would be their first new planet. Unlike Hayek, though, there existed no civilization, other than the rough field lined with support buildings to meet the logistics needs of the ongoing surveys. And large, nasty critters were something to definitely keep an eye out for.

Their arrival earlier in the day had been a rushed affair. Both of them had arrived at the assigned gate at Bowman Field an hour early, laughing when they discovered each had decided to make an early appearance. Upon checking in at the departure terminal, they were told to join a small convoy that was forming up near the gate.

"Let's see, you're on twenty-one. Okay. When you go through, check in with the Field Manager's office, it's a small building just past the gate, and let them know who you're assigned to. They'll get you squared away. Got everything you need?" Kim and Bill nodded.

The two made their way over and met up with the convoy leader.

"Ah, good. Smith and Clark. I was wondering when you two would show up. Glad you made it. Just hop in any truck that can fit you and your gear," he told them, pointing to a string of cargo trucks that were lined up behind several fuel trucks.

They spoke with several drivers until they found a truck with room. They threw their gear in the back, and with rifles slung over their shoulders and holding PDWs in one hand, they climbed into the truck bed, ducking under the canvas cover. Several other Explorers were seated on benches that ran along the sides of the bed. They recognized a few from training and nodded their greetings, and got nods in return. Most were too nervous to talk, just taking it all in.

After what seemed like forever, but was really only an hour and a half, a klaxon sounded. Bill could hear people shouting, "Five minutes to Zion crossover. Five minutes to Zion crossover. Stand ready and start engines."

Starters ground and truck engines began to rumble. soon every truck's engine was idling.

Four minutes later another klaxon sounded, the one-minute warning. Once again, people shouted, "One minute to Zion crossover. One minute to Zion crossover."

The final klaxon sounded, and this time the voices were yelling, "Zion crossover. Zion crossover. Go, go, go!"

Bill felt the truck he was in accelerate and thought *Hot damn! My first survey!* All thoughts of Meri were buried in the excitement.

Soon he could tell they were no longer driving on macadam, the smooth tire rumble and ride replaced with a rougher rumble and ride. Shortly thereafter, the truck came to a stop and the engine shut down.

The driver appeared at the back of the truck and told the seated Explorers it was the end of the line, and they needed to get out and report to their crews so he could unload the truck.

This time the Explorers helped each other out, forming a chain to hand out packs and butt packs. Rifles slung, and PDWs held, Bill and the others exited the truck onto the crushed rock airfield of Zion. Bill saw a sign stating *Welcome To Primary Base, Zion, Courtesy of the Corps of Discovery*.

The temperature was the same as on Hayek, as was the sun's position. It was a cool late October morning. *Just perfect for salmon fishing or rabbit hunting,* Bill thought, spying the small building with a sign stating *Field Manager.* Most of the people headed toward the building, with only a few heading toward buildings further down the field—clearly Explorers who had already been on Zion and were returning from a trip home. Bill could see several other buildings, one with a sign stating it was the mess hall; another was the sanitary facilities. Bill suspected that it was a combination toilet/bathing building.

Bill and Kim had to wait their turn, but soon they were inside the building talking to an admin type, an Asian-looking woman in her mid-thirties. "21's on the ramp getting refueled," she told them. "Head down the runway and you'll find her parked on the left side. Her number is painted on the tail. You can't miss her." She checked something off on her tablet. "Got you checked in so you're good to go. Stay safe out there."

As they exited the small building and began walking down the runway, they noticed that the only aircraft visible were CL-415s and C-123s. Bill surmised that this wasn't a forward enough base for the smaller Caribou and that the Monarch was probably not in use at this late a date in the survey.

Kim spotted Tail Number 21 first. A fuel truck was pulled up next to it with a hose stretching onto the starboard wing, where a man stood holding it. As they approached, they could see a man and a woman sitting in reclining lawn chairs, relaxing and enjoying the warmth of the sun. Sunglasses covered their eyes. Bill could see his reflection in them.

"Hi," Bill said. "We're looking for Mindy Hubert."

"That's me," answered the dark-haired woman, standing up. She looked to be in her mid-thirties.

Bill introduced himself and Kim.

"Great. Glad to have you aboard. Let's get your gear stowed and I'll give you the grand tour."

Mindy introduced the still-seated man, a dark-skinned twenty-something-year-old. "That's Doug Stine. He's the co-pilot. That makes me pilot," she said with a grin. Doug waved but didn't stir beyond that.

The trio entered the plane and Mindy, removing her sunglasses, showed them their workstations, bunks, hanging lockers, and storage lockers. Under each bunk was a drawer for their clothing needs while on a survey.

"We're kinda lucky with these birds. Everyone's got their own bunk, so no hot bunking, and each of you has your own workstation. We've got preliminary data, but they want the coastlines refined, so that'll be our job for the next couple of months. Luckily, we'll be operating in warmer climes. Wouldn't want to spend all winter up at these latitudes."

Mindy then gave them the ten-cent tour, showing them the galley, lavatory, fire extinguishers, and first aid kits.

"You guys know how to stow your gear in these?" she asked, pointing to the crash seats that also served as their workstation seats.

"I think we can figure it out," Kim said.

"Awesome. Well, get settled in, hang your flight suits in the lockers, and then join us outside. Might as well enjoy the weather while we can. We'll check you out on the equipment after lunch. Oh, and keep your rifles with you at all times. When you're in the plane, put your rifles here," she said, pointing to a rack to the left of the door. "Take-off is oh-seven hundred tomorrow."

It didn't take long to stow their gear, as most of the equipment they brought with them was to remain in their bags. Survival packs went into the storage lockers, flight suits in the hanging lockers, and secondary survival kits in the storage space under the crash seat. Bill was surprised at how tight a fit it was. Smaller items went into the drawers under his bunk.

Once done, the two stepped into the glare of the now-bright Zion sunshine. Sunglasses helped.

"Grab a seat," Mindy said, "and let's get acquainted." The two sat, placing their rifles in their laps, pointed in a safe direction.

For the next couple of hours Mindy quizzed them, then she and Stine talked about their experiences and the upcoming survey. Stine had come over from Earth the year before and had been flying as co-pilot with Mindy ever since graduating Survival School. He had attended an aeronautical school, so he had a heavy dose of theory and application. He was from South Florida and attended school in northern Florida. Other than that, he hadn't traveled much until joining the Corps.

Mindy had grown up in Denver, had been in the US Air Force and flown C-130s, but realized that it just wasn't working out for her. Between the wars and politics, she was fed up with Earth, so she managed to wrangle a position in the Corps as a pilot, despite being several years older than the average Probie. That was over five years ago, so she was considered an old hand by now.

Both Mindy and Doug had heard about Bill's Caribou incident. Other than a brief comment, with the follow-up of "I know who I can turn to when the brown fecal material hits the oscillating device," they didn't dwell on it too much. Bill was glad they didn't.

The survey was set to resume in the morning, now that Bill and Kim had arrived. They would be mapping around the Caribbean, which meant a multi-leg flight before they even started.

"Most of the fields we'll be landing at are like this, or worse," Mindy said, waving her arm around the airfield. "Don't expect much in the way of services once we leave here. The field bases are real basic— fuel depots, food stores, pit toilets, and outdoor showers. Some have basic repair shops. We'll be on flight and field rations for the next several months or so until we get leave, except when we happen to kill and cook something. I hope neither of you is a devout vegan?" she asked. Both shook their heads.

Mindy explained that the airfield they were on was the only place they didn't need to have all their survival equipment with them at all times, so to enjoy it while they could.

"Once we get out there, any time we land could be our last. So, don't take chances."

"Any idea on what we can expect out here?" Kim asked.

"Well, it appears we're on a Non-Impact Holocene Planet, which means it looks like this planet never went through the Younger

Dryas, so pretty much anything that existed before the Clovis Impact exists here."

Kim nodded, clearly understanding. Bill knew she had taken a paleoclimatology seminar in graduate school, despite working mainly on a GIS-centered degree.

Bill, on the other hand, was clueless. The University of Washington, while having a great GIS program, didn't really have a physical geography component, other than a single lower level course on basic physical geography. Admitting his ignorance, he asked what the "young dry ass" was and the "clover impact" were.

After recovering from their laughter at his mispronunciations, Mindy explained.

"As you probably know, the Earth went through a number of geologic eras, made up of epochs, and finally, stages or ages. We're currently in the Holocene Epoch, which started about 12,000 years ago, at the end of the Pleistocene Epoch. Some people don't think the Pleistocene ended, though, and consider us to be in an interglacial period, not a new epoch. Anyhow, according to certain experts, around 13,000 years ago a meteor or swarm of meteors impacted the Earth, or air-burst above it, in Canada. Possibly on the Laurentide Ice Sheet. It's called the Clovis Impact because it was first identified at a quarry that the Clovis civilization used to get the rocks to make their tools. By the way, the Clovis site was in New Mexico."

Mindy went on to explain how evidence of the impact was found on and around tools that were on the ground, but not under the tools, all of which had been excavated during archaeological digs in the late 20th and early 21st centuries. "Actually, not all that long ago."

The impact was so severe that it possibly caused fires to rage throughout North America. Another contributing factor was the massive melting of the ice sheet, which flowed into the Atlantic Ocean, cooling and diluting the salt water. This led to a colder, slower ocean circulation between the tropics and the northern latitudes. All of this led to a rapid cooling of the climate for approximately 1,200 years. This not only led to the collapse of the Clovis civilization but other proto-civilizations in Europe and Southwest Asia as well.

"The hypothesis is that the combination of fires, the cooling of the Gulf Stream, and sudden decrease in temperatures led to a mass extinction when most of the megafauna of the Pleistocene disappeared from the scene," Mindy wrapped up. "So, any planet that has megafauna usually didn't experience a Clovis Impact, and we refer to them as Non-Impact Holocene Planets."

"Wait a minute," Bill said. "I've been taught all my life that the megafauna was hunted to extinction by man. And now you're telling me it was a meteor that wiped them out?"

"That's the latest and greatest hypothesis," Mindy replied, shrugging. "All I know is that some planets have megafauna, and some don't, and that's how we differentiate them."

"I guess it makes sense," Bill commented, feeling cheated that he was clueless about this hypothesis.

"Not to sound ungrateful or anything," Kim said, "but what happened to the other two aerial surveyors that we're replacing?"

"Injuries" was the answer. "One got bit by a rattlesnake and the other broke her ankle trying to get to him to help out. Bad luck all around."

"Yikes," Kim said. "Were you on a survey?"

"Actually, no. This happened right over there, last week" Mindy pointed to the back of the aircraft, "before we even began our survey. Keep an eye out for rattlers. They normally won't bother you if you don't bother them, but sometimes you surprise them and they take offense."

As it was now approaching noon, Mindy recommended they eat at the base's mess hall. "Food's better than what we'll be eating for the next couple of weeks," she said, rising from her chair. The others followed suit.

"Now that we've got some replacements, we'll be heading out in the morning," Mindy said as the four walked. "We'll be based out of Carib." It took a couple of seconds to place Carib, but then remembered it was the Hayek name for the island he knew as Cuba.

"Based on the fact that none of you have much experience," she nodded to Stine, "including you, and that our commander broke her ankle and is no longer here, I'm assigned as Survey Commander. That means you do what I say, when I say it, without question. You can ask questions afterward, but not during. Got it?" she asked the three of them. Everyone nodded.

At the mess hall, they joined a rapidly growing line of people at the self-serve aisle. Just like on Hayek, Explorers were expected to serve and clean up after themselves, at least to the point of busing their trays. With the exception of the cutlery and trays, everything was compostable. The food was good, spicy, and filling, as usual. Bill particularly enjoyed the fresh bread slathered with butter. There was nothing quite like the taste and sensation of digging one's teeth into a piping hot hard roll with freshly applied butter just melting in it.

After lunch, the crew headed back to the craft where Mindy showed them the particulars of it and tested their knowledge on the various remote sensing and GIS software and hardware. To access the software, they used their Corps usernames but had to create passwords specific to the craft. The craft even had wi-fi, so one didn't need to be at a workstation to actually access the software. Of course, using the more powerful computers at the workstations was a lot easier and faster than trying to use a tablet while in a crash seat. Satisfied that the two knew their stuff, she proclaimed the survey ready to go. "You won't really have any duties until we arrive in Carib, so enjoy your free time during our flight down. Crap out, read, watch videos, play games, whatever. We might want you to spell us, though, so keep that in mind.

"We sleep in the plane, so be ready to go just after sunrise. I'd like to get as much flying time as possible, so that means an early pre-flight and takeoff. Besides, at barely 330 klicks an hour, it's gonna take us at least fifteen hours of flight time, and that doesn't include refueling stops. I figure we'll get there late Wednesday."

Mindy explained that small airfields were set up every 500 kilometers, giving the Corps a fairly widespread system, but one that wasn't impossible to make from any other field. They would be carrying a spare load of fuel with them to help out at the Carib base. The CL-415 was originally developed to fight fires, so instead of carrying water, they transported bladders of aviation fuel as part of their duties. C-123 Providers did the same thing. For overseas operations, airfields were developed near harbors and bays suitable for port operations, and the fuel was flown in and transferred to ocean-going vessels, usually small tankers. It took a lot of trips, but it was the most effective method developed to date for the rough field conditions the Explorers operated under.

Mindy excused herself to let the field manager know that CL-214-Z21 was ready to go. She told the crew to join her at the mess hall for supper in fifteen minutes and to bring toiletries, as they would be taking the last hot shower they'd get for a while. Leaving as early as possible meant bathing the night before. The three Explorers decided they might as well head over at the same time as Mindy, so they joined her for the short walk after grabbing towels, toiletries, and rifles.

After supper, the crew took showers and then returned to craft. The walk back was Bill's first exposure to a totally untamed wilderness. While he had experienced some of that on Hayek during survival training, this was a totally new experience. With the dark closing down on them, Bill felt exposed. Not only to the elements, as a cool wind had picked up, but also to the wildlife. He could occasionally hear the roar of some feline predator, along with the howl of wolves. He kept his rifle slung in front of him in the ready position, right hand grasping the stock with his finger along the trigger guard. The heft of the rifle felt comforting. And then a pack of coyotes howled close by, and he nearly lost it. Up came the rifle and clamped down went the sphincter. Looking around, he didn't see anything, but it didn't stop him from seeking the source of the canine cacophony. He was glad to see he wasn't the only one reacting—Kim had her rifle up, too. Then he heard Stine laughing.

"Oh, man. You should see you two, just from a couple of 'yotes."

"Yeah, well, we're not used to this stuff," Bill grumbled.

"You will be," Mindy said. "Or you'll be dead. Seriously, though, good reaction. Shows you're on the ball."

Still feeling the adrenaline coursing through him, Bill was a bit shaky boarding the plane. He wondered if he'd ever fall asleep after that.

Soon, though, the crew was settled into their bunks with the craft buttoned up. As the CL-415 wasn't designed for high-altitude operations, it had small portals that could be opened. Some of these were left slightly open—not enough for anything dangerous to enter, but sufficient to keep the interior cool and dehumidified. It also helped with any residual fumes in the fuel bladders under the cabin of the fuselage.

Bill awoke to the smell of brewing coffee. Rolling over and sliding aside the curtain from his bunk, he saw Mindy standing before a brewing pot in the tiny galley, cup in hand. *She looks like a lioness about to leap,* he sleepily thought. He looked at his chronograph; it was barely six o'clock. *Another hour before sunrise, but I guess I better get out of the sack.*

Bill had worn boxers and a T-shirt to bed, so when he sat up, he reached for his flight suit, which he had put on a small hook near the foot of the bunk. After getting his uniform on he dug a pair of socks out of the small drawer under his bunk. The drawer included socks, underwear, and his toiletries. Everything else was stashed in his primary survival kit. His tablet, which was in a small nook inside his bunk, went into the cargo pocket on his flight suit leg. Once his boots were on he was ready to go. It was warm enough in the cabin he didn't need his jacket, but he suspected he would need it once he stepped outside.

Raising an eyebrow in question, Mindy pointed to a small cupboard to the left of the coffee machine. Bill opened it and discovered three mugs. Grabbing one, he filled it and took a sip, nodding his thanks to the Survey Commander. He took a seat at the small table, which was about what one would see in a small camper, set between two lightly padded benches. The others stirred, and soon, all four were seated, sipping coffee.

Mindy said they'd get some breakfast first, and if anyone needed to visit the toilet it would be a good time to do so. "Partner up at all times," she cautioned. "You never know what nasty critter is out there looking for a free meal." After breakfast would come the pre-flight, then wheels up at first light, or as close to it as possible.

After coffee, rifles in hand, they headed to the mess hall, being sure to keep their heads on swivels for any sign of danger. Breakfast was like supper, serve yourself. Also like supper, there wasn't much variety, but plenty of food and the four ate well.

All four decided a trip to the toilet was in order. After all, it'd be a while before they saw another civilized toilet. And the one in the 415, while functional, wasn't as spacious.

On their way back to the plane Mindy made one more quick stop in the Field Operations building, asking the others to wait for her. Bill could feel the cold air tickle his nostrils. His breath condensed as he released it, which made him smile a bit. *Yep, fall is definitely here.*

Mindy came out in just a couple of minutes and announced, "We're set to go. Let's get back to the bird and get her in the air." She was carrying a cloth sack with the word *MAIL* stenciled across it. Seeing Bill and Kim eyeing it, she explained that every flight carried mail. "Mail's one of those important morale things. Better than coffee and beer. So, the Corps makes sure it gets delivered as soon as possible. We'll drop sacks off at every base en route, and it'll get distributed to the ground crews from there."

By the time they made it back to the plane the morning twilight was fading into sunrise. They could see the edge of the sun peeking up over the hills to their east as they pre-flighted the bird. Bill and Kim followed Mindy and Doug as they did the actual pre-flight. Mindy had wanted them with her so that all could take a hand and verify everything was okay. Bill got to remove the chocks under one set of wheels while Kim got the other.

Shortly after that Bill and Kim were seated in their crash seats while the two pilots took their seats and got things going. Within minutes both turboprop engines were roaring and the propellers were spinning. Everyone was wearing their headphones, so Bill heard Mindy call in for permission to take off. The tower granted it, providing her with the time, altimeter reading, and winds. Mindy gunned the engines and the big seaplane began moving. Soon it was on the threshold of the runway, and Mindy and Doug gave it more power. It began to roll down the runway gaining speed until suddenly it was airborne.

Looking out the port window, Bill could see land rapidly falling away as Mindy took the plane higher. The land looked similar to Hayek and Earth, with the notable exception of no signs of civilization. Anywhere.

Mindy announced, "Welcome aboard flight Zombie Two-One, bound for ports of call as yet unidentified. Please keep your seatbelts fastened until such time as the smoking lamp is lit. As this is a non-smoking flight, there is no smoking lamp, so don't wait for it to be lit." Bill chuckled.

"Our destination today is points southeast. We'll be landing in 1,000 kilometers for our first refueling stop at that garden spot of the world we know as the Great Salt Lake. And yes, it stinks as much here as it does on Earth. As you look out your windows you'll be able to see the Great Basin and Range system, made up mainly of desert, which is the main reason we'll be flying over it, so we don't have to drive through it. That is all."

Bill and Kim watched the terrain pass under them, both still amazed at the lack of signs of civilization. There were no roads or interstate highways, no dams with reservoirs behind them, and most obviously missing were the crop circles that indicated the center pivot irrigation systems so prevalent throughout the western United States. While it wasn't something he had really noticed on Hayek, mostly because he was focused on his training, he had still been aware of the obvious signs of agriculture there. Here, it was in-your-face obvious that there was no human civilization around.

Bill wondered what the forward bases would be like.

Chapter 17

After an hour of gawking Bill lost interest in the ground below, mostly due to the monotony. Other than basins and ranges, it pretty much all looked the same. He retrieved his tablet and decided to see if he could pull up the craft's wi-fi and tie into the GIS system.

Once he was in, he decided to find out where all the field bases were. One of the datasets was labeled *Secondary Fields,* so he pulled that one up first. Little dots appeared on the map of Ti'ichem. They seemed to radiate out from the airfield they had taken off from. On the west coast, there was a base in the San Francisco Bay, another one at the tip of the Gulf of Baja, where the Colorado River ran into it, and another in the islands that he knew of as the Alaska Panhandle. A final field was in one of the bays in south-central Alaska. Bill wasn't too sure, but he thought it might be Prince William Sound.

Looking to the east, he could see a string of bases scattered across the continent. There was currently only one in the Caribbean. *Boy, we'll really be out on the edge,* he thought.

He then decided to access some of the field reports to see what type of fauna he could expect. For the next couple of hours, he learned all he could about the fauna of Zion, along with some other items of interest. One of these, and most directly related to his duties, was that due to the massive amount of anthropogenic impact to the landscape on Earth, the shorelines of Zion were considerably different. While the overall picture remained the same, the devil was in the details: in this case, the shorelines, rivers, and other smaller features that can have a big impact.

Reading these reports took up several more hours, but by then Bill had run out of material to learn from. Looking out his window, he could see that the sun was fairly high in the sky; it was almost noon. Since Mindy and Doug were flying, he asked on the intercom, "I'm cooking lunch. Who's hungry?"

"Me," everyone replied.

"Flight rats for all," he declared, then took off intercom headset and made his way back to the galley. Digging into one of the cupboards, he pulled out four flight rations. Each ration contained a pre-made entree and a dessert. The flight rations differed from field rations in their variety, contents, and weight. The Corps actually had three types of rations. Flight rations were, obviously, for use in airplanes with amenities such as microwaves. While edible cold, they were better warmed, and the packaging was designed to allow for microwaving. These came in sealed dishes and included an accessory packet containing coffee or tea, sugar, and a non-dairy creamer. As flight crews could carry condiments and spices, none were provided. Nor were any utensils. Flight rations were broken down into breakfast and lunch/supper meals. Most were vegetarian, but some had fish or meat.

Field rations were more like the US Army's HDRs, Humanitarian Daily Rations, with the meals and some sundries in vacuum-packed retort pouches rather than cans. There were some differences between the Corps field rats, as they were called, and HDRs. For example, spoons weren't included, because each Explorer was supposed to already have a spork on them, and the variety of desserts was limited, with more effort spent on providing nutrition than variety and taste. There was no hard candy, only a fruit roll. A favorite of the Explorers was a rather large chocolate-covered coconut bar. Each field rat also came with a small chocolate bar, specifically designed for the tropics, so it wouldn't melt in the tropical heat (or even in one's mouth), crackers, and peanut butter. Bill was originally surprised by that but then figured that it made sense since the founders were originally Americans. An accessory packet similar to the flight rations was included. A major difference between the field rations and other rations was that it was the only ration that had field toilet paper included in the accessory packet.

The final ration type was the Emergency Ration, or E-rat. E-rats were more like the Safety of Life at Sea (SOLAS) rations that were kept in lifeboats on ocean-going vessels on Earth. Dense, nutrient-rich, and they allowed the user to eat them without much water consumption, but they didn't have much variety and were used only as a last resort—typically even after hunting, fishing, or trapping game and foraging for nuts and berries when trekking. No accessories came with the E-rats, just the block of dense, nutritional food.

As each meal was done heating, Bill took it to one of the crew members. First to be served, of course, was the Survey Commander and Pilot, Mindy. Doug had to wait until Mindy was done eating before he could take the time to eat. Mindy didn't want both pilots stuffing their faces in the event something bad happened to the plane. Bill also started another pot of coffee while heating the rations.

Kim thanked him and sat at the small dining table while Bill finished heating his lunch, then joined her.

Soon Mindy announced she was done, so Bill interrupted his meal to heat up Doug's. By this time the coffee was ready, so he grabbed some of the insulated spill-proof mugs and poured cups all around.

The flight continued for several hours, passing over mountain ranges and playas, until finally the Great Salt Lake, or Lake Timpanogos as it was known on Hayek, and on Zion, according to the maps Bill had looked at earlier, was below them. Mindy told the crew they would be landing shortly and to secure any loose objects and get buckled in. Bill and Kim made sure the detritus from the lunches was put away and then got into their crash seats and buckled up.

Mindy began speaking to the tower, getting cleared for landing and being provided all the necessary atmospheric information.

Bill was thinking that, since they were flying in a seaplane, they would land on the lake. He was surprised when he heard the sound of the wheels going down. They landed on a short gravel field near one of the several rivers feeding into the endorheic lake. As soon as they were down and slowing, the stench of the lake assaulted his nose.

"Yep, welcome to the world's stinkiest lake," Stine announced from the co-pilot's seat. Bill had experienced the stench before on a trip through Salt Lake City to Moab during one of his spring breaks. It still wasn't pleasant.

The seaplane taxied up to a small building with a sign above the door declaring it to be *Base Operations*. Mindy shut the engines down, and then the only sounds Bill could hear were the wind on the fuselage, the ticking of the cooling engines, and the water flowing in the creek.

"All out for a break," Mindy announced, unbuckling and leading the exit from the craft. "Be sure you've got your belt and rifle with you." She had struggled into her belt during the short walk from her pilot's seat to the exit. Bill noticed that it seemed second nature for her to grab her rifle from the rack attached near the exit. She opened the door, and before stepping out, charged the rifle and, holding it ready, looked around the airfield. It was obvious she wasn't looking just to take in the scenery. After a short pause, she jumped the short distance from the plane to the ground and waited for the others to catch up, all the while looking around with her head on a swivel.

Bill decided then and there that stuff was serious, and he better act like it. Slinging his belt on and buckling it, he headed for the door, trailing behind Doug and Kim. Doug had grabbed the mail sack and was carrying it in one hand while he carried his rifle in another. Grabbing his rifle from the rack, Bill ran the bolt back and forth, charging the rifle. Now he was ready.

When he hopped out of the plane onto the gravel apron he could see low trees near the airfield and the Wasatch Mountains to his east. Lake Timpanogos was visible to his west. He figured he was standing near where Salt Lake City was situated on Earth. Looking down the runway, he could see a small control tower, and near the base operations were several other small buildings and a hangar. Mindy and Doug were already performing their post-flight check while Kim kept watch, so he joined Kim in serving as the crew's backup. Soon the two were finished with their inspection and Mindy indicated that they should head to the base operations building.

Bill made sure to stay with the others, all the while spinning his head like a top taking it all in, while simultaneously watching for any threats. He kept the buddy concept firmly entrenched in the fore of his brain, sticking close to Kim.

A couple of men in their late twenties were coming toward the plane from the hangar and met the crew of Z21, rifles slung over their shoulders. Bill took that to mean it was a safe sign. The two were apparently mechanics and had a brief chat with Mindy to ensure all was well with their bird. Mindy let them know everything was running smooth, but the fuel and other onboard items were for the base on Carib, so not to touch anything. She also requested that they top off the tanks for the next leg. They agreed and left to get a fuel truck.

Base Operations was a small but fairly open building, about the size of a small rambler. Inside were the operations center with a large map on the wall, communications, and a combination mess/recreation hall. A basic kitchen was in the back. It was apparent that the base didn't have a large contingent, based on the amenities.

Two women, one black and one white, were sitting at one of the communications desks. One stood up and came to greet them. She greeted Mindy warmly: "Hey Mind, how's the wind?" in a strong New York accent.

"Fair as always," Mindy replied with a smile. She introduced the crew quickly. The woman's name was Roseanne Williams, and she was the area commander, in charge of all the ground survey crews in the area, along with all personnel involved in supporting the crews from her base.

Mindy asked Doug to open the mail sack, then reached in and pulled out several stacks rubber-banded together. Going through them she found the stack she was interested in and handed them to Williams.

"Mail call!" she announced with a grin.

Williams thanked her and set the packet down on a small table. "So, how long you here for?"

"Not long. Just long enough to fuel up, stretch our legs, and then hit the air again," Mindy replied. "Got anything you want me to carry? I'm heading to Carib."

Williams shook her head. "If you were heading back to the gate…"

Mindy shrugged.

Out the window, Bill could see the two mechanics fueling the aircraft. After they finished, the crew boarded and got settled in. They were soon back in the air, heading for the next stop along the journey to the Caribbean. *Don't think there'll be any boat drinks when we arrive*, Bill thought as they reached cruising altitude.

Chapter 18

The next leg of the flight brought them onto the Edwards Plateau of Texas. As they came in for a landing Bill could see the flat land stretch out seemingly forever. The base they landed at was rather spartan, similar to the previous base: a base operations building, a small control tower, a small aircraft hangar, and some limited living and storage buildings.

The sun was low on the horizon when they finally disembarked and made their way to the operations building. Nobody needed to remind anyone else about keeping rifles handy; it was becoming natural to grab one on the way out of the plane.

Once again, Mindy knew the area commander, and handed him the mail stack and requested refueling. She was offered sleeping quarters, but declined them, stating she'd rather keep the crew together on her bird. However, she did ask about showers and supper. Showers were available behind the operations building and supper would be served shortly, with plenty of food for all. The crew gathered their toiletries and towels and went into the showers, which consisted of a simple walled structure with wooden floors and solar-heated water in long black tubes attached to shower heads. As the water supply wasn't too voluminous, showers were kept short, with a simple rinse, lather, and rinse operation. Bill was beginning to gain a better, more personal understanding of what field conditions were like.

Supper was a hearty stew of imported vegetables, local herbs, and local elk venison, along with freshly baked rolls. "If we were flying up north we'd probably be having bison stew," Doug told them.

After supper, the crew returned to their craft and spent the night. The next morning they took off early for the leg to the Mississippi River, where they stopped at the base for lunch, to drop off mail, and to get refueled for the next-to-last leg.

By late afternoon they were approaching the base on the west coast of the Florida peninsula, just inside Tampa Bay. By the time they landed and opened the door, the cool air had fled the plane and was replaced with the muggy heat of a south Florida fall day. The heat and humidity reminded Bill of the sweltering week spent in survival training at Yucatan Base. *Better get used to it,* he thought. *Looks like we'll be in these climes for a while.*

A C-123 was parked next to them, with Explorers unloading material. A fuel bladder was on the ground with a hose running from the fuselage of the plane to it. Bill guessed that the bladder was being replenished by spare fuel in the hold of the plane.

After the post-flight inspection and request for refueling, Mindy again led the crew to the base operations building to see about a shower and food. This time, instead of stew, they had grilled fish and tropical fruits to go with the imported vegetables. The grouper was quite tasty, and Bill enjoyed every morsel. There was another white meat he was given, which he at first thought it was chicken. He learned shortly after tasting it that the meat was actually alligator.

The crew from Z21 was seated with the ground crew. The talk around the table that evening centered on a ground crew's incident with the alligator that was now part of their supper. The Survey Commander, Marcos, a young man of Filipino heritage, explained to them how the alligator had struck out of the bushes and grabbed the Explorer by one leg. Due to the closeness of the crew, and the overwhelming firepower, they were able to unload on the reptile, killing it before it managed to drag the Explorer all the way into the nearby swamp. The wounded man was currently in the base medical clinic stitched up and drugged out, awaiting a flight back to Hayek in the morning. "Looks like we'll be on a mini-vacation until his replacement arrives."

Bill had noticed that the majority of the Explorers in the base were of Southeast Asian, central African, or Central American heritage, and he asked about that.

"That's because we're actually more adapted to these tropical climates than you white," the Survey Commander said, laughing. "Think of it, thousands of years of evolution and acclimatization have left us more suitable for warm climates, while you'd do better in a cold climate. Just a factor of evolution."

Bill wasn't sure whether to believe him or not but decided to not pursue that line of questioning anymore.

Seeing the expression on Bill's face, Marcos broke out in laughter. "Sorry, man, but you had it coming." He explained how it was true that most of them were more suited to the tropics, but that was more a matter of upbringing that evolution. "Heck, we've got white guys that grew up in Florida and Louisiana on our teams. They're just as used to the heat and humidity as me."

After supper, the crew of Z21 made their way back to the plane. Bill was glad there would be some ventilation there, but he was starting to worry about some of the local fauna. The thought of being an hors d'oeuvre for an alligator wasn't his idea of a good time. He was wondering how to bring this up to the crew when Kim did. She had apparently been thinking along the same line.

"Only two things we really need to worry about buttoned up but with windows open here," Mindy said, "skeeters and snakes. And we've got screens, so neither will really be an issue." Coming from an experienced survey veteran like Mindy, Bill was happy to hear that.

Once in their bunks, the two pilots were out first; their job of flying the plane had been the most taxing, definitely more so than sightseeing or reading. Bill eventually turned off his tablet and went to sleep. Kim's light was still on, shining through the cracks of her bunk curtain when Bill finally closed his eyes.

As dawn broke, the crew arose, made coffee, and used the

lavatory at the base operations building. Breakfast was in the mess hall again, but without the alligator.

While they were eating they could hear a plane taking off, the C-123. Shortly after that, the ground crew from supper the night before came in, grabbed trays of food, and joined the crew of Z21. Marcos explained that the 123 was taking their wounded compatriot back to Primary Base to be evacuated to Hayek, where he'd wind up in the trauma center on Sacajawea Base. "We think he'll be able to keep his leg, but we'll know more when they finish with him," Marcos said before starting into his own breakfast.

After breakfast, Mindy thanked the area commander for the hospitality, performed the pre-flight inspection with the entire crew, and then loaded them up for the final leg to Carib.

Once they got to altitude, the temperature dropped enough to feel comfortable. While the C-415 could be pressurized, it generally wasn't for the flights that it was engaged in after crossing the Rocky Mountains. The landscape below them was scattered shrubs and everglades, extending as far as the eye could see. Soon they were approaching the southeast tip of the Florida peninsula and began another over-water flight. This meant putting on inflatable life preservers, which the crew did. As with most things in the Corps, better safe than sorry.

Three hours after taking off Mindy came over the intercom. "Land ho," she announced. "Mountains on the starboard side." Bill and Kim went to that side of the plane and looked out the portals to see the Escambray Mountains of Carib poking up from the sea. The island slid by parallel to their flight, and then they approached it on an angle. Bill could see how verdant it was. As they flew over the coastline he saw coral in the clear waters, and white, unpolluted sandy beaches.

"We should arrive at Carib Base in the next half hour or so," Mindy announced. "We'll be crossing the Sierra Maestras shortly. They're pretty high, so we'll be going up a bit. And I'm sure we'll encounter some turbulence, so grab a seat and buckle up."

Sure enough, as they crossed the mountains the plane bucked

and dipped, but nothing too violently. Soon they were over the mountains and approaching a bay that faced south into the Caribbean Sea.

Mindy got on the radio and informed Carib Base they were on approach and requested landing instructions. As usual, they were first in line to land. As a matter of fact (as had happened the entire time they had been flying since Primary Base) they were the only flight in line. Soon they were on the ground and taxiing to the lone hangar. "Welcome home, boys and girls," Mindy announced. "This'll be our home for the next couple of months, so let's make a good impression when we get in there. Don't want to piss off the locals."

As soon as the engines were shut down and they were exiting the craft, several Explorers came over to greet them. One was the area commander, a short man of obvious Asian heritage. "Mindy, you old goat. What they doing letting you off the reservation?" he yelled in greeting. The voice was booming and his grin was infectious. He gave Mindy a vigorous hug, pounding her on the back with his hands while she did the same to him.

"Cheng, you crusty old bastard," she replied. "Ain't you been killed yet?"

Releasing each other, Mindy introduced Cheng to her crew. Bill learned that Dave Cheng was a former US Marine ("once a Marine, always a Marine, except when you're an Explorer, and even then..."), of Hmong heritage from Sacramento, California.

"What'd you bring me?" he asked Mindy.

"All sorts of goodies," she said. "Your wi-fi up and running?" she asked.

"Yep."

She grabbed her tablet from her cargo pocket, activated it, and asked Cheng where to send the manifest.

Once he got it, Cheng looked at it on his own tablet. Mindy took advantage of the time to do the post-flight inspection. As she was wrapping it up, Cheng said, "Looks good. Let's unload after lunch."

Cheng pointed out the various building. Along with the

ubiquitous base operations building which housed planning, communications, recreation, and the mess hall, there were several residential cabins, one per crew, along with the shower facilities, latrines containing composting toilets, the hangar, and a supply depot. One small building was designated as the medical clinic, with a red cross painted on it. Bill could even see a small garden that was started, so the Explorers could have something other than frozen, canned, or dehydrated vegetables.

"We're too far out to rate a real doctor, but we've got a crackerjack Physician's Assistant," Cheng told the group, nodding to a light-skinned black woman in her early thirties. "Betsy's been a PA since Christ was a corporal and cut her teeth in Iraq." Betsy had been in a real shooting war. Bill realized; she must know her stuff and be able to operate under pressure. Betsy introduced herself as Betsy Finley.

As the group approached the operations building, Bill gave up any hope of escaping the heat and humidity of Carib when he saw that the building didn't have full walls. Rather, the bottom half of the walls were planked wood while the top half was screened. Obviously, there'd be no air conditioning. Fortunately, there were solar panels erected on roofs and tracking platforms, so Bill was hopeful he'd be able to use a fan to sleep.

"Welcome to the Ops Shack," Cheng said as he opened the door and stepped into the building.

Fan's had in fact been installed in the ceiling, keeping air flowing so it was tolerable. "Kitchen's out back, to keep the heat down in here," Cheng told them.

Looking around, Bill saw several maps, one of the island of Carib, another of several other islands, and an overall map of the Caribbean. Cheng saw Bill looking at them and said, "That's why you're here. Those maps are from the initial survey, so they leave a lot to be desired.

"Rack your rifles and gather 'round, and I'll explain the current situation and what we hope to accomplish over the next couple of months," Cheng announced, stepping toward the small-scale map showing all of the Caribbean after putting his rifle in the rack by the door. The others followed suit and were soon gathered around Cheng. Other than the one indicating the base, there were no other pins on the map.

"Right now, we're it on the island. Matter of fact, we're it in the entire area south or east of Florida." Looking toward Mindy he said, "The first thing I want your crew doing is mapping the shoreline around this island, then I want some DTMs of the island so we can make some topo maps for the ground crews who'll be arriving shortly." On the word DTMs, which he pronounced Dee Tee Ems, he looked at Bill and Kim. Both nodded, understanding that he wanted them to develop digital terrain models.

"We want both digital and paper formats. We've got the plotter here," he gestured to the large-format printer near a computer workstation, "so that shouldn't be a problem.

"The plan right now is to investigate the larger islands first, and then the smaller ones. If there's anyone there, we should be able to find them, but I'm pretty sure this is a sanitary planet. As you know, Parallel wants to open the planet to settlement as soon as possible, so we need to get crackin'.

"First you do the coastal surveys, then the inland ones. While you're doing those the first couple of ground crews are gonna be arriving and getting acclimated. We're also bringing in a couple of boats to help out, particularly on transport issues between islands."

Cheng pointed out the building toward the bay, only a hundred meters from the airfield, and said, "Now that the field's in, and all support structures, the engineering crew is down there putting in the dock. I expect they'll be done in a couple of days. Man, those guys are like freakin' beavers when it comes to building," he said, shaking his head.

"That's pretty much it. Get settled in today and I'll want you up mapping tomorrow. Any questions?"

Kim asked the same thing that Bill was wondering. "How are

they going to get boats down here? Aren't they too big for the planes?"

Cheng smiled. "Yeah, if they came in as boats. All of our equipment is pretty modular, so they'll fly them down in a couple of Providers, and the crews will assemble them here. Lots easier to handle that way, too. Expect things to start getting lively in the next week or so, once you've got the island mapped."

Cheng went on to explain to Bill and Kim exactly how a base developed out of the wilderness. The first step was to airdrop a construction crew some basic runway-building equipment, such as bulldozers, steamrollers, graders, and steel planking. Once a rough field was built, Caribous could fly in with more equipment and material to construct a field big enough for the Providers and CL-415s. At that point, it was a base and pretty much everything else was flown in, including the smaller boats that could be used for survey and logistics work. Larger vessels, such as tankers, could also be brought in, piece by piece, but it took many more flights. The two new Explorers remembered some of this from orientation day, but Cheng's fleshing it out cleared up many questions.

"Follow me," Cheng said, plucking his rifle from the rack and heading out the door. The rest followed like little ducklings, grabbing rifles as they went.

Cheng showed them to their quarters, which was another small half-screened building similar to the operations building. Cheng pointed out some of the features as they approached. These included solar panels and a rainwater collection system. Inside, it was set up with four hammocks, a small table with four folding chairs, and four canvas 'easy' chairs. The easy chairs were simply folding camp chairs with armrests and a high back. Two of them had rockers. Shelving ran around the perimeter of the building, obviously for use as 'dressers' and 'drawers'. The only electrical items were small fans above each hammock, adjustable LED lights on the support poles at one end of each hammock, and the fan and lights over the table and chairs. There was one outlet per hammock. Other than that, there was nothing. *Pretty spartan,* looking around. It was slightly cooler than the outdoors since the sun wasn't beating down on them.

"Home, sweet home," muttered Stine. He immediately claimed a hammock furthest from the door, and the rest followed suit. Kim and Bill both wound up next to the door.

"You're free for the rest of the day, so get settled in and I'll see you at supper," Cheng said, then left.

"Now that we've all chosen our sleeping arrangements, let's get our gear moved," Mindy said. "Leave your packs and secondary survival kits on the plane, but bring your uniforms, and keep your belts and rifles handy."

Being that they were at the tip of the exploration spear, nobody really knew what type of fauna existed in this timeline. According to Mindy, only a couple of timelines actually had any dangerous fauna on the islands of the Caribbean, or just about on any islands. "It's usually on the continents you'll find the big nasties. Here, it's just bugs and sometimes snakes. Hence the screens and plank walls."

Supper was grilled fish, along with rice and vegetables. Bill learned from one of the logistics crew, an Italian named Maria, that Bill's plane had brought in the frozen vegetable. "We haven't started getting regular supply yet, so we're pretty limited on what we've got on hand," she explained.

One of the many things that Z21 had carried in its hold was the daily alcohol rations for the base. Bill was surprised at that, never having heard about the Corps dispensing alcohol to Explorers, particularly in the field. Maria explained that it was a long-standing practice, actually taken from early US and British Navy traditions. Each Explorer was allowed one alcoholic drink in the evening while at a base. Since liquor had more bang for the buck, and because everything had to be flown in, the drink of choice was either whiskey or vodka. If one wanted, there was concentrated beer, but Bill wasn't sure how that would taste mixed with well or rainwater, so he decided on whiskey.

As the group sat and talked after supper, Bill took small sips from his glass, making it last. He wasn't much of a whiskey drinker, so it took him a while to make it through his ration. This was mainly because of the burning sensation it caused going down his throat, along with the sinus-clearing it induced. After an evening of getting to know others from the base, the crew of Z21 made their way back to their quarters and settled in for the night. The next day would begin the first of many journeys.

Chapter 19

The next day, Bill lay in his hammock listening to the early morning sounds. Along with Doug's snoring, he could hear a number of birds greeting the false dawn. He was about to jump out of his hammock and head to the latrine when he remembered the buddy rule. Looking around the room, he saw that Mindy was awake, so he got up and gestured toward the latrines. She got the idea, nodded, and climbed out of her hammock.

The two slipped into their flight suits and boots, put their belts on, grabbed their rifles, and headed out. After ablutions, it was off to the ops shack. Breakfast wasn't ready, but coffee was, so the two indulged themselves as they waited for the sun to finally rise. They were soon joined by Kim and Doug, neither of whom looked wide awake or rarin' to go. Doug barely grunted as he sipped his coffee, but became more animated as the cup was drained.

Mindy pulled out a map of Carib from the initial survey and explained that the day's flight would take them along the southern coast of Carib. "From Gitmo to the Gulf of Ana Maria," she said, running her finger from their location to a gulf several hundred kilometers to the west. It was then that Bill realized where they were—Guantanamo Bay! On Earth, this was still a US Navy Base on Raul Castro's Communist Cuba. Here, it was just another protected bay.

"I want you two to ensure we image and map every square meter along the coast. We'll be flying 1,000 meters AGL at 260 klicks, so you should be able to easily cover a three-klick-wide swath on each leg. The first leg out will be just along the shoreline, and the first return leg will be two klicks out, so be sure you cover everything and use the bathymetric system to get under the water. The second leg out and back will also be offshore. We want to make sure we get all the shoals and islands. The maritime units are gonna want that stuff, and it needs to be accurate."

Bill calculated that flying 1,000 meters above ground level, he should easily be able to capture a swath between three and four kilometers wide.

"When we make a turn to start the next leg, start converting the captured LiDAR data into DTMs. You can convert the final leg once we land. No need to develop the topo maps, that's what the guys at base'll do. Your job is to gather the data and do the basics."

Both aerial survey specialists nodded. Bill didn't have a lot of experience running the LiDAR (Light Detection and Ranging) equipment, but he had the basic knowledge, and converting LiDAR data into digital terrain models was an easy process for him. The imagery Mindy referred to was really nothing more than advanced overhead digital photography, where one had to line up the images in the proper order to show a complete overlay of the land.

"Great. Let's eat and get this show on the road," Mindy said, as the smell of cooking food wafted into their noses.

After breakfast, Mindy filed her flight plan with operations, and the four made their way out to the plane. After a quick pre-flight inspection, she contacted the tower and was given take-off permission. "First in line, again," she drawled over the intercom, sounding very much like a female Forrest Gump. The sun had broached the horizon less than an hour before, but the temperature was already climbing when the plane rose into the cooler air.

Once airborne, Mindy circled until Kim and Bill announced they were ready and recording. At this point, Mindy headed south to the coast, then turned west, following the coastline.

As with all long flights, this one soon became monotonous, despite all the work everyone was doing. Looking out one side, Bill saw a green island with uninterrupted vegetation extending as far as one could see. To the other side was an empty sea. He watched his displays, with brief interruptions for lavatory breaks, coffee runs for him and the crew, and to look out the windows. He noticed that they had turned north and then northeast, so he assumed they were entering the Gulf of Guacanayabo, one of the largest gulfs on the southern side of the island.

Eventually, they reached the Gulf of Ana Maria and Mindy announced the turning maneuver. The second leg was as exciting as the first, which means that it was endless wilderness with endless seas and the droning of the engines through the fuselage.

Soon it was lunchtime, and Kim offered to get everyone's feed on. As somebody was needed to man the LiDAR equipment and at least one person was required to fly the plane at all times, the crew ate in shifts. Bill ate with Doug, who had become more animated as the day wore on. It was obvious that mornings didn't agree with him.

Finally, they reached the third and final turn. After the maneuver, Bill could hear Mindy talking on the radio. "Carib Base, this is Flight Zulu 21, RTB. You copy?"

"Roger that Zulu 21, RTB at twelve twenty-seven hours. Advise when ten mikes out, over."

"Roger Base. Will advise when ten mikes out. Zulu 21 out," Mindy replied, affirming that she would notify them when she was ten minutes out from the field.

A bit over two hours later, Mindy again got on the radio to Carib Base. They were given the field conditions and cleared for first to land on the lone runway. "Again," Mindy drawled on hearing the flight order. The crew got another chuckle of out that.

Once on the ground, the two pilots exited to complete their post-flight inspection while Bill and Kim continued converting the third leg's LiDAR data to DTMs. The fourth leg's data was sent to the server in the operations building where either Kim or Bill would run the conversion. The two had decided to take turns daily; that way one of them could at least get part of the afternoon off. Kim had volunteered for the first day's run, so once the data transfer was complete she and Bill headed over to the ops shack, maintaining the buddy system, with rifles in hand and heads on swivels.

Inside, Kim got to work. Cheng asked Bill how the survey went. They were soon joined by Mindy and Doug, both of whom had changed out of their flight suits to the standard Explorer uniform, having showered after shutting out their flight plan. "No sense waiting until the last minute," Mindy said. Bill figured he would wait until Kim was done before taking his. The showers, like the latrines, were co-ed, but each stall had its own privacy curtain, so it wasn't as if they were showering together like the ground survey crews had to do in the boonies.

After Kim was done converting the data, she and Bill made their way back to the crew quarters, which Mindy had dubbed "The Swamp," to get their toiletries. After bathing, hanging towels to dry, and placing soiled clothing in mesh laundry bags, the two headed back to the ops shack for some downtime. Both had also traded flights suits for regular uniforms. Bill figured he would do laundry in a couple of days before he used his final flight suit.

Kim elected to take the time before supper to write letters, using stationery provided by the Corps. Bill had wondered why and then decided it was probably because it was less expensive than using flash drives. Since there was no internet, only a local intranet, email wasn't an option. Bill wrote a brief note to Meri describing the trip, the base, and his first survey. All in all, exciting, yet dull at the same time. It reminded Bill of his dad's comments about war being 99 percent boredom and one percent sheer terror.

After writing the letter and placing it in an envelope, he was stumped as to how to get it to Meri, so he asked Mindy.

"If you know her address, put that on the envelope, and just write the word 'SC Free' in the place where a stamp goes."

"'SC Free'?"

"Yeah, 'Survey Crew Free.' It means you're on a survey, so all postage is free for you."

"What if I don't know where to send it?"

"Address it to her last known posting. Somebody'll know where to send it on to. It may take a while, but it'll get there. Usually, most mail is delivered within two to three weeks, which ain't bad considering how spread out we are."

Bill addressed the envelope to Meri at her cabin on Sacajawea Base and placed it in the mailbox on the wall between the door and the gun rack.

By this time it was approaching supper, so he joined the crews as they formed a line to serve themselves from the buffet-style service.

Mindy waved him over to where she was sitting. Bill joined her and Mindy introduced him to a couple of Explorers, one a logistics engineer and the other a logistics supply specialist.

Bill learned there were only two supply personnel on base, along with the two mechanics he had met the day before, and eight engineers. There was also the kitchen staff, which consisted of the cook and an assistant cook, who was responsible for most of the cleanup details. Along with the crew of Z21 and the operations personnel (all two of them), that was it for base personnel.

Over supper, Bill learned that all the engineers were cross-trained in various civil engineering tasks, including light and heavy equipment operations. "We're sorta like Navy SeeBees," the engineer said, referring the US Navy Construction Battalions. "We do it all."

As the meal wrapped up, Cheng stood up and tapped his plastic drinking glass with his knife. Once the room quieted, Cheng said, "Good. Looks like the entire base is here. Kim Smith and Bill Clark, please rise."

The two did so, with befuddled looks on their faces.

"Explorers from Carib Base, let's give a round of applause for these two. They've just completed their first actual survey," Cheng announced, leading the ensuing applause.

Kim turned a bright shade of red, enhancing her brunette hair, while Bill felt the heat of a flush building under his tan. The room erupted in hooting and clapping.

Cheng gave each of them a small sky-blue uniform ribbon: the Survey Medal ribbon. "Just in case anything happens to you before you get back to Hayek, I wanted to make sure these were awarded. Put them on when you get back; it'll impress the guys and girls," he said with a grin.

"That is all," Cheng formally announced to the room, shooing the two newly bemedaled Explorers back to their tables.

That evening Bill had another whiskey for his daily ration, or 'tot' as he was learning to call it, then he turned in with the crew.

The days followed a similar pattern. The crew would arise before dawn and be in the air within an hour after sunrise, if not earlier. The first several days were spent mapping the southern coast of Carib, including all the archipelago chains that extended along it. As the mapping progressed further from base, the flights became longer and the mapping covered less ground.

The entire crew, base and survey, were finally given a day off after their sixth day of mapping. The crew all did laundry, hanging damp clothing all over "the Swamp." Bill found out that there was a cribbage board in the recreational portion of the ops shack, so he enticed Doug into a game, and promptly got skunked.

A resupply plane was expected. Nobody wanted to miss that, just in case there was mail or something special on board. Of course, meeting new or familiar faces was also a draw.

Shortly after four o'clock in the afternoon, the tower called the ops shack and said a Provider was inbound and twenty minutes out. Everyone headed out of the building to watch the plane land. Soon the orange high-wing craft was spotted, and in a couple more minutes it was on the ground, brakes and reverse thrusters kicking in to slow it rapidly. As it was a transient bird, rather than a semi-permanent fixture like Z21, it turned and parked on the apron.

The propellers wound down and the rear ramp lowered. Two Explorers stepped out, whom Bill surmised were the crew chiefs, responsible for loading the cargo and ensuring it was properly stored. If things weren't stored according to a specific calculation, it was likely the plane would have issues taking off and might crash. Cheng and the base head of logistics went up to meet them.

Soon Cheng waved the crowd over and requested they help unload the plane. This was a team sport, with the flight crews pushing containers of supplies out the door and logistics crews operating small forklifts to move the cargo to the supply depot. Bladders of fuel were emptied from their locations in the cargo fuselage into the small fuel truck that served as the airfield's fuel depot. Bill was dragooned into unloading loose items, one of which was a folding boat. He wondered about why such a small boat was brought to Carib and then he heard the assistant cook yell out, "It's here!"

The cook told Bill it was going to be used to capture some lobsters and crabs that lived in the bay. "Nothing like fresh lobster," he said, as he helped carry the boat off the plane. There were also oars, along with lobster and crab traps with ropes and buoys.

"Is this pretty much normal?" Bill asked, gesturing to the boat.

"Oh, yeah. Usually, they're brought in earlier. Not sure why it took so long this time."

One of the final items off the plane was a flitter, but unlike any that Bill had seen on Hayek. This one was a single-seater with a small metal medical litter slung under the bottom. The four propellers were in boxes rather than attached, which made it easier to transport.

When Bill asked one of the other Explorers about it, he was told it was an emergency response flitter. The four encased propellers were designed to fold up, just like old World War II Navy planes folded their wings. Unlike those planes, however, the flitter's propellers were developed to drop down, lock into place and engage while falling. It was designed to be carried in the support Caribou, and if needed, would be dropped out the back of the plane, land, and pick up an injured Explorer. Flitters could also hover, lower the basket, and then retract it to retrieve an injured Explorer if there was insufficient space to land. The Caribou, and its larger cousin the Provider, were the only Corps planes capable of deploying a flitter in mid-flight. Such actions were possible due to each plane having a cargo door in the rear that opened down into a ramp. These doors also made it easy for the Corps to airdrop supplies to ground crews.

"It's only got a 250-klick range, so it really is only for emergencies. The batteries can be changed, but that requires landing," Bill was told. "Either way, it's better than trying to haul somebody out on your back five hundred klicks."

The two mechanics jumped all over the flitter, attaching the folding propeller nacelles, the propellers, and then starting it up to ensure it flew. One of the mechanics took it for a quick loop around the field, then landed it inside the hangar next to the CL-415.

After the plane was unloaded, everyone was dismissed. The crew grabbed small overnight flight bags from the plane and walked to the ops shack. After they were settled in the transient crew quarters, they returned for supper. The co-pilot joined Bill and Kim, and explained that the crew was only going to remain overnight, or RON in pilot lingo, and be out early in the morning to get another load from Primary Base.

"We're one of the primary support craft for Carib, so we should be back every five days or so," she told him. It turned out that the Provider could make the trip from Primary Base in just two days, albeit two ten-hour flying days. Bill didn't envy the flight crew those long hours.

The next morning the C-123 took off early, and for once Z21 wasn't first in line for take-off.

Within two weeks the crew of Z21 had finished surveying the Carib coast and started mapping the interior. They began at the southeastern end of the island, close to the base, and worked their way from east to west, flying mainly north-south patterns. Each pass covered a swath between three and four kilometers wide and between 60 and 130 kilometers long, which meant they were turning every half-hour to hour. Bill calculated that they would have to fly over 38,500 kilometers just in surveys, not including transit time to and from the surveys. It would take almost a month just to cover this island. Of course, it was the largest island in the sea, so the rest of the islands should take far less time to map. It would just take more time to get to them.

Two weeks into the ground mapping survey, Z21 was inbound to base when they were advised to watch for a DHC-4 Caribou in the landing pattern. For the second time since their arrival, they were bumped from their number-one position for field operations.

As they landed, Bill saw the Caribou on the apron, with the pilot and co-pilot conducting a post-flight inspection. A number of other Explorers unloaded equipment from the rear ramp of the plane. *They must be the incoming ground survey crews that Cheng had told us would be here shortly,* Bill thought. He suspected the plane was their support craft.

Doug maneuvered their bird into the hangar while Mindy completed some paperwork. Bill was about to tell Kim he'd take over the data conversion once they got into the ops shack, despite it being her turn, but then noticed that one of the people inspecting the Caribou looked a lot like Meri.

Once the engines were shut down he was the first out the door, rifle in hand. As he approached the cargo plane he could tell it was most definitely Meri, and she hadn't even noticed him yet. Bill's heart skipped a beat. He couldn't believe it. Apparently, she was serving as the co-pilot. He saw her looking around and waved to her. A huge smile practically split her face and she waved back. She excused herself and began hurrying toward Bill, who had wasted no time heading in her direction. Bill enjoyed seeing the feminine way she walked, even with the rifle over her shoulder.

The next thing Bill knew he was holding Meri and kissing her. Breaking apart, the two laughed, with some embarrassment. "Well, that was unexpected," Bill said.

"And hello to you, too," Meri said, grabbing him around the neck and giving him another kiss.

Hooting and hollering had broken out around the assembled groups, with ribald shouts of "get a hammock" interspersed with catcalls and whistles.

This caused the two of them to blush, and Bill noticed that despite her tan, Meri flushed quite well. *Must be the red hair thing,* he thought. *She also smells great!*

Still holding onto his neck, Meri asked him "So, you gonna say hello, or what?"

"Hello, or what," he said laughing lightly.

"I've gotta get back, but hang around." She gave him another quick kiss and then returned to her post-flight inspection.

As Bill was waiting he heard a familiar voice and turned. It was his former roommate, Jordan Washington. The two greeted each other with hugs, then compared experiences while Bill waited for Meri. Jordan was on one of the ground survey crews as their main biologist. "I think they just want me here to identify what critters might eat them."

Once the plane was emptied, the air and ground crews were taken to the ops shack for a brief welcoming, and then to their quarters. Jordan left and joined his crew while Bill walked with Meri. He was thrilled to discover that her aircrew quarters were next to his. The ground crew quarters were next in line. Each crew consisted of four Explorers, and since there were four crews, that meant four more cabins.

The Caribou crew returned to their plane where they grabbed their equipment and returned to their quarters. Meri invited Bill in while she stashed her clothing and equipment. Like him, she would mainly be wearing flight suits, but she also needed her regular uniform handy.

After getting unpacked, they returned to the ops shack for supper. It was a crowded affair, with not enough table space for all. Bill and Meri, along with several others, elected to eat outside where picnic tables had been set up under an awning attached to the side of the ops shack. The tables had been made by the engineers the day before in the expectation that more seating would be needed.

Meri told Bill about finishing up survival school and how less than a week later she was assigned to flight Z45, which was the

Caribou. The pilot was a three-year veteran, most of it in Caribous, but also some time in Providers. The ground survey crews were a mix of veteran Explorers and Probies on their first survey. She told him that Matt Green was also a Caribou co-pilot, but his craft was operating throughout Africa, currently based near the Atlas Mountains in North Africa.

"Considering how much he likes the heat, I'm sure he's enjoying himself," Bill said with a grin. "What about Nicole?" Meri told him that Nicole was a co-pilot on a Provider, operating between the east coast of Ti'icham and both Eurasia and Africa.

"Unlike me, she only gets to see her guy about once a week," Meri finished with a grin, taking a bite of the freshly steamed lobster that was the catch of the day.

The two of them spent the rest of the evening chatting in the ops shack rec area, both happy just to see and be around the other. But, with early flights planned for all, they had to call it an evening. Bill walked Meri back to her quarters and got the kind of goodnight kiss that does little to settle a man down for sleep.

Indeed, just as he fell asleep, it seemed like it was time to get up.

"Rise and shine, lover boy. Daylight's burning," Mindy sang to him, shaking his hammock. Blearily he crawled out of his sack, looked at the dark outside, and said, "What daylight? All I can see are stars."

Slipping on a flight suit and boots, he grabbed his rifle and joined the exodus to the latrine. Next up was coffee and breakfast. As they got there, the crew of the Caribou came in. Realizing that the tables only sat four, Bill left his crew so he and Meri could sit together. She was obviously a bird of a different feather when it came to mornings, as evidenced by her cheery and energetic disposition, in contrast to Bill's monosyllabic grunting and all-around not wanting to be awake temperament.

Breakfast was followed by mission planning for the day's flight. For the first time in weeks, Z21 was tasked with something other than just mapping. They would be dropping off the ground survey crews at various points along the island's south side. One crew would be heading toward the eastern tip of the island from Carib Base, one crew would head north, and the remaining two crews would be dropped on beaches north of the base. Each would be separated by a distance of one hundred kilometers. Their missions were to explore inland, crossing the island, at which point they'd be picked up on the north shore. Each crew was expected to be out in the boonies for a bit over a week, with overflights and resupply every three days by the Caribou.

This was where Kim and Bill's work mapping the island would come in handy, as the ground crews would be working off the maps they had produced in the weeks leading up to the crew's arrival. The ground crews would be given a couple of days back at the base and then proceed onto the next survey once the mapping of those sections was complete.

After dropping off the final crew, Z21 would continue east and begin the day's aerial survey. They would continue doing surveys until it was time to pick up the ground crews. On the days that the Caribou was not involved in resupply they would be assisting Z21 map the island.

All members of both the air and ground surveys attended the final briefing shortly after breakfast. Radio and backup frequencies were confirmed, land routes identified and confirmed, and resupply matters discussed. Several potential extraction points for each crew were also identified on or near their routes, some appearing to be suitable for a rough airfield. Any possible extraction point for more than one Explorer would require clearing vegetation, ensuring the Caribou could land and take off. The Short Take Off and Landing (STOL) capabilities of the Caribou meant it could get into and out of rough fields of only 280 meters. Of course, it also needed clearance at the end of the runway so it wouldn't run into any trees. There was a reason some of the supplies brought in by the 'Bou Crew, as they were known, included detonation cord, plastic explosives, and blasting caps. The flitter would also live in the back of the Caribou in case an Explorer needed extraction and they were unable to land a cargo plane.

Their Caribou, with the tail designation Z56, would use the first day to scout out the possible extraction points to identify how suitable they were for operations. This involved some dangerous low-level flying, so they were to check in often.

At 0800 hours, the first two ground survey crews began their journey, while the remaining crews boarded the CL-415 for the trip.

Within minutes, the seaplane was in the air en route to its first drop off west of the base, only 100 kilometers away. The plane was soon there. Mindy circled the prospective water landing site checking for any potential hazards. Finding none, she put the plane down and landed on the water. As opposed to the relatively smooth landing on a developed field, the water landing was bumpy until they slowed sufficiently, and then the plane rocked from the waves while Mindy guided it toward the beach. Not wanting to get stuck, she stopped a short distance from the shore and turned the plane into the wind, which was blowing from the sea. Bill deployed an inflatable raft that could carry four people and their gear. As the raft would be needed again, the aircrew would ferry two Explorers to shore at a time. Mindy and Doug were needed to maintain the plane's stability in the ocean, so this chore fell to Bill and Kim.

Bill held onto a rope that was tethered to the raft while one of the ground crew boarded it. Once aboard, others handed him four paddles, two packs, four rifles, and four sets of belts laden with survival equipment. The extra rifles and belts belonged to Bill and Kim. Once the equipment was stowed, the second Explorer boarded, followed by Kim and then Bill. All four were wearing inflatable vests over their survival vests. They paddled to shore.

Soon the small waves were pushing them ashore, and the two Explorers, barefoot and with pants rolled up, hopped out of the raft and pulled it further on shore. They grabbed their equipment, put their belts on, slung their rifles, and set the packs down on the sand. Then they pushed the raft back into the waves where Bill and Kim struggled to get it back to the plane.

They repeated the sequence with the second set of Explorers.

As they returned, they saw the first pair had rolled down their pants and donned socks, boots, and packs, and were holding their rifles at the ready, facing the landward edge of the beach. Before leaving, Bill and Kim wished the crew a safe journey and shook hands with each of them.

Back at the plane, Bill grabbed a stanchion near the door and held the raft steady while Kim tossed the paddles onto the plane's floor. She then climbed out and Bill handed her the rope that was tethered to the raft. He opened the valve to deflate the raft, then hopped into the plane. Once the raft was deflated enough, Bill and Kim struggled to get it inside, where Kim closed the valve. They were panting and soaked with seawater when it was finally in. Leaving the partially deflated raft on the floor, Bill secured the door and yelled through the fuselage to Mindy "All secure!" while stripping off his life vest and dumping it in the raft.

As the two aerial survey specialists made their way back to their crash seats they could feel the plane transform from floating to forward motion; the rocking ceased, and the slapping of waves on the hull increased. They were barely buckled in when the plane broke free from the sea and rose into its natural environment.

A short time later they repeated the process with the second ground survey crew. This one also went smoothly, and soon they were back in the air.

The rest of the morning was spent conducting surveys of the island, with lunch consisting of flight rats. Mindy had started letting Bill take over as co-pilot while Doug ate, so Bill made sure to feed Doug first.

"At least wait until I'm outta the damn chair before you try to take over," Doug teased Bill as he unstrapped from the seat. For the next half hour, Mindy let Bill fly the plane while Doug ate and had a cup of coffee and Kim ran the remote sensing operations. All too soon, at least for Bill, he was kicked out of the right-hand seat and sent back to his workstation to process the data.

After several hours, Mindy made the final turn and flew east, back to Carib Base. As she approached the second insertion point, she attempted to raise the ground survey crew on the radio. Soon she was able to and confirmed all was well. "Stay safe out there."

She did the same thing with the first crew and reported to Cheng upon their arrival "home" at Carib Base.

Chapter 20

Once on the ground Doug and Bill carried the partially deflated raft to a spot on the apron where they took buckets of fresh water and rags and washed the salt off it. Leaving it to dry, they went to the Ops Shack to get something cold to drink. Bill thought of taking a shower but decided to hold off until the raft was dry, folded, and put away. *No sense getting all sweaty again,* he thought.

Stepping into the Ops Shack was almost like stepping into an air-conditioned room after having the sun beat down on them. Between the lack of direct sunlight and the circulation of air from the overhead fans, Bill could feel the evaporation of his sweat cooling his skin. It reminded him of a physical geography lab when they did an experiment on latent heat. *And this would be latent heat of evaporation,* he could imagine the teaching assistant say in his rather smug tone. He racked his rifle and stripped off his survival vest, putting it on a hook near the rifle rack. Doug did the same with his rifle, but couldn't be bothered to remove his vest.

As the two sat at one of the dining tables and drank some iced lemonade, they heard on the radio that Zulu 56, the tail number for the base's new Caribou, was inbound and ten minutes out. Soon the plane was on the ground and taxied to the apron.

"Damn, they're throwing all sorts of crap on our nice clean raft," Doug complained jokingly. Bill was just glad the raft didn't blow away with the prop wash from the powerful twin propellers. The plane's engines shut down, the props stopped spinning, and the crew was soon exiting. After completing their post-flight inspection Meri and the pilot, Sam Long, made a beeline for the Ops Shack. Upon arrival, Long went directly to Cheng, who was seated at the operations table, to brief him on the flight.

Meri went straight to Bill after racking her rifle, wrapped her arms around his neck and kissed him. Then she stepped back and wrinkled her nose. "What on Hayek have you been up to? You stink like a sweaty musk ox!"

"Oops, looks like the honeymoon's over," Doug commented sotto voce.

"Well, while you were having fun flying in the sky, I happened to have been paddling around in the ocean, numerous times, and wrestling with big yellow inflatables," Bill said, mock-indignantly.

"Sounds like fun, but you sit over there and don't even think of getting close to me until you bathe," Meri said, pointing to the chair Bill had just vacated on her behalf.

He plopped down while she got a lemonade and sat opposite him.

"There, now I can look at you and I don't have to smell you," she said with a smile.

"I guess that's better than nothing," Bill said.

"You can say that again," Doug muttered.

Bill asked Meri about her first day. She explained how the mapping Bill and Kim had done was really helping identify potential extraction points. "At one point I thought we'd need our own extraction, the way Sam took us so low. I figured we'd be pulling branches out of the wheel wells."

A short while later Doug tapped Bill on the shoulder and told him they should probably roll up and put away the raft now. "That way you can actually clean up a little so your woman friend doesn't find you so offensive," he said with a smirk.

Meri smiled up at him, raised her hand and waggled her finger, saying, "Toodle-oo." Off Bill went, promising to head straight for the shower after that. She agreed to meet him afterward.

Later, showered and changed into a fresh uniform, Bill joined Meri in the Ops Shack for supper. Meri and the other new Explorer were given their Survey Medals in the same manner that Bill and Kim had received theirs.

For Bill, the next several days were spent mapping, with evenings spent with Meri. He would have liked to do more than just talk with her, but conditions weren't quite suitable for anything else. He had to be satisfied with the evening kiss good night, which sometimes became quite steamy.

While Bill's craft was engaged in mapping, Meri's was involved in resupplying the ground crews and keeping track of them with some mapping in between.

Eventually, two of the crews announced they were ready for pickup, so once again Z21 landed on the water, this time on the north side of the island, and Bill and Kim got to do more paddling. As the ground crews boarded the raft, it was obvious they had been doing some rough traveling. There were stains on their uniforms and their boots were quite scuffed. Bill noticed, though, that they didn't stink like somebody who had been trekking around in the jungle for a week. He thought at first this was because they were outside, but even when the first group of Explorers was in the plane, he didn't notice much, other than an earthy undertone. Then it dawned on him; they must be using the hygiene tools he was issued and taught about in survival school. Along with survival shooting, it was one of the things drilled into them, which is why every base had showers installed as soon as possible. Clean Explorers were less likely to be sick Explorers, and clean clothes lasted longer than dirty clothes, as the grains of dirt and sand didn't remain in the fabric to grind it away like a fine sandpaper.

Once back at base, the new Explorers were awarded their Survey Medals. Fortunately, no Purple Hearts were handed out. Bill appreciated the fact that Cheng always made it a point to hand out the Survey Medals immediately upon earning them. And considering the mortality rate of ground crews, as evidenced by the wall of stars in the Corps' museum...

Each ground crew that was picked up got to spend two days at base loafing, and then it was back into the jungle for another romp across the narrow island. By the time the island was surveyed on the ground, the crew of Z21 had finished mapping it and had moved on to mapping other islands of the Greater Antilles.

One day a C-123 landed with nothing but boat parts and a maritime crew. After unloading the parts and moving them closer to the shoreline of Guantanamo Bay, the crew, along with the aircraft mechanics, supply guys, and engineers, began assembling the parts into a small ship or large boat—Bill wasn't sure which. First, the engineers set up a series of logs to serve as rollers to get the boat into the water when it was assembled. As the Explorers were assembling the vessel another Provider landed with fuel bladders full of diesel fuel for the sea craft. The bladders, which were on pallets, were dragged from the plane and positioned near the dock the engineers had built weeks before.

Within a day the boat was assembled. It was large enough for the three-person crew and a dozen passengers. Mindy stood next to Bill watching the workers push the boat out into the water, next to the dock.

"Looks like we'll be doing fewer water landings and take-offs for the foreseeable future," she commented.

Bill just nodded.

Mindy expanded on her statement for his edification. "This means we won't have to worry about water landings, shoals, coral heads, or other water hazards. Our threat level just plummeted."

With the addition of the boat crew the base had become officially crowded, and the engineers erected another building, this one designed exclusively for cooking, dining, and recreation. Once again the focus of the Ops Shack became survey operations, but some of the easy chairs were left for those seeking solitude from the larger crowds in the building that became known simply as "the Big Shack."

The first task of the new maritime crew was to ferry two ground survey teams to the island of Jamaica, barely 250 kilometers away. Once again, the maps provided by Z21 proved invaluable to the teams, particularly the nearshore bathymetry. The boat was able to make the journey with ease, dropping the two teams off on the eastern side of the islands so they could move westward. Then the boat crew circumnavigated the island, replicating Z21's work, but from sea level looking shoreward.

They were back at Carib Base two days later and picked up the other two crews for the first ground survey of the island of Hispaniola.

While the boat was ferrying Explorers and conducting its own surveys, the 'Bou Crew were keeping track of the ground crews and providing them with support. In the meantime, Z21 was still flying around the Caribbean, collecting data and making maps.

Two things became abundantly clear during the ground surveys. First was the lack of sapient beings. Second was the lack of large carnivores, just like on Earth.

After Cheng had declared the island relatively safe, he gave the Explorers the opportunity to do their own exploring, but with the caveat of having all survival gear with them all the time, notifying Ops anytime they left base, where they were going, and an estimated time back. All Explorers were required to carry two-way radios with them when leaving base.

Bill and Meri decided to explore more of Guantanamo Bay on their day off, looking for a secluded spot where they could spend some time together without the crush of others all around them. The airfield was on the seaward side of a peninsula extending into the bay from the west, so they decided to cross the peninsula and investigate the beaches on the tip of the peninsula. It was barely a kilometer walk, but being the first time out on their own, the two found it exciting. Exciting, hot, and humid.

By the time they reached the entrance to the bay they were

both beginning to get a bit warm, so Meri suggested they cool off. They were wearing shorts and short-sleeved shirts, so Bill stripped off his shirt, intending to keep his shorts on for modesty. He was surprised when Meri apparently had no intention of doing the same and was soon devoid of all clothing.

"What's taking you so long?" she laughingly asked, then ran to the water's edge and did a shallow dive into the bay.

Bill stripped his shorts off so fast he thought he was going to rip them, then ran to join Meri. Of course, he also wanted to get into the water fast so Meri didn't see the reaction she was causing his body. Diving in, he was surprised at how warm the water was. He had been hoping some cold water would help his condition, but it was not to be. When he came up for air he was within arm's reach of Meri, who jumped out of the water and came splashing down on him, wrapping her arms around him and kissing him breathlessly. Bill couldn't help wrapping his arms around her and returning the kiss, feeling her breasts on his naked chest, and then feeling her abdomen bumping against his erection.

Her reaction was just the opposite of what he expected. Instead of pulling away from him she wrapped her legs against him and pulled closer. "Make love to me here," she whispered in his ear, guiding herself closer onto him where he was barely penetrating her. The two made love frantically the first time, floating in Guantanamo Bay, with the waves slapping against them, seemingly in time to their lovemaking.

After the first bout, they made their way back to shore, hand in hand, where they made love again, this time more slowly. Afterward, the two lay on the towels stretched on the beach and looked up at the fluffy cumulonimbus clouds forming overhead.

"So, how long have you been planning this ambush?" he asked her.

"Only since I first met you. Do you know how much willpower that took not to jump your bones all these months, especially when we were at Lewis Landing?" Leaning over, she gave him a kiss, which stirred things up again.

They made love a third time before heading back to base, then rinsed off sand and salt.

As they approached the base buildings Kim came out of the quarters and spotted them. They must have been throwing off pheromones, had a glow on their faces, or looked like the cat that ate the canary. Whatever the case, Kim took one look at them and said with a grin, "I hope you used protection."

The look on Bill's face made it obvious he hadn't even considered that, because both Kim and Meri burst into laughter.

"What?" Bill asked plaintively.

"Silly, don't you know all women on field duty get birth control implants while they're in the Corps?" Meri laughed and leaned into Bill.

Bill's was relief palpable.

"I'm going to put my gear away and get a shower. See you after," she told him, giving him a quick kiss and headed to the 'Bou Crew cabin.

"Good thing you're making some good bank out here, boy, cause you're gonna need it to get that girl a proper ring," Kim said, as they watched Meri walk into her cabin.

"Y'know, I think you're right," Bill said with a grin, then trooped into the Swamp to get a fresh towel and a clean uniform.

Chapter 21

Over the next several months the two air crews, the maritime crew, and the four ground crews worked together to explore all the islands throughout the Caribbean. The crew of Z21 had the added pleasure of surveying the north coast of Suyu, or South America as Bill still thought of it.

The flitter was needed once on the island of Haiti. Bill had thought Haiti was a French word, because of the French settlement on the island he knew as Hispaniola, but apparently, it was a name from the original inhabitants on Earth, the Arawak. An Explorer made the mistake of stepping wrong while ascending one of the mountains. He broke several bones and had a number of severe abrasions from the ensuing fall. Fortunately, there was nothing as life-threating as a pierced lung or loss of limb, but there was no way the Explorer could continue with the survey.

The Caribou circled above the ground crew a thousand meters up, and the assistant cargo crew chief pushed the flitter out of the back of the craft. The flitter, flown by the Caribou's cargo chief, deployed the propellers once it had left the Caribou, flew it safely to the ground, and landed near the ground crew. The ground crew loaded the injured Explorer into the litter basket, and the crew chief took off. With no landing spots nearby for the Caribou, and with the base too far to fly the slow flitter all the way, he headed for the coast. When the flitter reached the coast, Z21 met them and transported both men to Carib Base. The flitter, which was left behind, was picked up the next day by the boat crew, who returned it to Carib to be reloaded aboard the Caribou for the next emergency. The Explorer was treated by PA Finley who made the medical decision to evacuate him to Hayek on the next resupply, which was due in two days.

"No sense him sitting here in the sand and sun under the palm trees when he can be home enjoying winter at its fullest," she said, informing Cheng of her decision.

Bill and Meri became serious enough in their relationship that they began talking about a future life together. They decided that once they returned to Hayek they would move in together. Bill thought they would have to live off base, but Meri informed him otherwise. Base housing arrangements were by the consent of those who were being housed, not those who housed them.

By March the entire Caribbean had been mapped, and all of the islands explored, at least to the satisfaction of the Corps of Discovery. All survey Explorers from Carib Base were pulled off duty and given a month's leave on Hayek, to begin once they crossed over. The ground crews would go through some refresher training and then be reassigned to another survey base on Zion after their leave. The flight crews were told they'd be receiving new orders, but to report to headquarters on Hayek at the end of their leave.

Rather than wait for one of the larger Providers to come in and take them out, one crew of Explorers loaded up in the CL-415 and the other three crews boarded the Caribou. Thus began a three-day flight back to the Initial Point. The two pilots decided to fly in formation the entire way, just in case any problems developed.

As they approached Primary Base, Bill was struck at just how busy the airfield was compared to the relatively backwater field on Carib. While Carib Base housed two airplanes, there were dozens operating out of Primary Base, most of them the bigger C-123s. There were also several seaplanes and Caribous on the apron. For the first time in a long time, Mindy had to put the seaplane into a flight pattern and was put in line to land. After landing, she told the crew and passengers to remain near the plane while she and the Caribou's pilot reported in at the Field Manager's Building for further instructions.

Grabbing a jacket from her hanging locker, Mindy exited the plane. A gust of cold air entered, reminding all that they had been in the tropics for several months, and that early spring on the Columbia Plateau was still downright cold. Everyone started digging jackets from their duffels or hanging lockers.

Mindy was back in five minutes and gave the crew the low-down. "They want us to cross over at the next gate opening, so we need to move the bird over to the waiting convoy." She pointed to a line of trucks and a couple of planes near the gate. "Crossover's tomorrow morning. My crew, stay on board tonight." She told the ground crews, "You can either stay on board or hang out in the transient quarters. It's up to your team leader."

The team leader looked around at his crew and said to Mindy, "If it's all right by you, we'll spend the night here. Wouldn't want to miss crossover." He grinned, reaching into his duffel to pull out a bottle full of an amber liquid. Holding it up so Mindy could see it, he said, "And if it's all right by you, I'd like to celebrate a bit by sharing this with everyone as a reward for a great survey. We all survived!"

An entire bottle split between eight people wouldn't amount to anyone having more than a couple of shots, so Mindy agreed, but not until they had moved the birds into line. Soon, all were sipping from canteen cups, enjoying the sweet-tasting liqueur. Bill, who had gotten used to sipping whiskey, was surprised at the sweet scent and flavor and asked what it was.

"Nectar of the Irish gods" proclaimed the ground survey leader. "Irish Mist, a mix of Irish whiskey and honey mead. And remember, it's for sippin', not sluggin', lad."

Everyone decided to avail themselves of the dining opportunity presented by the base rather than consume flight rations, as they had every night since leaving Carib. After several months of flight or field rations or Carib Base's cook's relatively plain cooking, they were ready for a change.

Soon they were seated and eating. Meri and Bill sat together, as usual, and made plans for their leave, which included spending lots of time with each other, a lot of it without anyone else, and some spring salmon fishing on some of the rivers of Cascadia. Bill had heard about the 50 kilo Chinook salmon, or hogs as they were called, and was hoping to catch one, just for the experience.

After supper, the crews took showers and retired, sleeping on the planes. Bill felt a bit sorry for the Caribou crew, as they didn't have the same accommodations as the seaplane. Rather than having bunks, they slept on the floor of the cargo plane. But he didn't feel sorry enough to give up his bed, and Meri adamantly refused to share his bunk with all the others in the same plane.

Early the next morning, the crews were awake and waiting. Crossover was expected to take place at eight fifteen, as soon as the incoming resupply was on Zion. They made coffee in the plane and those who ate chose flight rations.

Fifteen minutes before crossover Primary Base radioed Z21 and requested confirmation that all passengers and crew listed on the manifest Mindy had provided earlier was correct. Mindy was quick to respond, then turned and gave the crew and passengers a thumbs-up. She started the engines, making sure they were warmed up early.

The same warnings that were issued before Bill's crossover from Hayek were announced on Zion, only this time he heard them through the aircraft's radio. Mindy put it on the intercom for the ground crews who were sitting in the bunks. Crossover was actually announced for the incoming traffic, with the warning to remain stationary until given the go-ahead to transit back to Hayek.

When crossover happened the crew got to watch it from a different perspective, and they were amazed at the number of trucks that came rolling through the gate. Bill didn't quite know what to expect, but this was far more than he had figured on. Of course, having dozens of planes and thousands of personnel scattered around the globe, the supply needs were quite large, particularly fuel, aircraft parts, and food.

Soon the departing convoy was given orders to begin movement through the gate. Mindy gave the CL-415 more throttle and taxied the plane forward through the gate and onto the tarmac of Bowman Field, where she was directed to park the plane on the apron. Mindy shut down the engines and announced over the intercom, "Welcome home, guys." Cheering broke out and Bill realized that, even though he was still considered a Probationary Explorer by the Corps, he was now a veteran. He noticed the other Explorers putting their ribbons back on their uniforms, so he did the same. He had to pull his out of one of the drawers under his bunk where he had stashed it after Cheng's ceremony. He put it on, looked up, and saw Kim grinning at him, wearing hers.

"We made it!" she practically shouted, reaching over and giving him a high-five. Bill hadn't felt this proud since getting the letter accepting him into the Corps.

"We sure as hell did, didn't we?" he said.

"Listen up!" Mindy announced. "For those just finishing their first survey, we've got to check in with headquarters before we go on leave. I'll get a jeep to drive you to your quarters so you can dump off your gear, but don't take too long. Just store your rifles, dump your gear, then get on over to headquarters. I don't know about you, but I'm ready for some serious downtime away from you ugly mutts."

The ground survey crew was the first out, as they didn't have any equipment or clothing stashed in the plane, just their primary survival gear, backpacks, rifles, and duffels with uniforms. The plane's crew emptied their lockers and drawers into their duffel bags, then retrieved all their secondary survival equipment from under the crash seats and stowed them in the duffel bags. Stepping out of the plane, each wore their survival vests under their jackets, their suspenders and belts over the jackets, backpacks on their backs, and carried partially-filled duffel bags in one hand, and rifles in the other.

"The problem with living in a plane is all the crap you gotta carry," Doug said as they staggered to the waiting jeeps. The ground crew was already gone.

"See you in a few," Mindy told Bill and Kim as she dumped her gear in the rear of a jeep and jumped into the front seat. Nodding to the driver she gave him her address while Doug loaded his gear and climbed in, precariously perched on the small bench seat with his feet on the pile of equipment.

Bill and Kim loaded their gear into the other jeep and Bill deferred to Kim, taking the rear seat and letting her sit up front. "Welcome back," the driver said. "Where to?"

They gave the driver their addresses, and with a "hang on" they were on the way. The cold spring air felt refreshing on Bill's face, but he was glad it was only for the mile-long trip. As they were moving Bill pulled his tablet from his pants cargo pocket, where it had been living the past several months, and activated it. Seeing the basewide wi-fi network connect, he sent a quick email to Meri to meet after they processed through headquarters. Almost immediately he received a response stating she would meet him there.

After getting dropped off, Bill lugged his gear up the steps of 117 Jaskey Lane. He dug his ID from his wallet, inserted it, and heard the lock disengage. He shouted "Hello" into the house. There was no answer and the house smelled like it hadn't been lived in for several months. It had obviously been taken care of, though, because Bill didn't see any dust anywhere.

He headed to his room where he left the rifle on the bed, the backpack and duffel bag on the floor, and then his belt and vest on the bed. After divesting himself of all unnecessary items, he put his rifle and PDW away in the gun safe, then headed down the stairs to the first floor as Jordan came in.

"Hey, took you long enough," Bill said, ragging on Jordan a bit.

"Yeah, well, we had the slow co-pilot driving," Jordan shot back, meaning Meri.

"Oooh, low blow," Bill said. "Hurry up and put your stuff away. I'll walk over with you."

Jordan disappeared into his room and within minutes was back. Because they were relatively close to headquarters, they were among the earliest to arrive. It was their first time in the building, never having had a reason to go there before, so they weren't quite sure what to expect. What they saw was an open foyer, with oil paintings and large-format photographs on the wall showing various Explorers. There was a desk at the end of the foyer where an older Explorer sat. From what they could see, it wasn't obvious she was a survivor of some incident. Knowing the Corps as they did, the two men suspected she probably had some type of traumatic disability that kept her desk-bound.

"Good morning," she said, and then asked them if they were just off Zion. The two nodded, just as Mindy walked through the door.

"Mindy! How good to see you," the receptionist said, standing up. As she came around the desk Bill could see her using a cane.

She and Mindy hugged, and then Mindy to Bill and Jordan. "Boys, this is Glenda Slater. Glenda, this here's Bill Clark, one helluvan aerial survey specialist. The other is Jordan Washington, biologist, and all-around ground pounder."

Glenda shook both their hands and congratulated them on a successful survey. Turning to Mindy, she said, "I'll notify the Commandant your team is arriving. Why don't you take the crew into the large conference room." She left the group and walked down the hall and into the Commandant's office.

While she was gone, others from the Zion team came into the building, including Meri, who sidled up next to Bill and took his hand. Bill realized it was the first time that they were going to be seeing the Commandant since the two had become lovers. *No wonder she's holding on for dear life*, he thought.

Mindy directed the Explorers into a rather large conference room, big enough to handle all six crews. Soon all twenty-four were gathered in the room. Mindy told them it was tradition for the Commandant to welcome them back and then they would check in with Glenda to formalize arrival on base and taking leave.

Commandant Lewis came into the room trailed by Glenda and greeted the assembled crew. Spotting Meri, his face broke out into a huge smile. To the group, he said, "Welcome home! I'm certainly glad every one of you made it back alive, but I guess you can say I'm especially glad that a certain co-pilot made it back." With that, he came over to her for a hug. She released Bill's hand and hugged her father back.

After the hug, Lewis said, "Sorry, she's the only one that gets a hug. But, I sure am glad to see all of you." He proceeded around the room shaking the hand of every Explorer. When he shook Bill's hand, Bill could feel a sense of warmth and welcome coming off the Commander, like a father welcoming home his son. This made Bill think of his father, whom he had been corresponding with for the past several months, using old-fashioned paper letters.

While Lewis was welcoming them, Slater had pulled out several bottles of whiskey along with enough tumblers for all. Pouring two fingers of the liquid in each glass, she began handing them out. Bill wasn't sure what the protocol was, but since nobody was drinking, he held on to his glass.

When everyone had a glass, Lewis raised his and said, "To you!" then took a sip. Bill was about to raise his glass, but nobody else did. Then Lewis said, "To the Corps," and that's when the veteran Explorers took a sip. Bill and the other new Explorers followed suit. Lewis made a final toast, "To absent companions" and drained his glass. The others did, too. Bill thought, *Damn, I'm glad I took up drinking whiskey months ago. No way I would have been able to do this without choking on it.*

Lewis then said, "As of now, you're all on leave for thirty days. Check out with Glenda before leaving, and have fun. And, stay safe out there," he finished with a chuckle.

As the others said their farewells and headed out the door, Meri and Bill hung back, with Meri still holding on to Bill's hand.

Lewis took one look at them, then said with a grin, "So, looks like you two kind of hit it off, eh?"

Meri nodded. "Daddy, it's gone way beyond hitting it off. We're moving in together."

Lewis looked at them sharply, then grinned again. "Hell, it took you long enough. I thought you'd move in together months ago after you spent the weekend at Lewis Landing."

Holding out his hand to Bill he said, "Take good care of her."

Meri let go of Bill's hand, which allowed Bill to take the Commandant's. After the two shook, Meri grabbed her father in a bear hug and said, "Thank you, Daddy."

He asked the two what they were planning on doing.

Their first course of action was to get set up in housing together, then they were planning on spending their month off traveling the west coast of Ti'icham.

"We're not sure what after that, but I'm sure somebody will work to keep us together," Meri said, shamelessly batting her eyes at her father, who just laughed.

"Well, go get checked out and get your housing arranged. Will you have time to join an old man for supper any time soon?" he asked.

The two agreed, and after arranging a date and time to show up at the Commandant's residence, they went to make their new living arrangements. Bill thought, *It's a good thing she knows what she's doing, 'cause I'm clueless.*

PLANET 42

Chapter 22

Meri took them to the housing office, and twenty minutes later they were standing in the living room of their new living quarters, a small one-bedroom apartment in the family section of the base.

"Say, shouldn't we be married if we're going to be living here?" Bill blurted out.

"Well, that's certainly the least romantic proposal I've ever heard of," Meri said, crossing her arms over her chest and giving Bill a mock glare.

It was then that Bill realized what he had said, and Meri laughed at the look on his face. He tried to explain that it wasn't a proposal, just an observation, but she wasn't buying it.

"If you're going to propose, then do it right!" she said. "In the meantime, let's get our stuff and get moved in."

The first thing they did was to set the biometric lock for the gun safe to operate for both of them. Since there was a lot of stuff to move, they had rented a small electric Kenji then went to Meri's cabin for her belongings. Bill had been surprised to find out early in their relationship that she didn't live at the Commandant's, that it had been her idea to move out once she started training. "That way people won't think that I'm the Commandant's daughter. I'm just another Probie."

Soon, all they owned was in the little apartment, which now looked even smaller. Fortunately, it had some basic furniture, but that was all. While the Corps supplied all housing necessities for new arrivals, it didn't do so for those who moved out of their initial housing. They took the small truck to the base exchange to get some of the other essentials for living, such as pots, pans, cutlery, coffee pots, mugs, dinnerware, et cetera. And then to the commissary for some basic foods, but nothing that would spoil if left in the refrigerator. It was almost nightfall when they were finally finished unloading and putting everything away.

Rather than try to cook, they decided to have their first night back on Hayek at the old standby, the Cave Bear Cave. They dropped off the Kenji at the rental shop and walked to the Cave. Dinner consisted of stew and beer. While they had had plenty of stew during their survey, beer was another matter altogether. Very few ever drank the concentrated beer provided as their daily tot, eschewing it for whiskey or vodka. Bill enjoyed the feeling of carbonation in his nose when he took his first draught of the brown ale he had ordered.

The next couple of days were spent getting settled into their new digs. Along with getting organized, they had supper with the Commandant one evening The two took turns describing their adventures and then told him about their plans to ride up and down the coast to see the sights and to spend a couple of days fishing for chinook on the Nch'i-Wana. Bill couldn't tell if the Commandant was happy or not that his only daughter was shacking up with a new kid, but he decided not to worry too much about it. It appeared that Lewis was accepting him as part of the family and that was good enough for him. Considering how much Bill had worried about "the Colonel's" opinion before joining the Corps, this was quite the mindset change for him, one that he didn't really notice had developed.

As they left the Commandant's quarters, Meri gave her father a hug while Bill simply shook his hand.

By the third morning, the two were ready to take off, so they each packed a bag, grabbed their rifles, and headed off to the skytrain station to catch the maglev to Cascadia. Bill had looked at a map before they left, finding small cities in the same locations on Hayek as they were on Earth. He wasn't sure if that was simply because the geography was ideal for trade, or if some underlying cultural desire was at play.

The maglev stopped in Tahoma, then headed south toward the small city of Multnomah, situated at the mouth of the Willamette River where it joined the Nch'i-Wana. As they traveled south, they saw a volcano with a large crater. Bill realized that he was looking at Mt. St. Helen's, and asked Meri about it.

"Oh, Loowit. That erupted about forty years ago. Caused a bit of problem in Milton, I hear. What, with all the ash."

Wow, Bill thought. *Some things don't change.*

Multnomah, on the location of Earth's Portland, was more a working city than a place for hipsters, but there were a few fishing guides who operated from the small city. Meri had contacted one of the guides the day before, so they were set to get out on the wide river and hopefully catch some fish.

And they did. Bill was amazed at the size of some of the salmon they caught, and after catching, and releasing, his third one, his arms were feeling like noodles. The two decided they would keep one salmon, the smallest, and share it with the guide. They took their portion to a restaurant located near the small boat dock and had it grilled on an alder plank. Bill was amazed at the amount of wildlife he saw, including dozens of bald eagles, flocks of swans, ducks, and geese. There were also flocks of birds so large that they created shadows as they flew overhead. In the water, he saw river otters near the banks and a small family of giant beavers near a suitably sized giant beaver lodge.

The backdrop for this experience was the cone-shaped mountain Wy'east, rising east of their location. Bill still couldn't think of it as anything other than Mt. Hood.

The next morning they were back on the maglev and Bill was getting, yet again, another education about his new home. He was glad to see all the wildlife but wondered how it was possible to feed people without displacing all the animals, as had been done over most of Earth. As the train slid south, he could see miles and miles of forest, with only a few farms located near small towns and cities along the maglev route. There was nothing that looked like the typical agribusiness he knew from drives up and down Interstate 5 back when he lived on Earth. Nor was the landscape marred by the high voltage electric towers he was used to seeing. It seemed most homes were powered with solar, wind, or both, and most towns had small nuclear reactors. Bill had asked Meri about the reactors and what they did with the spent fuel, learning that most of it was reprocessed and reused. What little spent fuel couldn't be reprocessed was actually placed on another parallel planet, supposedly out of harm's way. Bill wondered about that, and what exactly that meant, but didn't push the issue.

They soon crossed the pass over the Klamath Mountains and entered the northern part of the long central valley of Yokut Canton. It was here they saw larger farms, but still, nothing that resembled agribusiness. A few short stops along the way where people boarded or disembarked, and soon they were entering the Ohlone Bay area, which Bill knew as the San Francisco Bay. While some things looked familiar, most did not. About the only things that were even remotely similar to his experiences from trips to the Bay Area before were the Golden Gate, without the bridge, and the two bigger islands in the bay, Alcatraz and Angel. Other than that, the bay looked bigger, more natural, and had far fewer humans. They spent a couple of days there, then down the coast again to some smaller settlements along the coast. Eventually, the two wound up near the tip of Baja California, where they lazed in the sun for a few days before making the trip north to Cascadia to visit the town of Squamish. The small town on the Salish Sea was where Bill remembered Vancouver, British Columbia, being. The mountains overlooking the town were just as beautiful and imposing as he remembered.

Finally, the two returned to Sacajawea Base to spend a few days at "home" where they spent some time salmon and steelhead fishing on the Naches and Yakima Rivers.

The Friday before their leave was up both received emails stating that they were to report for more training. Bill's training was mostly refresher training on remote sensing platforms, mainly digital aerial imagery along with infrared sensing. Meri was going to spend more time in training on the S-1 Monarch as co-pilot, and both would be spending a day on navigation skills.

"Y'know," Meri said after they had finished reading their emails, "they wouldn't be putting us through this training unless they were planning on using us for an initial survey."

Bill raised his eyebrows and felt a thrill course through his body. *The ultimate survey!* "That'd be awesome!"

A relaxing weekend spent in the apartment, around Milton for some non-essential shopping ("ooh, look at this rifle"), and supper with the Commandant, and the two were ready to report for training Monday morning.

Chapter 23

Monday morning finally arrived, and Bill and Meri reported to their respective training modules. Bill was back in Room 204, this time with only two other Probies, one of whom was Kim Brown. All three wore uniforms, along with their primary survival equipment, but the major difference about them that stood out was that now all three wore a ribbon indicating that they had been on a survey.

Jim Merriman, Bill's initial instructor/evaluator for GIS and remote sensing, was the same Explorer leading this training. After a brief welcome, he had the Probies go through some basic diagnostic testing to determine their depth of knowledge on the two main types of remote sensing platforms that they would be operating. While everyone knew the theory and how to convert the data into useful formats, only one person knew how to actually operate the equipment, and she was a graduate of Cascadia Technical Institute.

"Pretty much what I expected. Seems like this is never actually taught in schools on Earth," Merriman said, shaking his head and looking at the two Earth-educated Explorers.

Merriman released the Hayek-educated Explorer to her next training module, signing her off as suitably trained. He then spent the next several hours working with Bill and Kim to bring them up to speed on the three main systems they would be using: digital aerial photography, near infra-red sensing, and far-infrared sensing.

"You've got two things you're doing when you're out there on a Monarch. First is getting imagery that can be used to create some basic maps for the secondary surveys, which you guys have already used. The second thing relates to our primary mission, which is to identify potential civilizations or human settlements, be they permanent or temporary."

By lunchtime, the two were almost up to speed. Merriman wanted them back after lunch to ensure they had everything down cold. By mid-afternoon, he was sure they were familiar with the equipment and software. Rather than release them, though, he ran them through various scenarios until quitting time.

The following day Bill was assigned to refresh his navigation skills. This time, there were more Explorers in the class. While Bill had done some navigating on Zion, he didn't have a lot of experience with old-fashioned navigational tools, such as the sextant. Most of his skills were with GPS, maps, and compasses. Once again, the Hayek-educated Explorers were much more familiar with the tools used on an initial survey, so after they passed the tests they were free to go. Bill, Kim, and a few others had to stay for more training. Bill was beginning to realize that, despite all the time already spent on Hayek and in the Corps, the education he had received wasn't quite up to snuff. His consolation was that Kim, despite having a master's degree, was in the same boat.

"There's a reason we issue you chronographs," the instructor said; "it's so you know what time it is where you started. If you can figure out local noon, then you can calculate what your longitude is. The sextant will help you determine your latitude. That means you'll be able to calculate, with some degree of accuracy, your location on the planet."

The Explorers were taught how to use the sextant, and then how to determine local noon.

"It's best if one person uses their chronograph to determine local time while the other keeps Alpha time. That way you know what the time was from where you took off and what the time is from where you're at," the instructor advised them. Alpha time was the time at

Milton, the entry point for every survey gate. Twelve hundred Alpha meant it was noon in Milton.

He then showed them how to tell local noon using a stick in the ground. "The sun crossed the sky at 15 degrees every hour, so that's one degree every four minutes. Put the stick in the ground, making sure it's vertical. Then every minute put a tick mark in the dirt at the top of the shadow. The tick marks will eventually form an arc. The top of the arc is noon. Knowing that the tick marks represent one minute, you can calculate back how many minutes ago noon occurred. From there, you calculate the Alpha time and local time, which should be noon. So, if it's zero eight hundred hours Alpha, and your watch is showing 1500 hours at local noon, how far east are you?"

Before Bill could even make the calculation Kim raised her hand. The instructor nodded at her and she replied, "Seven hours, or seven twenty-fourths of the planet."

"Exactly! Now, a planet consists of 360 degrees, a circle—well, sorta, but close enough for our purposes. So, how many degrees would that be?"

Bill thought about it. *Let's see, 360 divided by 24 is 15 degrees. Hey, wait a minute, we just covered that. Okay, so 15 times seven is 105 degrees.* Bill raised his hand and responded, "One hundred five degrees" when the instructor nodded to him.

"Correct. So, where are you?" he asked the assembled class. "Here's a hint, you can use a map."

The students dug out their tablets and pulled up maps of Hayek, which was more akin to the worlds they were surveying than the heavily anthropogenically-altered Earth. Soon they all found that it would put them either in the Atlantic Ocean near Eurasia, or on the western tip of Africa.

The instructor had them run more exercises, breaking them down from simple degrees to the full degrees, minutes, and seconds required for finding one's absolute location.

He then had them work on the sextant, and assigned them homework to work on it in the evening when the moon, the planets, and the stars were out.

At the end of the training, Bill and the others were feeling much better about their navigation skills.

"Tomorrow we'll practice taking sun shots from a Monarch, so meet at Bowman Field," he said, dismissing the class.

When Bill arrived back at the apartment he found Meri already there, getting supper ready. The two had already discovered that Bill's camp cooking wasn't quite up to speed for real-world adventures in living, so Meri had taken over that task, leaving cleanup to Bill. Supper was a simple stir-fry which was soon gone. Afterwards, he and Meri went outside to find a good place for practicing using a sextant at night. They spent several hours in an open field and even managed to take some star shots of the North Star with the sextant Bill had brought with them.

The next morning Bill reported to Bowman Field where he and the others got to sit in a Monarch and practice taking sun shots. That didn't take too long, so the rest of the morning was spent going over the Monarch. As Bill had actually qualified as a co-pilot in one, he had less to learn than some of the others, but he paid attention nonetheless. After all, he thought, he wasn't going to be piloting a Monarch if he was assigned to one as an aerial surveyor. After going over the plane inside and out the group was given the afternoon off and told to report in the evening, after supper, so they could take star, planet, and moon shots from the Monarch.

While Bill was going through his rudimentary navigation course Meri was getting a refresher on flying the Monarch, which meant many hours in the plane, oftentimes operating as pilot. During initial surveys the pilot and co-pilot typically took turns flying the plane, with the automatic pilot often relieving whoever was on pilot duty for hours at a time. It was the only way to keep the plane in the air for a week at a time with only two main pilots. Bill thought that was definitely not something that would fly in Earth aviation, but, as he remembered, *We're not on Earth anymore, Toto.*

They had been in refresher training for less than a week when both got an email announcing their next assignments; co-pilot for Meri and aerial survey specialist for Bill, both on the same Monarch on an unnamed planet referred to solely as Planet 42. They were to report to the departure terminal at Bowman Field Friday morning, to meet the Survey Commander of Flight S-1-42/2. Monday morning they would be passing through the gate.

At Bowman Field, they were told where to find the Monarch and its crew. They had borrowed a cart and hauled a week's worth of uniforms and equipment with them. Duffel bags and secondary survival kits went into the cart while the two wore the rest of their regalia. Hauling the cart down the ramp, they spotted four Monarchs sitting together. One of them had the tail number they were looking for, S-1-42/2. It was obvious the last three letters had been freshly painted. Bill now understood that the last digits of a tail indicated the assignment of the plane. As Z21 was the twenty-first plane on the planet Zion, this plane would be the second one on the planet designated as Planet 42. They could see drop tanks under each wing.

As Bill and Meri approached, Meri shouted, "Ahoy in there." A male head popped out the pilot's window and yelled back, "You Lewis and Clark?" Bill and Meri got a chuckle from that and confirmed they were. "Well, c'mon in and I'll show you around."

At the door on the opposite side of the plane, they met the young man who was waiting for them. Bill could see a Survey ribbon with a small metal pine cone and two small metal acorns on it, indicating that he had been on seven surveys. Each pine cone meant that the Explorer had been on five surveys, and the acorns indicated a single survey. He held out his hand. "Ben Weaver, pilot. You must be the primary co-pilot," he said, to Meri.

"I guess so. I'm assigned as co-pilot, while my ersatz fiancé is an aerial surveyor."

Bill shook Ben's hand, which had that rough feeling one gets from working with one's hands outdoors.

"Great. Well, come aboard. Karen's trying to get us some better flight rats, but she'll be back soon. I think logistics wanted to use up the worst tasting rats."

In the plane, Ben showed them to their assigned bunks and where to stow their gear. "Bill, you put your secondary kit under the crash seat behind the co-pilot. Meri, put yours in the co-pilot's seat. Rifles go in your hanging lockers. When we're airborne you wear all primary survival gear."

The inside of the S-1 was similar in layout to the CL-415 but smaller. More space was dedicated to remote sensing platforms and there appeared to be larger computer drives. One such was by itself inside a crash cage that was surrounded by a Faraday cage for further protection against electromagnetic pulses. Ben pointed it out to Bill and told him that Karen would show him the particulars on it.

There were two computer workstations, one on either side of the fuselage. The port side workstation had a picture posted above the monitor of a petite blonde woman holding a toddler. Both workstations had three monitors, which Bill assumed was for each of the three sensing platforms he'd be running: visible light, near-infrared, and far infrared.

Pointing to the picture, Ben informed them, "Karen Wilson's the Survey Commander and head aerial survey tech. It's her third initial survey, so she's pretty familiar with how to run things."

"It's our first," Bill said. "How about you?"

"Second. First as pilot. Initial surveys are so draining; you only get to participate in one every couple of years."

Meri, having grown up listening to her father's tales, knew just how grueling initial surveys were, but Bill didn't. He thought they'd be flying along and taking images, and naively said so.

Ben and Meri both broke out laughing, and then Ben explained. "Think of it this way. We'll be up in the air for a week. Just the four of us. We're all qualified as pilots or co-pilots for a reason: we all need to fly the plane. You'll be doing your job AND flying. Very little sleep for a week, then off for a week, then back up for little sleep for a week.

Get the picture?"

"Uh, I guess so. Then again, isn't that what we signed up for?"

"That we did," Ben affirmed.

Outside, they heard a female voice yell, "Hey, gimme a hand here."

At the door, they found Karen Wilson towing a cart full of flight rations. Before unloading the rations she introduced herself to Bill and Meri. She had a Survey ribbon and a Purple Heart. The Survey ribbon had several of the small metal pine cones on it.

Once the rations were aboard, Karen gathered the crew around the small table next to the galley and filled them in on the assignment. "Parallel's just opened a new planet, and so far there's no sign of human activity. No visual signs, radio, television, nothing. So, keeping with protocol, they're launching a bunch of Monarchs. We'll be out a week, off a week, then out a week, until we've covered the planet. Our particular mission is to survey the northern hemisphere from the Tropic of Cancer to the Arctic Circle. We'll be flying at around 9,000 meters for the most part, but that'll vary between night and day." She was referring to the solar-driven electric engines that powered the plane in flight at altitude, and the impact that the lack of solar energy at night would have.

"Right now the first flight is already running a survey around the Initial Point. When they're done, we go in. They'll have covered a radius of 150 klicks around the initial point, but since we've got that sector, we'll start our survey from the IP." The Initial Point was where the Corps entered the parallel Earth and began their surveys. Most IPs were at the same location as Bowman Field.

"Our job," she said, referring to Bill and herself, "is to scan everything using visible light, near IR, and far IR. We'll be running analyses looking for any signs of civilization, such as straight lines, heat sources, you know, the usual. We'll be taking turns, so when you're off, sleep. At the altitude we'll be operating at we should be able to cover about 3,200 square kilometers per hour. While that sounds like a lot, remember, the Earth has over 500 million square kilometers!" she finished with a grin.

To the two pilots, she said, "Your job is to keep the bird in the air. We'll also be relieving you guys for short spells to try and give you a full eight hours off at least once a day, but it's pretty much gonna be watch on, watch off, for a week. I'll try to expand the night off watches to be six hours, but no guarantees. When you're off, sleep!

"Any questions?"

Nobody had any, Ben because he had already been there, Meri because she had already heard it all from her dad, and Bill because he didn't really know what to expect or ask.

"Great. So, all your gear is stowed?" Karen asked them, looking mainly at Bill and Meri. They nodded.

"That's it for orientation. Report here Sunday night. We'll remain in the bird overnight and head out Monday morning."

She shook each of their hands, saying, "Great to have you aboard. Meri, you and Ben go over the bird and make sure we're good to go. Bill, let's you and I go through the equipment we'll be using."

Karen showed Bill where the cameras were located, made sure he could get his workstation up and running; and then showed him how to transfer data to the protected server and the two backup field tablets stored with it.

"Those are there just in case we go down. We always try to bring back as much data as possible, so in the event anything happens, we'll transfer the data. You and I'll be responsible for doing that and we'll be the ones toting the tablets."

She also gently grilled Bill about the Caribou incident, making sure he was sound enough to fly with the team.

"It's not often they assign two rookies to an initial survey" she said. Bill could tell she was wondering why, but couldn't offer an explanation.

Several hours later, the crew took a break and headed to the field's cafe where they joined other Explorers who were assigned to Planet 42's initial survey. Bill was surprised to find out how many were still probationary Explorers: practically a third of them were.

After lunch Karen dismissed the crew, saying that, in her opinion, the craft was ready to go. "We might as well have a last hurrah, or two," she said, and offered to treat for a beer at the Cave Bear Cave. "I can't stay too long, the little guy is waiting for me," referring to her son, who was pictured in the photograph on her desk. Bill didn't ask why a man wasn't in the same picture. He figured she would tell them if she wanted to.

The four, along with another Monarch crew, headed for the Cave, where they restricted themselves to a couple of pitchers of beer between them all.

Karen left before the others, admonishing them to report to the Monarch no later than eighteen hundred hours Sunday. "We'll do supper at the field. Crossing is at zero seven hundred. They want us through early and fast so they can use the gate to resupply a secondary survey."

After finishing the beers, Bill and Meri gave their farewells and headed back to their apartment for what would be their last privacy for some time.

Chapter 24

By early Sunday evening, the Monarch crew was gathered in the plane and settled down. Wilson wanted them up at five o'clock in the morning to pre-flight the bird and make sure they were ready to cross over by seven.

Seconds before the alarm went off, Bill was awake, staring at the bottom of the bunk above him, where Meri was sleeping. When the alarm did go off it caused a general stirring in the cabin.

Bill hopped out of his bunk and started the coffee pot which had been set up the night before. By the time everyone was up and dressed the coffee was ready, and each had a cup before beginning the crossover preparations.

Ben and Meri began their pre-flight inspection while Karen and Bill, who had far less to do, started up their equipment and made sure everything was good to go. Then the crew went to the airfield's cafeteria to get the last meal they would have for the next week that wouldn't be coming out of a retort package, the flexible metal bagged modern equivalent of canned food.

By six thirty, the four were back in the Monarch wearing all the required survival equipment, seated in their respective seats, and wearing earphones, listening to ground control organize the gate opening and aerial convoy departure. Soon the Monarchs were told to start their engines. They were already in line, so they didn't need to do anything else until given the go-ahead to cross over. Bill looked out the window next to his workstation and saw a long line of trucks waiting for the gate opening.

Precisely at seven, the gate came to life, and seconds later the order was given for the Monarchs to move through it. Ben gave the bird more throttle and it began moving forward, following the lead bird. In less than a minute they had crossed from the smooth surface of the tarmac onto the gravel apron of a new crushed gravel airfield. Through the windshield, Bill could see a small control tower near the middle of the field with a small operations building behind it.

Over the earphones, Bill could hear the new control tower giving the four Monarchs directions to park on the apron next to the control tower and shut down their engines. All Explorers were to report to the operations building immediately thereafter. Ben taxied the bird and maneuvered it so it was parked on the apron and off the runway. Shutting the engines down, Ben announced their arrival on Planet 42.

Everyone unbuckled, gathered their rifles, and clambered from the plane, joining others making their way to the small building. On the opposite side of the apron was a parked Monarch: the first bird on the planet, the one that had run the initial survey around the initial point.

When they stepped out of the plane everyone became hyper-vigilant. Unlike Hayek or Zion, there was practically no human presence here prior to their arrival to scare off predators, other than the engineers who had built the field and the small operations crew. Everyone's heads were on swivels as they headed for the relative safety of the building.

Soon, all sixteen Explorers were inside being greeted by the Survey Commander, another older Explorer. After welcoming everyone, she gave them a simple situation report on their findings so far: nothing. She then confirmed the flight operations for each crew and made sure they had the correct frequencies for the long-range radios, reminding them not to use them other than for emergencies.

"So far, it looks like this is a non-impact planet. We've seen some mastodons wander by, and a couple of giant sloths, but haven't seen any large predators yet. Keep your eyes out when you're on the ground," she admonished them.

Once she confirmed routes, frequencies, and verified that all planes were prepared to go, the Survey Commander gave the order to begin taking off in tail number order. Bill's plane would be the second in the air. She shook the hand of each Explorer, giving the Corps' standard farewell of "Stay safe out there."

Taking care when returning to the crafts, the crews boarded, engines were started, and survey equipment activated. Within minutes, each pilot informed the tower they were ready to begin and requested permission to take off. The control tower gave 42/1 permission and then announced each plane could take off in two-minute intervals.

Two minutes later Monarch 42/2 was taxiing to the end of the runway. After reaching the end, Ben turned into the wind and pushed the throttles to the max. The plane accelerated rapidly and was soon airborne. Rather than make a beeline to where they would begin their survey, Ben took the plane up in circles around the airfield, gaining altitude.

As the plane was climbing Ben announced over the intercom, "Welcome aboard Monarch 42/2, destination somewhere east of here. The captain, that's me, has turned off the seatbelt light, but please don't get up and make this little bird wobble with your funky gyrations. The smoking lamp is unlit, so please don't light up stogies, blunts, or other noxious weeds. I expect we'll arrive at our cruising altitude in twenty minutes, so please sit back and enjoy the brief break—it's the last you'll see for a week!" He got the requisite chuckles from the crew.

Once the Monarch arrived at cruising altitude, Ben announced that he was transitioning from avgas to electric-powered flight. Looking out the window, Bill could see one propeller start up, and when it was running, the other stopped and feathered, reducing the drag on the plane. Karen and Bill got to work prepping the remote sensing equipment. Mission planning had the plane running north-south runs from the Arctic Circle to the Tropic of Cancer, so Ben started the plane north from the IP for the first leg.

Bill started the first imagery capture using all three bands of the spectrum, while Karen watched over his shoulder. When she was sure he had a handle on it, she told Meri to take a break. "We're gonna be up here a while, so no sense burning energy you don't need to."

To Bill, she said, "Run the first analysis when we turn at the Circle. It'll take us about nine hours until turnaround, so, in the meantime, just watch the screens to see if anything jumps out."

Karen and Meri made their way back to the crew quarters to sit, read, and relax. In the meantime, Bill took a photograph from his shirt pocket and taped it to his workstation. It was the picture of Meri that he had on Z21. He then paid attention to the three screens, looking for anything out of the ordinary. As with his first survey, Bill was amazed to discover just how boring it could be. For the most part, all he was doing was staring at the screens while Ben supposedly flew the plane. Bill suspected he had turned on the autopilot and was just checking his position periodically.

Four hours in Meri relieved Ben, who grabbed a bite to eat and then crawled into his bunk for a quick nap. Karen microwaved a couple of flight rations and brought one to Bill, and the two sat together, watching Bill's monitors and chatting. Bill learned that Karen's toddler, John, was two years old and that his father was an Explorer, serving as a flight instructor at Bowman Field. He also learned that the Corps liked to ensure that at least one parent was at Sacajawea, or at least not on an active survey when children were involved. "They don't like to leave anyone an orphan," Karen said.

Two hours later Karen relieved Bill. Ben was still taking a cat nap when Bill retired to the crew quarters to relax, so Bill elected to read a mystery novel he had found at a bookstore in Ohlone when he and Meri were on leave. It involved a Ranger from the Hayek Public Safety Force investigating an environmental crime involving strip mining and a murder in the gold fields of Yokut. Bill wasn't sure if it was a true story, based on a true story, or pure fiction; his knowledge of Hayek laws was still fairly nebulous.

Six hours later it was his turn back at the computers. As he was taking over he wondered what the protocol was for visible light imagery at night. He was amazed he hadn't thought of it before and asked Karen.

"The pictures are mainly for secondary surveys to develop maps. We'll get good enough imagery with the IR for our purposes," she told him.

By now it was dark, and they were only a couple of hours from turnaround, so Bill focused on the IR monitors.

As the night progressed the watches got shorter. Fortunately, there wasn't much physical or mental demand for any of the positions at this time, so none of the crew were taxed. Unfortunately, it was boring as hell, which led them to doze constantly.

When turnaround came, Meri was flying. She banked the plane to starboard and flew east for twenty minutes before turning south. While she was doing the eastbound leg Bill saved the data they had on one computer that was designed specifically for GIS operations. By the time Meri had the Monarch headed south Bill had the remote sensing platforms up and running to capture the data for the 4,700-kilometer run to the Tropic of Cancer.

The analysis didn't take as long as he expected, mainly because he wasn't looking for changes, only for signs of life. Any straight lines or clustered heat sources were identified. Bill had to check those by reviewing each and every one of them. There were no straight lines, and the only heat clusters he found turned out to be large mammals, most likely mammoths or mastodons.

The night passed quietly, with Karen and Bill taking turns, while also relieving Ben and Meri. The crew got into a set routine, with fixed hours at each station and time off for rest, but nobody got more than six straight hours of sleep at any one time. At times Karen had to force the two new Explorers to stop working and rest.

By the end of the week, the Monarch had made twelve north-south runs and covered a swath extending just east of the Great Salt Lake. As they passed over the lake Bill commented about not having to smell it at this altitude. Despite being exhausted, the others chuckled at such a lame joke.

As they hit their turnaround over the Pacific Ocean west of the southern tip of the Baja Peninsula, Karen announced, "That's it for this run. Take us back to the IP, Ben." Cheering broke out among the crew. Finally, they'd be able to sleep for more than six hours at a time. Karen told Bill to shut down the remote sensing equipment and to run the final analysis as they made the 2700-kilometer trip home. She made copies of all their imagery and analysis onto a portable hard drive that she would turn over to the Corps for further analysis. She also wrote up a succinct report of their findings: to wit, no sign of civilization or human groupings.

Almost nine hours later 42/2 was circling the IP airfield, and using the short-range directional radio Ben contacted the control tower for landing instructions. Upon given clearance to land and the weather conditions, Ben took the plane down and gently set it on the runway. As he did, the crew burst out cheering again. As they taxied down the runway toward the apron Karen went back to her locker and retrieved a bottle of Tullamore Dew Irish whiskey.

"I may not be Irish, but this is a hell of a lot better than champagne for celebrating," she said. "We'll have some once the engines are shut down." She handed the bottle to Bill and dug out four plastic cups from the galley.

When Ben shut down the engine Karen poured each of them a glass and said, "To a successful survey. We made it home!" then tossed back her drink. The others followed suit. "We'll let the Commandant give his toast, but I wanted to give the first one." She put the cork back in the bottle and secreted it back into the duffel bag.

All four grabbed their rifles from their lockers before Bill opened the door, and when he did they were greeted by the Survey Commander and her assistant, both armed as usual.

She told them that the gate would be opening the next morning at zero seven hundred hours for ten minutes and that the crew should be ready to go through it. "Take only your soiled clothing and rifles, and leave the rest here. I'll have mechanics go over everything and get you resupplied." At a glance from Karen, she affirmed, "With good rats. I know the kind of crap logistics likes to push off on crews, but that don't fly with me!"

The crew were given a week off and told to report back to the gate the following Monday.

Chapter 25

After a week off, Bill and Meri were beginning to feel human again, when they returned to Planet 42 for their second run. By now, the crew was familiar with each other and their idiosyncrasies, and because they genuinely liked each other, they were looking forward to another week of stress and lost sleep.

When they walked through the gate this time, they could see their Monarch waiting for them. Ben even commented that it appeared to have been washed, by the lack of bug splatters on the windshield and leading edges of the wings. They threw their duffels into the plane haphazardly and then continued on to the operations building where they met with the Survey Commander. She told them their replacement should be arriving at any time, and to stand by until they did. That way the crew could be updated on the survey findings and also be told where to begin their survey.

Rather than hang out in the Monarch, the crew decided to hang out in the operations building, which, like other operations buildings on every base the Corps established, had a bit of a dining/recreation area. This one was smaller than most, though, needing only to handle the small operations staff and transient air crews.

It was shortly after lunch before the radio squawked and a voice started calling for the base.

The Assistant Survey Commander responded, and gave the incoming plane weather conditions on the field and directions on where to park. Soon, the Monarch was on the ground and everyone went out to watch it taxi up.

"I bet they're having a small celebration," Karen commented to her crew, sotto voce.

Soon the crew disembarked from the S-1 and were briefing the Survey Commander. After listening to what they said she released the crew and told them they could cross over to Hayek in the morning.

She then turned to the crew of 42/2 and told them where to begin their survey, which was almost 2000 kilometers to the east. "Nothing's been found, so far, but that doesn't mean it won't be. If I'm correct you should be crossing over the Mississippi near the end of the week, so keep a sharp eye out."

Karen was then ordered to get her flight underway, so she and Bill boarded the Monarch while Meri and Ben conducted their pre-flight inspection. Within minutes Ben was in the left-hand seat, Meri in the right and Bill and Karen strapped into their crash seats. Upon getting clearance from the tower, Ben gave the bird some throttle, taxied down the runway, and in a repeat of the week before, took the bird up.

The flight to their first run was longer than Bill expected because Karen wanted to start it at their southern terminus, which put them far into what was the eastern side of Mexico on Earth, over the Sierra Madre Oriental. It was well after dark when they arrived, and Bill had been given the opportunity to fly for some of that time, simply because he and Karen had nothing to do.

Once on station, the two aerial survey specialists got their equipment up and running and began collecting imagery as Ben turned the plane north to the Arctic Circle. For the next week the same routine as before took place, with Bill and Karen focused on data collection and analysis, but giving Ben and Meri breaks from flying. Different than the first survey, though, the four had now gotten into the groove, so they didn't feel as tired when they finished as they had the first trip out.

Bill had hoped to find anything, such as mounds or streets as they crossed into the Mississippi River valley, but as with the prior thousands of kilometers, there was no sign of civilization.

Finally, on the seventh day out, Karen ordered Ben to return to base. Considering they were now almost 3,000 kilometers to the east, and at the Arctic Circle, which was still white in early May, Bill was surprised to find that it took them as long to get home as it took to get to their starting point. Then he remembered, despite knowing it from the many runs toward and away from the North Pole, *Duh, lines of longitude converge at the poles! Man, I must be more tired than I thought.*

The next several weeks followed the same pattern. They would survey a week, usually extending the survey range out another 950 to 1,000 kilometers, then they would have a week on Hayek to recover and wear something other than a flight suit, survival vest, and survival belt. It also gave them the chance to eat something other than flight rations, which, while good, weren't something one wanted to live on indefinitely. Ben, seeing Karen be greeted by her husband and son when they came home each survey was glad that he didn't have any children. *How the hell does Karen manage with a toddler? I'm exhausted when we get back, and kids are nothing but energy vacuums.*

By the time they had covered Ti'icham and the Caribbean, they were pretty certain no civilizations existed anywhere in the western half of the northern hemisphere. Reports that they were getting from the crews covering the tropics and the southern hemisphere were presenting the same findings - nothing! Ti'Icham, Suya, and the Caribbean were void of any signs of civilizations or even proto-civilizations. No roads, no temples, no signs of agriculture. If there was anything down there, the Explorers surmised that they hadn't progressed beyond the migratory hunter-gatherer stage.

By the time June rolled around the Surveys were just reaching the western edge of Eurasia. Nothing had been spotted in Greenland or Iceland, but the crews were told to keep a sharp eye out. As the Survey Commander told them, "Most civilizations started out in Eurasia, particularly in Mesopotamia. I expect you'll be over that area by late June or early July, so be careful.

When the crew of 42/2 arrived on Planet 42 after another week off, they were surprised to find that 42/1 had already landed. They discovered that the co-pilot had gotten ill their fifth day out and they were unable to help him. It turned out the poor Explorer had a ruptured appendix, and they barely made it back in time to save his life.

So, instead of starting out further east than they expected, their initial point would be almost three hundred kilometers closer to the IP. Karen decided to start the survey at the Arctic Circle just to get on station sooner. "If I can manage it, I'll end us at the Arctic Circle so we can get home faster," she told the crew as they prepared to take off. Taking the Great Circle route northward, they arrived at their start point twenty hours later.

The first run south took them over what was Scotland on Earth, down through the Irish Sea, over the Iberian Peninsula, east of the Strait of Gibraltar, over the Atlas Mountains, and finally over the deserts of North Africa where they eventually made their turn northward. The sun was just coming up over the desert when they made the turn, and even at more than 9,000 meters altitude Bill could see it was just like the desert on Earth, barren.

As they headed north Bill could see the planet change color under him, going from the dun of desert in the morning to the aquamarine of the Mediterranean by late morning, and then the verdant green of western Eurasia by noon. Bill found the terrain below much more interesting than he had found that of Ti'icham, probably because it was vastly different and didn't look quite as boring.

As they conducted the survey, the crew followed their, by now, usual routines. Fly, work, eat, nap, repeat. As the week was winding down and they were making their final run of the southbound leg, Bill could just make out the mountains of western Eurasia poking out above the darkening land below them. The mountains were bathed in the ruddy color of the setting sun, a condition known as alpenglow. It reminded Bill of sunsets seen from his dorm room overlooking

Washington State's Mt. Rainier. *We'll probably be right at their bases when we make the next run tomorrow afternoon,* he thought.

Right after he thought that, Karen told the crew to get a good look at the mountains. "As soon as we turn north for the next run, that'll be it for this trip. Once we get to the Circle let's head for the barn" she announced.

That evening they crossed the Mediterranean, and once more over the Atlas Mountains of North Africa. The rest of the night was spent crossing the barren North Africa desert, both southbound and northbound. They finally cleared the desert and crossed the shoreline of the Mediterranean Sea by mid-afternoon. A little over two hours later they left the Mediterranean and once again began flying over land, just on the western edge of the Eurasian Alps.

Far below Bill could see large, fluffy cumulonimbus clouds piling up. Knowing just how dangerous it was to fly in such clouds, and especially in such a light aircraft as the Monarch was, Bill was glad to know that they were out of harm's way.

Chapter 26

Bill was sitting at his workstation, running another analysis on the imagery his cameras and other remote sensing equipment had picked up. Staring intently at his screen and looking for any signs of human habitation, he was surprised when the cabin around him lit up with a brief flash. His computer screen went blank and the interior lights of the craft shut off. Sparks flew from his computer, and he felt the hair on his head stand on end. Simultaneously, he felt, more than saw, a brief electric bolt extend from his computer to his left leg cargo pocket of his uniform. At practically the same time, he heard Ben exclaim, "What the hell, over?" Bill picked up the scent of ozone, as if a small electrical fire had taken place. He suspected it was his computer and reached toward the bulkhead to his right for the small fire extinguisher.

As he was releasing the extinguisher from its clamps, Bill looked to his right, toward the front of the craft, beyond the crew crash couches, and saw beyond Ben that all the flight screens were blank. As a matter of fact, there didn't appear to be a working light or electronic device on the craft. The only light in the aircraft was coming through the windshield and the side portals.

Bill finished releasing the extinguisher and pointed it at his computer just in case it burst into flames, but the smoke dissipated, leaving him holding a loaded fire extinguisher with no fire to extinguish.

"Shit!" Ben yelled. "Fire on the port engine!" Bill looked out the small portal to the left wing and saw flames coming from the engine. Looking out the opposite portal to the right wing he was relieved to not see any flames. Bill could still see the large cumulonimbus clouds several kilometers beneath them.

Meri came charging through the main cabin, passing Bill's workstation and jumped into the co-pilot's seat. Bill could see her and Ben making frantic motions, attempting to put out the flames. Bill looked back out the port window and watched as fire retardant spewed into the engine until eventually the flames were put out.

While this was happening a rumpled Karen joined Bill in the main cabin area, taking a seat in the workstation across the plane from Bill's. It was obvious she had just been rudely awakened.

"What's up?" she asked Bill, who was now in the process of putting the fire extinguisher into its cradle.

"Don't know. All the power went out with that flash and the port engine caught on fire. Looks like the fire's out, but still no power."

"Hey guys," shouted Ben to the crew, "We got a problem. No power. Looks like we might have to ditch. Bill, can you find me a spot to land this thing, preferably on a lake or flat plain?"

Bill looked hopelessly at his blank monitors and yelled back to Ben "Stand by. The computer got fried, so I'll have to check a back-up."

Bill reached into the cargo pocket of his pants and pulled out a small tablet, which he subconsciously noticed was warmer than usual. Swiping the screen he waited for it to wake up. Nothing happened. He swiped the screen again. Still nothing. He pushed the power button on the side and held it, waiting for the familiar vibration indicating the unit was powering up. Still nothing.

With a perplexed look on his face, he turned to Karen and asked her to check her tablet. Pulling it out, she went through the same ritual as Bill, getting the exact same results.

"Uh, guys, we got another problem," Bill announced to the flight crew. "Something killed our tablets. Do yours work?"

Bill heard some talk between Ben and Meri, but couldn't hear what they were saying. Meri pulled her tablet out, swiped it, looked at it and swiped it again. Then shook her head. "Mine's dead, too."

Meri put her tablet back in her pocket and grabbed the yoke, allowing Ben the opportunity to get his tablet out and try it. Ben's results were the same as everyone else's, a dead tablet.

Bill, still holding his tablet, thought for a moment, and then asked the others if they saw a lightning flash extend from any electronics to their tablets. Ben said no, and both the women said they didn't have their tablets with them, as they were sleeping.

"What the hell could have caused all our electronics to fail?" Bill wondered aloud.

Ben said, "Well, it doesn't matter what caused this, we're gonna have to put this bad boy down safely, so secure the craft and get strapped in. We'll be deadsticking it the entire way."

Ben and Meri remained at the controls while Bill and Karen scurried around the craft's cabin, securing all loose items. They were soon finished and moved to the crash couches directly behind the cockpit. The crash couches were designed to be suitable for rough landings, or if that weren't possible, to be deployed from the aircraft. Each contained explosive charges for ejection, parachutes, and a simple survival kit, all one needed to trek thousands of kilometers of uncharted territory.

"We're secure," Karen told Ben, letting both pilots know that the cabin was clear of potential flying debris, including the two crew members who were strapped into their crash couches.

Ben and Meri spoke among themselves, plotting how best to land the large plane. Fortunate for them, it was designed more as a powered glider than a typical powered aircraft, and they had had extensive simulator training on landing it without power.

Ben looked over his shoulder and ask Bill, "What's the closest body of water you think we're near"

Bill thought about the latest bit of data he had just processed and asked "Other than the Med? One of the lakes to the west or south of the Alps. Freshwater, smaller waves, and you could probably get us pretty close to shore. I'd opt for one east of the Alps, toward the south. That way we could make our way down toward the Med. Otherwise, we'd be forced to go north, maybe up the Rhine or some other river, and that means we'd have to cross the Channel or the North Sea. We're probably about 50 klicks from the nearest big lake."

"Okay. Well, we're descending into the Alps, so I'll try for one of the southern lakes."

"If you can, get the southernmost lake. I'm not sure if the others have outlets or if they're all hydrographically enclosed," Bill responded, unable to restrain himself from using geographic terminology learned in school. "Lake Geneva's pretty big, and it's got an outlet."

Bill saw Ben nod his head, and then sat back as Ben and Meri worked together to get the dead plane on the ground.

After what seemed forever, but was probably about 20 minutes, Ben announced that he had a string of north-south running lakes in sight and was heading for the largest, which appeared to have shallow water on its eastern side. By now, Bill could make out large Eurasian mountains on both sides of the craft. He continued to watch as their peaks gradually rose above them.

"Prepare for impact," Ben said loudly. "Remember, that means relax!"

Bill thought to himself, *How the hell am I supposed to relax when I'm about to crash into a lake at a high rate of speed?* but he tried, closing his eyes and humming tunelessly to himself and practicing some of the meditation methods he learned in a yoga class he took several years ago.

Within seconds the craft slammed into the lake, bounced, and slammed into again. Bill was thrown against his restraints, slammed back into the crash couch, thrown against his restraints again, and then slammed back into the couch a second time. The violence soon ended, and Bill could feel the plane rocking on waves.

"YEAH!" Ben yelled. "Damn, we're good!" he said, letting go of the yoke and turning to Meri for a high-five. Cheering broke out among the crew. They were alive, for now. But the fun was just beginning. Here they were, stranded on a continent 10,000 kilometers from the nearest help. All they needed to do to survive was cross two continents and an ocean, using only their brains, feet, and a few tools from their survival kits.

Bill unstrapped and looked out the starboard portal and saw that Ben had managed to land them within a hundred meters of land, near shallow water and a beach. "Nice job," he said, reaching over to pat Ben on the back. Meri looked back and he gave her a grin and a thumbs up.

"Listen up," Karen said. "We've got to get this plane to shore and salvage all the stuff we can. Bill, did you back up the data to the protected drive?"

Bill nodded his head in the affirmative. The protected drive was an external storage device that was protected in a combination crash case and Faraday cage. The crash case was very similar to the black box on Earth airplanes, while the Faraday cage was a metal screen that surrounded the case, designed to keep electromagnetic pulses from damaging it. It was plugged into the onboard computer daily for the short time it took to transfer the digital data derived from the remote sensing devices on the plane, along with whatever spatial analysis had taken place between transfer times. It was also designed to be able to transfer the data to the two field tablets stored with it in the event a plane went down and the survivors needed the spatial data to get home. Exactly like what just happened.

"Okay. While the rest of us are getting the bird to shore I want you transferring the data to the field tablets. You carry one, I'll carry the other. Any questions?" she asked, looking around at the three crew members. Everyone shook their heads in the negative, and Bill began the process of retrieving the protected servers and the field tablets, hoping that they had survived whatever electronic storm had killed the plane and all their other devices. While he was doing that the others opened the access hatch of the plane, which, fortuitously, was on the same side of the plane as the shoreline.

While Bill had his head buried in the rear of the craft retrieving the equipment, which was shoved into a small nook designed to protect it, he heard a splash, followed shortly by Ben yelling, "Christ, that's cold!"

Within seconds, Bill had the case out of the nook and extracted the server and one of the tablets. He turned on the tablet and was relieved to see the screen light up.

"We got power," he yelled, letting the other know that the tablet was working. He powered up the battery operated drive, turned on the wireless access, and connected the tablet to the drive through the automated wireless connection. Rather than transfer all the data he had, which encompassed most of the northern hemisphere between 23 and 70 degrees north, and from the western edge of Ti'icham to practically their current location (less the data lost since the last transfer) on the western edge of Eurasia, he focused on transferring useful data. In other words, data that would help them get home.

The transfer took several minutes. While the transfer was taking place Bill started the second field tablet and was, again, relieved to see it work. He set it up to receive the same data as the first tablet. As the transfers were taking place Bill took the laminated photo from his workstation and put it in a shirt pocket. Soon, the data he wanted was transferred and Bill put the server back in the case. Carrying the equipment with him he walked to the front of the plane where he could see Meri and Karen operating a manual winch that was attached to an attachment point just inside the hatch to a line that stretched to a tree on the shoreline. Bill looked out the door and saw an almost nude Ben sitting on the bank, wearing only a pair of wet briefs. He was curled up with his knees to his chest and his arms wrapped around his knees, it was obvious he was cold and trying to preserve body heat.

"How goes it?" Bill asked the two women.

"Slow," Meri said, looking back over her shoulder. "I think the water's a wee bit chilly," she continued.

Bill thought, *Glad I'm not the one that had to swim. Who knows what kind of critters are out there.* That thought prompted Bill to ask, "Anyone keeping watch?"

"Crap! I can't believe I didn't think of that," Karen said. Turning to Bill she ordered him to get his rifle and stand watch.

Bill returned to the main cabin of the aircraft and retrieved his rifle from his locker, along with a loaded magazine. He inserted the magazine into the rifle as he returned back to the hatch.

Upon arriving at the hatch, he charged his rifle, pulling the bolt back and then forcing it forward, seating a round in the chamber. Ensuring the safety was on, and keeping the rifle pointed away from anyone else, Bill took up a position behind the two women, looking over their shoulders to the shore. His main goal was to keep an eye out and ensure Ben didn't get eaten by any nasty critters.

Within minutes the plane was within feet of the shore. Karen stripped off her boots, socks, and flight suit, grabbed Ben's flight suit and survival vest, and then jumped out of the plane into knee deep water. When she got to shore she tossed Ben his clothing and vest, which he gratefully accepted and put on. Returning to the plane she said, "Okay. We gotta get this thing unloaded. Let's form a chain and start handing out gear. Personal rifles and survival gear first, then crash couch emergency kits, all the available food, and last the group gear. Bill, you keep watch until Ben's got his rifle, then help carry stuff to shore while Meri passes stuff out. Got it?"

Bill kept watch while Meri retrieved Ben's rifle. She handed Karen the rifle, already loaded with a magazine, and waited while Karen carried it over to Ben and returned. Ben loaded his rifle while Karen returned to the craft.

Bill set his rifle by the door, stripped off his boots, socks, and flight suit, and jumped into the lake. He was immediately shocked at how cold it was. *How the hell did Ben manage to swim that far in this water?* Grabbing his rifle and discarded clothing, he carried them to shore and set them on the ground, close to hand, making sure his rifle was on top of the clothing pile with the barrel pointed away from the group.

For the next fifteen minutes, he and Karen carried survival

equipment between the plane and shore, taking turns standing on shore and carrying the equipment slightly further inland to make room for more equipment. This gave each of them a break from the frigid waters. The first things Meri handed out were Karen's rifle and emergency pack. Then came Bill's pack, followed by Ben's and Meri's. It took a while for Meri to disengage the crash couch emergency kits from the crash couches, but eventually, she got them detached and passed them through to Karen and Bill. The food was the standard field rations used while conducting surveys. The group survival equipment, retrieved last, was mainly the emergency raft and its supplies, their parachutes, and the limited boat building equipment.

"That's it," Meri called. Bill turned to the pile of equipment and thought, *I wonder how much of that we'll be taking?*

Bill got dressed while Meri made the cold crossing, holding her rifle, boots, and dry clothing. Bill admired the view of the partially clad Meri. "Yikes, that's cold!" she exclaimed upon exiting the plane. The others couldn't help but smile at this, knowing that all of them had spent considerably more time in the water than she.

When Meri got to land she handed a burnt item to Karen, saying "Somehow, I don't think our power outage was natural."

Karen looked at the object. "What it is?"

"If I'm correct, it's an EMP bomb. See the timer?"

"What's an EMP bomb?" Ben asked.

"Electromagnetic pulse bomb," Meri answered. "It's a large electrical discharge in a small area. It basically fries all electronics within a short range, like the inside of a Monarch."

"Who the hell would put one of these on a Monarch?" Karen wondered.

"GLF," Meri said. "Gaia Liberation Front. In other words, Gaia Firsters."

"Gaia Firsters? Aren't they just some fringe group on Earth?" Ben asked.

"Looks like they just got a lot more local," Karen said.

"Unfortunately, no. Some Explorers might be involved," Bill

said. The others looked at him in shock. He then went on to explain about his conversations with Commandant Lewis and Janet Babbitt, and what really happened to the Caribou.

"And you didn't tell me?" Meri said.

"I couldn't," Bill replied. It was obvious he wasn't too happy about not having done so.

After a few moments of silence, Meri said, "I bet this is because of me."

"Huh? What makes you think that?" Karen asked.

"Simple. My dad's the Corps' Commandant. If the GLF decided to act against the Corps, wouldn't it be smart to take out the head, and in this case, the entire family? It's what the revolutionaries did to the Romanov's in Russia back in 1917."

"Well, nothing we can do about it from here," Karen said, tossing the burnt object onto the ground. "So, first things first. Let's get a fire going then set up camp. No sense worrying about something out of our control, and it makes no sense going anywhere until we figure out where to go and how to get there. Besides, it'll be night soon, and I don't know about you guys, but I don't plan on being dinner for a smilodon or other big, hungry critter. Meri, you stand guard while we set up camp. Bill, you set up Meri's hammock. Ben, get a fire going then set up your hammock. I'll get a trip wire line out."

Soon a fire was blazing and hammocks were set up around it. Close enough to benefit from the heat and smoke, but far enough away so they wouldn't catch fire, even from stray sparks. Experience had taught them that wild animals generally didn't come near fires, so it should prove relatively safe. Even so, the trip wire that surrounded the encampment was designed to create an alarm if anyone or thing ran into it.

Bill had retrieved his PDW, or personal defense weapon, from his crash couch emergency kit, and set it in his hammock. He figured he could sling his rifle under the hammock in the hammock sling designed to hold it while he slept, but still have a means of protecting himself. Like the others, though, he kept his rifle with him at all times.

Meri maintained watch, not looking at the fire, but rather at the surrounding terrain, her head practically on a swivel, while the others ate and discussed the plans for the evening the future. Meri could hear and respond, but her main focus was on keeping watch.

Dinner consisted of flight rations. Usually microwaved while in flight, the rations were designed to be eaten cold or heated in boiling water over a fire or on stoves. In this case, they used their individual wood burning stoves to heat their respective meals, reserving the fire for safety and warmth.

Karen led the discussion, mainly on the first night's watch schedule, and then a more general planning session on how to get back to Ti'icham. "Just to be clear," Karen said, summarizing their condition, "any hope of rescue is out. We've got no radios, we're too small to register as something worth investigating on any of the sensing platforms the Corp uses, and there's always the possibility they'll find something and shut this planet down. That means we walk, swim, row, whatever it takes to get back to the IP. So, let that sink in. We're on our own."

One thing that became obvious during the discussion was that a boat would be needed. Luckily, they had the supplies necessary to make one. It was now just a matter of figuring out exactly where they were and which route to take.

Ben relieved Meri so she could eat and then gave her back the first watch after she finished eating. Karen would take the second watch, Ben the third, and Bill the final watch. Since it was early June, and they were at a relatively high latitude, there was plenty of daylight, meaning less night, so each person had a relatively short watch, less than two hours each.

Shortly after eating, Karen, Ben, and Bill climbed into their hammocks. Bill's hammock contained not only his PDW but also his summer sleeping bag with a silk liner. Enough to stay warm without overheating, even at the altitude they were at. Despite the stress and excitement of the crash landing and subsequent preparations, Bill was tired enough that he was soon sound asleep.

All too early, Ben was tapping on his hammock side, whispering "Bill, get up. Your turn to stand watch." Awaking rather abruptly, he slid out of his hammock, his PDW in hand. He had slept with it just in case. As he had been asleep for several hours his eyes were already adjusted to the lack of light. Looking around, he could see the fire burning low, mostly embers but with some smoke, due to the benefit of some green wood thrown on it.

Ben muttered, "G'nite" and crawled into his hammock. Ben placed his PDW in his hammock and picked up his rifle from the sling under the hammock. Soon, Bill could hear Ben's snores merge with those of the others.

Looking around, he could make out the outlines of trees. The moonlight shone on the water, making things even brighter, despite the fact that the moon was in a quarter-moon phase. He could make out the outlines of mountains across the lake. Looking up, Bill saw the sky filled with stars, the Milky Way making a wide streak across the heavens. A meteor streaked across the sky.

It's been one heckuva ride just to get this far, he thought, bringing his attention back to ground level, where most threats would materialize. *I wonder if we'll make it back?*

Bill remembered a conversation he had had with "the Colonel" one time about adventure being somebody else far away in great danger. *Looks like this might be an adventure,* he thought, scanning the area around him, *'cause we're sure in danger, and we're sure far away from home.*

Chapter 27

The first dawn after the crash landing found Bill watching his surroundings, seeing things magically appear with the lightening sky. The morning twilight faded into daylight, and Bill was able to see more and further. During the night he had stoked the fire with wood that they had gathered the evening before, so when the others began awakening they could warm themselves between packing their equipment. Across the lake, he could see a mountain range with snow still at the top.

Meri was the first awake, having been the first to stand watch. Giving Bill a quick 'good morning' kiss she suggested they take turns changing out of flight suits and into field uniforms. "They'll be a lot more useful," she said, stripping off her flight suit.

"Hey, you're supposed to be looking *out* for me, not looking *at* me," she complained when she noticed Bill ogling her. Reluctantly, Bill turned his attention away from her and back to the surrounding forest until she announced she was dressed.

As she stood guard Bill repeated her actions. The commotion of their interchange awoke the others, both of whom crawled out of their hammocks, grabbing their rifles from the under-hammock slings as they did.

Breakfast consisted of flight rations warmed in boiling water.

"From what I can see, we've got a couple of day's worth of flight rats, then it's on to field rats, hunting, foraging, and survival rats. I'd like to hold off on eating any more of the rations until we absolutely have to," Karen told the crew as they ate their morning rations around the fire.

"Bill, were you able to pull any imagery of where we are?" Karen asked.

Bill shook his head in the negative. "Nope. The last stuff I backed up was from before the last turnaround."

Karen bit her upper lip, in obvious deep thought.

"Okay, here's what we're gonna do. I want to bring all our supplies with us, which means either rafting down a river or hauling them by hand. If we have to haul them by hand, then we'll need to make some travois," she said, referring to the frame structure consisting of two long poles lashed together with crosspieces and used to carry cargo and pulled by people or pack animals.

"I'd rather we go the easy way, rather than hauling everything by hand, so the first order of business, after determining where we are, is to see if this lake has an outlet. If it does, we'll follow it. I don't know of any lakes in this part of the world that don't feed into an ocean or a river that feeds into one. Bill, do you?"

"Not to my knowledge, but I'm not as good at European geography as I am GIS," he replied.

Karen thought for another minute, and then told the group what she wanted done. Ben and Meri were to go along the lake's shore to the south to see if they could find an outlet while she and Bill stayed at the campsite. Bill was to determine their location, which meant using the sextant to take sun shots.

"Your chrono still set for Alpha time?" she asked Bill, who nodded his agreement. "Good. At least that's one thing we don't have to worry about. You keep yours set to Alpha and when noon rolls around I'll set mine to local. That way we'll always have a pretty good idea on where we are."

After breakfast, Ben and Meri gathered their equipment, donning survival vests, belts, and backpacks. Karen told the two to take a PDW and try and bag a deer or something like it if they saw one. "Save the rifle ammo for when it's really needed," she cautioned.

Meri gave Bill a kiss before the two pilots began their westward trek along the southern shore of the lake. With no operating radios, there was no way to communicate other than by using whistles, voices, mirrors, or shooting. And, any shooting done wouldn't be for signaling, rather for food or safety.

"Y'know," Karen said, after Ben and Meri were gone, "I bet we're just north of Marseilles. If that's the case, we could be at the Med in a couple of days."

"As the crow flies, we're probably less than 200 klicks from the Med," Bill offered.

"Hmm. Twenty klicks a day by foot, yeah, more than a couple. More like ten or so. I'll have to keep that in mind. In the meantime, get the sextant and take a sun shot. I'll keep watch out, and when you're done clear a space on the beach for a stick so we can find out when local noon is. I figure we've got plenty of time, but I don't want to be scrambling."

Bill dug the sextant out of the pile of group survival equipment and sought out the best place on the beach to take a sun shot. Soon, he had things lined up and he was able to determine their latitude. After a quick calculation, he announced to Karen that they were at 45 degrees and no minutes north.

Digging out the field tablet that he had recovered from the crash box Bill decided to find the line of latitude they were at and follow it until he found a lake surrounded by mountains. It wasn't long before he found one, and it was one of a string of four, so it seemed to fit the bill.

"It's possible we're at Grand Lac de Laffrey," he said, mangling the name with his abysmal French pronunciation. Looking closer, he then said, "Doesn't look like there's an outflow river, but there is a river to the north of us, the Isère. Looks like it loops around and feeds into the Med. Too bad we didn't make it another 150 klicks north, we could have landed in Lake Geneva and rafted down the Rhône the entire way."

Karen looked at the snow-capped mountains surrounding them

and said, more than asked, "You want us to walk over that?"

Bill shook his head. "No. I don't think we need to. Looking at the topo map, I think we're on a high valley over the river. There looks to be a break in the mountains at the northwest end of the lake, and that should lead us straight down to the river. That is if this planet's like Hayek."

"Well, let's wait 'til the others get back and then we'll decide. In the meantime, let's find our longitude so we're a little more accurate on our location."

As noon approached Meri and Ben returned to camp from the north, having walked all around the lake. As Bill suspected, the only outlet they found was a small stream on the north end, not large enough for a raft.

"Looks like we hoof it then," Karen decided.

"One other thing," Ben said. "We found a fire pit."

Bill didn't catch on at first until Karen asked, "Are you sure? Was it a real fire pit or just a lightning strike?"

"It was real," Meri answered, holding up a stone artifact.

"Crap. That just raised the stakes. We may have gone from a Class III to a Class II planet."

Bill recalled that a planet without hominids was classified by the Corps as Class III, but if there were any, it was marked Class II and shut down to further exploration, exploitation, or settlement.

Karen took the artifact from Meri, examined it briefly, then handed it to Bill.

Damned if that doesn't look like a spear point, he thought.

"Okay, everyone pay special attention to the surroundings and keep an eye out for any hominids," Karen told them. "Also, while we can't scuttle the Monarch, let's get everything that could possibly identify us or Hayek out of there and burned. You two," she said, pointing to Meri and Ben, "get back inside and pull out anything that's a potential identifier. That means all flight manuals, logs, whatever. We need to get them burning, now."

She turned to Bill and told him to complete his task.

"I'll hold onto this," Karen said, referring to the artifact, "just in case we make it back. The Corps'll want it as evidence."

As the sun began to reach its zenith Bill began marking the tip of the stick's shadow every minute. Within twenty minutes they could tell when it had been noon, so they calculated their longitude, finding out that Bill had been correct in his assessment of their location.

Meri and Ben went back into the Monarch while Karen kept watch. They soon emerged with armfuls of manuals and other paper items. Karen had them toss everything on the fire, piece by piece until everything was burned. While the two were engaged in their pyromaniac behavior, she went into the floating craft and double checked to ensure no identifiers were left behind.

She soon returned to the fire, legs dripping with lake water. "Looks good. Too bad we can't sink that bird, but it's designed not to be. I locked it, though, so unless whoever had that fire has axes, ain't nobody getting in."

As the last of the paper was burning Karen said, "I guess it's pretty much settled. We walk. Let's get a few saplings cut and limbed so we can make the travois. Let's start out with two and see if that'll do. Meri, you keep watch while we get it done."

Soon there were enough saplings to construct the travoises. Karen dug out one of the parachutes they had salvaged from its pack and used the parachute cord to tie the frames together. The parachute straps were used to make shoulder straps for the travois. That way nobody would have to hold onto them, thereby freeing their hands to carry rifles.

As Karen pulled the chute out, she discovered that it had been sliced.

"Look at this!" She held up the cut fabric. Everyone could see that it was a neat slice, and one guaranteed to ensure the parachute would fail when deployed.

"Those bastards weren't dickin' around," Ben said.

"Well, we'll repair it later. Let's get the travois done first," she said, stuffing the parachute back into its bag.

Karen had the men sling the travois over their shoulders while she loaded the equipment on them. It soon became apparent that even wearing their packs, there was too much equipment and food to carry on just two travois. One more was constructed and that sufficed.

"Rather than getting a late start, we'll spend the night here again and head out in the morning. It's not like we need to get anywhere in a hurry," she said with a wry chuckle after they had set the travois down. "Bill says the creek you two found will lead us to a larger river that feeds into the Med, so we'll follow that down."

Once more, hammocks were strung, wood brought in to feed the dwindling fire, and trip wires set out. Bill and Meri decided to try their hand at fishing while Ben and Karen kept watch. Rather than use the issue Cuban yo-yo reels, the two of them had elected to pack small packable fly rods. It was their lucky day: they had strike after strike. Soon they had a string of trout and whitefish on shore, enough for all without digging into any of their limited rations.

The fish were cooked over the fire using a field expedient grill made from the limbs of one of the saplings they had cut down to make the travois. The burning wood added flavor that the lack of seasoning couldn't. After eating, Karen made sure all fish remnants were disposed of away from camp. "No sense tempting hungry critters," she commented.

Karen decided to go with a rotating watch schedule, so that the first person on watch one night would be the second on the next, and so on. As Bill had the last watch the night before he was given the first watch and told to wake Meri after his watch ended at twenty-two hundred hours. The other three crawled into their hammocks while Bill took the first watch. After two non-eventful hours he roused Meri, and when she was up, attired, and standing ready with her rifle, he slung his rifle under his hammock, grabbed his PDW, and crawled into his hammock.

The cool morning air woke Bill as the sun was climbing over

the mountains to the east. As he climbed out of his hammock, PDW in hand, he saw mist rising off the lake. Ben had stoked the fire, so a cheery blaze rose from it. Suspended over the fire was a pot of boiling water.

"Hey," Ben quietly said to him from the fire, not wanting to wake the others. Bill grunted.

Bill joined him at the fire, sitting down on a log strategically placed by the fire. He set the PDW on his horizontal thighs, and faced his palms to the fire, feeling the warmth seep into him.

Using a bandana as a hot pad, Ben poured some of the hot water into a cup and handed it to Bill. "Here. It looks like you need some coffee." He took the proffered cup, thanked him, and took a sip. The first sip was hot and he could feel it coursing down to his stomach.

Before Bill was halfway through the coffee he could hear Meri and Karen stirring. Soon, they joined Bill and Ben and each had a cup of coffee. "Might as well enjoy it while it lasts," Karen said wistfully.

After the coffee was gone, Karen ordered the others to pack up their hammocks, ensure their canteens were full, and to get ready to move out. "Once we're ready, then we'll have a quick breakfast. I'd like to be on the river by this afternoon, if possible." Meri added more water to the pot over the fire so they could heat some flight rations for breakfast.

While Meri was doing that, Karen asked Bill how far away he thought the river was. Bill pulled out the field tablet, activated it, and pulled up the Hayek map. He used the ruler tool to estimate the distance from their location to the river.

"If this is the same terrain as Hayek, then we should be about five or six klicks from the river. It's flat about half way and then we drop about 500 meters in elevation to the river valley," he told the others

"So, if we average three klicks an hour, we should be there in about two hours," Karen said. "A couple of hours to build some rafts, so we oughta be well on our way downriver by noon, then. Okay. Well, everyone pack your hammocks and get your gear on. Packs can stay off until after breakfast, but from now on, unless we're stopped for an extended period, you keep all your survival gear on you at all times." The others nodded their assent at these words.

Soon, all the gear was packed, everyone was wearing their full field uniform, including survival vests and belts, and had their packs placed on the ground next to them. Breakfast was a hurried affair, and the retort bags from breakfast and the day before were buried in the fire pit and covered with rocks.

"Well, no sense wasting time. Meri, you take rearguard and keep an eye out to the front, back, and sides. Ben, you take point. Bill and I'll be in the middle. Everyone keep heads on swivels. Remember, this is a non-impact world, which means there are some truly dangerous critters are out there."

The three designated pack animals put their packs on and then picked up the travois by the improvised shoulder straps. It was a bit awkward, Bill thought, but a lot easier than trying to carry everything by hand or on their back. *And, we're not leaving anything useful behind.*

Within minutes the quartet was walking along the eastern shore of the lake, heading north. Fortunately, there was enough of a beach they didn't have to bushwhack through trees. All four carried their rifles at the ready and were constantly scanning the ground and trees for any potential threat. As they walked, Bill thought about what Janice Goodland had said in one of her survival classes. "A lot of threats come from above, trees, boulders, the sky, but for some reason, none of us look up. Do so, constantly! It might save your life."

After an hour they had made it around the lake to the northwest corner where the gap between the mountains became obvious. Working their way through the forest wasn't as difficult as Bill had thought it would be. This was mainly because it appeared to be old growth forest with minimal undergrowth, most of which appeared along the edge between the lake and the trees. Some quick work with a machete got them into the forest, where the walking, while darker and cooler, was easier.

The trip downhill was somewhat daunting, between not having

a trail and hauling the travois while wearing their packs and survival gears and carrying their rifles. But, they eventually made it, coming out on a gravel bar on the river.

The river didn't appear too deep but it was relatively swift and had the cloudy look as if from glacier runoff. Touching her fingers to the water, Karen said what they all were thinking, "Yep, it's cold."

Looking around, Bill took in with his fisherman's eyes the fact that the water had been higher just days before. "Looks like it's dropping," he commented. The others look around and Meri agreed with him.

Picking up a stick from the gravel bar Bill tossed it into the river and watched it rapidly disappear downstream. "Quick and cold. Most likely snowmelt."

"Well, doesn't much matter," Karen said. "We need to get down to the Med and get a boat built, so let's get crackin'."

The three Explorers hauling the travois dropped them to the ground and placed their packs on top. Karen told Bill and Ben to cut enough trees to make two rafts, while she and Meri kept watch.

The two men identified trees that would be suitable for the rafts and began chopping them down. Each raft required two skid logs with a half dozen top logs. The skid logs were short, barely two meters long, but wide and heavy, to support the top logs which rested on them. Each top log was four meters long and a third of a meter in diameter. After a couple of hours of chopping, and several blisters, Bill and Ben had all the logs lined up on the riverbank ready to be assembled. Feeling the sting of broken blisters on his hands, Bill commented, "Guess I'm not as up to chopping as I used to be."

Karen gave them guard duty, as a way to rest, while she and Meri assembled the rafts, placing the top logs over the skid logs and lashing them together with parachute cord. In just a couple of hours, both rafts were ready, and the two women chopped down saplings that would be useful for poling and maintaining control of the rafts. Karen tied ropes to the ends of each raft so they could be dragged or held on to.

"Before we start this flotilla, let's make sure all the gear is strapped down. Does us no good to get to the Med if we can't build a boat," Karen said. She then directed the trio how she wanted the equipment lashed to the raft decks. "Wear your vests and belts, but keep the belts unbuckled. If you fall in and start going under I want you to get out of them quickly. Rifles over your shoulders."

Once all the equipment was lashed to the rafts, they were pushed into the river. Karen ordered Meri on one and had Bill hold the tow rope. Karen and Bill pushed the raft into the frigid waters, then they pushed the second raft partially into the river, where Karen jumped on it and Ben held onto the tow rope. Ben then sat down on the gravel bar, and using his feet, pushed the raft out into the river. Fortunately, the site they had chosen to build and launch the rafts was on the downriver inside curve of the river, so the current didn't pull the ropes out of the men's hands.

"Hop on," Karen commanded, and both men launched themselves onto the rafts, which dipped perilously, touching the bottom of the river briefly. Fortunately, the part of the river bottom that they touched was barely a couple of inches. *I wouldn't want to do that in deep water,* Bill thought.

Slowly, with assistance from the four Explorers poling, the rafts moved out into the river and were soon swept up into the current. Bill estimated that they were going about seven knots, or about thirteen kilometers per hour. *Heck, with that speed we might just make the Med in just a couple of days.*

Chapter 28

It was just after noon when the crew launched the two rafts. While not very maneuverable, they were better than walking and carrying all the survival equipment.

Karen ordered the others to maintain a close watch for any rapids because while they were in what appeared to be a relatively flat valley, the mountains still reared above them on all sides.

The four ate a meal of unheated flight rations while drifting and poling. Bill decided he much preferred his flight rations heated, as he spooned the cool, gloppy food into his mouth. *At least it's not freezing,* he thought. *Just imagine how much fun it would be warming these up under armpits just to thaw and eat them.*

About two hours before sunset Karen gave the order to pull over to a gravel bar that had a small stream feeding into the river just below it. "Let's get the rafts up on shore as fast as possible, and keep an eye out," she hollered to the trailing raft.

The four poled the two rafts until they bumped up against the gravel bar and the two men, holding the tow ropes, jumped out and pulled the rafts up as far as they could as fast as possible while Meri and Karen poled toward shore, assisting them. The two women then hopped off their rafts and help pull the rafts further up the gravel bar until they were completely ashore.

"Let's tie the tow ropes to trees just in case the water rises overnight," Karen commanded, and immediately did as she said, tying her raft's rope to a sturdy looking tree above the riverbank. Meri did the same for the raft she and Bill had ridden in.

While Karen kept watch, the other three gathered firewood, strung a trip wire, and set up hammocks on the edge of the riverbank. Soon a fire was going and flight rations handed out to each. Karen had each Explorer fill their canteen cups with water from the river and set them by the fire to heat up to warm the flight rations.

"Well, unless we take some time to hunt, we're gonna go through these things pretty quick," Karen commented, holding up a flight ration entree retort bag. "So, either tonight or tomorrow morning I'm gonna want one of you to kill some game. I don't want us using any more rats until we absolutely have to. In the meantime, whenever we pull into a campsite I'll want you two to set out some snares," she said to Bill and Meri "but one keep watch while the other sets them." The two nodded their agreement.

"I think I saw a spot just a bit upriver that looked like a game trail, so after you eat, stake it out. If you see anything, take it. If not..." she shrugged her shoulders. "Remember, save rifle ammo and use a peeder."

Karen then enforced the Corps of Discovery's hygiene rule, requiring each explorer to take a quick shower using their bottle showers and to at least wash underclothing and socks, which were hung over branches to dry. Uniform shirts were washed in the small stream that fed into the Isère River and also hung over branches. By the time the four were clean the water in their cups was boiling, so they immersed their flight rations for five minutes to heat them up. Once heated, the pouches were open and the food eaten directly from them, as nobody wanted to take the effort to wash dirty dishes after the day they'd had.

With an hour left until sunset, Meri and Bill headed upstream to stake out the game trail. Both had their rifles at the ready and were carrying all their primary survival equipment, including their packs, but Bill had the added weight of his PDW, which was slung over his shoulder. They soon came to a point where they could see the game trail but were far enough from it to not be obviously visible to any animal that might poke its head out. Bill verified that the wind was blowing downriver, so their scent wouldn't give them away, and the two sat down on the gravel bar. Meri kept her rifle at the ready but Bill set his down and held onto his PDW. Bill's PDW not only had iron sights, but it also had a small low power rifle scope mounted on it. As the effective range was considered 100 meters for game, it wasn't a big scope, barely seven centimeters long, but it was good enough for what he needed it to do.

The two sat quietly for some time, as the sun dipped over the mountains on the horizon and the long twilight of a northern latitude summer day commenced. Bill spotted motion in the forest near where the game trail came out to the river and readied his PDW, sighting down the scope with one eye, but keeping the other open in the event something outside the scope's field of vision caught his eye.

Soon a deer emerged from the underbrush, and just as Bill was about to take the shot he was nudged by Meri. Looking over at her she used her chin to indicate he should look into the forest again. Doing so, he spied a tan color amidst the green of the forest. It took him several seconds before the outline of a lion appeared to materialize amongst the leaves. When Bill finally realized that he was staring at a Eurasian cave lion, he turned back to Meri with eyebrows raised. She indicated she would shoot the lion while he shot the deer.

"On three," she mouthed. She had her rifle aimed at the lion, but was able to hold up three fingers of her right hand, then dropped one, indicating the count was on. Bill stopped watching Meri and did the count in his head while aiming at a point just under the deer's left ear. On the silent count of three, he squeezed the trigger. At the same time, Meri fired, then ran the rifle's bolt back and forward. Both stood and looked at their kills. The deer Bill had shot had dropped like a stone, the unblinking open eyes indicating its death.

There was thrashing in the brush where the lion had been, and the two waited, weapons at the ready, while the thrashing died down. Only after there had been no more noise for several minutes did the two take the chance of approaching where the lion was last seen. Meri spotted it first, lying sprawled on the ground, still twitching. "Put a bullet in its brain," she told Bill, "just to be safe." Bill did so and the twitching stopped. The two still waited several more minutes to ensure the deadly creature was dead before approaching it. Bill, heart beating so fast he thought it was going to burst his rib cage, grabbed a stick and poked the lion in the eye to see if there would be a reaction while Meri kept her rifle aimed at it. The lion did not move. Bill looked over to Meri and noticed her hands were shaking. *Glad I'm not the only one scared shitless,* he thought.

The two decided that dragging the kills back to camp would be the best option, but neither wanted to not have a guard, so Bill was elected to do the dragging while Meri kept guard. Both kills were back at the camp before it got too dark, and Karen and Ben took over cleaning the game.

"Tomorrow, let's see if we can gather some berries before taking off. I'd like to get some pemmican made before we start across the ocean," Karen told the crew. Bill remembered the pemmican he'd made during survival training, a combination of dried meat pounded into a powder, rendered fat, and berries.

"We should probably also keep an eye out for nuts, like acorns and such," Meri suggested. "Great for flours and stews."

"Good point," Karen agreed. "See to it," she said to the crew. "In the meantime, let's get what fat we can off these guys and dry the rest of the meat over the fire."

Since Bill had carried the game in Meri volunteered to gather sticks that would be hung over the fire, out of reach of the flames but close enough to drape the meat over and make jerky. "Y'know," Bill said, "the word barbecue comes from the Arawak word barbacoa, which basically means a wooden framework for drying meat on." Meri just looked at Bill as if he had lost his marbles.

"Really?" she asked. "We're out here struggling to survive and all you can do is lecture on the etymology of a word?" Shaking her head she returned to her task with a wry look on her face.

By the time the sticks were arranged over the fire full dark had fallen, and Ben had taken watch. Karen advised everyone to pay particular attention as the smell of cooking meat might draw some unwanted guests. Bill and the two women then began the task of slicing the meat into thin strips and separating what fat they could find on the lean animals. The fat went into a pot near the fire to be melted and eventually mixed with cold water to clarify it.

The trio was finally done cutting and trimming by the time Ben's shift was up, so Bill took over guard duty. Once all the meat strips were hung over the fire the three not on watch called it a day and climbed into their hammocks. Bill continued to look around, knowing that the pre-impact planet that they appeared to be on harbored some predators that have never developed a fear of man, and might consider Bill a tasty treat.

At the end of Bill's watch, he awoke Meri who had the joy of the worst watch that night, the mid-watch. She muttered as she climbed out of her hammock and Bill, once stashing his rifle and grabbing his PDW, was grateful to climb into his.

It seemed that Bill had just closed his eyes when he was rudely awakened by what sounded like several people cackling with laughter nearby. The sound sent chills up his spine, and he exited his hammock as fast as he could, PDW firmly grasped in his hands. He noticed that Ben and Karen had done the same, with both of them replacing their PDWs with rifles. Meri was just inside the ring of hammocks looking all around while the eerie sound continued.

"That sounds just like hyenas!" Ben said, eyes wide open. Karen grabbed a flashlight from her pocket and flicked it on, shining it outside their small encampment. Sure enough, a couple of pairs of eyes reflected back at her. "Bill, shoot them!" she shouted. Bill took aim with his PDW and fired twice at one set of eyes and watched it drop. The loud sounds scared off the other, but Bill heard a crashing in the bush behind them and turned just as a large hyena came rushing into the campsite, headed straight toward Meri. With no time to give warning, Bill turned and fired several shots at the large canine, at the same time Ben did with his rifle. The animal flipped in the air, obviously hit by Ben's larger bullet, while the two women turned to face the latest threat. Meri fired one round into the predator's head, silencing it forever.

Karen yelled at them all to turn out and keep an eye out. "Hyenas hunt in packs!" she warned, flashing her light in all directions.

Noises of running animals were heard, but thankfully they were all heading away from the encampment. Only then did Bill start shaking. He wasn't alone, and Meri came over to him and hugged him fiercely, practically sobbing.

Karen toed the dead hyena in the middle of the camp and then ordered Ben to toss it into the river. "Let's get that carcass out of here. No sense attracting any more critters." Looking around the shocked group, she then told them that from now on, any time they were doing food preparation, there would always be two people on guard. "And keep your flashlights ready! I don't want them used unless absolutely necessary, like tonight."

Bill helped Ben, as the hyena was much heavier than expected. Bill estimated that it must have weighed at least 100 kilograms.

Sleep was out for the crew for the rest of the night, so they stayed up until the sun rose, at which time they ate some of the meat in a stew that Karen made. While Bill and Meri were hunting the day before Karen had gathered some edible plants she found in their camp, so for breakfast, she added them to the stew. All agreed, it was certainly better than eating just plain deer meat, and then the discussion promptly turned to their favorite breakfasts.

The four took down and packed their hammocks after breakfast. They then stripped all the washed clothing from the branches, which they also packed. Karen deemed the jerky sufficiently dried for travel and had the crew pack it in resealable plastic bags that they carried in their survival pack for this exact reason.

"The plan for today is just like yesterday's, but without the chopping and hauling" Karen informed the other three with a slight smile. "We'll drift downriver and stop a couple of hours before supper. If anyone sees some game worth taking, and it's at a spot we can easily land, take it. We don't necessarily need it for tonight, but I'm thinking long term, specifically when we try to get to Ti'icham."

The four then loaded up the rafts and set off downriver. They stopped occasionally along the way, usually for bathroom breaks, and once because Ben saw, and shot, a goat. Eventually, the Isère River connected with the Rhône River. When it did Karen had them pull over onto a sandbar for a lunch of dried jerky. Bill, looking at the Hayek map on his tablet, informed the group that they were only about 300 kilometers or so from the mouth. "At this rate, we should be on the shores of the Mediterranean in a couple of days" he announced.

After lunch, the crew set off again. While the current was fast, it was not as clear a river as the Isère, which led Bill to complain to Meri about the missed fishing opportunities. She was sympathetic, but then told him not to worry, she was sure they'd have plenty of opportunities to fish over the next six to twelve months. That shut Bill up in a hurry.

Two hours before sunset they pulled over onto a gravel bar on the east side of the river, where they grilled and ate the goat Ben had shot. Karen said she didn't want a repeat of the night before, so after supper, they would move their camp to a spot downriver. Before taking off, Meri and Karen scrounged around in the bush for edible plants while Ben and Bill kept watch. It wasn't long before the two women were finished, and the foursome once again boarded the two rafts and continued their journey downriver, stopping less than a kilometer later on a gravel bar on the west side of the river.

The night passed uneventfully, and the next morning they were on the river again after a quick breakfast of, yet again, dried jerky. Bill was beginning to tell the difference between deer and lion, and he found that he actually preferred the taste of lion.

Chapter 29

Two days later, the crew found themselves approaching the mouth of the Rhône. Karen had them pull ashore at a gravel bar where large oak trees reached their branches out over the river.

"This looks as likely a place to build the boat as any," she announced one they were grounded. "Here's the plan: we're gonna construct a standard dugout outrigger canoe. I want it to be as close as possible to those used by the Polynesians, so it's gonna have to be fairly big, at least eighteen to twenty meters. I'd prefer we use linden wood, but if we don't find any small leaved-lime trees nearby we'll have to use oak. Whatever tree we use, though, I want a minimum width of one meter. It'll be tight, but if we string a net between the canoe and the outrigger we'll have a little more room to relax in. We've all built smaller boats in survival school, so any questions?"

The three shook their heads in the negative, and Ben said, "Just tell us what you want done, when, and how, and we'll get it done."

Karen nodded her appreciation and then started giving orders. The first order was to set up camp, string the hammocks, and set out the trip wires. She also had the crew gather plenty of firewood. "Once we've got the camp set, then we'll get cracking on the canoe and food supplies."

It didn't take long for the crew to set up camp. Karen didn't like leaving the camp alone, so she ordered Bill and Meri to remain behind while she and Ben conducted a quick search around the area for a small-leaved lime tree, or, if they couldn't find one, another suitable tree. "Try catching some fish for supper," she said as the two headed out to find a suitable tree.

Meri took sympathy upon Bill and offered to keep watch while he fished. Thanking her, he retrieved his fly rod from his pack and soon had the line and dry fly laying on the water, drifting. Within minutes there was a strike, and Bill could feel the fish struggle as he reeled him in. After catching a second fish he offered to trade places with Meri. She was glad to do so, and after he had put his fishing gear away she got hers and was soon fishing. As was becoming the case every time they went fishing, she wound up reeling in the bigger fish. By the time she had reeled in a second fish Karen and Ben had returned.

"We found one," Karen stated without preamble. "It's about a hundred meters downriver. We'll drop it tomorrow and begin digging it out. Fish for supper?" she finished.

Meri held up the four large fish and said, "One for each. If you're hungry for more I can catch them."

Supper consisted of the fresh fish grilled over the fire and some dandelion greens that served as a salad.

As they ate Karen outline the plan. "It's gonna take several days to build the boat, and before we launch I'd like to have more food on hand, especially pemmican. I'm sure we'll be eating enough fish as we cross the ocean, that we'll probably be sick of them. So, let's see about getting some game and finding as much green stuff as we can carry. That'll mean weaving baskets for storage, along with doing some serious hunting."

Looking around at the three crew members eating their supper, she continued, "Bill and Meri, you two work together. Ben and I'll be a team. When one team is working on the boat, the other should be either working on baskets or out hunting. Everyone's got their survival book?" she asked.

Bill patted his vest pocket where the waterproof book, the size of a deck of cards, resided. Feeling its outline he nodded to her. The book was modeled on the British Special Air Service's survival book but adapted for Corps needs. Along with showing how to navigate, make boats, traps, baskets, survive on land and sea, and other items that would help a lost Explorer, it also gave primitive methods of food production, such as pemmican, jerky, and other foods that could be made from foraging.

The evening passed without incident. When Bill was on watch, though, he could hear the howl of wolves in the background. After the hyena attack the other night he was justifiably nervous on watch, and even when he wasn't on watch. He seldom put his rifle or PDW down, even when emptying his bowels.

The first priority was building the boats and baskets, so while one team worked on the boat, the other worked on the baskets. Felling and limbing the tree took a full day, as did flattening the bottom and molding the front prow and the stern. Other than survival training, none of them had ever used an adze, so it took a while to get fully comfortable with it. The canoe took shape. First, the outline was completed, followed by the hollowing of the interior, with a center block left in place for the mast. They then constructed the outrigger and attached it, along with a tiller. The mast they cut and trimmed from a tall sapling, and finally, they used a parachute to make the sail.

After a week the outrigger was ready to sail and the storage baskets were made. Then the hunting began in earnest. In an effort to ensure they didn't lose anything to hungry animals, one team would always remain behind while the other team hunted, and usually, each team was successful every day. It helped that the local fauna had no fear of humans or experience with rifles that could kill further than a lion could pounce.

On one of their final hunts before launching the canoe, Bill and Meri wound up on the shores of the Mediterranean. Stopping, they looked south to the endless waves. "Sure is empty out there," Bill commented as the two stood on the beach holding hands, rifles slung.

"And big," Meri replied quietly.

Bill felt Meri's hand slip from his as she turned to head back up the sandy beach in search of game. As he turned, he could see a tear slipping down her face.

"Hey," he said in an attempt to cheer her up, "we've made it this far. Nothing's gonna stop us now. Not even the GLF."

She smiled back at him and replied, "Damned right! Nothing's gonna stop us."

Dear Reader,

Thanks for buying *Surveyor*, the first in the *Corps of Discovery* series. I hope you enjoyed it.

As an independent author, I don't have a marketing department or the exposure of being on bookshelves. If you enjoyed Corps of Discovery, please help spread the word and support the writing of the rest of the series by writing an Amazon review or telling a few friends about the book.

Thanks again,

James S. Peet
Enumclaw, WA

This is my first novel, but the second novel, *Trekker*, will be out soon, so if you'd like advance notice of it, please join my e-mail list at **www.jamespeet.com**. This is my blog site where I'll be posting updates on novel progress, along with whatever else tickles my fancy.

Following is an (unedited and totally raw) excerpt of *Trekker*.

Trekker

Book II in the
Corps of Discovery Series

James S. Peet

Chapter 1

Bill Clark wouldn't say he was a particularly skittish guy, but when your erstwhile fiancé fires a rifle off in your ear at two in the freakin' morning, it tends to make you a bit skittish. That's pretty much what happened to Bill, just minutes after crawling into his hammock. Granted, Meri Lewis wasn't shooting at Bill, nor even that particularly close to him, or even shooting in his direction, and he wasn't even asleep yet, but any shot within twenty feet is too close when you're not expecting it.

Bill's first reaction was to roll out of his hammock holding his personal defense weapon at the ready. Unfortunately, rolling out of a hammock involves gravity, and after slamming his face into the ground of Planet 42, courtesy of said gravity, he staggered to his feet. Scanning around the gravel bar in the light of a half-moon Bill could see the love of his life aiming for another shot at whatever it was that had perturbed her in the first place.

Bill looked in the direction that Meri was aiming, and as she shot again, the muzzle flash showed him the threat, a lion just outside the trip wire line. Bill brought his personal defense weapon, a PDW-1, up to add his support when he heard a crashing sound from the lion's position. He also heard more crashing through the nearby forest. At that moment Karen Wilson announced her engagement in the fracas by shining a small, powerful flashlight into the dark. Bill could see that the lion Meri shot was down, and possibly dead.

"Keep your eyes peeled," Karen warned, shining the light around with her left hand, rifle in her right. "Lions hunt in packs."

As she was doing so, Ben Weaver made an appearance, also armed with the Corps's ER-1 rifle, a bolt action rifle with a low power scope mounted on it. It was identical to the one Meri was using and Karen was holding.

After several tense minutes, with no other sounds, not even the usual night sounds of bugs and birds, Karen said, "I think they're gone."

She ordered Bill, who was armed the lightest, to throw some more wood on the fire. Meanwhile, Bill could hear Ben mutter, "That's it for sleep." Bill silently agreed with that statement.

Meri Lewis came into the fire's circle of light and Bill looked at her questioningly, obviously concerned for her. She shakily smiled back at him and said she was okay, just scared. "No doubt," Bill said.

After circling the camp, Karen came back to Meri and asked how she was doing.

"Fine, but I can't wait to get off this beach.".

"Yeah, well, another couple of days and we should be good to go," Karen said. Then, looking back to where the lion Meri shot was hidden by the brush, she continued, "I'm thinkin' that bad boy you shot'll add to the larder."

Ordering Ben and Meri to keep watch, she and Bill went to the lion and dragged his carcass back to the campfire, managing to not set off the tripwire. Dragging it back in required both of them, it was that large, and neither was willing to set down their weapon as they did.

As the fire roared to life, Bill shouldered his PDW, then he and Karen cut up the dead animal while Ben and Meri continued to keep watch. It had only been a couple of weeks since their sabotaged survey plane had crashed in the Eurasian mountains on this unexplored planet, a parallel Earth. They weren't quite used to the fauna they had to deal with. One thing was obvious, the animals, particularly the predators they had encountered so far, were not scared of humans.

Before setting out on the survey they had been told that it appeared the planet was a non-impact planet. This meant that the meteors that were suspected of slamming into the Laurentide Ice Sheet during the late Pleistocene, causing major flooding and climate change and leading to the extinction of most megafauna, never happened in this timeline.

Not only were the four crew members stranded 10,000 kilometers from any help, but they were also dealing with megafauna of the late Pleistocene. Not that all the animals were bad, but in just a couple of weeks they had been attacked by a pack of hyenas which were larger than their African cousins, and now a pride of lions. Fortunately, technology in the form of rifles and flashlights had triumphed over fangs and claws.

"Y'know," Bill said, "I was taught in survival school that fires kept the critters away. Sure doesn't seem that way to me."

"Well, I'm gonna disagree there, man o' mine," Meri said, smiling at him, her blue eyes laughing. "So far, other than that hyena, nothing's come into the camp. I spotted that lion out beyond the trip wire. I think it was trying to figure out how to get in but the fire kept it away."

Bill mulled that over and then, reluctantly, agreed with Meri. When it came to survival stuff and megafauna, he considered her far better versed in it than he. After all, he was only from Earth, while she was a native Hayeker who earned a bachelor's degree in Exploration Science. And if that wasn't enough, she was also the only child of the Commandant of the Corps of Discovery.

"Either way, we'll be out of here in a couple of days," Karen said. "Unfortunately, we can't carry as much food and water as I'd like, so we're almost at the limit of what we can carry. Simba, over there, might just top up the larder once we dry and jerk him.

"One thing I want to do is sail fairly close to land until we pass through the Strait of Gibraltar. That way we can continue to get fresh game. Which reminds me, I want you two," she indicated Bill and Meri," to gather up makings for bows and arrows tomorrow. I figure we'll be in that outrigger for about a month, so that should give us plenty of time to get them made."

The four sat and waited for sunrise, which, thanks to the time of year, came early. Mid-June was still fairly cool at night, but the days on the southern coast of what was France on Earth were getting quite warm. As the sun came up fish started jumping in the Rhône River, apparently feeding on bugs on the water.

Karen suggested lion for breakfast. Knowing how much Bill and Meri enjoyed fishing, she said, "We'll be eating enough fish as we cross the Atlantic. No sense in burning out on it early." Soon lion steaks were grilling over the campfire, pierced by sticks that were held by hungry Explorers. The rest of the lion would be turned into jerky, and some of that would be made into pemmican, depending on how much fat they could render from the lion.

The day before Karen had spied a number of oak trees several hundred meters from the river. She informed the crew that she and Ben would take a couple of baskets the crew had made and collect as many fallen acorns as they could find.

"When we get back we'll have a nut cracking party," she said, deliberately looking at first Ben and then Bill, both of whom raised their eyebrows and made mocking gestures of protecting their privates. The two women laughed, a much-needed break from the stress of the morning.

"I'll want you two to stay around camp and keep an eye on the meat. Take a moment to check the snares, and if you find any edible plants, collect them. We're gonna be pretty shy on veggies when we cross the ocean. And keep an eye out for whoever made that point," she said. She was referring to a stone artifact Ben and Meri had found on the opposite side of the lake from where they had crash landed. The two had discovered a fire pit and the point, but no other signs of humans or other hominids.

Breakfast over, Karen and Ben each grabbed a small handmade basket and headed off into the forest east of the river. While they were gone, Bill and Meri did a quick walk around to each of the snares that had been set out the day before. The found several rabbits and a couple of squirrels in the traps, all dead, and all destined for the lunch stew pot. Smaller animals were consumed fresh while the larger animals were being turned into long-term storage food, such as jerky and pemmican.

They collected the dead animals and reset the snares, moving them to new locations near the old location, but still along the game trails.

As they made their way back to camp, which was visible through the trees, they heard a shot. Bill recognized it as being from one of the rifles that each of them carried. Both Bill and Meri, rifles raised in the ready position, as always, stopped and looked in the direction of the shot, which was several hundred meters away. Another shot rang out.

"I hope they're shooting at something they found," Bill said, implying that he hoped they weren't shooting to protect themselves.

Meri said, "Me, too", understanding exactly what Bill meant.

One of the most frustrating things about being stranded was the lack of two-way radios. While they each originally had one, the same electromagnetic bomb that destroyed their plane also fried all the electronics inside said plane, with the exception of one server, two field tablets, and a solar charger that were in a combination crash box/Faraday cage. Not being able to communicate, even a couple of hundred meters, meant that something could be happening to one pair of Explorers and the other pair would know nothing about it. The only means of communication they had, other than yelling or shooting, was the small whistles each Explorer was issued.

The two continued their short journey back to the campsite, stepping over the tripwire line, and into the circle of hammocks.

Bill took the dead lagomorphs and rodents from Meri and began the process of cleaning them. This entailed decapitating them, removing feet, gutting, and then stripping the skin off them. Bill had done a lot of hunting before joining the Corps, and killed and cleaned a fair amount of game, but it was still a task he didn't like. Mainly it was because he liked animals, and didn't like seeing them suffer or die, despite how much he enjoyed eating them. As he cleaned the animals, he thought about this, and then came to the realization, *If I didn't kill them, I couldn't eat them. Then I'd be dead.* That brought back memories of his father, who would often say, "You don't work, you don't eat. You don't eat, you die."

Looking at the first squirrel before cleaning him, Bill thought of what he had read in an old western novel back in his Earth days. A squirrel ain't nothing but a rat with a cute, fluffy tail. *Alright, cute, fluffy-tailed rat, into the pot with you.*

Bill's father was a career military man in the US Air Force, so he was a bit taken surprised when Bill announced, after graduating college, that he had joined the Corps of Discovery on Hayek as an aerial survey specialist. Hayek was the first parallel planet discovered when Dr. Tim Bowman had invented the gate that would allow people to move between parallel Earths. It was hard to believe that Bill's conversation with his dad was only a year ago. In that one year, he had been through several months of training, had a propeller blade slice into a plane he was transitioning in and decapitate the instructor pilot, spent several more months on a survey in the Caribbean, and then the last two months on the Initial Survey of Planet 42, the one they were currently stranded on. His job had been to use remote sensing platforms for mapping and, most importantly, to determine if any humans, civilizations, or proto-civilizations existed on the planets they were surveying. On the recent flight, Ben was the pilot and Meri the co-pilot. Karen had double duty. Not only was she the survey commander, the one in charge of the survey, but she was also an aerial survey specialist.

Bill had met Meri just before starting Explorer training, and the two had hit it off so well that they had moved in together after their first survey. When they moved into the small apartment Bill had said something to the effect of, "Geez, just like married people." Meri took that, in jest, to be a poorly worded marriage proposal. Ever since then she had called him her "erstwhile fiancé." Bill was secretly pleased with that and was planning on having the phrase changed by dropping the "erstwhile" part. Of course, that was before they crash landed in the Alps a couple of weeks ago.

It was still several hours before lunch, so Bill wrapped up the cleaned game in fresh leaves and set them in the shade. They would go in the stew pot an hour before lunch, with whatever edible plants they could find.

Less than a half-hour before Ben and Karen hailed the camp, giving the two camp sitters fair warning that it was them and not some hungry pre-Holocene predator coming in for a snack.

Meri asked if all was alright, and was told it was.

"We shot this monster sized bull," Ben said by way of greeting, dropping his basket of acorns by the fire. "The thing's over two meters at the shoulder and must weigh at least a thousand kilos."

Karen nodded her agreement with Ben's description and then said, "I think it's an auroch, or something similar. Either way, the damned thing's huge and should have plenty of fat on it." She set her basket of acorns next to Ben's.

The emphasis on fat was actually a pretty important one for the stranded Explorers. First, there aren't many animals that eat well enough to develop the marbled fat that domesticated grain animals had, which meant that all the protein the four stranded crew members were getting was lean meat. Fat contained plenty of calories, more than lean meat, so it was greatly desired. The other benefits of fat included making pemmican and soap. Pemmican is a long-term storage food item made from ground up dried meat, clarified fat, and whatever nuts or berries could be found and added. The crew was hoping to carry as much as possible for their journey across the Mediterranean from their present position at the mouth of the Rhône River, and then across the Atlantic Ocean to North America, or Ti'icham as it was called on Hayek. Soap, of course, was useful for staying clean, something the

Corp of Discovery considered one of the most important things Explorers could do when in the boonies, other than survey, that is.

"After lunch, Ben, you take Bill and clean it," Karen ordered. "Hang whatever you can't carry in the tree near where you shot it, so take some rope with you. It's probably gonna take several trips, and I'd like to get as much in before night. And definitely, before it attracts too many predators. We've already seen just how nasty some of them can be." And, then, with a grin, she said, "Meri and I'll just stay here and crack some nuts."

"Bad, Karen, just bad," Bill said about the bad joke shaking his head in disbelief.

After lunch, the two men gathered their rifles, some rope, and headed out beyond the trip wire. Ben knew where they were going, so Bill followed. The two walked with rifles ready, heads moving all around and up and down, looking for any potential threats. Both had been taught in survival school that threats could come from anywhere, including above, where some predators like to hang out and jump their victims.

They not only had their rifles with them but also all of their primary survival gear. This included a backpack full of survival equipment, a web belt full of survival equipment, a survival vest full of survival equipment, and their Corps of Discovery uniforms, with pockets full of survival equipment. Bill estimated they had well over two thousand dollars, or about two-fifths of a troy ounce's, worth of survival equipment on each of their bodies. The Corps standing rule was that any time an Explorer was on a survey planet they carried their rifles and wore vests and belts. If they stepped away from the group, they took their packs. This was emphasized so much that every probationary Explorer, or "Probie" as they were called, was required to wear all survival equipment during training. It was now second nature to Bill.

As they walked through the forest, Bill could smell the rotting vegetation. It reminded him of the Cascade Mountains he used to hike in.

The two arrived at the dead auroch. Bill was amazed at its size. *That thing's larger than a bison,* he thought. Luckily, no other scavenger had arrived yet, but buzzards were starting to circle. As Bill kept watch, Ben commenced cutting the big bovine. It had already been gutted, so now the task was to quarter it, and hang the meat out of reach of scavengers. It didn't take Ben long, and soon they had over half the big bull in the air, strung between several large branches.

Bill cut a sapling down with a hatchet he kept on his belt, and the two strapped a large chunk of meat to it. Ben then used his canteen to wash the blood off his hands. No sense getting his rifle stock all sticky with blood. When Ben's hands were finally clean and dry, Bill picked up one end of the pole and Ben the other. The two, with rifles still at the ready, staggered back to camp with their heavy load.

When they arrived they found the two women had already cracked open all the acorns and were leaching them in several small pots of boiling water to extract the tannin. Acorns were edible only after the tannin was removed, and boiling them in water was one way of doing that. The acorns would be used as flour to make a form of bread, and it was also used in stews.

"Drop it here," Karen said, indicating a spot near the fire. "We'll take care of it."

After the men dropped their burden, they removed the rope holding the meat to the stick. Bill took the rope, Ben took the pole, and then two men, nodding to the women, simply turned and headed back to the kill, rifles at the ready.

By the time night had fallen the two men had made several trips to haul in as much of the auroch carcass as possible. Karen called for a two on, two off watch for the night, just because that much meat would most likely attract predators and scavengers. The two men were told to sleep first and were given four hours. They collapsed in their hammocks after a quick supper of stew.

It was two o'clock in the morning when the two men were awakened. *At least nobody's shooting this time*, Bill thought, recalling Meri's activities the morning before. Karen had made coffee for both men, but told them to nurse it, as she didn't want to use it all up in one night. Both men stood watch with rifles at the ready and flashlights handy. The light from the campfire threw a circle around the camp, casting long shadows into the dark forest. Bill and Ben kept a watch for any reflections from eyes that might be staring at the camp.

Over the course of the next four hours, they didn't see anything approach, nor were the trip wires activated. But, they could hear from the site of the auroch shooting, hyenas laughing, and then Bill heard a wolf howl in the distance. *Great, just what we need,* he thought, *now it's either regular wolves or dire wolves. Hope they don't come 'round here.*

James S. Peet is a modern day Renaissance Man. He's lived on four continents, six countries, and visited countless more. He's been a National Park Service Ranger, a police officer, a tow-truck driver, a college instructor, a private investigator, a fraud examiner/forensic accountant, an inventor, and an entrepreneur. His other writing endeavors include several articles on modern sea piracy, economics, and the private investigation of fraud. He lives on the top of a small mountain in the foothills of Washington's Cascade Mountains with his wife, dogs, barn cats, and whatever adult daughter returns to the nest. He's attended 10 colleges and universities, two law enforcement academies, and has three degrees (all in geography) and multiple certificates (he really likes learning). *Surveyor* is his first novel in the *Corps of Discovery* timeline. Be sure to watch for future releases.

Made in the USA
Monee, IL
01 August 2020